PRAISE FOR LINNY MACK

"Linny Mack's debut novel, *Changing Tides*, is a **captivating tale** that explores the intricate dance between love, loss, and rebirth. With a narrative that will keep you on the **edge of your seat**, and an ending you won't see coming, this **story will break your heart** and piece it back together, one beautiful shard at a time."

–Buck Turner, bestselling author of *The Keeper of Stars*

"Mack's **striking debut shatters your heart** in fourteen different ways before masterfully piecing it all back together by the end. Cape May, Sophie, and Liam, will have a place in my heart forever."

–Lily Parker, author of *The Best Wrong Move*

"A **breathtaking debut**, *Changing Tides* is a masterclass in slow-burn romance, brimming with depth, heart, and hard-won healing. Featuring **beautifully drawn characters** in their 40s, it celebrates love not as a reckless leap but as a **courageous journey**—one where finding each other begins with first finding ourselves.

–Shaylin Gandhi, author of *When We Had Forever*

"This story of two broken people struggling to heal themselves grabbed hold of my heart and refused to let go. **An ode to fate and found families**, *Changing Tides* is a satisfying, slow-burn romance that will make you believe in second chances."

–Lindsay Hameroff, author of *Never Planned on You*

"Every page of Mack's debut was filled with the warmth and comfort of found family, the **bittersweet nostalgia** of childhood summers, and the yearning excitement of new love. Her characters have found a forever home in my heart!"

-Christy Schillig, author of *Wish You Weren't Here*

Chasing Stars

Chasing Stars

LINNY MACK

Page & Vine
An Imprint of Meredith Wild LLC

Paperback ISBN: 978-1-964264-11-0

For the ones who chased the stars and found each other instead.

Chapter One

"This can't be it..." I mutter to myself, squinting through the front passenger window at the dilapidated Craftsman bungalow before me. It's not how I remember the house on Monarch Street, but then again, I haven't laid eyes on it since I was nine years old.

I reach for my oversized tote bag and rummage around for the paper that my mother's lawyer gave me. I toss out sunglasses, lip gloss, my wallet, my mother's checkbook, a folder of important papers, and a mess of crumpled receipts. Finally, I find it at the bottom of my bag. The address is scribbled in smeared gel-inked chicken scratch, but it is legible: *503 Monarch Street. Cape Property Management.* A barely legible phone number is scrawled beneath it.

I exhale sharply causing the impulsive trauma bangs I just got to fall into my eyes. I brush them out of my face, cursing myself for running to my stylist last week when I lost control of *literally* everything in my life. "Not my hair, though. Nope. I've got control of my hair, and to prove it to myself, I want bangs," I told her. Ten out of ten do not recommend doing that.

I groan and squint out the window again. The lawn is cut, thanks to the property manager I guess, but the garden is way overgrown. The cedar fence is rotting and broken. Some of the siding is coming off. The exterior is not promising. "Well, there's only one way to find out." I force optimism into my self-talk, throwing open my driver's side door more aggressively than I intend. It catches in the late September sea breeze and bounces back at me, hitting my calf. "Ow!" I shout as I get out of my teenage Toyota Camry. "Stupid car." So much for optimism. I slam the door shut and stomp up to the sidewalk, shading my eyes as I take in the house up close.

It's possible it looks more promising from the front yard than the front seat of my car. I squint. The outside definitely needs some work and curb appeal, but I think I can make it look decent for listing photos. Lord knows I can't pay anyone. I have to use my inheritance money very wisely now that I'm no longer gainfully employed—hence, the bangs.

I spent five years as a personal assistant at a high-end interior design firm on the Main Line in Pennsylvania, hoping to break into actual design work. But my entry-level job remained entry-level. Last week, after returning from bereavement leave following my mother's funeral, my boss called me into her office and told me she no longer had use for an assistant.

"People just aren't hiring interior designers like they used to—not with all of the online platforms that they can use to DIY," she said.

She had to let me go. I understand it, I really do. The design industry is hard, and she needs to keep every penny she earns. Times are tough, but now what am I supposed to do? I packed up my desk, went out to my car, and screamed into the abyss. And then I got bangs.

I pull my tote bag higher up on my shoulder and trek across the front lawn, the dried yellow grass crunching beneath my Chelsea boots. I don't have a key—I didn't know this house still existed until last week—but I wanted to have a look at it for myself before going over to the property manager's office. I walk up the concrete front steps, holding the rotting wooden railing while carefully avoiding a splinter. *That would be the icing on the cake.*

The small porch is really just a stoop, large enough for a couple of people to stand on while they ring the doorbell. A memory flashes in my mind—my mother, in this very spot, helping me tie my shoes before I ran off to catch lightning bugs. It's a heady mix of grief and nostalgia. I close my eyes, letting the feelings wash over me. I shudder and blink my sadness away.

Focus on the task in front of you, Jenna.

The front door is a faded brick red with stained glass windows on either side, caked in dirt and grime. I use the cuff of my shirt to wipe away some of it and attempt to peer in, but it's dark inside. Just for kicks, I try the handle. Locked, of course.

I turn and walk around to the side of the house. The gate to the weather-worn fence takes no effort to push open. Immediately inside the gate is a side door with paned windows, offering me a view inside of a narrow hallway with an ancient stackable washer and dryer beside a large sink basin. A little girl's bathing suit is draped over the side of the sink. My heart sinks.

My bathing suit...from twenty-five years ago.

I had wondered where that one went; it was my favorite. The brightly colored print looks like a Lisa Frank folder design. I lean against the buckling aluminum siding and catch my breath. For years, my world of possibility was reduced to pill bottles, insurance calls, doctor visits, and 'how-are you-doings' that I never could quite answer. In the blink of an eye, all of that's over and here I stand—no job, no plan, nothing but a Lisa Frank bathing suit that made me feel like a mermaid all those years ago—in front of a house that once held so much promise.

I sigh and close my eyes as grief for the last twenty-five years without my dad consumes me. And now I have lost my mom too. I'm all alone. My eyes well up and soul-crushing sadness almost envelops me when the sound of someone clearing their throat brings me back.

"Can I help you?" a curt male voice asks, startling me.

His voice abruptly pulls me from my private moment. I whirl around, unable to formulate words, my jaw hanging open. Standing before me is an attractive man about my age, and he doesn't look happy. He is tall and lean, with a mop of curly hair falling over his forehead and sinewy forearms peeking out from the rolled sleeves of his pale blue button-down.

"What are you doing walking around my yard?" he asks again, squinting at me, arms folded across his chest.

"Your yard?" I scoff. *There we go. There's my voice.* I put my hands on my hips and frown. "This is *my* house."

The man smirks, a small chuckle escaping. "No, it's not."

Frustration bubbling, I take a step toward him. "*Yes,* it is. And who are *you* anyway?"

He ignores my question. "This isn't your house, lady, and we're not in the business of allowing squatters, okay?" He cocks his head in the direction of the street. "If you don't mind, I'd kindly ask you to exit the property."

Now I'm frustrated, and I suck in a shuddering breath, fighting back the sting of tears threatening to betray me. This is the last thing I need.

"This *is* my house!" I fold my arms across my chest indignantly. "I haven't been here in nearly twenty-five years, but it is." I open my tote bag and rummage for that folder of important papers, pausing to turn off Mom's med reminder app on my phone. I had forgotten to delete the app and now it's blaring, reminding me once again that I don't have a mother anymore. She's gone. Once again, the wave of grief crashes into me and I pause, closing my eyes to collect myself.

The man waits patiently for me to regain my composure. I'll give him that.

My hands tremble as I continue to fumble through the black hole that is my bag. "Aha!" I shout when I find it. I thrust the folder into his hand. He might be good-looking, but I'm not sold on kind yet.

The man offers me a tight smile as he opens the folder, eyeing me as he reads. Then he closes the folder, his expression more somber after reading. "I'm sorry about your mother," he offers with sincerity.

I exhale. "Thank you. See? It is my house," I retort, frowning at him and holding my hand out for the folder.

He hands it back with a sheepish smile, ducking his head. "So, it is."

"You never told me who you are," I remind him, shifting my weight to the other hip. "Are you just some nosy neighbor?"

He barks out a laugh, shaking his head. "No. I'm Miles Corbin. My family's real estate firm manages this property."

"Okay, Miles," I mutter sarcastically. "And you just so happened to be driving by, checking on it?"

He chuckles again. "No, a *nosy neighbor* called me and reported a suspicious woman peering in the windows. It's a small town, what can I say?"

His hazel eyes dance with amusement, and I want to be annoyed, but I can't even muster that anymore. Now, I'm just tired, and the sharp bite of the late afternoon chill is creeping in, reminding me that autumn comes much earlier by the seashore.

I crack a smile, trying to keep him in my good graces. "Okay, Miles, who can I see about getting myself a key?"

"Why don't we go back to my office and chat?" he asks, gesturing back toward the street. I'm hungry and tired, and I just want to go inside and fall onto the twenty-five-year-old mattress, but I don't have a key, or a hotel room for that matter, so I have no choice but to follow the annoyingly handsome stranger back to his office.

We walk around the front of the house, and I glance back at it, longingly, blinking back tears. There are so many memories tied to this little bungalow, but now that I'm alone, unemployed, and forced to live on the little inheritance my mom left me, I have no choice but to let it go. I pause on the sidewalk as Miles gestures toward a sand-colored Subaru Outback, with two surfboards on the roof rack, parked in front of my Camry. "Do you just want to follow me over?"

I nod somberly, hugging myself for warmth no one else can offer, and walk around to the driver's side. How did I get here? I mean, I *know* how I got here but, in this moment, I have never felt more alone. And then, we both notice it at the same time. A flat tire. A completely *undriveable* flat tire. I must have ridden over a nail. I groan and close my eyes, tipping my head toward the sky.

"Well, I guess you're riding with me then." Miles smirks, and I glare at him like he's the reason my world is falling apart.

"You can't be serious." My voice cracks, filled more with defeat than anger. "I don't even know you. Have you ever *seen* a horror movie?" I cross my arms protectively and take a step back. "The pretty girl trusts the handsome guy, and then—" I drag my finger across my throat. "Cue the spooky music."

I don't mean to sound cruel but I'm fraying at the edges—cold, heartbroken, and overwhelmed. I'm one flat tire away from completely unraveling, and he is standing before me with that maddening smirk, his lips turning upward at the corners.

"This is the last thing on earth I need right now," I grumble, fighting the tears pricking the back of my eyes.

At this, Miles softens, stepping closer as he pulls a business card from his wallet and hands it to me. He holds up his hands. "I promise you—I am who I say I am. Come on, Jenna. I'll take you to the office to get your key, and then maybe we can get something to eat and talk about your options." He offers me his arm but drops it when I don't take it.

I reluctantly follow him to his passenger door. His seat is cluttered with empty fast-food bags, which he hurriedly tosses in the back so I can climb in. Before he closes the door, I glance up at him, my brow knitting. "I don't think I told you my name. How did you know it?"

"I saw it on the papers in your folder." He grins proudly and shuts the door, whistling as he walks around to the driver's side.

"Oh," I say, but he doesn't hear me. Warmth bubbles in my chest—he took note of my name. Lately, I've felt so lonely, I don't bother to force the flicker of yearning back down.

Miles climbs into the driver's seat and turns the ignition, shooting a glance in my direction. "Ready?"

I let out a defeated sigh. "I guess."

He shifts into drive and pulls onto the street. "So, you think

I'm handsome?" His lips quirk into a playful smile.

I roll my eyes, but my stomach flutters with unfamiliar tingles. "Don't push it," I murmur.

Chapter Two

Jenna is quiet on the short drive to my office in downtown Cape May, not quite walkable from her house. Coldplay's "The Scientist" plays softly on the radio as Jenna stares out the window. I keep stealing glances at her, but she never looks my way. Her dark brown hair falls in waves around her shoulders, and every time the breeze blows through the cracked windows, I catch a whiff of her shampoo. She rests her elbow on the door and leans against it. I swallow my awkwardness and clear my throat.

"So, when was the last time you were in Cape May?" I ask hesitantly.

"When I was nine."

"I see... How old are you now?" I ask and then wince because I don't think you're supposed to ask women that.

Jenna doesn't flinch though. "I'm thirty-five."

I let out a low whistle. "That's a long time."

"It is. How old are you?"

"I'm forty-one." I force a laugh to lighten the mood. The urge to crack a joke about AOL chat rooms and the A/S/L days bubbles, but something tells me Jenna isn't in the mood for nostalgic joking. She gives me a quiet, polite smile and nods, turning back to the window. *Message Received: doesn't like small talk*. That's fine with me because before I can ask her anything else, we're pulling into the parking lot at Cape Realty & Property Management, the business my father started three decades ago, now run by my brother Nate and me.

Nate's locking the front door just as Jenna and I get out of the car. "Yo," he says over his shoulder, looking surprised to see me. "I thought you had left for the day."

"I got a call about someone trespassing on Monarch." I give Nate a wry smile and gesture teasingly at Jenna. "Turns out, it was the owner."

"No, shit." Nate laughs, holding his hand out to Jenna. "I'm Nate, this guy's younger and much better-looking brother." He winks, glancing at me for my reaction. I could punch him.

Jenna smiles but it doesn't reach her eyes. I hardly know her, but I get the sense that she's just being polite to both of us so she can get this over with and get the hell out of here. "Hi, I'm Jenna." She gently pulls her hand back and wipes it on her jeans.

"Well, I'll leave you to it," Nate says, sidestepping. "I've got to get Caden from the sitter." Nate is a newly single dad. His wife passed away from cancer when Caden was three. Now he is raising his four-year-old son alone and is far more responsible and dependable than I am. I love to josh him for it too, but truthfully, I am really proud of my little bro.

I take out my keys and unlock the door that Nate just locked, motioning for Jenna to follow me inside. Our office is an open-concept space with a variety of seating arrangements—my desk, Nate's desk, and our assistant Linda's desk. A casual seating area with a sofa and end tables sits off to the side when you walk in. Big floor-to-ceiling windows cast the room in the glow of the setting sun. Instead of taking Jenna to my desk, I motion for her to sit on the sofa, so it won't be in her eyes.

"It gets really bright in this room in the afternoon," I say, awkwardly. It's not often that a pretty girl makes me fumble my words, but something about Jenna unsettles me. We just met but it's like she's carrying a silence that I feel the need to fill. There's a heaviness in her eyes, as if she's somewhere else entirely. For some reason, I want to know where. It's because she looks so downtrodden, it tugs on something deep inside of me. It's an unfamiliar feeling.

"Why don't you sit here so the sun doesn't blind you and I'll be right back?" I don't wait for a response and instead, turn and walk to the back of the office where we keep the residential keys and paperwork in a locked cabinet.

Jenna settles on the edge of the couch, flipping through the fall edition of *Cape May Magazine,* though it's clear to me that she isn't really seeing the pages. From the back of the office, I take a minute to study her before digging for the key. She looks drained, shoulders slumped, T-shirt rumpled, like she threw it on in a hurry and doesn't have the energy to care. There's a tiredness in her brown eyes, a sadness behind them. Despite all that, she is very beautiful—striking even. Her shiny brown hair catches in the afternoon light, highlighting her olive complexion. She has full pink lips that look like they haven't smiled in some time. I have to actively stop myself from thinking about how they might taste. Her voice breaks my stare, and I thank my lucky stars she can't see me from where I'm peeking, or else she'd definitely think I'm a perv.

"Are you finding it?" she calls, sounding a bit impatient.

"Be right there," I call back, unlocking the cabinet. I know exactly where the box for 503 Monarch is because I have never touched it. My father took on the property about twenty-five years ago as a favor to a friend. He said the family had just endured a tragedy and wanted to hold onto the house, but they wouldn't be using it. They didn't even want to rent it out. It never made any sense to me—they paid it off and then left it untouched for years. When my dad retired, he told Nate and me that the weekly landscaping was to continue until further notice, and that is literally all we've done since we took over Cape Realty fifteen years ago.

Until today, I've never put a face to the name—and it's a pretty one at that. I take the keys out of the lockbox and swing them on my finger, whistling as I walk back toward Jenna.

Jenna stands and holds out her hand for the keys. "Great.

Thank you so much. "You don't have to drive me back, I'll call an Uber," she adds hurriedly.

I laugh. "Whoa, hold on. Let's sit down for a minute." I motion toward the couch. "What's the rush?"

Jenna rolls her beautiful brown eyes and plops back on the sofa. "I am hungry. And I'm tired, and I just want to get in my house, eat, and go to sleep."

"Okay, well. You should know that I can't just hand you the keys... There is paperwork to file." I scratch my jaw, mulling over what I'm about to say next. "I can file it tomorrow but let me make copies of the will and death certificate so I can do it first thing in the morning," I say, knowing full well that I shouldn't be skipping this step.

Jenna sighs with relief. "Thank you." She hands me the folder of paperwork.

I start to turn and walk away but pause and, as an afterthought say, "You know you can't stay in that house tonight, right?" I frown.

"What? Why not?" Jenna's jaw falls open in disbelief.

"Because the utilities haven't been turned on in years, Jenna. There's no heat or electricity. It's dropping down into the fifties tonight... Honestly, I've never even been inside it. You don't know what you're walking into." I wince when her face falls.

"Now what am I supposed to do?" She bats at her eye, and panic grips me—she might actually cry. "And I can't drive my car." she groans, and my heart lurches in my chest.

I take a step closer and awkwardly pat her shoulder. I force myself to ignore the spark that ignites my fingertips. "Listen, let me make these copies, and then we'll drive back over there and check things out, okay?" I know I'm going above and beyond for this woman, and it's not just because she's beautiful—though I'm sure if my buddies were here, they would say otherwise.

Jenna sniffles and wipes at her eyes, and that's when I realize she really was fighting back tears. "Thank you, Miles," she says quietly. She sits up straighter and I think she may feel better.

I swallow hard. "You're welcome, Jenna. Let me get these copies."

☙

Twenty minutes later, we're back in front of 503 Monarch. The air is cool, and the sun dips behind the trees. It's going to be dark inside the house, but Jenna is hell-bent on getting inside, and I am not going to let her down now. She starts for the front door, and I catch her wrist without thinking. There it is, that electric buzz again. I shake my head and shift my focus to anything—everything—but this beautiful woman in front of me and her full lips that I'd kiss until she was smiling again. "Hold on," I rasp, then clear my throat. "Let me get a flashlight."

Jenna nods and waits on the sidewalk while I walk around to my hatchback. I suck in a breath, open my car emergency kit, and pull out two flashlights. I close the trunk and hand one to Jenna. "Let's do it," I say, putting my hand in the middle of her back in a way that feels too familiar. I immediately pull it back, and she shoots me a small smile and an eyebrow raise, like she knows I feel awkward.

I take the lead, bounding up the steps and unlocking the door. It's an old steel door and requires a little umph to budge. I push my shoulder into it and force it open. It creaks, hinges groaning in protest, but I get it. On the other side is a dark entryway with oak floors and an oak staircase to our right with cobwebs in the corners of the bottom steps. Jenna hesitates in the entrance.

"Come on, it's okay." I offer her a reassuring smile.

"I'm coming," she says, with a shuddering breath. "I'm just in my feelings a little bit."

I force a sympathetic laugh. "I get it," I say, even though I don't, and I never know what women mean when they say that.

"I haven't been back here since I was a little girl," she reminds me, following me down the hallway to a small kitchen. There is a round breakfast table with a thick layer of dust coating it. Jenna sneezes and it might be the cutest sound I've ever heard. *Uh-oh. Reign it in, buddy.* I move to flick on a light before remembering there is no electricity. I shine my flashlight at the cabinets. "Pretty standard kitchen from the '90s," I mutter.

Jenna pushes her lips together and nods, running an index finger through the layer of dust on the table. Beyond the kitchen, a living room comes into view. Drop cloths cover the couches and end tables. Dusty family photos remain on the mantel. Jenna steps closer and shines her flashlight. She picks a frame off the mantel and dusts the glass off with her sleeve. I don't want to hover too much, but from here it looks like beach photos of her and her parents. She is so quiet, and suddenly I feel that I'm encroaching on what should be a private moment.

I have the unshakeable urge to make light of the situation. There is a big box TV from the '90s on a corner cabinet. "There's a throwback for you, huh?" I gesture toward the TV. "I haven't seen one of these things since...well, probably since the late nineties." I chuckle awkwardly—I often deflect with humor when I'm uncomfortable. This is definitely uncomfortable.

Jenna smirks. "I know. Wow," she muses. "It's weird to be in here without them." She shivers. "I want to look at all of it and none of it at the same time."

Silence hangs between us for a few moments while I wait for her to continue. I can't take my eyes off her though. Jenna is not like other vacationers who come to Cape May for the sunsets and a good time. I get the feeling she's not here to escape—she looks like she's been through the wringer and hasn't found her way out yet. Jenna sniffles again and meets my gaze—for a second, it's like she can see right through me.

"You're right, though. I can't stay here tonight." She hugs herself, rubbing her arms for warmth. It's chilly in here. And Jenna is wearing that defeated look again—I suddenly feel the overwhelming urge to fix it for her.

"You can't," I agree, shaking my head. "But we can come back in the daylight and see how it looks tomorrow," I assure her.

"Okay." She nods and steps toward me. "But what do I do in the meantime?"

I smile. "I have an idea, come on." I cock my head back toward the kitchen.

This time, she grabs *my* wrist. "Miles." I turn and look at her wistful expression. "Thank you."

I'm in so much trouble.

Chapter Three

Miles parks his car in the alley behind the Washington Street Mall, right in front of a sign that reads *NO PARKING ANYTIME*. He turns off the engine and looks my way. "Let's get something to eat and I'll help you figure out a place to stay." He smiles, and I force myself to ignore the little flip my heart does when he reveals his dimple. "Come on, everything will be okay."

I glance at the sign and arch an eyebrow. "Okay, but just so you know...you're parked in a no-parking zone." Normally, I'd insist on finding a place to stay first, clinging to the kind of control that a plan offers—but I'm starving and this stranger seems to know what I need most right now.

When he grins at me, he looks like a mischievous teenager. "I know the manager." He winks. "Come on." Throwing open his door, he walks around to mine, opening it at the same time I reach for the handle, taking me by surprise. *Who is this guy?*

I'll admit, I'm warming to him. We might've gotten off on the wrong foot, but I'd be lying if I said he didn't rescue me today. Sure, I would have called a tow truck and a cab, then found a hotel, but it was really nice to have the support of a stranger. I'm used to figuring things out on my own. My dad died when I was nine, and after that, it was always just me and my mom, but she worked a lot. I was a latchkey kid, and I had to fend for myself *often*. It made me independent—and it made me adept at taking care of her when she needed it—but I forgot how nice it is to have help.

"Okay, I trust you. Lead the way, rule breaker," I say, falling in step beside him.

Miles leads me out of the alley and into the Washington Street Mall. It's almost exactly as I remember, and on this Friday evening, the shops are bustling. The town has the mall decorated for autumn with pumpkins, hay bales, and corn stalks throughout. Twinkling lights adorn the trees, giving the walk a magical feel. Miles stops in front of The Ugly Mug, a historic landmark restaurant that I remember from my childhood. It was old even then. I make a mental note to look up when it opened. Miles swings open the door and a few patrons look our way. A group of guys at the corner of the bar erupt into cheers.

"There he is!" one shouts.

"We thought you ditched us," another adds.

"But he's coming in with a pretty lady, so maybe he *is* ditching us," the first one says again.

"It's after Labor Day, bro. No more vacationers." The third guy shouts, laughing at his own joke.

Even though it's clear his friends are teasing him, my face burns and I look at the floor.

"Shut up, you stiffs." He pulls out a barstool for me, then takes the one closest to them. "This is Jenna. She's an out-of-town *client*."

There's no mistaking the emphasis on *client*—and for a fleeting moment I wonder what it might be like if I was more. Maybe Miles is just a kind guy, but he definitely lets his gaze linger a bit too long for someone I just met.

"Client, right. Maybe for now." One of them laughs and elbows the guy next to him in a knowing way.

Miles groans, and if I'm not mistaken, his ears turn a little pink. *Embarrassed? Maybe.* "I shouldn't even bother introducing you to these assholes," he mumbles to me.

I raise my eyebrows and give him an amused smile, then, reaching across him, I hold out my hand to the nearest guy. "I'm Jenna," I say confidently.

"Danny," he says, taking my hand.

The middle guy takes a sip of his beer before answering. "Jack."

I glance over at the quietest guy nursing a Corona as he watches the baseball game on TV. "Hi, I'm Jenna." I speak directly to him.

He gives me a tight smile. "Liam."

I can't help but notice all these guys are wearing wedding rings. Miles isn't, though. At that thought, a spark of something flickers in my chest—Hope? Curiosity? I force it back down. I don't have time to self-analyze. Suddenly, the bartender appears, saving me from inappropriate thoughts about the charismatic stranger perched next to me. *What can I say? It's been a while.*

"Hey, Miles. Who's your friend?" the pretty bartender asks. Her strawberry blonde hair is clipped half back, and she wears tight black jeans and a short-sleeved V-neck shirt with the bar's name on it. A tattooed sleeve of hibiscus flowers winds down her arm. On her other wrist, a single tattoo of a word I can't make out.

"This is Jenna." Miles motions toward me, his voice low. There's a faint flush to his cheeks but he's already brushed off his friends' teasing with the ease of a guy who doesn't take himself too seriously.

"Miles is the property manager for my family home," I add. "We just met today when he caught me trying to break in." I snicker, surprising myself. There's a glimmer of something—relief, maybe?—that catches me off guard. Perhaps it's the promise of food, or maybe just the sense of normalcy that comes with sitting in a bar with strangers. Whatever it is, for the first time in a *long* time, I feel the tightness in my chest lessen ever so slightly. It's not gone, but I feel myself starting to relax.

"I'm Melanie." She smiles. "Don't pay any mind to these schmucks." She gestures at the three married guys. "They like to give him a hard time, but really, they should be going home to their *wives*." She rolls her eyes, and I instantly like her.

I laugh softly. "Okay." I glance at Miles who seems a little more relaxed. Melanie puts a draft beer in front of him, and he immediately takes a sip.

"What can I get for you?" Melanie asks, leaning on the bar. "Then, you have to tell me what brings you to Cape May. It's not often a lady joins these guys for happy hour."

I hesitate, knowing my funds are tight and not knowing Miles's intentions for this pit stop.. "Uh...I'll just have what he's having." I gesture to Miles.

"Miller Lite? Okay." She turns to grab it, giving me the opportunity to ask Miles some questions.

"So, you know everyone in this town, huh?" I squint at him curiously.

He laughs, completely unselfconscious, and my stomach does a little flip. "Well, I grew up here, and it's a small town. Hence the phone call about a strange woman peeking in the windows of your house," he says.

I nod slowly. "Gotcha." Then, to the guys who seem to have already forgotten about us. "And you all live here too?" I ask, cocking my head in their direction.

"We all grew up here, on Perry Street," says Jack, the guy in the middle. "We've known your boy here since he was six years old, scoring in the wrong soccer goal."

"That was one time!" Miles protests. "I was learning."

I laugh until my phone buzzes. I glance down and freeze. A reminder for Mom's next doctor's appointment—one I forgot to cancel. The air shifts. The lightness I was feeling evaporates

"Surfing is definitely more your sport," Danny adds, and finally, Liam tears his eyes from the TV and laughs.

"Whatever." Miles chuckles easily as Melanie sets my beer down.

"So, Jenna. Tell me about yourself, and I'll tell you if you should steer clear of this guy." She juts her thumb in Miles's direction and laughs.

I inhale sharply and take a sip of my beer for courage. *How much do I really want to share with these strangers?* "Well, my mom died a few weeks ago..." I start.

Melanie cuts me off. "Oh, I'm so sorry." She reaches for my hand, squeezing it with an apologetic smile.

"It's okay. She was sick for a long time." I shudder as I take a deep breath, then offer her a grim smile so she knows it's okay. "I lived with her in an apartment for the past few years so I could take care of her. And my parents bought our house in Cape May when I was a little girl...but when my dad died, I assumed my mom sold it. I didn't even know we still owned it until last week. So, since the apartment lease was up, I packed my things and headed East. Miles found me poking around the yard earlier." I shoot him a wry look.

Smirking, Melanie cocks her head in Miles' direction. "What a way to pick up a girl," she says, her eyes twinkling with amusement.

I shake my head, and a nervous laugh escapes. "Oh...no. That's not what this is."

"That's not what this is," Miles reiterates, wincing and glancing sideways at me.

"Okay." Melanie holds her hands up in defense, smiling as she backs away. "Let me get you guys some menus." She comes back a moment later and hands them to us. Miles doesn't even open his. "So, are you planning to live in it now?" she asks. "We don't get too many year-round newcomers." Cape May is a gorgeous Victorian beach town that draws tourists year after year, but in the off-season, things seem to be much quieter.

I lift my gaze from the menu. "I think I have to sell it," I say, regretfully. "I lost my job, and I could really use the money."

Miles flicks his gaze my way. "I don't think it's exactly in a livable condition right now," he says. "I mean, maybe. But you'll have some work to do before you can sell it. We can talk about that tomorrow."

I sigh. "So much for a quick buck," I mutter. Then, to Melanie, "Can I have the cheeseburger, please? Medium."

"Make that two," Miles chimes in, handing Melanie both of

our menus.

Melanie taps on the computer kiosk, her nails clicking against the screen. "Got it. So where are you going to stay then?" Melanie asks me, but it is Miles she's looking at with a raised eyebrow.

"Actually...I was thinking," Miles cuts in. "Liam, is Ellie's guesthouse open?"

Liam coughs and clears his throat. "I can ask her," he says, picking up his phone and hammering out a text message.

Miles turns back toward me. "Ellie is Liam's next-door neighbor. She's a dear friend to all of us. She has a little guesthouse on her property. If it's open, I'm sure you can stay there tonight." He awkwardly pats my shoulder in an effort to be reassuring. "In the morning, I'll pick you up, and we'll figure out the house situation."

"Guesthouse is booked, but Ellie says she can stay in one of the rooms in the main house. She'll get it fixed up right now," Liam calls from his spot across the bar.

I scrunch up my nose. "Is that awkward? Me staying with a strange woman I've never met before."

Miles barks out a laugh. "I mean, you're welcome to stay with me." He takes a swig of his beer. Heat pricks the back of my neck.

Melanie pats my hand. "It won't be awkward. Ellie is in her seventies, and she is the kindest soul. She'll make you feel comfortable." She gives me a reassuring smile as a food runner brings out our burgers.

"That was fast," I say, and suddenly, I'm starving. I take one bite of the burger and all bets are off. It's a good thing I'm not trying to impress anyone because I devour it like I haven't eaten in weeks, all traces of dignity gone by my second bite. Miles eats his equally fast. We must be a sight.

"I got to jet," Danny announces from his spot on the corner. He walks over to us and puts a hand on Miles's shoulder. "Miles, call me if Jenna needs anything with the house." He pulls a business card from his pocket and hands it to me. "I'm a contractor," he adds with a smile.

"I probably can't afford you," I grumble, wiping my mouth with a napkin. "But thanks." I take the card and drop it into my tote bag, probably never to be seen again.

"I'm out too," Jack says, throwing some money on the bar. "Kid sports tomorrow. It was nice meeting you, Jenna." He smiles and holds up his hand in a wave to everyone as he and Danny exit together.

I am finishing my burger when Miles says, "Liam, do you mind giving Jenna a lift to Ellie's since you're right next door? I have something I need to take care of."

A wave of nerves swirl in my belly, threatening to send that burger right back up. Liam seems kind enough, but his quiet, serious demeanor puts me on edge. He's a stark contrast to Miles's happy-go-lucky energy and easy charm that has already started to wear down my walls. I shoot Miles a concerned look, but suddenly he's all business like I'm another task on his to-do list. It stings more than I'd like to admit.

"Sure thing. Whenever you're ready, Jenna. My wife is going to kill me for being out this long while she's home with the babies." Liam chuckles, and it puts me at ease.

"Okay. I'm ready." I push back my barstool and fumble in my purse for my wallet. "Melanie, can I have my check?" I call. She's the only bartender working and things are picking up. I note the flyer sitting next to me: *Fridays in September: Open Mic Night.*

Miles waves his hand, shaking his head. "Don't worry about it. I got it." He stands and throws three twenties on the bar. "Let's get your bag out of my car."

If I were anywhere but Cape May—with its small-town-everyone-is-family feel—I'd probably call a ride share and book it to the nearest hotel, but something stops me from doing the one thing I know is most rational. Maybe it's Miles, maybe it's this town that inherently feels like home, or maybe it's just that I'm realizing now how damn lonely I've been all this time. Either way, something about Miles makes him seem instinctively trustworthy. So, I blindly follow the two men out of the bar to get in a car with the second strange man in one day.

☙

As it turns out, Liam is totally and completely fine. As we drive over to Ellie's house on Perry Street, he tells me how he met his wife, Sophie, when she was staying at Ellie's cottage. I listen intently and the nerves in my stomach settle almost immediately. It's already seven p.m., and I know most of the anxiety I was feeling is due to the condition of the house, losing my mom and my job, and the uncertainty of my life before me. It has nothing to do with the kind stranger driving me to a place I can stay for the night.

He pulls into the driveway of his house and kills the engine. A pretty woman that I assume is his wife stands on the porch, holding a baby girl. He gestures toward them. "That's Sophie and our daughter, Leah. Come on, I'll introduce you."

I gather my small duffel bag and purse and climb down from his enormous truck. Liam looks like the kind of guy who *would* drive a pickup this big. I walk around in front of the truck, where Sophie meets us in the driveway.

"You must be Jenna." She smiles. "I'm Sophie. This is Leah." She gives the squishy baby a little nuzzle and her chubby hands grip Sophie's cheeks.

"Hi." I force cheerfulness into my voice, hoping to contradict the melancholy I feel inside from the absence of my own family. Liam clears his throat and gestures at the sage-green Victorian house next door. "That's Ellie's house." He reaches for Leah. "Soph, why don't you walk Jenna over?"

"I'd be glad to." Sophie smiles, the epitome of a warm fire on this cool autumn night. "Let me take something from you." She reaches for my tote bag.

I shake my head. "Oh, no. You don't have to. I've got it."

"I insist," she says, patting my arm. "Ellie will be having her evening tea right now. Maybe we can join her." She takes my tote bag and links her arm through mine. Nothing will ease the pain of the loss of my mom but the kindness I have encountered today is slowly melting the ice around my broken heart.

When we reach the front door, I expect Sophie to knock, but she lets herself in. "Ellie, we're here!" Sophie calls. She turns to me and motions for me to follow.

Ellie steps out of the kitchen, wiping her hands on a dish rag. "Oh, hello!" She smiles, her warm countenance instantly making me feel safe. "I'm Ellie. You must be Jenna."

"Yes." I nod, offering a tight smile. "Thank you for letting me crash here tonight."

Ellie waves her hands. "Nonsense! Robert and I love the company." She turns toward the kitchen. "Leave your bags. He'll bring them up to your room. I've made us some tea."

I smile for real this time, marveling at the way this small group of friends came together today to help me, a newcomer.

Sophie shoots me an I-told-you-so look and grins. "Come on," she whispers.

In the kitchen, Ellie has set the table with four saucers and some Italian cookies I remember from my childhood. I pull out the nearest chair, suddenly desperate to sit down. "Oh, I wish you didn't go to any trouble. I really just need a warm bed tonight," I say meekly, tucking my hair behind my ear.

"This is what she does." Sophie looks at Ellie with fondness. "She *loves* taking care of people."

"I do." Ellie nods, bringing the teapot over. She pours hot water into each of our mugs and offers me a basket of tea bags. "Pick any kind you like," she urges.

I do as I'm told, and we sit quietly together while our tea bags steep. I know as soon as my head hits the pillow, I will zonk. Tomorrow I will figure out what's next. *What's next* has been a question I've been chasing the answer to since my dad died. After he died, my mother and I moved into a town house.

The day we sold my childhood home felt like closing the door on a whole life we were leaving behind. By the time I left for college, my mother was ready to downsize again. She moved into the two-bedroom apartment that we'd shared after her diagnosis. When she died, there was no home to sell, no place to return to. Just a month-to-month lease that ended with everything else. The Cape May house came as a great surprise—a leftover piece of my family history. I came here feeling hopeful, but instead, I'm disappointed. I have no plan and even worse, no money to make one.

"So, Jenna, tell me about yourself." Ellie's voice interrupts my thoughts.

"Oh... I... Well, I just discovered last week, during the probate of my mother's will, that our house here still existed." The words tumble out of me before I can stop them, rambling and messy. "I'm planning to sell it, and I naively thought I'd be able to stay there while I do, but I'm not sure if that will be possible." I exhale loudly and take a sip of my tea, hoping it'll settle the discomfort inside me. "I don't know what I'm going to do. My aunt lives here in town, but...we're estranged."

Ellie slurps her tea, making me smile. I can already tell she is a warm light to everyone she meets, while at the same time, unapologetically herself. "Who is your aunt? Maybe I know her."

Just then, Robert interrupts us with a peek in the kitchen from the hall. He's holding my bag. "Hi, everyone," he says. Then, turning to me, "You must be Jenna. I just wanted to introduce myself and say goodnight," he says, chuckling. "You know we old people can't stay up too late. I'll just drop your bag in the purple room, if that's okay?"

I grin, nodding. "That's more than fine, thank you," I say. "And thank you for letting me stay here."

"You're welcome, dear. Goodnight." And then he's gone.

Ellie smiles after him. "That man has more creeks than our porch swing, but he's my favorite place to rest." She sighs, a content smile crossing her face. "Now, tell me about this aunt of yours."

I hesitate. If she does know my Aunt Leona, I'm not sure I want her to know I'm back in town. But Ellie has a kindness about her and I get the feeling she can make everyone she meets spill their guts. I don't want to alienate myself by keeping secrets from the people who are helping me. "Her name is Leona Walker. She is my late father's sister. But I haven't seen her since a year after he died. My mom and aunt didn't exactly get along." I scrunch up my nose. "I have a cousin too—I saw him more when I was in college, but I think he lives nearby. His name is Jake."

Ellie dips her chin, and just when I think she may judge me for being estranged from family, she reaches for my hand. "Sometimes, cutting toxic people out of our lives is the best thing we can do—family or not. I'm sure your mother had a good reason." She pulls her hand back and takes a sip of tea. "Your aunt is in my book club, but I don't know her well. I do know though that you and your mother are different people, and it sounds like your aunt is your only family left. Maybe you should try reaching out."

I don't have the energy for this type of conversation—not after the day I've had. It's taking everything in me to smile and take this stranger's advice with a grain of salt.

Maybe Sophie can sense it because she interjects. "Jenna, you must be exhausted. Where did you say you drove here from?"

I clear my throat. "Oh, Bucks County, Pennsylvania." I stifle a yawn. "I am very tired, yes."

Sophie rises. "Ellie, why don't I show Jenna to her room?"

Ellie smiles. "That would be lovely."

"Thank you for the tea," I offer, standing. "And I will think about what you said."

"You're welcome, dear." Ellie turns back toward me. "And Jenna? Don't fret. Everything looks better in the morning."

I sure hope she's right.

Chapter Four

Miles

I arrive at Ellie's at eight-thirty on Saturday morning. I forgot to get Jenna's number last night, so I'm really taking a chance on her being awake this early. I'm also taking a chance on a coffee order. On my way over, I stopped by Coffee Tyme and got two options for Jenna to choose from. I climb Ellie's front steps and hear laughter through the front door before I even knock.

Having grown up on this street, I've known Ellie my entire life. My parents still live across the street, but I don't feel like I can just walk into Ellie's house the way Liam does. I balance the two to-go cups in one hand and grab the crab-shaped door knocker with the other.

"Come in!" Robert's jovial shout carries outside.

Juggling the coffees, I open the front door and peer down the small hallway to the kitchen. Jenna is laughing—a true, genuine belly laugh—as she wipes her eyes. She is absolutely radiant when she laughs. The realization startles me. Ellie and Robert sit side by side and they are laughing too. I wonder what I missed that was so funny. "Good morning," I say, prompting everyone to look up.

"Oh! Hi." Jenna smiles and stands. She is wearing a pair of lounge shorts and an old, hooded sweatshirt that says Drexel University. Seeming self-conscious, she pushes her bangs out of her face. Catching her off guard awakens something in me I don't have a name for—a pull that is equal parts warmth and curiosity. "I didn't expect you so early on a Saturday," she admits. "Or I would have been ready."

I shake my head. "Totally fine. I, uh, forgot to get your number yesterday so..." I trail off, keenly aware that Ellie and Robert haven't taken their eyes off us.

"What's that?" Jenna asks, eyeing the cups I'm holding.

I shift awkwardly and set them on the table. "I didn't know what you liked, so...I got two. You can choose. I got just a regular coffee with cream and sugar, or a pumpkin spice latte." I raise my eyebrows, hoping that one of those will suffice.

"Ooh. Pumpkin spice, please. I haven't had one yet this season." She picks up the cup with PSL scribbled on the side and inhales before taking a sip. This Jenna is an entirely different person than the one I met last night. Unfortunately, that only makes me more interested in getting to know her. Against all my better judgment.

"So, what is on your agenda today?" Ellie asks me, pointedly.

"I thought I'd bring Jenna back to the house so we can assess it for the list price. We can possibly see about her staying there in the meantime," I say, glancing at Jenna for her approval.

She nods and smiles in between blowing on her coffee. "Great. Yes. Let's do it." She pushes her chair in. "Ellie, Robert, thank you for breakfast. And thank you for letting me impose last night." She turns to me. "I'll get ready as quickly as possible." Picking her coffee up, she turns and heads up the front staircase.

I rock back and forth on my heels, bracing for the grilling that I sense coming. Ellie is known for her unsolicited advice.

"So, Miles," Ellie starts. *There it is.*

I turn to her, unable to hide my amusement. "Ellie." I grin.

"Just what are you planning to do with Jenna?" She cuts right to the chase. Ellie knows I've been a bit of a serial dater since my divorce. In all honesty, it's because I do get lonely, but I hesitate to let myself get close to someone again. It killed me that I failed at being there for my wife. I come from a close-knit family with parents who love each other—a shining example. Yet, I failed. If there's one thing I learned from my short marriage, it's both people have to make the conscious decision to make it work. I don't know why, but Erin and I never seemed to be moving in the same direction. We wanted different things. I want—or wanted, since it probably won't happen *now*—kids. She didn't. She was very career-focused and didn't care about spending time with my family. I thought she would embrace them since she left her own to live here with me when we got married, but no. It was a constant battle of wills.

After a year of disagreement, Erin said she wanted out. Small town life was not for her. It crushed me, but I didn't let anyone see that. Instead, I threw myself headlong into distractions—work, surfing, and casual dating only. That's why Ellie is probing me now.

"I'm not doing anything, Ellie, I promise." I hold up my hands. "I get the feeling she's had a hard time. I'm just trying to help her out." I raise my eyebrows at the two of them. "I know you think I'm some sort of Casanova, but believe it or not, I don't try to take home *every* woman I meet. Otherwise, she might've just come home with me last night." I chuckle at my own joke.

Ellie and Robert don't get a chance to respond before Jenna comes thundering down the stairs. "Who would've gone home with you last night?" she asks, eyeing me suspiciously.

"Oh, my friend's puppy. I really want another dog, but I just don't have the time to devote to two of them." I'm impressed with my own recovery and shoot a warning glance toward Ellie.

Jenna gives me a look like she doesn't quite believe me. "You know, they say dogs need companions, just like people."

"Pete's fine. He doesn't need a companion." I chuckle, taking a sip of my coffee.

"Your dog's name is Pete?" Jenna asks with a giggle.

"Yep. He's a Boxer. It suits him. Come on, let's go." I salute Ellie and Robert. "Thanks again, guys."

Ellie and Robert rise from their chairs and come around the table. Robert pats Jenna's shoulder. "It was nice to meet you, dear," he says, excusing himself to the living room while we all walk to the door.

At the front door, Ellie pulls Jenna into a hug. "Think about what I said about your aunt," she whispers as she pulls away.

"I will, I promise," Jenna says, pulling back and moving to pick up her bag. She stops when she sees I'm already holding it. She gives me one of those cute, annoyed smiles but doesn't try to take it from me.

Once we're in the car, I glance at Jenna. "So, what's this about an aunt?" I ask casually.

She sighs. "My aunt Leona lives here. She is my dad's older sister...but I haven't seen her since about a year after my dad died. My cousin Jake went to Drexel with me, so I've seen him on occasion and kept up with him on Facebook...but we're not exactly friends. I think he's a personal trainer or something. Ellie thinks I should reconnect with them since they're my only family left." Jenna fidgets with her seat belt strap. "I'm just not sure where I'd start."

I purse my lips—they must have really gone deep last night getting to know each other. I think I know Jenna's cousin, Jake, but I want to be sure before I blurt it out. "What gym does your cousin work at?" I ask her.

She shrugs. "I don't even know. My aunt lives in a condo now, I think. But I'm not sure exactly where Jake lives. And I won't be knocking on Aunt Leona's door without him, that's for sure." Jenna leans her head back on the seat, staring out the window as we head north toward Monarch Street. Then, as an afterthought, she adds, "Their last name is Walker."

That's when it dawns on me. "Jake Walker. That's it. I know who he is. He surfs at my beach. He's younger than me but I've hung around him a little." My memory of Jake is he's a single guy who works at the Local Fitness on the west side and surfs every chance he gets. "He works at my gym. I could take you there," I offer. As far as I know, he's an okay guy, but Jenna seems hesitant.

Jenna scrunches her nose and shakes her head. "I think I'd rather figure out the house stuff first."

"Okay." I don't push it. I turn down Monarch Street and park behind Jenna's silver Camry. "Is there anything you want to get out of your car?" I ask, putting my own in park and unbuckling my seat belt.

"Oh, good idea. If I'm going to call a tow truck, I should probably get the rest of my things." Jenna unbuckles her seat belt and hurries out of my car with me at her heels. She opens her trunk, and I watch as she struggles to pull out a very large suitcase.

After a minute, I reach in and grab the handle, giving it a swift tug. I flash her a satisfied smile and she rolls her eyes. "Anything else?" I ask her.

"Just my sunglass—" She walks around to the driver's side but abruptly stops and looks my way, narrowing her eyes. "This tire was flat last night."

I nod in agreement. "Indeed, it was."

"And now it's not."

"Correct." I chuckle. "You're observant."

Jenna puts her hands on her hips and cocks her head at me. "Did you change my tire this morning?"

"No. I changed your tire last night. After Liam took you to Ellie's." I grin.

"Miles." She swipes her tongue over her lips. "I didn't even have a spare."

"I know. Even if you did, your car was locked. Luckily, I had one," I say, pleased with myself.

Jenna lets her tote bag drop to the street. She strides definitively over to me and wraps me in a tight hug. "Thank you," she murmurs into my T-shirt.

Unsure if I should hug her back, I awkwardly pat her shoulder blades. "It was nothing," I say, pulling back. This woman barged into my life less than twenty-four hours ago and she already has me doing nice things for her because I can't stand to see the defeated look on her face for another second. *What have I gotten myself into?*

Chapter Five

Miles pulls away from my embrace and I'm instantly self-conscious about my impulsive hug. My gaze darts away before it lingers on him and I step back, fidgeting with the hem of my shirt. "Sorry. It's just...no one has done anything this nice for me in a really, *really* long time," I admit, tilting my head.

Miles runs his hands through his tousled hair. "It was nothing," he says with a casual shrug. "I wanted to. But maybe before you leave town, I should show you how to change a tire."

Memories flood my mind and suddenly I'm eight years old again, hanging out the backseat window while my dad changes the front tire on my mom's station wagon.

He kneels next to the axle and cranks, all the while telling me, "Someday, Jenna, I will teach you how to change a tire. It's something all girls should know how to do."

"Why, Daddy? I'll have you do it for me," I say, gleefully.

Dad shakes his head. "I may not always be nearby. You'll need this life skill one day."

If I close my eyes, I can see him winking at me with black grease on his hands.

I shudder at the memory running through me and tears prick the back of my eyes. I missed out on so much life with my dad, and being back here is a stark reminder of everything I don't have. No dad, and now, no mom either. *It's not fair.* Miles interrupts my thoughts with the clearing of his throat.

"You okay? You went somewhere else for a minute." Miles eyes me cautiously, like he's afraid I might break.

I shake away the sadness. "I'm good. Yeah. Let's check out the house."

Before he can stop me, I trek across the lawn and back into memories of the past.

☙

It doesn't take long for me to realize I'm in way over my head. In the daylight, the house looks more promising but not promising enough to walk away from this with a pretty penny. Not to mention, my mother didn't do anything to pack this place up. Memories are everywhere, but a musty stillness clings to every corner, every surface. It's as if the house itself has been holding its breath, waiting for life to resume inside its walls. Yellowed family photos line the shelves and walls in tarnished frames. Dust blankets every surface, muting the colors underneath.

Aside from the signs of life frozen in time, the faded wallpaper is peeling like withered leaves, cobwebs fall from the ceiling like ghosts, draping across corners and doorways. Areas of drywall are cracking, spreading like spiderwebs. The ceiling in the kitchen has dark water spots speckled in an uneven pattern.

"That might not be good," Miles points his pen upward. The look on his face tells me he *knows* it's not good.

"The brown spots?" I ask, furrowing my brow.

"It could be a sign of a leaky roof." Miles treads lightly. "It just means we need to have the roof looked at."

"Okay." I let out a shaky breath, continuing on to the laundry room.

Laundry from 1997 still sits in the dryer. My small colorful bathing suit draped over the sink basin. I let my fingers trail the fabric for a moment before walking away, Miles at my heels. In the adjacent bathroom, the toilet has a ring around the water line. Rust creeps like ivy across the faucet. I glance at myself in the tarnished mirror, a shadow of the girl who once lived here, and take a breath to steady myself. *Okay, it's dirty, but it's not that bad.*

The house is buried in layers of dust as thick as ash. Drop cloths cover the living room furniture, but somehow, dust still found its way underneath to the cushions. An old cordless telephone sits on the end table next to the couch. Time has settled here, like an old friend overstaying their welcome. I climb the stairs and poke my head into the hall bathroom. There are old shampoo bottles and hand soaps in here. The bar soap in the shower is so stuck to the shelf that I fear I'll need a chisel to get it off.

Maybe it's my imagination but as soon as I walk into my parents' bedroom, I can smell her. My mom. That warm, familiar trace of her perfume. I know it's impossible—she hasn't set foot in this house in twenty-five years. But it's here somehow and it's clinging to the air like she never left.

"You could have warned me it would still smell like you," I mutter, pacing slowly around the room. I tug open a dresser drawer. Empty. Then another, nothing in there either. Did someone clean these out, or were we not here long enough that time to unpack?

Miles leans quietly in the door frame, watching me carefully. He coughs lightly and I look his way.

"You know," he says, his voice low, "they say if you can smell the scent of someone who has passed on, it means they're still with you. Maybe your mom is here."

My cheeks warm—I didn't think he heard me.

He lets out another awkward cough and when I look at him, he looks away.

"Maybe," I say softly. "I think I've heard that too."

I brush past him and step into the hallway.

In the other bedrooms, morning light filters through grime-streaked windows, casting everything in a sickly yellow glow. Drop cloths cover the beds but somehow the ancient sheets still smell musty with traces of dust settling in the creases.

"First order of business is to strip the beds," I mumble, crossing the room and pushing apart the rest of the frayed curtains. The house needs serious cleaning. It's also freezing in here. *Ah, right, no utilities.* "God, you really kept everything exactly as we left it," I say, looking up at the ceiling like she'll hear me better that way. "If you're still here, can you at least help me figure out what the hell to do now?"

Miles keeps his distance as he follows me from room to room making notes on a small pad of paper, presumably assessing the home's potential value. After opening drawers and closets, looking at family photos that no one had the opportunity to put away, and wiping my silent tears, I trudge back down the steps with Miles in tow.

I walk into the living room and lift the drop cloth to reveal an old tan sofa with small burgundy dots in the fabric. I remember the day this sofa was delivered. My mother was thrilled with her brand-new living room in her brand-new beach house. She wouldn't let us eat in front of the TV after that. I suck in a breath and plop onto the sofa willing to take the risk of dust clinging to my black leggings.

"Now what?" I say, more to myself than to Miles.

Miles pulls the drop cloth further off the sofa and sits down next to me, leaving a bit of space between us. A part of me wishes he would move closer. Although that would probably be as terrible an idea as the bangs.

"Well. If you want to stay here, we can start by having the utilities turned on and getting a cleaning crew in here." He offers a reassuring eyebrow raise. "It needs work but it's not unlivable."

I shudder. "I want to put it on the market and run for my life," I admit. "But I have nowhere to go. My lease was up when I left." My voice catches as I fight back a new round of tears. "This feels like *a lot.*" Everything in my life has felt like a lot lately, but I don't say that to Miles. I'm not usually a big crier but with the turns my life has taken, it feels like all I do anymore.

Miles scoots closer and awkwardly drapes an arm around my shoulder. "Hey, it'll be okay," he says, but his reassurance feels limp.

I suck in a sharp breath. "If you listed it tomorrow, what do you think I would get for it?" I ask, nervously chewing on my lip.

"Oh gosh. Probably not what you're hoping." Miles doesn't look my way.

"$500K?"

Miles stifles a laugh, then points his finger downward.

"$300K?" I venture. My mother had some medical bills that her Medicare and secondary insurance didn't cover. Now, they're my medical bills.

Miles meets my eyes, then makes the same downward motion with his index finger.

"That bad?" I groan. I thought that in a beach town, even the worst of the worst houses go for top dollar. *I guess I was wrong.* "How much, then?"

"That depends, do you have any money to invest in renovations or upgrades before we list it?" Miles's face softens. I'm sure he's trying not to completely crush me.

"Not really. I have some money in my 401(k) I could tap into if I wanted to take the tax hit. My mom worked really hard up until she got sick, but she was a renter. She had very little savings and nothing with equity." I sigh and throw myself backward on the couch. "This is bleaker than I thought."

Miles leans on his elbows, staring at the floor. He's quiet for a few minutes, probably thinking about my options. The morning sun casts a golden glow through the patio door, highlighting Miles's physique perfectly. Even though it's the last thing I should be thinking about, I take this moment to study the sharp edges of his back, the curve of his shoulder into his bicep, and the way his gray T-shirt hugs his lean muscle. His wavy hair curls at the nape of his neck, and in his profile, I see the perfect amount of stubble.

He interrupts my assessment of him. "So, I'm thinking you have a couple of options. First, we can try listing it for $225K. You won't get that. People will see the inside and try to lowball you. We may be able to sell it for the upper one hundreds or lower two hundreds and you can walk away." He pauses, turning back to me, studying my face while giving me a moment to digest.

I sit up straighter. "Or?"

"Or...you can have the utilities turned on, a cleaning crew come in, and you can stay here—take time to think about what you're going to do and fix the house up at the same time." Miles shrugs.

"But I really can't afford to fix it up too much," I say, chewing on my lower lip.

"Listen, I'm not saying new countertops or floors or anything like that. But paint can go a long way. You can refinish the cabinets, replace the rusty hinges. Fix up the yard. There are all kinds of things you can do." Miles is so encouraging that optimism flutters in my chest—though maybe that's just the budding attraction I feel toward him.

"Okay." I mull this over for a minute. "I probably can't afford your friend Danny," I admit. "Unless he takes a credit card."

Miles huffs out a laugh. "I actually think he does, but that's beside the point. Think about the things you can do and make a list. Maybe there are some things I can help with."

I nod. "Okay. Well, at the very least, I'll stay a few more days."

Miles claps his hands together. "Attagirl! See, you can do hard things, Jenna. I believe in you."

"Miles?" I ask, my meek voice barely above a whisper.

"Yes?"

My face contorts in embarrassment. "I don't even know where to start. I feel so overwhelmed."

Miles stands and holds a hand out to me. "Come on, I'll call a cleaning company, and you call the electric company. You've got this."

I sigh begrudgingly, channeling the sharp independent girl I know is inside me. *I've got this.*

Chapter Six

I don't realize I'm whistling as I unlock the office door Monday morning. I spent most of the weekend with Jenna, helping her clean up the house so she could stay there. There were a few awkward moments where her emotions got the better of her—ordinarily, that would send me running. There is something about tears that makes me feel useless—like I'm supposed to fix it, but I never quite know how. For some reason though, I didn't run. I *wanted* to stay. I feel drawn to Jenna like I've never experienced before, like a current I can't fight. She's guarded but that's probably because of everything she's dealing with right now. After nearly forty-eight hours getting to know her, I admittedly, still don't know that much—but I want to. Aside from her warm brown eyes and genuine, disarming smile, there's a brokenness about her, cracks beneath the surface she's trying to hide. I want to know more about her. I can't exactly explain why but, it's not my usual MO—not by a long shot.

"Yo, dude." Nate comes up behind me, scaring the shit out of me.

I nearly jump out of my skin. "Geez, warn a brother, will you?" I huff, whirling around to face him.

"Sorry. Why are you so jumpy?" Nate reaches around me to push open the door and walks inside. I follow him.

"I'm just tired, I guess. I spent all weekend helping Jenna with her house. I didn't even surf. Maybe I need to decompress." I walk to my desk, drop my briefcase—that really has nothing in it—and boot up my desktop.

Nate gives a low whistle. "Whoa. You spent all weekend with that girl?" He raises his eyebrows. "When was the last time you did *that*?"

I hold up my hands. "Hey, it wasn't like *that*," I say, hesitating. "I just get the sense that she's been through a lot. I feel bad about that so I'm helping her out."

"So, she's sad, and you didn't hook up because you feel bad for her? That doesn't sound like you," Nate says, a smirk playing on his lips. Nate is the most honest and loyal guy I know, but we've always been polar opposites. It's not that I'm not honest or loyal—I am, to my friends and family. But, with women? I protect myself. I go after what I want, and for the past two years since my divorce, I haven't really cared about who I hurt. I'm not proud of that. Of *course,* Nate finds it hard to believe that I can spend a weekend with a woman and not have sex with her. "Is she weird?"

I bark out a laugh that surprises us both. "Not even a little bit."

"Huh." Nate rocks back in his chair. "Well, I'll be."

I crumple up a piece of paper and throw it at him, laughing. "Shut up."

☙

By late morning, I can't take it anymore. I want to know what Jenna is up to. No, I want to see her. I actually remembered to get her number this time, so I shoot her a text.

What are you up to?

It takes her a few minutes to respond, and they're the longest minutes of my life. What is happening to me? *Who is this girl?*

Finally, after about five minutes her reply comes through.

Jenna

I'm going to buy some paint! How is work?

I smile as I read the text, and I'm definitely not mistaking the curious look Nate gives me.

I ignore him and hammer back a reply.

Whoa, whoa. Don't buy paint yet. We need a home inspector to come out first.

Jenna's reply comes at a rapid speed this time.

Jenna

Too late.

I groan, throwing my head back.

"You good over there?" Nate asks, not even bothering to hide his amusement.

"Jenna bought paint." I frown. "I wanted to get her a home inspection first."

"I think she might need a *different* kind of inspection from you." Nate chortles at his own joke.

I ignore him and reply to Jenna.

I am going to set up a home inspection for you. Don't paint anything until after that.

Jenna

Ugh. Fine.

I must be smiling at my phone again—Nate cocks his head at me, a little brother twinkle in his eye. "You like this girl," he observes with a hint of amusement in his voice.

"I don't." I shake my head. "I mean, not like *that*. I'm just being nice." I shrug. "I'm doing what you would do if you got to her first." I laugh, brushing him off. So what if Jenna was the last thing I thought about before I went to sleep last night—and the first thing this morning? So what if I'm already thinking of ways I can see her again? I am not a relationship guy anymore but damn if Jenna hasn't made me second guess that.

"Right." Nate nods, a sarcastic smirk playing on his mouth.

But even as he says it, I am already texting Jenna back.

Have you eaten yet? Want to get some brunch?

ᘓ

Jenna agrees to meet me at a small cafe downtown for brunch. I want to see her, but I don't want her to know that I can't stop thinking about her, so I arm myself with information about the house. I don't even know why I want to see her so badly. I've got some soul-searching of my own to do. Since my ex-wife, Erin, no woman has pulled me in like this. Typically, I'll ask a girl out, she'll say yes—a vacation fling sounds fun. We'll hang out for a week and then she'll go back to her life, and I'll go back to mine. It's really the perfect arrangement: I'm never lonely, and I never have to commit to anyone. Jenna fits the mold—she is just passing through—but I can already tell she'd be different for me. Only since I've met her have I started feeling like something is missing. It's a foreign feeling and suddenly, I'm questioning everything.

When I walk up to the café, Jenna is already sitting at an outdoor table waiting for me. She's scrolling on her phone and doesn't notice me at first. I pause before she does and let myself take her in. Her brown hair, in its naturally wavy texture, is blowing in the autumn breeze. She's wearing oversized black sunglasses and black leggings. Her running shoes look brand new, and I wonder if she has ever worn them. Maybe she's like me, has good intentions of running, even goes as far as buying the shoes, but then never actually runs. She has on a long-sleeved shirt, but she rubs her arms when the breeze blows, telling me she's chilly. She's beautiful, and I am completely taken aback by her.

I glance down at my own outfit. Nate and I keep a pretty casual office, unless we have home showings. I'm wearing loose-fitting jeans, a thermal, and my gray Hey Dudes. This is an outfit I would wear on a date, yet I'm strangely self-conscious. I don't know what's happening to me around this girl. I run a hand through my floppy hair and suck in a breath. It's now or never.

A soft breeze drifts in as I approach, and Jenna rubs her arms again. "Are you cold?" I ask her.

She looks up from her phone, giving me an easy smile and pushing her sunglasses onto her head. "Hey."

"Hey," I say back. For a moment, our eyes lock, and we linger there, suspended in whatever this is that's brewing between us. Mesmerized by this woman, I clear my throat. "If you're chilly, let's eat inside."

Jenna nods. "Okay. Yeah. That sounds better." She shivers a little and I resist the urge to wrap an arm around her. I'm not even trying to sleep with her, yet her every move makes me want to reach out and touch her.

We walk toward the door, and I put my hand on her lower back as I open it with my other. She smiles at me over her shoulder, and I can't tell if it's meant to be encouraging or if she's being polite. I quickly remove my hand once we're inside, just to be safe.

The hostess leads us to a corner booth, and Jenna slides in across from me. I sit down and look over the menu, forcing myself to act normally. All it took was a weekend helping Jenna to turn me into this rom-com cliche.

"So..." Jenna says nervously. "Was there something you wanted to talk about?" She raises her eyebrows.

Something I want to talk about...right. Because it would be weird to have asked her to brunch otherwise. I chew on my lip, trying to remember my excuse.

Before I can answer, a server comes over, interrupting us. "Hi, folks. My name is Julie. I'll be taking care of you. Can I interest you in some coffee?"

"Yes!" Jenna says quickly. I chuckle as she shrugs sheepishly. "This is my first cup today. The coffee maker in that house is ancient. I couldn't even figure out how to turn it on." *Note to self, buy Jenna a coffee pot. No. Don't do that. That's not something property managers do.*

I laugh. "Yes, please," I say to the server. When she walks away, I clear my throat, finding my voice again. "I set up a home inspection for you. It'll be tomorrow afternoon. I don't know the guy, but Danny does. He'll be there with us so he can give us advice if we need it."

Jenna sighs, relief crossing her delicate features. "Thank you, Miles. Really. I don't know what I would do if I hadn't met you." She pauses and as an afterthought says, "Probably cry. Since lately it seems like that's all I do."

The server returns, placing two piping hot mugs of diner coffee in front of us.

"I'll give you two another few minutes," she says before walking away.

She slides the mug toward her and inhales deeply before fixing her coffee thoughtfully.

I stifle an awkward cough, scratching my stubble. "I'm happy to help," I tell her, reaching for my own cup of coffee.

Our hands brush when I reach for it and my knuckles tingle. Jenna gives me a hesitant smile before pulling her hand back and reaching for her mug. If I'm not misreading the situation, there is something mutual in the way her eyes meet mine—uncertain but open. Our eyes meet and the conversation stalls again, both of us looking to the other to speak first.

Jenna swallows and averts her eyes. *She must feel it too.* Hope bubbles in my chest. *There's a connection here.*

"So, what do you think you're going to get?" she asks, forcing me out of my thoughts.

"Probably pancakes with chocolate chips in them and on top." I grin. "I'm a child."

Jenna lets out a genuine laugh, her shoulders relaxing a little. "That actually sounds great."

The server returns to take our order, and Jenna blurts out *my* order before I even get a chance, eyeing me mischievously as she repeats it to the server.

"And for you?" the server asks.

"I'll have what she's having," I say, meeting Jenna's gaze, forcing my eyes to remain there and not down at those lips again.

The server finishes jotting down our order and disappears. Jenna picks up her mug and takes a sip, never taking her eyes off me. She seems good today, like maybe she's coming to terms with the house stuff.

"So, you bought paint." I arch an eyebrow at her.

"I did. But I won't use it yet, I promise!" Jenna giggles. "I let myself get excited for a moment about the idea of fixing the place up."

I can't hide the grin threatening to give me away. "It's okay, you're allowed to be excited. It would be weirder if you weren't." I take a sip of my own coffee.

Jenna's brow furrows. "I just have a lot of mixed emotions surrounding this house," she admits with a shrug. "And if I start to feel excitement creep in, it's quickly followed by crashing guilt or sadness." She winces and for the first time I get a glimpse of the weight she's carrying.

"Do you want to talk about it?" I ask, fighting the urge to reach for her hand.

Jenna sighs. "Not really." A look of guilt crosses her features. She gnaws on her lower lip. "It's not you... It's just every time I try to talk about it, I feel like I'm going to break open. I'd rather have a nice brunch."

I offer her an understanding smile. "I get it. Well, if you ever want to, I'm here."

Jenna tilts her head, smiling back at me. "Thank you, Miles. I appreciate that."

I clear my throat as the server sets our identical plates down. "So, what else did you do this morning?"

"Oh, I talked to the girl who works in the hardware store. Her name is Joy and she had blue hair." Jenna busies herself cutting up her pancakes and dousing them in syrup.

I chuckle, "Oh, I know Joy. That's my buddy's little sister."

"She seems nice. And I saw they're hiring in case this house drains my bank account." She says it like she's joking but I wonder if that's something she's really worried about. I tuck it away in the back of my mind.

"You'll be fine," I say, my voice soft. This time I do touch her hand. The warmth of it sizzles my palm. It's meant to be friendly, reassuring, but when her gaze meets mine, she licks her lips. My chest tightens and I pull my hand back. If I'm not careful, this business relationship is going to turn to pleasure real quick.

We finish up brunch and I pay the bill while Jenna is in the restroom. She pretends to be mad at me when she comes back but I think I see appreciation behind her eyes.

We walk outside and stand on the sidewalk. The cool breeze is back so as much I want to linger here with her, I keep it short.

"I'll give you a call later and let you know about the inspection tomorrow," I say, shoving my hands in my pockets to keep from touching her.

"Thanks, Miles." And before I know what's happening, Jenna rises on her tiptoes and presses a soft kiss to my cheek. It's quick, warm—and completely disarming. Before I can even respond, she's grinning and waving goodbye. "I'll see you later," she calls over her shoulder. And then she's gone and later can't come soon enough.

ଔ

I meet Jenna at her place the following afternoon around two. I watch her from the entryway. She is a bundle of nervous energy, and I have to actively force myself not to check her out as she buzzes around the house, telling me the things she has done since I was last here. There's a warm front coming through the region this first week of October, and Jenna is wearing cut-off jean shorts and a mock-neck pullover that hugs her tiny waist. I'm so distracted by the curve of her waist and her toned legs as she flutters around the kitchen that I don't even hear Danny and the home inspector come in the door.

"Yo, Miles." Danny claps me on the back. "You good, dude? I was talking to you, and you didn't even blink." He laughs.

I shake my head to snap out of it. "Just a little drowsy, I guess." I hold out my hand for Danny's buddy, a stout guy about ten years older than us with a gray beard. "I'm Miles," I say as he gives me a firm shake.

"Tommy Russo," he says, his voice gruff but polite. "Danny and I go way back."

I chuckle. "Danny and I go way back, too. Thanks for doing this for us," I say.

Danny eyes me suspiciously, "Us, eh?"

Luckily, Jenna doesn't seem to hear him from the kitchen. "I just mean I'm the property manager, and I'll be the one selling it. So yeah, us." I shoot Danny a warning look.

Danny ignores it and laughs, elbowing me knowingly. "Right. I'm sure it's got nothing to do with the homeowner being a pretty, out-of-town girl." He winks, and even Tommy chuckles.

Jenna interrupts my roasting when she sashays down the small hallway. "Hi! I'm Jenna." She smiles at Tommy, holding out her hand.

He takes it and shakes it delicately, shooting a knowing glance in my direction. "Tommy."

So, these two have *checked her out.*

"And it's nice to see you again, Danny." Jenna smiles. "I appreciate you helping us out."

Danny coughs and gives me an aggressive shoulder squeeze. "No problem at all."

"Well, there's not much you need to do, Jenna," Tommy says, walking back toward the front door. "Danny and I are going to take a look at all of the important areas, and we'll come find you when we're done."

"Okay, that's great." Jenna rocks forward on her toes. "I'll be here."

"I'm going to tag along if you don't mind," I say. "I'd like to assess for listing purposes."

"Whatever you want," Tommy says.

An hour later, I don't have great news for Jenna. Tommy found termites feasting on the foundation off the side of the living room. It looks to be the only area where the foundation is ruined, but we can't be too sure until he digs in a little more. The house will have to be fumigated, and she can't sell it in this condition—at least not for what she wants. In addition to the brown spots on the kitchen ceiling, the roof shingles are missing in a few places, so the roof will eventually need to be replaced. The old pipes are corroded. While they aren't causing an obvious problem, they may be contaminating her drinking water. She'll need new siding and to fix the concrete in the driveway and sidewalk. The HVAC system is twenty-five years old and probably close to being on its last leg, though, by some miracle, Tommy was able to get it running. Some of this stuff, Jenna can leave up to buyers, but many will want it in the contract that it will be taken care of as a condition of the sale. Jenna has a lot to think about.

We're standing on the front lawn, waiting for Tommy to finish writing things down and I'm trying to figure out how to break the news to Jenna. "Well, here's my report," Tommy says with an apologetic sigh, tearing a carbon copy from his clipboard. *Old school. I like it.* "Do you want to lay it all out there for her, or shall I?"

"I'll do it," I say, giving him a tight smile.

"Yeah, you probably need to *lay* it all out there for her," Danny says, then he cackles. "I could think of a couple of ways to *lay it out there*."

I narrow my eyes, shaking my head at him. "What does that even mean?"

Danny shrugs. "Just that she's hot, you know."

I shake my head at him. "Are you fifteen?"

Tommy laughs and shakes my hand. "Miles, good talking to you. If you need anything at all, recommendations for other contractors, maybe?" He looks sideways at Danny and then cracks a smile. "Give me a buzz. Danny, always a good time." Tommy claps Danny on the back and heads back to his truck.

When he is gone, I let out a puff of air. "Man. She's going to cry," I mutter.

"Yeah, she is," Danny agrees, shaking his head. He's enjoying this too much. "She'll have you to comfort her though."

"Can you stop?" I shoot him a warning glare. Then I groan loudly. "I hate when women cry."

"Me too." Danny shakes his head. "Which is why I'm going to leave you to it." He gives me a quick fist bump and turns to go.

"Thanks," I call after him with a wave.

He looks over his shoulder. "Later."

ℭ

I find Jenna in the living room, fidgeting with the remote for the ancient television. "I don't think that thing is going to work—even if you can get it to turn on." I chuckle, sitting down next to her.

Jenna pulls her knees up under her and turns to face me, wincing. "It's bad, isn't it?" She pushes those lips into a thoughtful pout, and I struggle to focus.

I fidget with the paper copy of Tommy's findings. "It's not great," I start slowly, delicately. "But you have options."

Jenna shifts nervously. "Okay...options are good." She chews on her lip. "Lay it on me."

I try very hard not to think about other ways I could be laying it on her. *Thanks a lot, Danny for putting that visual in my head.* I'm so distracted by her proximity that I have to shift my body further away to stay focused. "Okay, so, the biggest issue right now that cannot wait...you have termites. A *lot* of termites. And they've destroyed the foundation in the back corner of the house."

Jenna hops off the couch abruptly. "Eww! That is so, so gross." She scrunches up her nose and begins pacing the living room.

"They won't come inside. At least, I don't think they will. But they will destroy the joists in your floors and the framing in your walls if we don't get rid of them. And you need the foundation fixed in order to sell. If you sell as is, you won't get what you want for the house at all." I pause, watching her carefully.

Jenna stops pacing and stands in front of me. "How do we fix it?"

"Well, you're going to start by getting it fumigated. You can't stay here while they do that. Danny said he'll give you the friends and family rate to fix the foundation issues and dig a little deeper to make sure everything is secure." I wince, knowing this isn't what she wanted to hear.

Jenna presses her fingers to her temples and for a moment, I expect an outburst—but she doesn't lose her cool. Instead, her shoulders rise with a shuddering breath, and when she speaks, her voice is tight and controlled.

"I just don't know how I'm supposed to do all this." She sinks into the couch beside me, not dramatically but like someone who is at the end of their rope. She covers her face with her hands for a moment, then looks at me, her eyes glistening with unshed tears. "This house is starting to feel like more trouble than it's worth." A single tear rolls down her cheek.

I sit there awkwardly, unsure what to say and fighting the urge to catch the tear with my thumb. I am terrible at this. Every time Erin cried, I reacted the same way. This time, though, I can't help myself; I reach for her knee and curve my palm over it, giving it a little squeeze. "Hey, it's okay," I whisper. "I will help you."

"How are you going to do that? I can't take money from you. And geez, now I have to find somewhere to stay again." Jenna looks sideways at me, sniffling, but doesn't pull away from my touch.

I have the embarrassing sense that my palm is sweating on her bare knee, but I don't pull away either. I am addicted to the tingling sensation her touch leaves on my skin. "You can stay with me," I say, cautiously.

Jenna sits all the way up and squints at me, shaking her head. "No, no. I can't do that."

I pull my hand away and meet her eyes. "Why not? It'll only be for forty-eight hours max, and I have an air mattress. You can take my bed. I'm sure you can stay here while Danny's crew works. It's just the fumigating that you need to leave for."

Jenna hesitates, chewing on that plump bottom lip again. *I swear to God, I am going to bite it so hard if I ever get the nerve to finally kiss her.*

"Okay," she says after a beat. "Yeah. Hotels are expensive, and I really don't want to impose on Ellie again," she admits. "We're friends, right?"

I grin and pat her thigh as I stand. "Yeah. Friends. I have to make a call."

I leave her there before she can say anything else, wondering how in the hell I'm ever going to stay just friends with this woman. I even like her when she cries.

Chapter Seven

Jenna

I never wanted to be a damsel in distress, but I certainly plummeted right into that role this past week. First, my mom died. That part, sadly, I was prepared for—she was sick for a long time. But it still broke me. Then I lost the job I poured the past five years into. My boss didn't even pretend to be sorry to let me go. Somewhere in that spiral, I thought it might be a good idea to get bangs. I was wrong.

Finding out about this house felt like a lifeline—until I saw it. It is a damn money pit. I don't even know how it's still standing. I'm not sure how *I'm* still standing. Maybe I am dissociating. Maybe none of this is real.

Except it is.

And so are the bangs.

But when the sunlight glows through the back bay window, I can picture what it could be—a home. If money were no object, I'd knock out the wall between the kitchen and the dining room and open up the whole downstairs. I'd love to vault the ceilings in the family room, add in some skylights. Open shelving with seashore-themed decor. I'd bring in soft coastal tones, white oak, and breezy linens. Warm and calm.

The kind of place I could call *home*.

These are the sorts of designs I'd assist with at work. It's crazy to imagine doing it for myself.

But when I look around at the old linoleum, peeling paint,

and the mystery spots on the kitchen ceiling, the dream fades away.

I barely sleep after Miles leaves. I order Chinese food and eat it while scrolling TikTok on my phone, since it's the only form of entertainment I have in this godforsaken house. I toss and turn all night before finally waking up with the sun.

I pack enough clothes for three days, go for a walk, and Google some DIY projects that are probably way harder than they look. When I've paced the house long enough, I sit on the front stoop and wait for Miles. He's taking me to Frank's Auto this afternoon to get my tire fixed, then showing me his humble abode.

I'm trying desperately not to read into his kindness, but it is difficult. It's not every day an unfairly attractive, single guy does nice things for you without some kind of ulterior motive. The last thing I need is to get mixed up with a local, especially one that looks like him and treats me like I matter. But dare I say, I might be interested. In a fling, of course. It could *only* be a fling. I am not staying here. I don't have a plan yet, but I know it's *definitely not* staying here and falling for a surfer with kind eyes and a dimple that makes my knees weak.

Miles's horn startles me from my thoughts, and I nearly jump out of my skin. He rolls down the passenger window and laughs at me. "You all right over there?" His hazel eyes sparkle with amusement. "You jumped two feet in the air."

I hop off the stoop and grab my duffel bag. "I'm good," I say, trying not to look directly at his handsome face—or that boyish dimple. "You scared me is all."

"Sorry." Miles grins, but he doesn't look sorry at all.

I roll my eyes. "So, are you going to follow me over to Frank's?"

"Somebody has to make sure you don't blow that donut." Miles winks, and my stomach flutters. I'm not sure if it's Miles making me nervous or the thought of blowing out his spare tire on the way to the mechanic. I force myself to ignore the feeling and walk around to the car.

Miles cracks open his driver's side door and leans out. "Why don't you follow me? Since I know where it is." It's not really a question, and an embarrassingly large part of me likes his take-charge attitude way too much.

"Yes, sir," I say, grinning as I get in the car.

Before I close my door, I hear him mutter only to himself, "Ooh, so the lady likes it when I tell her what to do. Noted."

☙

We drop off the car with no trouble at all. I even meet Frank of Frank's Auto himself. His eyes lock on Miles and he does a double take when he sees me standing beside him.

"I didn't know you knew Miles when you called," Frank says, eyeing me curiously. But whatever surprise he's holding onto disappears and he cracks a joke, promising to have my tire replaced in no time.

"Do you want to wait here for it?" Miles asks.

I wave a hand. "No, no way. You have to get to work. Just take me over to your place and we can get it after you're done." I have always found that life feels easier when I accommodate other people instead of asking them to accommodate me. My mom used to tell me that it was making myself small when I should be the same size as everyone else. Even on her deathbed, she told me my feelings, my hopes, my fears, they all matter. I don't always believe that, and that's why it's a struggle for me to inconvenience Miles.

"I took the rest of the day off." Miles grins, like he's proud that he kept a big secret for an entire hour.

"You did?" I ask, not even trying to hide my shock. There's a part of me that hopes he took the day off to hang out with me. I swallow that hope and say, "I guess you can do whatever you want when you own the place." I nudge him with my elbow, fighting the urge to lean my body into his.

"Well, no. But I've worked a ton lately, and I haven't really had any downtime." He scratches the stubble on his chin and flicks his gaze to mine. "So, tell me what you want to do. Cape May is your oyster." His smile is infectious.

I giggle and it sounds foreign to me. It's been a really long time since I've been even remotely interested in a guy. My friends got married and have their own lives. I'm happy for them for sure, but after I'd gone to multiple weddings on my own, I started to wonder if it'd ever happen for me. That's the headspace I was in when my mom got sick, and then everything kind of halted. I couldn't possibly go on a dating app and look for a boyfriend when I spent every waking moment with my mom, wondering if it might be our last chance.

I haven't even been on a date in over a year. And as for sleeping with someone, it's been way longer than I'd care to admit. I've never been quick to jump into bed with a new partner but Miles kind of makes me want to try again. The way he's looking at me now makes my heart hammer in my chest—a stark reminder that I better pull it together. *He is just a nice guy. That's all.*

"I don't know." I tilt my head thoughtfully. "Why don't you start by introducing me to Pete."

"Pete," Miles repeats, a smirk playing on his lips. "The first thing you want to do is meet my dog?" He barks out a laugh and my chest pulls tight at the sight of his dimple again. "I can live with that. Come on."

☙

Ten minutes later, we're at Miles's condo complex which overlooks the beach. He pulls his car into the lot and hops out, jogging around to my side to open my door. That's when I feel it. Butterflies again. I couldn't say the last time I felt them like this, but now they swarm my insides with every nice thing Miles does for me. I climb out of his front seat while he opens the back passenger door and grabs my bags. I try to take them, but he refuses. There they are again, *flit flit.*

"I'm on the second floor." He gestures to the upstairs condo and grins. "Better views. Follow me."

Miles leads me up two flights of stairs to a landing with a

condo door on either side. He walks to the one on the right. The building is a cream-colored stucco and the doors are slate blue. There is nothing hanging on his front door, unlike the one across the landing, but there is a doormat that reads *I like it dirty.* Heat creeps up my neck when I read it and I smirk.

"You like that?" Miles winks, unlocking the door.

"I mean–" I stammer, searching for something to say that won't further add to the blush I feel creeping all the way across my face

As soon as the door opens, a loud, joyful bark echoes through the foyer as the sweetest copper colored boxer barrels up to greet us. He has a white chest and black mask on his face making him look like a mischievous bandit. His wrinkled forehead furrows with curiosity as he sizes us up. His underbite tugs into a playful smile as he immediately bypasses Miles and launches himself at me, nearly knocking me over. I catch his white front paws, and he stands on his hind legs, bending his head to eagerly lick my arm.

"Pete!" Miles snaps. "Get down."

Pete obeys but then proceeds to walk around and sniff my rear. I giggle and shove him away. "Well, hello there, Pete! Nice to meet you too." I skirt away from his wet nose and cover my butt.

"He doesn't get out much." Miles chuckles awkwardly, scratching the nape of his neck. "He's not so great with the ladies."

"Well, you better teach him a thing or two then." I tease, following Miles past the entryway.

"I'm trying." Miles rolls his eyes. Then shooting Pete an exaggerated scowl. "Come on, man. You're making me look bad."

I laugh heartily and ruffle Pete's ear. "He's fine." I give Miles a reassuring pat on his bicep.

Miles turns back to me, his expression unreadable. He almost looks nervous as he clears his throat. "Come on, let me show you the space."

Miles leads me down the small hallway to his open kitchen. "This is it," he says, holding out his hands. I walk around, admiring the modern finishes. The cabinets are white on top and navy blue on the bottom with shiny quartz countertops. The walls are pale gray throughout. There is a round table with four chairs in a breakfast nook off the kitchen. In the living room, a gray sofa sits in the center between two white end tables, facing a large TV mounted above a gas fireplace. But the real showstopper is the double sliding doors leading to a balcony overlooking the ocean. I gasp when I see it.

"Nice, huh?" he asks with a grin.

"It's amazing." I walk to the sliding doors and my eyes drift across the gentle rise and fall of the tide. "I would sit out here every day."

"Open the door," Miles urges, so I do.

I step onto the balcony and inhale the smell of the ocean. It's the first time I've laid eyes on it since I've come back to town. To my right, four surfboards lean against the side of the condo. There are two Adirondack chairs with a small table in the middle. To my left, a huge and inviting woven hammock. I walk over to it and finger the material—until I catch Miles watching me.

"You can lie in it," he says, the corners of his mouth lifting in amusement.

I try to laugh it off, but I'm caught—I'm completely starstruck by this condo and he knows it. I shake my head quickly, warmth creeping into my cheeks.

Miles cocks his head toward the door. "Come on, you can have my room." He slides open the door and I sheepishly follow him back inside and down the hall. "This is the only bathroom." He gestures into a small bathroom with a tub-shower and small vanity. Not five feet from it is a door he pushes open. His room.

A king-size bed sits centered against the wall with nightstands on either side. Miles must have cleaned up for me. No man's room looks this neat. It smells of lemon Pledge and cologne. There's a tall dresser, a mirror hanging on the wall, and a desk. There's no TV in here and I find it low-key sexy that he can't be bothered to watch TV in the bedroom. The bed is made with a white down comforter and sage green sheets. A dog bed sits in one corner and in the other, a hamper, full to the brim with men's clothes. I sit on the edge of the bed, smiling up at him. "Are you always this neat?" I marvel.

Miles lets out a little gasp, like I called him out on his secret. He rocks back and forth on his heels, something I've discovered to be a nervous tick of his. "I might've cleaned up for you." He chuckles, scraping his hand along his jaw. "I definitely changed the sheets, too. Just so you know."

"Noted and appreciated." I beam.

We stare at each other for only a few moments, but it feels much longer. I imagine hopping off his bed and into his arms. He'd catch me and hoist me up, my legs curling around his waist as he cups my jaw and kisses me hungrily, like I've never been kissed before. I'd run my fingers through his wavy brown hair and tip my head back, so he could kiss my neck, letting out a little groan as he hardens beneath me. But that doesn't happen, and I am embarrassed when he disrupts my lustful fantasy. *God, it has been too damn long.*

"Jenna," Miles says, a teasing note in his voice that makes me feel exposed.

I blink, realizing he must've said my name more than once. "Sorry—what?" I shake my head to play it off but my grimace betrays me. He can't possibly know what I was just thinking but I'm self-conscious anyway.

Miles laughs and shakes his head. "I was asking... Do you want to learn to surf?"

Chapter Eight

Miles

I don't even know why that came out of my mouth. Maybe it's because I haven't been surfing since I met Jenna. Maybe it's the warm air that makes me nostalgic for summer. Suddenly, I can't wait to get back in the water. The ocean in New Jersey is often still very warm in October, but when Jenna hesitates, I quickly add, "I have a wet suit that will fit you." I can't hide the hope on my face or the rasp in my voice, and I'm sure she notices.

"Okay." Jenna shrugs, chewing on her lip. "Yeah. Why not? I'm a strong swimmer—how hard could it be?" But she sounds like she's trying to convince herself.

I nod and walk toward my closet, rummaging through the back for Erin's old wet suit. It should definitely fit Jenna, but I debate whether to tell her whose it is. In the end, it's better to be honest—what do I have to hide? Finally, I find it and turn around so she can see. I clear my throat. "This was my ex-wife's. She left it here when things...well, you know." I scratch my chin and look down at the floor.

Jenna's grin falters and she licks her lips.. "I get it. It's fine." She shifts, looking away from me. "I, um... I don't have a bathing suit to wear under it, though." She scrunches up her nose as she meets my eyes.

I meet her gaze and then stifle a chuckle so she doesn't feel silly. "You don't need one," I tell her, my mouth twitching with amusement.

"I don't?" she asks, furrowing her brow. "But I thought..." She pauses. "I'm just naked under it?" Her cheeks turn a shade of pink that does something to my insides. She fiddles with her hands.

"Yep. Naked underneath." I exhale, a low whistle escaping. I turn away from her so as not to embarrass her further. And to clear the visual permeating my mind. Jenna. Naked. Under a tight-fitting wet suit. *Fuck.*

"Okay." Jenna nods. "I'll go get changed." She strides over, taking the wet suit from me, and heads right for the bathroom.

"Yep. I'll do the same," I say, but she doesn't hear me. *God I'm fucked.* It's maybe the first time in my life that I actually *hope* the ocean is cold.

ଔ

After stopping for a slice of pizza, it's nearly two o'clock. I take Jenna down to The Cove. It's the perfect spot for beginners and often quieter than some of the other surfing beaches. This is the beach I have surfed all my life, and it's also the spot where my life was saved when I was fifteen. I don't tell Jenna—I don't want to freak her out before she's even in the water. But this place has always been special to me. Year after year, summer after summer, The Cove remains. The same surfers and families show up, hang out, trade boards, and teach the youngins' how it's done. It's where I learned to surf and it's the perfect spot to teach Jenna.

I pull into the small parking lot and kill the engine, turning to face her. "You ready?" I ask, raising my eyebrows.

Jenna wipes her palms on her thighs and meets my gaze, exhaling slowly. "As I'll ever be, I guess."

"Hey, it's not too crowded," I point out. It's midweek in October so it's exactly what I expected. Usually, the same regulars surf before or after work and that's about it. Cape May isn't known for its surfing, so the surf community appreciates any waves we can get. I gesture out the windshield at the small waves breaking on shore. "It's actually pretty flat today. Perfect for learning."

Jenna nods, but she doesn't look any more confident. She chews on her lip, making no move to get out of the car.

"You said you're a strong swimmer, right?" I ask, giving her an encouraging smile.

She nods. "Yes. I took swim lessons for all of my childhood, then I was on swim teams in my teens. My dad was an elite college swimmer." She swallows hard. "Okay, let's do it," she says, throwing open her car door. "It's now or never." She shoots me a tentative smile.

"You'll be fine," I promise, following her lead and taking down my seven-foot longboard off the roof rack.

"I hope you're right."

ꕤ

Once we're down on the sand, I start with the absolute basics. I lay the board flat and crouch down next to it, pulling out my wax stick and rubbing it on the board's surface.

"What's that for?" Jenna asks, kneeling next to me.

"This is wax. It keeps the board from getting too slippery, so you have traction." I glance over at her.

Jenna takes in a shaky breath. "Okay. That's good. I don't want to fall, if I can help it," she admits.

I push my lips together thoughtfully, resting my hand on hers. I'm really going out on a limb here, but she doesn't pull away. I will my heart to stop racing. "Jenna," I say slowly, "You will probably fall. But when you do, I'll be right there to help you up."

Her lips press into a tight smile and she nods. "Okay. I can do hard things," she breathes, nodding as if trying to convince herself.

"You can," I agree, handing her the wax stick. "Here. Help me wax."

She takes it and starts rubbing it on the board, but not firmly enough. I put my hand on top of hers and she looks my way. "Can we do it together?" I ask, my voice catching ever so slightly. She can probably tell I'm nervous.

Jenna grins. "Show me how it's done," she murmurs and my stomach drops.

Together we make wider, firmer circular motions. I ignore the tingling in my palm from where our hands touch. Jenna's breath catches, and I can't be sure if it's nerves about surfing or if, like me, she's affected by our closeness. I don't get a chance to find out. As soon as the board is waxed and I pull my hand away, we're interrupted.

"Jenna Rossi, is that you?" A surfer shielding his eyes and emerging from the water with his board shorts and rash guard plastered to him calls out.

We look up at the same time. Jake Walker—Jenna's cousin whom she hasn't seen in years—walks toward us, dripping wet. He drops his board at his side.

"Holy shit, Jake!" Jenna shrieks, jumping up and throwing her arms around her cousin. "I didn't expect to see you here."

Jake laughs. "I can safely say you are the *last* person I expected to see here." He pats her back and pulls away, looking her over. "What are you doing here?"

Jenna turns back to me, smiling. "Miles is teaching me to surf."

I wait for Jake to recognize my face and when he does, he gives me a nod, holding out his hand. "What's up, man? Don't you go to my gym?"

"The Local Fitness on 9?" I shake his hand.

"Yeah. So, how do you know my cousin?" He squints at me, and I can't tell if he's feeling protective or curious.

Jenna interrupts. "He's the property manager of my house that I didn't know was *still* in the family until last week." Jenna huffs out a breath.

"No shit," Jake says, scratching his head. "Oh—hey, I'm really sorry about your mom." He gives her a grim smile.

Jenna blinks rapidly and folds her arms over her chest, like she's trying to comfort herself. It looks to me like she may be fighting back tears. "Thanks. I miss her so much." Her voice is thin and her jaw trembles as she gives a small shake of her head. She is clearly eager to change the subject. I guess when you're estranged from your family, they don't attend your mother's funeral. The thought tugs at my heartstrings. *Who did Jenna lean on at her mom's funeral?*

Jake must sense the awkwardness because he gestures toward the water. "Well, these are perfect baby waves for learning," he says.

"That's what I told her," I add quietly. Jenna glances my way, something like relief flickering in her eyes—as if Jake's confirmation steadied her first-timer worries.

Jake shoots me a look, reaches for Jenna's shoulder, and cocks his head. "How long are you here for? Let's catch up."

Jenna sucks in a breath and nods. "A while. My number is still the same."

"Cool. Well, it was great seeing you." Jake wraps Jenna in what looks like an awkward obligatory hug. He turns to leave, then glances back, pointing two fingers at me with a sly smirk and a wink. It's like he is daring me to do with Jenna what everyone seems to think I always do.

I know that look—I've seen it often—like people assume my bedroom has a revolving door and I'm always looking to add a name to my list. The list isn't as long as they think. I like dating but I don't sleep with every woman I take out. Regardless, the gossip mill spreads. I usually let it roll off my shoulders—let people talk. But for some reason, it matters to me if Jenna thinks that too.

"Miles," he says with a smug salute.

I hold up my hand in a wave. "Later," I call.

And then, we're alone again at last.

Chapter Nine

Jenna

As soon as my torso hits the ocean, it comes back to me—the fearlessness. I used to live in the waves. My parents would prop up their chairs at the water's edge of this very beach and watch me jump in the waves for hours on end. My dad would bring his surfboard and a cooler, and we sat here nearly every day in the summer of 1997. He promised me the next summer, I'd be big enough for him to teach me how to surf. He never got the chance.

Miles is an excellent teacher. Before we hit the waves, he gives me a land lesson on how to pop up quickly. In the water, he shows me how to paddle out on my stomach, dipping the nose of the board under each wave until we're past the break. He didn't bring a board for himself, but he stays next to me the entire time, steering my board to the perfect spot. My lower back tingles each time his fingertips graze it. *Focus on the surf, Jenna.* Once we make it past the break, I sit up and let out a breath.

"This looks good," Miles says, turning the board around to face the shoreline.

I suck in another shaky breath, and Miles lowers his lean body under the water. It's only now that we're alone, with no noise except for a stray seagull, the waves crashing, and the thumping of my heart, that I take the time to appreciate Miles in his snug-fitting wet suit. His body is lean and muscular. His skin still has that end-of-summer glow, likely from spending so much time at the beach. Like a true thalassophile, Miles immediately dove under a wave as he ran into the water and now his wet hair curls at the nape of his neck. Water clings to his long eyelashes. He licks his lips as if he likes the taste of saltwater. *God, he is gorgeous,* and at the same time, his love for the sea reminds me so much of my dad that my chest aches.

The thing about surfing is once you are out past the break, you can sit on the board for as long as you like. You can float peacefully out here, watching the waves crash against the shore. I have the urge to ask Miles if we can sit for a while. That sounds better than riding a wave in and falling on my face, but I don't say that. Miles shivers, and because I'm a recovering people pleaser, I feel guilty that he's cold.

"It's chillier than I thought when the sun goes behind the clouds." He ducks his head under the water again.

"Uh-huh." I shudder when he reappears. "I thought it was just my nerves."

Miles cracks a smile and puts his hand on the rocking board to steady it. "Listen, a longboard is the best thing you can learn on. Lots of room for you to find your balance. And I'll be right here next to you the whole time, okay?"

I nod but don't say anything.

"These are tiny waves. You should be able to get up. Here's what we're going to do." He glances behind him at the building swell, causing my board to bob up and down. "You're going to lie on your stomach and paddle as hard as you can to reach the tip of the wave, then you're going to push yourself up as quickly as possible and try to stand. Got it?" He raises his eyebrows.

"I think so," I breathe, moving to lie on my stomach.

"Attagirl." He pushes the board as I begin to paddle, and it happens before I have a chance to think about it. The wave catches my board and carries me in. "Pop up, now!" I hear Miles shout.

I push up as forcefully as I can but I only make it to my knees, not a full stand. Nevertheless, the board carries me all the way to shore, and it is more fun than I've had in a long time. I don't realize it until Miles surfaces next to me, but I'm laughing.

"That was pretty good!" he says, patting my shoulder. "I bodysurfed right next to you."

"You did?" I ask, my eyes wide.

"I told you I would be with you the whole time." In a move that both startles and arouses me, he brushes a droplet of saltwater from my lash line. I lean into his hand and close my eyes at his touch. Miles coughs, a stark reminder of where I am, who I'm with, and just how easy it would be to fall into this. "Want to try again?"

ঔ

It takes me two more tries before I can stand, but we finish out the lesson with a good run. I make it all the way up, only falling when I reach the place where the water is too shallow. Miles is laughing as he runs up to me.

"That was incredible!" Miles hugs me, lifting my feet off the ground. He puts me down just as quickly, his hands falling away like he realized he was holding me too long. His smile is still wide but there is something flickering behind it—maybe he is worrying he crossed a line. "I've never seen someone get it in three runs. You're a natural." He pushes a damp chunk of trauma bangs out of my eyes, then takes the board from me and walks toward the beach.

I can't imagine what I look like right now, but strangely enough, I don't care. My heart is racing, but I'm not sure if it's because I *actually* surfed or because of Miles. "That was exhilarating," I breathe, plopping down on the sand next to him. The October sun is sinking lower, and the sky is turning gold.

Miles sits down next to me, handing me a towel. He glances sideways at me, resting his arms on his knees and letting his legs fall open. I'm distracted by him, and I can't look anywhere else. "I've been surfing since I was a kid." He turns back to the water. "I have probably done it three hundred and sixty days a year for twenty years. I've had a few scary moments out there. But I always go back."

"Why do you think that is?" I ask. "I can't think of *anything* I've loved that much for that long." The words taste bitter, and I let out a quiet laugh to soften them.

Miles doesn't seem to notice. He shrugs and turns back to me. "I think I'm always chasing that rush of adrenaline. But...I also feel at home out there. I can't explain it. My favorite thing to do is paddle out right when the sun starts to go down. I float on my board, watching the first stars appear and just...exist. I like knowing there's this vast, incredible universe out there and I get to be a part of it, but it's *so* much bigger than I am. When I'm ready, I ride the wave in, and it's like I'm chasing the stars above me. I can't really explain it well..." He pauses. "It's the closest I'll ever get to religion."

"Wow," There are no other words right now. I tilt my head back, watching the first stars appear in the clear autumn sky. "It is really beautiful out here. And so peaceful."

"It is," Miles agrees. "But now I'm freezing." He stands and reaches for my hand.

I giggle, my teeth chattering as a shiver escapes. "Me too. And I'm going to be sore tomorrow. I used more muscles today than I have...well, maybe ever."

Miles gathers our things, then drapes a large beach towel around my shoulders. "How about I drop you at my place to shower and I go pick us up some dinner?"

"I can't argue with that." I meet his gaze, and his lips twitch. *I could get used to this.*

Chapter Ten

The heat is blasting on us as I pull into my spot at the condo complex and put the car in park, but Jenna is still shivering. "Do you like tacos?" I ask, hoping she'll say yes.

"I love them." She grins. "Is that what you want to eat?"

"There's this awesome little hole-in-the-wall in town. If you're up for it, I'll get a variety and bring them back here." I raise my eyebrows at her.

"That sounds great. And...you said I could shower?" The corners of her mouth turn upward and something twinges in my chest.

I nod, ignoring the heat that creeps under my skin. *It's probably better if she showers when I'm not here.*

"Yeah." I suck in a breath, my mind already wandering to places it shouldn't. "The towels are in the cabinet above the toilet. You can use whatever products you find." I unbuckle my seat belt and turn to the backseat, pulling my keys out of my bookbag. "I'm just going to run in and change and then I'll grab the food."

Our gazes linger for a second too long before we simultaneously open our doors, making me think she is feeling whatever this is too. My insides are twisted in knots by this girl—as if she actually reached through my chest and tangled them up herself. It's been a long time since anyone has made my heart pound like this.

I've never admitted to anyone that I surf in the dark so I can be alone under the stars—not even my ex-wife. It has always been my thing, my private ritual. A way to clear my head, open myself to whatever the universe has in store and just *be*. I may use it to tempt fate a little, too. Ever since I nearly drowned at fifteen, I've been chasing that adrenaline rush, that *Final Destination* moment. Erin hated that about me, which is probably why I never told her about the night surfing.

I run up and change and when I come out, Jenna's already in the bathroom with the shower running. I jog down the steps, pulling my phone out of my bookbag to order the tacos and get back to Jenna as fast as possible. That's when I see I have five missed texts from Nate.

Nate

Yoooo, where are you, Miles?

Did you forget about this showing today? I thought we were tag teaming it.

The messages get angrier from there. *Shit.* Instead of replying, I plug my phone into the car speaker and call while I drive. He answers immediately.

"Good, you're alive. Now I'm going to kill you." What sounds like a joke comes out shockingly threatening.

"Nate. I'm sorry, man. I don't know what happened," I lie. I *know* what happened. Jenna happened, and I completely forgot about this showing when I took the afternoon off.

Nate exhales loudly. "I had Caden running around, being annoying as hell because you didn't show. Now I don't know if we're going to get a sale from this," Nate grumbles. Caden's maternal grandparents take him on some days and weekends to give Nate a break. Today, they were bringing him back, and I was supposed to relieve him but I'm a dick. Or, I was thinking with my dick. Probably both.

"I'm sorry," is all I can say, and I make sure Nate catches my remorseful sigh.

"Let me guess. You were with Jenna again." Nate's voice is impassive, and I can't tell if he's teasing or genuinely angry that I blew him off for Jenna.

"I taught her how to surf," I say, smiling to myself. *I've got it bad.* This *is bad.*

"Well, I guess we know where this is going." Now he sounds shockingly judgmental. "Just don't hurt the poor girl, okay? Dad will kill us if you blow up this twenty-five-year relationship. It won't look good for Cape Realty if you have a scorned woman telling everyone to stay away from the owner," he cautions. He's probably right. It isn't a good idea. That's never stopped me before though. Besides, Jenna is different than the others; I'm invested in her.

"Relax, dude. Nothing has even happened." *Yet. Nothing has even happened yet.* I know full well the direction our newfound friendship is headed. I also know I need to be careful. Nate's right, our reputation is on the line. My dad has told us repeatedly that this account is special. I could ruin it on one lustful night if I'm not careful. "Why does Dad even care so much? It seems to me like he wouldn't even know them if they haven't been around for twenty-five years."

"I don't know, man. You know Dad. He makes business contacts and considers them friends for life. He's always been very specific about Jenna's property. The last thing you want to do is hurt a client and then, in turn, hurt our business," Nate warns, but it's my father's voice I hear in my head. *Keep your pecker in your pants, Miles.*

I say what I have to say to express my remorse and hang up as I pull into the taco place. I order all of my favorites plus some chips and guac, but it feels like an eternity before it's ready. I hightail it home, and I have to actively stop myself from running up the stairs back to Jenna. When I open the door, she isn't there. I set the food on the counter and peer down the hallway. My bedroom door is shut—she must be getting dressed.

Without thinking, I push open the bathroom door, without realizing the light is still on.

"Oh my God!" Jenna shrieks.

I slap a hand over my eyes. "I'm so sorry. Oh my God." I start to back out of the bathroom, but Jenna's giggle stops me in my tracks. I slowly remove my hand from my eyes, dragging it down my face. I take her in, starting with her feet and slowly scouring her towel-covered body until our eyes lock. My heart rate quickens, and I suck in a sharp breath.

Jenna bites her lip, tilting her head, a teasing glint in her eye—almost like she wanted me to walk in here and find her this way. Suddenly, I'm afraid that I'm misreading the situation, but Jenna takes a step closer. Her cool fingers wrap around my wrist, tugging me closer to her. *She is coming onto me.*

"Miles." The way she says my name pulls my gaze to her. I glance up, and my eyes catch on her lips. *Those lips again, my God.* I meet her gaze, and it is full of questions, but also, maybe...desire? "It's okay. I wanted to thank you for today." Jenna's voice comes out in a whisper.

I swallow hard. "By...waiting for me in a towel?" My neck heats. All the logic and reassurance that I spouted out to Nate not twenty minutes ago is already out of my head. I want her. *Fuck. I'm in over my head.*

"I didn't exactly plan that part, but..." She pauses and our eyes lock. Jenna lets out a soft breath. "If you keep looking at me like that, I'm going to start to think you're interested." She runs her fingers up my forearm, and my skin goose pimples in response.

I throw my head back and look at the ceiling, then back at Jenna. My heart is thumping, but I reach up and tuck a wet strand of hair behind her ear. "Oh, I'm interested." My voice comes out husky. "This is all I've thought about since we met."

Jenna lets out a soft, nervous laugh then catches her bottom lip. "Really?"

My cheeks heat and I know I'm blushing. "Okay, well, not *all* I've thought about," I mumble, raking my hands through my hair.

"But...yeah."

"I've thought about it too," She admits, biting the corner of her lower lip. I feel myself harden at her words.

Something is *happening between us.* My mind races. If I kiss her right now, I'll do nothing else but carry her to bed. It will take the utmost self-control to stop myself from ripping off that towel and doing unspeakable things to her. I groan.

"What's wrong?" Jenna asks, pulling back. "I know you feel something between us too...or I wouldn't have waited here like this." *So she admits it.*

"Oh, I feel it," I reassure her. "It's just, normally, I'm impulsive with these things, and...I want to be careful with you."

"Why?" Jenna asks, her voice low. She takes another step closer. She reaches her left hand up and drapes it around my neck, running her fingers through the hair there. "I won't break."

I sigh begrudgingly. "I know you won't break. But I am having so much fun with you... I want to do things differently." I lean my forehead into hers, and my dick moves, letting me know he thinks I should go for it.

"Miles," Jenna breathes, pressing her nose into mine.

"Jenna. I can't. Not yet anyway. I need to be sure," I rasp, internally berating myself. *Since when are you the good guy?*

"Um...okay." Jenna's voice breaks slightly. She takes a step back, biting her lip and looking away.

"It's not that I'm not into you. Believe me, I am *so* into you." A war of emotions rages inside me, but I take a step back too. "Your mother's account means so much to my dad. I... I don't want to do anything to mess that up."

Jenna bats angrily at her eye and it tugs at something deep inside of me. If I make this girl cry, I'll hate myself. I want to be close to her, but I don't trust myself not to screw it up. I reach for Jenna's hand, and she takes a step towards me, but she doesn't say anything. She's so vulnerable standing here in this towel. I need to make this better for her. I hold open my arms and surprisingly enough, she walks into them.

I wrap her in a tight hug. "Our tacos are getting cold," I whisper into her hair.

Jenna nods and backs away, catching her towel right before it falls. She bites back a smile, but her pink cheeks tell me she's embarrassed. "Yeah." She lets out a defeated sigh. "Okay. I'll get dressed."

I step back and smile wistfully at her, allowing myself one last lustful look at her in a towel. "I'll see you out there."

Chapter Eleven

Jenna

"Oh, you stupid, stupid girl," I mutter under my breath after Miles leaves me in the bathroom. "What were you thinking? Of course he's not interested. He's just being *nice.*" I stare at myself in the mirror. My cheeks are flushed, and my eyes are glassy with unshed tears.

"I will *not* cry over this."

I don't really know what I was thinking. Maybe that it's been a long time since I've felt a warm body on mine. When I was taking care of my mom, I didn't *feel* lonely. I was too busy. But now that she's gone, the silence is deafening.

Miles has softened that for me. There's something between us—I swear there is. But maybe this wasn't the best way to put myself out there.

Truthfully, I only hoped he'd catch a glimpse of me. I didn't mean to completely throw myself at him. And yet here I am, standing alone in the bathroom, mortified.

Guys have rejected me before. It doesn't happen often—I rarely put myself out there—but it's happened. The last time a guy rejected me, it was a new colleague at work, only he wasn't a newbie like me, he was a real designer. He took a liking to me, brought me under his wing. I misread the situation and let's just say, I will not be making the first move on a colleague again anytime soon. Nope.

But Miles was definitely giving me the *fuck me* eyes when he saw me in that towel. I know I didn't imagine that. He's been so kind to me this whole time. Maybe he's confused about what he wants—or maybe I once again misread a man's intentions.

"Ugh!" I groan at my reflection and I'm immediately embarrassed that Miles might've heard it.

What a shit show this has turned out to be.

I am not stupid. I am not desperate. I'm just...lonely.

Sometimes lonely people do reckless things. I don't have anyone left in this world who loves me exactly as I am. That's a tough pill to swallow. I never thought I'd be thirty-five and completely alone. But here I am.

I've done a great job distancing myself from people. Not on purpose—but Mom came first. I couldn't take care of her, take her to doctor's appointments, make sure she took her meds, look after myself, *and* nurture relationships with others. So I didn't and now, I'm all alone.

When I was a teenager and I felt lonely or left out, I would plop on the couch, sighing dramatically and say, "What can I say? I'm not everyone's cup of tea."

My mom would smile, eyes twinkling and say, "No, you're not. But that's because you're champagne." Then she held open her arms and hugged me until the ache went away.

I close my eyes now, sinking into the memory, letting it wrap around me like one of her hugs.

God, I miss her so much.

What I wouldn't give for one of those hugs now.

Then just like that, I see her again—not as the frail, sick woman in the hospital bed—as herself. Strong, warm, stubborn as hell. That last night, I sat by her side, holding her hand until she went. Just before she closed her eyes for the last time, she'd turned to me, her gaze watery.

"Promise me that you'll never let the world convince you that you're anything less. You're not their cup of tea because you're champagne. Don't you forget it."

My eyes sting. I close them and then with a shaky breath, I

slowly look in the mirror. I hardly recognize the girl staring back at me, but I know I'm in there somewhere—trying to claw my way out from under this mountain of grief.

I step into my leggings and pull a soft black T-shirt over my head—no bra, but who could tell? *Hopefully Miles.* Then I run a brush and some product through my damp hair, letting my natural texture do its thing. I twist back my bangs and secure them with a hairpin.

With one last look in the mirror, I remind myself, "You're champagne."

Then, I open the door.

ଓ

I find Miles in the kitchen, a flat top griddle on the counter, warming our tacos. There goes my heart again. *He probably didn't want to eat cold, soggy tacos either. This means nothing.* I have to keep reminding myself of this. Not ten minutes ago, I stood in front of Miles in a tiny white towel. He could have taken me right then and there, but he didn't. *He's just not that into you,* my inner mean girl whispers.

"Smells good," I say, taking a seat at the counter where Miles is working.

"They better. I slaved over them all day," he jokes, turning toward the fridge. He comes back and sets a Corona in front of me. "Tacos and Corona. They belong together." He picks up his beer and takes a long drag of it.

I'm not feeling much like giggling at his jokes right now. We had such a great day, but I would be lying if I said my ego wasn't bruised. *Why don't you want me?* I scream internally. I haven't let myself think beyond this week—after all, I'm not staying here—but rejection like this serves as a stark reminder that I am really and truly alone in this world. I have no one to depend on but myself. I just want a little pity sex to cheer myself up. Maybe if I remind Miles that I'm not staying, we can just have our fun. Maybe then he'll change his tune. *Now that's desperate.* Miles removes the tacos from the griddle and shuts it off.

He makes me a plate of tacos and sets it in front of me. "Spicy chicken, carne asada, coconut shrimp." He points at each one as he says it.

"Thank you." I force a smile and pick up the chicken taco first. We eat in awkward silence for a few minutes before Miles clears his throat.

"Jenna, listen." He scratches his jaw, his voice uneven.

I hold up my taco juice covered hand and shake my head. "Miles, don't. It's okay," I say, even though it's not and I'm not. He doesn't need to know that. I avert my eyes and pick up my beer, taking a long sip.

"No, I'd really like to explain." He looks down at his hands and then back at me. I sigh and wait for him to continue. "I was never serious with anyone but my wife. And even then, I must've kept her at too much of a distance, because she left me. I couldn't make her happy. I tried so hard, but I couldn't make her stay."

"Miles..." I utter, but it stops there.

He shakes his head. "No. Just let me get this out." He runs his fingers through his floppy waves and then looks back at me. "Since my divorce, I haven't been...monogamous. Erin broke my heart." He runs his hands down his face, and I wonder if he's self-conscious. I keep listening. "It's just easier not to commit. Find a companion for a week or two, scratch the itch...then move on. That way, nobody gets hurt." He winces as he says it and I wonder if he knows how bad it sounds.

I start to open my mouth to speak, but he cuts me off. "I was content doing that. Not feeling anything, keeping myself closed off." He pauses, licking his lips. Then he looks me in the eyes. "Then I met you. I don't want to be closed off anymore."

"Miles," I breathe. "You don't have to feed me the bullshit. It's cool. We're cool. We're friends, okay?" It's not just him I'm trying to convince.

"No," Miles says, more firmly than I expect. He walks around to my side of the counter and pulls out the stool next to me. "No, Jenna. That's not what I'm saying. I like you. I'm having a ton of fun getting to know you. Do you know how often that happens to me? Never." Miles takes my hand, and I let him, not knowing what else to do.

"So, then what?" I ask, shrugging.

"I need to just take my time here," he admits softly.

"Why? To make sure you don't get bored with me in a week? I may not even be here that long." It comes out harsher than I mean it to.

Miles flinches, like I just slapped him. "No...I—" He grimaces and then shrugs, defeated. "Maybe," he admits. It's only then that I realize this is hard for him too. Something softens inside me.

"Well, I can respect your honesty, I guess." I sigh, spinning back toward my once again cold plate of tacos.

"I appreciate that," Miles says, looking slightly relieved. He eats his last taco in two huge bites before getting up and putting his plate in the dishwasher. "I am going to set up the air mattress... Like I said before, you can have my bed."

"Okay." I don't argue—there isn't anything else to say. I'm not sure what I'm feeling. Rejected still, of course, but also, maybe a little hopeful. What if I'm the girl who changes Miles?

Don't be foolish, Jenna.

Miles heads into the living room to set up the air mattress. The pump starts, then stops, then restarts again. After the third time, I hop off my stool, put my plate in the dishwasher just as Miles did, and go investigate.

"What's going on?" I ask, peering into the living room, raising my eyebrows.

"It's not inflating," Miles huffs. "There must be a hole somewhere."

I move further into the room, my brow furrowed. "Well, come on, let's flip it over and see if we can find it." I move to one end and flip my side over to find a two-inch gash on the bottom. "That was easy," I announce.

Miles walks over to examine it. "Jack, that asshole. I let him borrow it for his hunting trip. He probably knew it had a hole in it when he gave it back," Miles grumbles.

"Do you have any patches? Or duct tape?" I ask, tapping my chin.

"Duct tape? No. I'll just sleep on the couch." Miles rolls up the air mattress with a tight breath, a flicker of annoyance in the crease of his brow, but he shakes it off just as fast.

"Miles, you can't be serious. You're like six feet tall. You'll have to sleep in the fetal position," I scoff.

"I'm six-foot-two actually." He snickers. "I'll be fine."

"No. Let me sleep on the couch. I'll fit better," I insist, putting my hands on my hips.

"No. No way. The light coming in from the sliding glass door will wake you up at dawn." Miles perches on the arm of the couch, refusing to let me win.

We're both quiet for a minute. I hesitate to suggest it, but I know he certainly won't. "Miles," my voice squeaks. "Your bed is pretty big... We could put a pillow between us."

Miles studies me for what feels like an eternity before answering. "You'd be okay with that? After everything I just told you?"

I shake my head. "Yes. I told you I appreciate your honesty." I don't have to worry about him putting his hands on me, *unfortunately.* And I hate how much that disappoints me.

"Okay. That'll work," Miles agrees.

Thirty minutes later, we settle on opposite sides of his king-size bed, a large body pillow between us. Miles glances over. "You good?" he asks.

I nod and force a tight smile. "Yep. I'm good."

"Good." Miles exhales. He reaches over and turns out the light on his bedside table. "Night."

"Good night, Miles," I say quietly. I try to sleep but I toss and turn. I can't remember the last time I shared a bed with a man. *How sad is that? Thirty-five and celibate.* If Miles is awake, he doesn't let on. It seems like he's sleeping peacefully. *Typical man.* Eventually, I must drift off, but it's one of those restless sleeps where I feel awake every hour. I'm not even surprised when morning comes—my anxiety wakes me up first.

I am, however, surprised to find that I'm in Miles's arms, a soft snore emanating from his peaceful slumber. His legs are intertwined with mine, his arm draped over the curve of my waist, his breath hot against my neck. And somethings poking me. Desire blossoms in my belly as his body molds against mine. I know I'm playing with fire, but I scoot closer, savoring the press of his body against me. Just for a few moments—before he wakes, or before I come to my senses and extricate myself from his grasp.

I am in so much trouble.

Chapter Twelve

I'm already awake when Jenna inches her ass closer to my morning wood. At the risk of seeming like a perv, I pretend to sleep, so I can enjoy the feeling of Jenna pressing up against me for a few minutes. Her body is warm against mine, and she smells like coconut shampoo and clean laundry. Her hair tickles my face, but I don't dare move.

My heart is pounding in my chest. I shift forward, and Jenna lets out the faintest sigh. *She wants this.* It would be so easy for me to let my fingers graze over her stomach or down her thigh—to turn this from an accidental cuddle to something with purpose. The alarm bells ringing in my head keep me from doing that though. The safest option is pretending to sleep. Then I don't have to apologize for the very obvious situation poking her either.

The minutes slip by too quickly before Jenna peeks back at me, gently lifting my arm off her waist and tiptoeing out of the room. I wait until I hear the soft click of the bathroom door before I drag myself out of bed. I adjust myself, careful not to remind Jenna that my dick woke her up, then throw on some deodorant and a clean T-shirt. I run my fingers through my hair and pad into the kitchen to start the coffee.

I'm sipping a hot mug of coffee and looking out the sliding glass door when Jenna finally appears at my side. "Good morning." She smiles at me.

"That it is," I reply, smiling back.

We hold each other's gaze for a moment before I clear my throat. "There's coffee in the pot." I cock my head toward the kitchen.

"I'll get some in a minute," Jenna says. She grabs the door handle and slides it open, walking out into the crisp autumn air. Because I'm a lovesick puppy, I follow her. Jenna leans against the railing, looking out at the waves. The morning glow of the sun kisses her cheekbones, and I'm struck by how beautiful she looks in the morning without even trying. But it's more than that. It's the way she seems to fit here without effort. I've lived alone so long now, my condo has felt like my quiet place, my escape from long, busy days. But with Jenna standing barefoot on my balcony, her scent carrying in the sea breeze, I realize, I don't want her to go. Before Jenna, my days felt like background noise. Now, even the quiet hums with something new. She has turned my ordinary into something to look forward to, I can't deny that.

I step beside her and take a sip from my mug, with a satisfied "ah" sound. "There is nothing like a hot cup of coffee on a cool morning," I say, because it's true, but I also need something to say to fill the silence.

Jenna hums in agreement, then turns to me. "Frank called. My car is ready."

"I know," I reply. "He called me too." I don't let on that *really* I called Frank first. I lean sideways against the rail, watching her. She looks nervous and it's the first time I've ever seen her this way. It's adorable and a major turn on. *Focus, buddy.* "I can drop you on my way to work. Danny is going to stop by your house sometime today to give you an official price for the foundation work. Then you can decide if you want to use his crew or shop it out."

Jenna nods. "Okay. Thank you. Really. I couldn't have gotten through this without you." She looks like she wants to reach for me but holds herself back—God, I wish she wouldn't. It's taking everything I have not to give in first. The memory of her body against mine this morning is still seared into my skin like a cruel reminder of everything that I'm missing. I already miss her warmth. I know what the right thing to do is, but every part of me wants to be wrong.

"Do you think it's safe to go back to the house now after fumigating?" Jenna asks, tilting her head.

I take another sip of coffee and swallow hard. *I don't want you to go back to your house.* The thought alarms me. I am usually ready for girls to leave the next morning, but I don't know if I'll ever be ready for Jenna to leave. "Maybe. I can call for you and see what they say," I offer

"That would be nice, thank you." Jenna smiles, pushing off the railing. "I'm going to get that coffee now." She turns to go, and I can't help myself anymore. I have to know if she realizes how cold my bed was after she left it.

"Jenna?" Her name catches on my breath, thick with everything I'm holding back.

She turns and looks at me but doesn't say anything.

"Were we...cuddling?" I ask, a stifled smile playing on my lips.

"We were absolutely cuddling." Jenna grins before disappearing inside.

This fucking girl.

ꕤ

I take my time getting my day started. The longer I can prolong my time with Jenna, the better. I take Pete for a walk on the beach, then take a shower, since I didn't after surfing last night. I'm used to falling asleep with saltwater on my skin. I get out, throw a little gel in my hair, and brush my teeth. I give myself a little mirror pep talk, reminding myself that an important client is off limits until I can decide if I'm capable of being with someone for more than a week.

I slip out of the bathroom in my towel, avoiding Jenna but also hoping she sees me. It would give her a little taste of her own medicine. I put on dress pants and a button-down today as I have a couple of new client meetings this afternoon. I make sure to spray enough cologne to catch Jenna's attention.

She's waiting on the couch with Pete snuggling up to her, engrossed in *Good Morning America*, when I come out. She quickly clicks the TV off and turns to face me, a small smile playing on her lips. "It's been a while since I've watched actual TV."

"Anything good?" I ask, gesturing to the now black screen.

Jenna shakes her head and stands. "Nah," she says, picking up her packed duffel bag. *She probably can't wait to get away from me now.*

"All right then, let's hit the road." I cock my head toward the front door and start walking, she trails behind. I can't resist. I turn, gesturing to her overnight bag. "You packed already? Had enough of me?" I murmur, stepping closer to her.

Jenna blinks, caught off guard. "Oh...no. I just thought...just in case," she stammers, shrugging.

I nod. "Okay. Just so you know...I am not in a hurry for you to go," I add in a low voice. I reach to take her bag from her, and she doesn't object. Our hands graze, and it takes everything in me not to pull her close. I can't force the girl to stay, especially after I turned down her advances last night, but I'd be lying if I said I'm not disappointed.

"It's probably for the best...if the house is safe," Jenna says awkwardly. "I mean...I'm not staying in Cape May when this is all over. Better if we're just friends." Her eyes flick past me to the door and back to mine. She shrugs, forcing a smile. I get the sense that she is trying to convince herself, not me.

"Okay," I say again. I always knew she was leaving. But after these past few days with her, I really wish she wasn't.

ଓ

Jenna is quiet on the ride to Frank's, so I don't hesitate to answer the phone when Nate calls. I'm already on thin ice with my ever-forgiving and ever-responsible younger brother.

"You're on speaker," I say instead of hello. The least I can do is warn him.

"Good morning, Miles." Nate's curt voice comes through the car speakers. Then more cheerfully, "Hi, Jenna."

"Hi," she says back in a singsong voice, then goes back to being quiet.

"I just wanted to see if you were actually going to show up to work today," Nate says, antagonizing me.

I keep my voice level. "I am." I exhale to steady my brewing frustration. "I am taking Jenna to pick up her car and then I'll be in."

"Okay...then we need to talk," Nate says, and I don't like the forewarning in his voice. I snag a glance in Jenna's direction, but her expression remains stoic as she stares straight out the windshield. "I'll call you back, Nate," I say, ending the call before he can reply. Then, I'm pulling into Frank's Auto.

When I park, I glance over at Jenna again. She slowly turns and looks at me.

"Do you want me to come in with you?" I offer.

Jenna shakes her head. "It's okay. I think I've got it from here." Then she pulls me into a hug that gives me a strange sense of goodbye. I don't like it at all. "Thank you for everything, Miles." Her breath skims my neck, sending a chill up my spine.

I pull back and search her face for answers. "I'll call you later about the fumigation," I say uncertainly.

Jenna shakes her head. "It's okay. Maybe it's just better if I call." She gives me a grim smile.

"Okay." I nervously drum my thumbs on the steering wheel and meet her gaze. "Why do I feel like this is you saying goodbye to me?" I furrow my brows.

Jenna blushes. "It's not. It's not goodbye. Just...see you later." Jenna gathers her bag at her feet and opens the car door. "We'll talk soon, Miles, okay?"

"Yeah. Sure," I mutter. And then she's gone, leaving me feeling bereft.

This is not goodbye. It can't be.

Chapter Thirteen

"That son of a bitch," I mutter, staring at the invoice Frank slides in front of me—*PAID IN FULL.*

Frank sucks in a breath and raises his eyebrows. "That's not the reaction I'd expect from having your bill paid for you."

"I just...didn't know." I sigh, exasperated. "Why would he do this?" I grumble. "He should *not* have done this." I know why Miles did this; he feels bad for me. I'm trying desperately to keep my guard up around him and he keeps knocking it down. I hate it.

"Maybe the guy likes you." Frank shrugs with an amused glint in his eye. "I took the liberty of giving you a little tune-up too. You were *way* overdue." Frank looks pleased with himself.

"Thanks, Frank," I mumble, offering him a smile so he knows it's not him I'm mad at.

He hands me the keys with a warm smile. "Don't mention it."

"See you later." I wave, rushing out the door. I whip out my phone to call Miles immediately and yell at him for paying my two-hundred-fifty-dollar bill, but Danny's name flashes on the screen.

"Hi, Danny," I huff into the phone.

"Hey Jenna—everything okay?" Danny asks warily. I must sound exasperated every time this guy talks to me.

"Oh, it's nothing. I'm sorry. I just picked up my car and found out Miles paid the bill," I grumble, climbing into the front seat. Attached to my steering wheel is a Post-it note. *Thank me later.*

- *M.* I groan. He must've beaten me here at some point, though I have no idea when he would have done that.

"Wow." Danny lets out a low whistle.

"Wow, what?" I snap. It comes out harsher than I intend.

"No, nothing. It's just...he must like you." Danny laughs, and for some reason, it annoys me.

"That's what Frank said. It's not funny. I'm not staying here. I don't want to be indebted to anyone," I whine, banging my hands on the steering wheel in frustration. The horn beeps angrily. I'm not used to people doing nice things for me. In fact, I've had to do most things myself for most of my adult life. *Of course* Miles is super thoughtful, and one might even say this is a romantic gesture. But he's really complicating my feelings about selling my house and leaving Cape May—and him—behind. He's making me want to stay.

Danny chuckles. "You're going to have to tell him that."

"I've *tried*," I say, sighing in defeat. *Well, first I tried to hook up with him, but Danny doesn't need to know that.*

"Try harder. The Miles I know doesn't do nice things for girls he doesn't care about... Just think about that." Danny is quiet after that.

"I have. I know," I mutter. I don't say this to Danny, but the problem is, I don't *want* Miles to care about me. I don't know what I'm doing with my life *at all* right now. I'm alone, I'm unemployed, and I'm floundering. I should not be getting tangled up in some fling. Sure, last night was a moment of weakness. And of *course* I liked waking up in his arms this morning. But a new relationship in a new place is the last thing I need. Neither of us is in the position to catch feelings right now.

"Listen," Danny changes the subject, "I have an hour free to come do an estimate. Are you home?"

Home. I try not to think about how the word makes me feel like a foreigner in a strange land who desperately wants to find her place, but not knowing where it is. "Not yet, but I'm five minutes away or so."

"Great. I'll meet you there," Danny says. He hangs up before I can reply. I guess Miles will have to wait.

☙

An hour later, I'm sitting on my front stoop when Danny comes around the side of the house, writing on his clipboard. He startles when he sees me. "Geez!" He flinches, jumping backward.

"Sorry." I smile nervously, standing. "I didn't want to follow you around, but I'm also anxious as hell to hear the news." I shift my weight and look at him expectantly.

"I'm sorry to have to tell you this, but there is more damage than you probably thought." Danny grimaces. "The damage to the foundation and the structural beams is extensive. You're looking at about seven thousand dollars for those repairs—and that doesn't include anything cosmetic after we repair the wall." He furrows his brow. "And we're going to have to rip this fence out. The termites have been feasting on that, too." He turns and gestures to the old wooden fence that separates the front yard from the back.

"I thought you were giving me the friends and family rate." I force a half-hearted smile.

"Unfortunately, that *is* the friends and family rate. I'll tell you what..." Danny gives me that pitying look again. "I won't charge you to demo the fence."

I suck in a breath. "Okay." I nod. "That's fair. Now I have to figure out how I'm going to pay you."

Danny shifts uncomfortably. "I take cards, but there is a three percent fee. How about I have my secretary call you to work out a payment plan?"

Relief floods me instantly. "Really? Thank you!" I throw my arms around his neck.

Danny stiffens and carefully peels me off. "Hey, anything for Miles. I know it's what he'd want me to do."

"So, when can you start? Actually...the better question is...can I live here while you work?" I scrunch up my nose, embarrassed. "I don't have anywhere else to go."

Danny nods. "You can. We will be working off your sunroom so you can just avoid that area. We may wake you up early with our construction noise though."

I shrug, relieved. "It's okay. I am an early riser."

"Okay, well, then I'd say we're looking at a couple of weeks before I can start. We're a little backed up." Danny starts walking toward his truck. "I'll call you as I get closer to a start date."

"Thank you so much, Danny," I call after him.

He turns back and smiles. "Don't mention it. And Jenna?"

"Hmm?" I raise my eyebrows.

"Go easy on Miles. He means well." With that, Danny climbs into his truck and drives off.

☙

My next task, if I'm going to be sticking around for a few weeks, is to find some temporary income. I clearly won't be using my design skills here in Cape May, but I need something in the interim. Then I remember I saw a Help Wanted sign at the hardware store. The woman, Joy, mentioned it was just seasonal help when I asked, which might actually be perfect for me since I don't plan to stick around.

Without thinking twice, I hop into my newly tuned-up car and drive over there. I stride into the hardware store and spot Joy sitting at the counter, scrolling on her phone. No one else is in the shop. *This place really is a ghost town in the off-season.* Joy's face lights up when she sees me.

"Hi, Jenna!" She hops off her stool and comes around the counter. "Are you back for more paint?" Her eyes glimmer with excitement.

"Uh, no," I start. "Actually, are you still looking for holiday help?" I wince. I should not be embarrassed about applying for a retail job. Joy gets it, she works here. Sometimes, you do what you have to do to make ends meet. My ends are nowhere close to meeting, so beggars can't be choosers.

Joy squeals, clapping her hands. "Yes, we are!" She walks back around the counter and rummages underneath it for something. She reappears a moment later with an old-school paper application. "Does this mean you're staying?"

I suppress a grin, unable to hide my amusement as she pushes the application in my direction. I chew on my lip, hesitating. Joy is *so* nice, but is this really what I want? "I..." I falter. "For a little while, maybe. Some things came up with the house, and I can't list it as is, so..."

"This is *so great!*" Joy claps her hands, delighted. "I'll hire you on the spot."

"You'll hire me?" I ask, raising my eyebrows.

"Yeah. I own the store." Joy smirks. "I thought you knew that."

"Nope." I shake my head, a giggle escaping. "I definitely just thought you worked here."

"Well, now you know!" Joy hops onto her stool. "So, when can you start?"

I let out a laugh. "Does tomorrow work?"

Joy laughs with me, which I appreciate. If she only knew.

"So, most of the time, weekdays are really slow. It is the off-season after all. I'd like to have you work Fridays, Saturdays, and Wednesdays, if that would work for you?"

I shake my head. "To be honest, anything works for me."

"Great!" Joy takes the application and shoves it under the counter. "I'm not even going to have you fill this out. Just put your number in my phone."

I do as she asks and hand the phone back to her.

"Yay!" Joy squeals, her enthusiasm is contagious. "I'm so excited. Tomorrow you can come in and I'll train you on the register. You'll never be working alone, my older brother, Leo, works here too, so one of us will always be around to help you."

"Great. That's great." I let out a sigh of relief. "Well, I'll see you tomorrow?" I raise my eyebrows.

"Ten a.m." Joy grins.

"I'll be here." I smile. "Thanks, Joy. You're really helping me out."

"Anytime, Jenna. And *you're* the one helping me out." She winks. "I'll see you tomorrow."

I step outside and immediately feel a little bit lighter.

I got a job.

Now there's just one thing left to do—deal with Miles.

Chapter Fourteen

Jenna's at my office door when I return from my new client meeting, and immediately I sense something is wrong. Her brown eyes flash with something like frustration, and she exhales out of her nose like she's trying to keep her cool. *She looks mad?* I clear my throat, drape my sport coat over the chair, and set my bag down, bracing myself.

"Jenna," I say cautiously. "I wasn't expecting you. I called the extermin—"

"Miles. What the hell?" *Definitely mad. At me.*

From his desk, Nate coughs and pushes back in his chair. "I'm just going to get a late lunch," he says to no one in particular. We ignore him.

"What's wrong?" I step closer to her, concern tightening my chest.

"What's wrong?" she bellows. "You paid for my car, Miles. What. The. Fuck?" Jenna pulls out the chair in front of my desk and drops into it. *She's hot when she's angry.*

"I was being nice," I offer. "I thought it would be a relief. You don't have to pay me back."

"Don't have to pay you back? Miles, of *course* I have to pay you back." Jenna gives me a stern look, folding her arms across her chest.

"Fine. Pay me back, then. Venmo me right now." I sit down on the other side of my desk.

"I will," she mumbles.

"Okay, great." I put my hands behind my head and lean back in my chair, smiling at her smugly.

She straightens and looks at me, her expression softer now. After a deep breath, she says, "Just... *Why* did you do that, Miles? I told you I can take care of *myself*. I don't need a white knight." She huffs, folding her arms across her chest. Her frustration with me is real. I can't help wondering if anyone has ever done anything nice for her or taken care of her for that matter. I'm fighting every instinct I have to walk around the desk, unfold her arms and wrap her in a hug, among other things.

"I did it to be nice," I repeat, meaning it. But after these past few days with Jenna, it's more than that. I've come to care about her—more than I expected to. I don't want to see her struggle even though she's clearly capable of handling things on her own. The day I showed up to help her clean, she was already elbow-deep in it. She's the one who called the utility companies, talked to Danny about the work, and made a plan for how to move forward. Clearly, she doesn't want my help, but I want to give it anyway. It's a foreign feeling. With Erin, doing things out of love slowly turned to obligation. But with Jenna, it's different. I don't feel obligated—I *want* to carry some of the load for her.

"Don't be nice to me, Miles," she says firmly. "I'm *not* staying here." There it is again. The tone of voice she uses when she's trying to convince herself of something.

"I *know* you're not staying," I say, stifling a smile. "You never let me forget it."

Jenna sighs. Then, quieter, "It's just...if you keep being so nice to me then..." she trails off.

"Then what?" I press, holding her gaze.

"Then I'm going to want to. Stay, I mean." She chews on her lip.

I bite back the grin threatening to betray me. I like the idea of her staying, but I won't say that out loud. Not yet anyway, not until I'm sure I can be what she needs. "So, stay, Jenna. It's a great place to live." I hold out my hands as if to say, *take a look around.*

Jenna narrows her eyes. "No. I'm not staying. I don't even know what I'd do here."

I chuckle. *So, she's stubborn.* "Okay, fine." I raise my hands in surrender.

Jenna sits there quietly for a few moments. I boot up my computer while I wait for her to talk again. I busy myself, clicking through my inbox, taking a sip of water, rummaging through my drawer.

"It's just—I don't know how to handle you doing these things for me, Miles. For so long, *I* am the one who took care of another person. My world revolved around my job and caring for my ailing mother. So, when you sweep in here and do these things, it makes me really uncomfortable." Jenna eyes me cautiously, gnawing at that lower lip that drives me crazy.

I let out a long, slow breath before I speak. "Wow. I'm sorry, Jenna. I didn't think of it like that. I just thought I was being nice." Embarrassment warms the back of my neck. Here I thought I was sweeping her off her feet and I did the exact opposite.

"It's okay," Jenna says quietly. "I *do* appreciate your help. I just...need some time to adjust to my new normal. I'm trying to figure out what to do next and where I belong." Her voice cracks but she doesn't falter.

"Okay. I'm sorry." I look at her and our gazes lock, neither of us speaking.

Finally, I can't take it anymore. I swallow the knot in my throat. "Is there anything else you want to talk about?"

A slow smile creeps across Jenna's face. "I got a job," she offers.

"A job," I repeat, returning her smile. "Even though you aren't staying here?"

She ignores me. *This girl is too much.* I try to ignore the hope that blooms in my chest at the idea of her staying. Until she tells me otherwise, I should take her at her word.

"Where?" I ask when it's apparent she is only going to tell me if I do.

"The hardware store. It's just holiday help," she assures me. "Did you know Joy *owns* that place?" She quirks her eyebrows in surprise.

"I did, yes," My lips twitch.

"She was the first person I actually felt like I could be friends with here," Jenna says matter-of-factly.

"Hey." I scowl at her defensively. "What about me?"

"Besides you." Jenna smirks, pursing her lips.

"Good. I'm glad." I smile at her and my cheeks warm. "I took the liberty of calling the exterminator. Your house should be fine to stay in tonight." I force myself to hide the disappointment from my voice. I was really hoping she'd need another night with me. Just thinking about the way we woke up today makes my dick move. I need to think logically. I refused her advances last night. I can't just change my mind today. That wouldn't be cool. *But dammit, I want her.*

"That's good since I already went inside." She laughs, and I think maybe I'm forgiven.

I'm not feeling much like laughing anymore though. "When can I see you again?" I ask, urgently. I don't even bother to mask my desperation at this point.

"Oh, Miles..." Jenna sighs. "Maybe it's a good idea if we take a few days of space...let whatever this is"—she motions between us—"simmer a little bit."

"I don't want to let it simmer, Jenna," I admit, and it sounds harsher than I mean for it to.

"But *I* do," Jenna reaffirms. "I put myself out there last night, and you turned me down. I realize now that was probably for the best." She doesn't let her gaze drop and neither do I, wondering which of us will break first.

Of course it's me. I groan, running my hands down my face in exasperation. "Jenna."

"Miles." She bites back a smile as if she knows this is torture for me.

"I didn't turn you down because I don't want you," I rasp. The emotion in my voice catches me off guard.

Jenna pushes her lips together. "Maybe. But you still turned me down. I'm taking that as a sign from the great big universe you love so much." She is nowhere near as rattled by this as I am. In fact, I'd go as far as to say she is unbothered.

I peer at her from across the desk, but I don't say anything right away. "I don't think the universe is giving signs to the little people." I sigh.

Jenna huffs out an exasperated breath. "Well, I do." She pushes back in her chair and stands to leave. "I'll see you around, Miles. Okay? And thanks for my car."

"You're welcome, I guess," I grumble, slumping back in my chair. I let her walk out the door. What else can I do? I can't force her to like me. The bell over the door jingles, and she's gone.

"Finally. I thought she'd never leave." Nate's voice interrupts my pouting. He pulls out his chair and plops down, turning to face me.

"Did you listen to our entire conversation? I thought you went to get lunch." I scowl, making it clear that I'm not in the mood for his shit.

"Of course I listened to it. I just said that so you could have some privacy. I believe you are supposed to thank me." Nate laughs. When I don't join in, he says, "Damn, you've got it bad for this one."

I scoff. "I do not."

"You *so* do. You're sitting in here pouting like your prom date dumped you." Nate chortles. Nate is doing exactly what younger brothers do, but the frustration in me is starting to build.

"Nate. Shut up. I'm not heartbroken. I just like her. But it doesn't seem like she's into it." It comes out sulky. *Maybe I am sulking. I'm not used to girls telling me no, even if I said it first.*

"I'm no relationship expert, bro, but I think you're going about it all wrong." Nate leans back in his chair.

"Oh? How so?" I raise my eyebrows.

"Well, I can tell just by talking to Jenna that she's an

independent girl. She is used to taking care of herself—she might even be proud of it. So when you come in and pay for her car, it's not the same thing as buying her a coffee. Do you get what I'm saying?" Nate gives me a look that tells me I should have known this. "I don't get the impression that she's looking for someone to save her."

"Oh yeah? Then what is she looking for? I thought girls liked to be swept off their feet." I run my hands through my messy hair, groaning. I'm in over my head.

"Some girls do. Erin did, for sure. But I'm betting Jenna is looking for a partner. Not a savior." Nate gives me a pointed look.

"You seem awfully sure of yourself," I mutter. The truth is, normally, I am pretty sure of myself too, especially when it comes to the ladies. Jenna makes me feel like a clueless teenager who has no idea what he's doing.

"It's just a matter of listening to her, bro. Really *listen* to what she has to say. Even I heard her say that she can take care of herself." Nate arches an eyebrow at me.

"I have. Or I thought I had." I groan. "Fine. I'll try it your way."

"Hey, you aren't doing me any favors. I'm just trying to help you." Nate whirls back toward his computer.

"I know you are. I appreciate it," I say, determined to get back to work and put Jenna out of my mind for a while.

A few hours pass and I'm mostly successful at quieting my mind. One thing is still nagging at me though. If Jenna is so determined to take care of herself, why didn't she Venmo me? *It's not much to go on but it's something.*

Chapter Fifteen

Jenna

A week later and I'm settling in nicely. My house is starting to feel like mine—despite how much needs to be done to it—and I'm at least waking up with a purpose. The hardware store makes for good temporary employment until I figure out what I'm going to do next. Joy has trained me in every aspect of the store. I can ring people up, look up prices, and even do a refund. I know how to check inventory and help customers find what they need.

I'm exhausted though. I haven't worked retail since high school, and it's been years since I've spent this much time on my feet. It has taken everything in me not to verbally bemoan my aches and pains—I don't want Joy to second-guess hiring me.

I have just enough money to scrape by, but I need to make some or I'll never be able to pay Danny for the foundation work, list the house, and get the heck out of this town. There are just *too* many memories here, and it's getting harder and harder to tuck them away in the back of my mind.

I've been packing up family photos and heirlooms bit by bit, but I can't do it for very long. Every box I pack with family treasures is like pouring salt in an open wound. Earlier this week I was sorting through my mother's old cookbooks when I came across a photo of my mom and me in the backyard, picking tomatoes. In the photo, I'm holding up a tomato I had taken a big bite of, and the juice is running down my chin. I'm grinning at the camera, and Mom is beaming at me. I froze right there in the kitchen, my grief overwhelming me, and I ended up in a puddle on the floor. That's the thing about grief, you can think you're doing okay, but it is always there—sneaking through the smallest crack and wrecking you all over again.

"So, it's Saturday night. Any big plans?" Joy asks, jarring me out of my memory. She's counting the cash in the register while I straighten the display. We're still open for another hour, but Joy likes to get a jump start on closing when it's slow.

"If you count scrolling my phone until my eyes blur, then yep," I mutter sarcastically.

"Jenna! Come on, that's no way to spend a Saturday night," Joy chastises with a grin.

"Well, my TV is from 1997, and I still don't have cable or internet, so that's what I'm doing." I lift a shoulder. "I don't mind it. When I get really bored, I stream Netflix on my phone. I just get tired of holding it in front of my face. Besides, I'm so exhausted, I'll probably be asleep before ten." I give her a lazy smirk, feigning a yawn.

"No," Joy whines. "Come with me and Leo to the brewery. They're having a fall festival with all the seasonal beer flights."

"I don't know," I say, knitting my brow.

I have worked with Joy's brother Leo a few times now. He seems nice. Miles mentioned that they're buddies. Leo reminds me a lot of him—just less responsible. We had a lot of downtime when I worked with him the other day. He told me he teaches surfing to vacationers in the summer and spends the off-season working here for his little sister. He can't stand a nine-to-five, or so he says. He's nice enough though, and Joy's offer is tempting. It beats staying home alone feeling sorry for myself again.

Then again, Leo and Miles are friends, and I haven't spoken to Miles since I left his office last week. He's reached out a few times, but I've kept my responses short. I don't want to encourage him when I'm still planning to leave. Maybe I *could* be swayed to start over here in Cape May, but Miles told me himself he's not great at commitment. I've been through enough—I have to protect my heart. If I go tonight, Miles might be there. As much as I desperately want to see him, I really *don't.* It'll only make this harder. The best thing I can do is keep things between us friendly and professional.

Lately, I've been thinking that it's time for a big change, but I don't know what. The more I look at the old photos in the house, the less I recognize the girl I used to be. I've spent so long taking care of my mom, it's almost as if I've lost myself completely. Now I realize I've been going through the motions for years—content with mediocrity. It was as if I had to get through my mother's illness, wait for her to die, and *then* figure out who I am and what I want.

The truth is, I had been discontented at work for a while—never being awarded the opportunity for promotion. Never being trusted enough to make project decisions on my own. I never had the courage to make a change because I was so exhausted in my personal life. I used to wake up every morning at 3 a.m., check on Mom's breathing, reposition her if needed. Now, I sleep through the night—I'm free. But as soon as that thought creeps into my head, I berate myself for feeling that way. Grief is so complicated. No one tells you that it can also be laced with relief.

I could move out near Morgan and start completely fresh. Morgan is my oldest friend. She's seen me through my darkest days. I don't have anyone else now, so why not move out near her? I can start over there and put myself first for the first time in a *long* time. But something doesn't feel completely right about that and I don't know why. And then, it's as if the universe hears my thoughts.

The front door jingles before Joy can convince me, signaling we have a customer. A soft gasp escapes me. If I was tired before, I'm wide awake now. My cousin Jake saunters in, followed by my Aunt Leona, and I was not prepared for this in the least.

"Jenna." Jake sounds as surprised as I feel. "What are you doing here?" he asks me for the second time in a week.

"I work here." I level my voice. *Be cool.*

"You work here?" Jake's brow furrows, but he appears to recover quickly. "I thought you—" He pauses and clears his throat. "Never mind."

"Jenna Rose Rossi, is that you?" Aunt Leona's voice is sharper than I expect. She peers around Jake's shoulders, eyes sweeping over me. Then, raw emotion clouds her features, her eyes glistening. "I haven't seen you since you were a girl," she says, her voice barely above a whisper.

"I know," I murmur. "I'm sorry for that." My eyes sting as I fight back unexpected tears. I wasn't prepared to see my father's sister tonight. In the hardware store of all places.

"How long have you been back?" Aunt Leona asks, her voice tender with surprise.

I suck in a breath and glance at Joy for encouragement, but she's way too enraptured by the scene before her. I turn back to Jake and his mom. "My mom died... I thought you heard," I mutter, pushing down the resentment that no one from my dad's side of the family so much as reached out to me. I assumed they would have heard through the cousins my mom kept in touch with, but maybe not. "I didn't know she still had our house here until a couple of weeks ago. I came back to sell it, but it needs too much work, so I'm staying for a bit." I continue, raising my eyebrows with a soft exhale. It's been so long since I've seen Aunt Leona, and suddenly, I want nothing more than to fold her into a hug—despite her falling out with my mom. I don't know what happened between them, but suddenly, none of it matters. It's like seeing my dad again. I can't help it; my eyes fill with fresh tears, and I have to bat them away.

"I did hear about your mother," she says gently, her voice thick with emotion. "I'm so sorry, dear." She steps closer, reaching for my hand. I let her take it. "I know things were...strained...when your father passed, but I want you to know—I've always missed you. When you and Jake were in college together, he used to fill me in on how you were doing. It warmed my heart." Aunt Leona gives a sad smile. "I'd love to know how you're doing now."

"Thank you," I say, and it lingers in the air because I can't think of anything to say next.

Joy clears her throat. "Was there something I could help you find, Mrs. Walker? It's just...we're getting ready to close." She comes around the side of the counter, linking her arm through Aunt Leona's. "Let's go look around." Then she leads her away, like the gem she is, giving me a chance to collect myself a little.

I reach for a tissue and blot my eyes when Jake speaks.

"I'm sorry. I didn't mean to catch you off guard." His voice is quiet, almost remorseful. "I didn't even know you worked here."

"No, no, I know you didn't." I sniffle, throwing the tissue in the trash.

"Are you still hanging around Miles?" Jake asks, catching me by surprise.

"Um...not really. Why?" I walk behind the counter and busy myself with the dust cloth again.

"I'm just wondering... He doesn't have the greatest reputation." Jake shrugs. "I'd hate to see you get hurt."

Before I can respond, Joy and Aunt Leona return to the register with two battery-powered smoke alarms. "I can ring you up right here, Mrs. Walker," Joy says cheerfully, walking behind the counter.

I step out of her way and my gaze shifts to Jake. So many questions fill my mind. *What do you mean his reputation isn't great? What do you mean I'll get hurt? Why do you care? Why do I care?*

My aunt pays for her items and Joy makes awkward small talk. I want to ask Jake about Miles's reputation but what does it matter, really? We're barely even friends. I'm not staying. In a few weeks, Miles will be nothing more than the guy who helped me sell an old house with ghosts of the past hiding in the walls.

Joy hands Aunt Leona her bag and Jake takes it from her. "Let's get that lunch, okay?" He cocks his head—like he's concerned and trying to decide for himself if I'm okay.

"Okay," I squeak.

Aunt Leona pauses in front of me. "Jenna, dear, please come have dinner with me? We have so much lost time to make up for." She squeezes my shoulder, and I don't pull away.

I nod. "Jake has my number. We can set something up."

"I would love that. Come along, Jake," she says, and he follows her out the door.

When they're gone, Joy breaks the silence first. "Oh my God! What *was* that?" she demands, an excited curiosity bubbling in her voice.

"That was...my cousin Jake and my estranged aunt that I haven't seen in twenty-five years." I suck in a breath, leaning on the countertop with my head in my hands.

"I know Jake. I had the biggest crush on him in high school," Joy says, and her eyes look starry. She shakes her head, snapping out of it. "And I guess if you're estranged, you were *really* surprised." Joy lets out a low whistle.

"I saw Jake the other day at the beach when I was surfing with Miles, but yeah. I wasn't expecting to see my aunt like that."

"It could've gone worse," Joy assures me. She scrunches up her face like she's mulling something over. "Wait back up...surfing with Miles. Miles Corbin?"

"Yeah. He's my property manager, why?" I ask, suddenly wondering if there really is more to this guy I can't stop thinking about.

"Well, he's quite the Casanova." Joy laughs. "He's friends with Leo. Just be careful, okay?"

"Yeah, so I've heard," I say wryly. "It's fine. I'm not staying here anyway." I wave my hand dismissively.

"That's what I'm afraid of. Girls who aren't staying are *exactly* the kind of girls Miles likes." Joy rolls her eyes as she locks the register drawer.

"Whatever. What do you say we hit the brewery?" Suddenly, I desperately need a change of subject and scenery.

"I say, you're on!" Joy reaches into the cabinet and grabs our jackets, tossing mine to me. "Let's get you cheered up."

Chapter Sixteen

Miles

I'm carrying my shortboard out of the ocean when my Apple Watch starts ringing. It's Leo. Not exactly who I hoped it would be. I haven't stopped thinking about Jenna, which is annoying because she is clearly not thinking about me. Every time I reach out, her replies are short, polite, and distant. I haven't even asked if I can see her again—I'm not sure my ego can take the rejection. I did take Nate's advice though—I will not try to fix things for her anymore. Not unless she asks. I've thought a lot about what she said the other day and I realize if Jenna has spent the last few years taking care of her mom, it probably means she put herself last. She was probably shouldering everything, trying to keep her mom comfortable while her world fell apart, hardening herself in the process. Her independence is her armor. So, while I hate that she wants to do everything on her own, I get why she doesn't want to let someone in. I'll just have to let her come to me.

"Yo," I say, into my watch. "What's good?"

"What's up, brother?" Leo's voice bellows and I get the impression he's had a few drinks already. "You coming over here?"

"Coming over where?" I set my board down and wipe my dripping brow with a sandy towel.

"The brewery, man. Did you forget about the fall festival?" Leo just keeps shouting louder. I can hear the background music. There must be a DJ. The Cape May Brewery is having a festival where all its fall and Halloween-themed beers are on special. I completely forgot. I know Danny, Jack, and Liam were planning on going too.

"I did forget," I mutter with a sigh. "I just finished surfing. I'm pretty tired." I didn't bring a change of clothes or anything, I'd have to speed home, change, and go back out. And if I accidentally sit down on my couch? Forget it, I'm not going back out. Leo and I are buddies and have been since we were teenagers, but if my other friends aren't around, I'm not exactly jumping to hang out with just Leo. He's a bit much sometimes, and he's never really grown up.

"Come on, man. The guys are coming, it's Saturday night," Leo pushes. "Joy is on her way with her new friend."

Jenna.

I sigh. I *am* tired. I doubt Jenna wants to see me—she's barely spoken to me in the last week. And yet, after hearing that, I know I'm going to go, because I desperately want to see *her.* If only to see how she is doing. Does she look happy or stressed? Anxious? I have to know she's doing okay. *I'll keep my distance.*

"All right, I'll be there in an hour or so," I say, hanging up before he can answer.

☙

An hour later, I am walking into the brewery, and the parking lot is packed. I'm sure it's mostly locals, but there is always a good number of weekenders down in Cape May for fall festivities. There's a chalkboard out front that reads *Boos & Brews.* I pull open the door and spot them immediately. Joy, Leo, and Jenna are crowded around a small high-top table with three flights in front of them. I swallow hard, collecting myself. Jenna laughs at something one of them says, and her face lights up. She looks completely fine, and now I feel stupid for wanting to check on her. *She doesn't need you.* I don't care though. In this moment, Jenna radiates warmth, and I just want to be near her. I can't remember the last time I felt this way.

I rushed home, rinsed the salt water off my body, and threw on a pair of jeans and a navy blue thermal. I didn't so much as glance in the mirror before running over here. Now I wish I had.

Leo spots me from across the bar. "Yo! Miles!" he shouts.

Jenna's smile falters. *She really must not like me.*

I take a deep breath and walk toward them. My confidence is in the toilet. I have never felt this insecure around a woman before. I hate it. "What's up, guys?" I say as I reach their table. "Hi, Jenna." I look directly at her.

She meets my gaze, and her cheeks flush. "Hey, Miles," she says quietly.

No one speaks for what feels like an eternity. "Where's everybody else?" I ask Leo.

"Bailed. Naturally." Leo shrugs. "Kids and shit." He scoffs.

I force a laugh, but the awkwardness that has fallen over their table since I arrived is palpable. "Got it," I mutter. Figures my married friends bailed. They always do. If Jenna wasn't here, I would have bailed too. "Well, I haven't eaten, so I don't know how much I want to drink," I admit.

"You? Not drinking?" Leo roars. "What, are you pregnant?"

I roll my eyes. "I didn't say *not* drinking. I just have to get something from the food truck first," I clarify, my gaze settling on Jenna.

"Oh, you must've worked up an appetite surfing," Joy teases, flicking her gaze between Jenna and me.

"You were surfing?" Jenna squeaks.

"Yeah," I say, and nothing more.

"But it's so dark out," Jenna insists, concern clouding her face.

Leo barks out a laugh. "Yeah. When we were fifteen, Miles almost drowned surfing in a hurricane. Ever since, he tempts fate every chance he gets." He rolls his eyes, willing me to take his bait.

Jenna's jaw falls open, and I'm not sure if she's reacting to Leo's revelation or my night surfing. Either way, it sends a rush of warmth straight through me.

My eyes flick to hers. "I told you, I love to surf at night." My voice comes out husky.

"Yeah. But I thought you were just trying to impress me. Miles, that's *really* dangerous, surfing in the dark like that." Jenna frowns.

"You don't need to worry about me. Besides, it's not *that* dark," I reply curtly. It sounds harsher than I mean it to. Jenna's cheeks redden, and the expression on her face is unreadable, but she doesn't reply. "I'm going to get something from the truck. I'll be right back," I mutter, turning to walk away.

"Wait." Jenna's voice stops me in my tracks. "I'll come with you. I haven't eaten either, and I've already had too much beer."

"Okay." I start walking.

I hold the door open for her, and she ducks under my arm, turning back to look at me with a smile I can't read. We approach the food truck in silence. It's dark outside, but the area is well lit. The air is crisp and cool, reminding me that these nice outdoor evenings are numbered. I quietly peruse the chalkboard menu while Jenna bounces back and forth on her feet, like she's cold.

"Are you cold or do you just like dancing around?" I smirk, running my hands through my surf hair.

"I'm cold. Well, cold and nervous maybe," Jenna admits, looking down at her feet.

When she looks up again, our eyes lock. Her cheeks are pink and flushed. Pink cheeks, pink earlobes, luscious pink lips. I wonder just how much she's had to drink. My lips twitch with amusement. "Why are you nervous?" I haven't been alone with Jenna in days and to be honest, I'm nervous too. But this is the last thing I expected to hear from her tonight. She's been avoiding me for a week. I'm confused to say the least.

"*You* make me nervous, Miles." Jenna pushes my shoulder with the palm of her hand, sending an electric jolt down my arm.

"Me?" I scoff. "Please. I think you're just tipsy. I'm a puppy dog," I banter back. It's the only way to swallow the irritation rising in my throat. I have to make light of it so I'm not a jerk. *I will not be rude to Jenna.* I repeat the mantra in my mind. I just can't take the hot and cold with her. It leaves me feeling like I'm floundering.

"I'm not." She shakes her head.

"You've been ignoring me for days, Jenna," I say carefully. It's hard to remain coherent when I'm this close to her.

"I have not," Jenna replies, crossing her arms.

I roll my eyes. "Well, every time I've reached out to you, you've given me very brief answers." We step closer to the food truck as the long line moves at a snail's pace.

"I know," she admits with a shrug. "You scare me, Miles." Her voice is quiet.

"Now that's what every guy wants to hear," I mumble, throwing my head back with a sarcastic chuckle. Then I meet her gaze and I can't ignore the warmth that runs through me.

"You scare me in a good way." Jenna bites her lower lip. "In a terrifyingly good way." *Is she swooning at me?*

I groan and rub my forehead. "Jenna, don't play these games with me." I feel restless and irritable. But I also want to push her up against the back of the food truck and kiss her senseless. The tension between us is sizzling.

"I–I'm not playing games, Miles," Jenna says warily. "I guess, I just miss your company."

At this, I soften, but just a little. This girl is going to drive me insane. How can I want her so badly and feel so irritated by her hot and cold demeanor at the same time? It's a lethal combination—when I finally get my hands on her, I'm going to have my way with her until she screams my name. "You've got a funny way of showing it," I retort, side-eyeing her.

"Come on, Miles. You miss hanging out with me too, don't you?" She pushes a lock of brown waves behind her ear.

I eye her cautiously, but before I can answer, it's our turn to order.

"What do you want?" I ask her, changing the subject.

"I'll have whatever you're having," Jenna replies, inching closer to me. She puts her hand in the back pocket of my jeans, cupping my ass. My dick moves in response and I feel myself tense.

I suck in a breath and look at her before ordering two pulled pork sandwiches. "Jenna," I say hoarsely.

"Miles. I miss you." Jenna leans on me. *This has got to be the booze talking.* "Despite everyone telling me to stay away from you, I do. I miss you."

I pull away from her and hand the cashier my card. "Who is telling you to stay away from me?" I frown. She almost had me caving, but now my guard is back up.

Jenna shrugs. "Joy...Jake." Jenna rocks her neck back and forth, lips pursed in thought. "That's about it, I guess."

We step aside to wait for our food. "Yeah? And why are they telling you to stay away from me?" I fold my arms across my chest and lean on the side of the truck, trying to mask my growing irritation.

Jenna steps closer. "It doesn't matter what they say." She brushes her fingers along my cheek. "There's something between us."

I meet her fiery brown eyes and those fucking lips. All I want to do is grab her face and devour it in frustration, but I don't.

"I know you feel it too," Jenna whispers. "I tried to ignore it, but..."

Now I'm completely vexed. I stand up taller and tower over her, looking down. I fight the urge to touch her but let my breath linger on her ear. "Maybe I do," I rasp. "But you're probably better off taking your friend's advice and steering clear of me."

Our food comes up and I grab it, turning to find a table. Jenna trails behind me.

This is going to be a long night.

Chapter Seventeen

I don't know how I got this drunk. *I mean the alcohol, obviously.* The sandwich I ate with Miles did nothing to soak up the beer sloshing around my stomach. Now Joy is talking to some guy she met; Leo is off doing who knows what. Last I saw, he was inserting himself into a bachelorette party. I'm sitting alone on a wobbly stool at our high top, feeling a little woozy when Miles places a glass of water in front of me.

"Drink this," he says, lips pressing into a tight smile.

I narrow my eyes but a teasing smile tugs at my mouth. "What did you put in it?"

"It's water, Jenna," Miles says curtly. He doesn't have the patience for me tonight. That became apparent as soon as I started flirting with him at the food truck.

I don't know what comes over me when I'm in his presence. Logically, it makes zero sense for me to get involved with him. There just seems to be a magnetic force always pulling me toward him. I can forget about it if I'm not near him, but if I'm in the same room as him? There is no forgetting. I want him. I don't want to want him, but I do. Even if it's just for one night. *Which would be a whole different kind of mistake, I'm sure.*

It's got to be the alcohol heightening my awareness of him. He's standing so close to me, watching to make sure I drink the water. Sober me would find his watchful eye annoying but buzzed me thinks it's sweet. I sip the water and smile up at him. Miles has never looked broody before. Normally, he's happy-go-lucky. Now he just looks royally pissed. *It's so hot.*

"How are you getting home?" he asks. Before I can answer, he adds, "You're not driving."

"I'll Uber or something and get my car tomorrow," I say, blowing bubbles in my water glass through the straw. It shoots up my nose and I cackle.

Miles isn't amused. "I'll take you home. Let's go." He starts to put on his jacket.

I frown at him. "Why do you get to say when it's time to leave? I'm having fun." The truth is, I stopped having fun about an hour ago when Joy ditched me for a guy with neck tattoos. I also wouldn't mind a car ride with Miles, but I don't want him to know that.

"Well, I'm ready to go, and your two friends left you, so what's it going to be?" Miles lifts a brow, already turning toward the door. He doesn't wait for me; he starts walking toward the door.

"You're so bossy," I say, wrinkling my nose. I hop off the stool and gather my things quickly, following him out. "Would it kill you to wait for me?" I call through the crowd. A few people around us glance my way.

He turns and gives me a devilish smirk over his shoulder. "You move too slow."

Miles waits on the sidewalk as I step through the door out into the cool air. I'm never going to get used to the ten-degree difference of a seashore town. I shiver, and Miles notices—but for the first time since I've known him, doesn't say anything about it. I expect him to open my car door, but instead, he goes right around to the driver's side.

"It's unlocked," he says flatly. Not that I wanted him to open my door or anything, but he's really turned the cold shoulder to me.

Miles is quiet as he drives to my house. I want so desperately to talk to him. I have to find a way to tell him how I feel. I don't exactly know how that *is* yet, but I do know I want to be near him. It feels too strange not to be. After we ate our sandwiches, he mostly avoided me. I *know* I don't want that.

"Miles," I say quietly. He doesn't look at me, keeping his eyes on the road. "Miles," I say more firmly, prompting him to give me a sideways glance before turning back to the road. "What did I do wrong?" I whisper. "You're freezing me out."

Miles sighs, scratching his chin. "You didn't do anything wrong, Jenna," he says exasperated.

"Clearly, I did." I roll my eyes.

Miles pulls off the dark, wooded road and onto the shoulder, a flicker of unease tightens in my chest. He turns to face me. "Jenna. You didn't do anything wrong. I am just dealing with some personal stuff, okay?" He licks his lips and looks down at the gear shift.

"I feel like it's me, though," I say quietly, shifting my body toward his.

Miles shrugs and turns his eyes back to mine. "Maybe it's you a little bit," he admits.

Suddenly, I'm sober. *I knew I wasn't imagining his cold shoulder.* It never crossed my mind that my flirting might actually be hurting him. "Then talk to me about it, please."

"I just can't take the hot and cold with you, Jenna. I told you I like you, but I'm trying to be careful. One minute, *you're* freezing *me* out, making it seem like it's the last time you're going to see me. The next, you're putting your hand in my back pocket." He drags his palm down his face. "It's really confusing."

"I'm sorry," I whisper again, suddenly embarrassed by my behavior. Miles has been nothing but kind to me. He doesn't deserve this roller coaster I've put him on. I sigh. "I guess I am wrestling with the idea of starting something with you when I'm not planning on staying. I don't want to hurt you."

Miles lets out a dry laugh. "Hurt me? I'm worried about hurting you."

I crack a smile. "So, we're both looking out for the other." I bite my lower lip, hoping it will entice him.

"I guess so," he rasps, looking me in the eye. My stomach flutters, and I don't look away.

"So, now what?" I ask, not bothering to hide the hope in my voice.

Miles sighs. "Now, I take you home. And maybe we try to stay in the present moment and not worry too much about what comes next." He shifts the car back onto the road.

"Okay. I can do that." I swallow the lump in my throat. "I'm glad we had that talk," I say, resting my head on the seat. "And even more glad you didn't drag me into the woods and murder me." I giggle.

For the first time tonight, Miles smirks at me. "Yet. I didn't murder you *yet*." He winks, and his smile turns genuine.

I'm devastated when he pulls up in front of my house.

"Okay, this is your stop." He looks at me, his eyes suddenly tender, like he doesn't want me to go.

"Miles," I murmur.

"Yeah?" He asks, his voice quiet but earnest.

"Will you stay with me tonight?" I sound desperate, and I don't mean how it comes out, but suddenly I really don't want to go in there alone. "It's just...*really* lonely in there." I cast my eyes downward, not daring to see him tell me no.

Miles exhales. "Tell you what? How about I stay until you fall asleep? I can't leave Pete alone."

I nod. For tonight, that would have to be enough.

ଓ

The last thing I remember before falling asleep is Miles sitting at the end of my childhood bed, whispering that he'd call me tomorrow. How is it, then, that the smell of brewing coffee wakes me up on Sunday morning? I glance at my phone on the bedside table: ten fifteen a.m.

I lurch out of bed, irrationally suspecting an intruder. Sometime during the night, I kicked off my pajama pants. I throw them on and jog down the steps, the scent of coffee and breakfast growing stronger the closer I get. Then I'm in the doorway, finding Miles standing in my ancient kitchen, scrambling eggs. Pete is at his feet, waiting for something to fall. There's a coffee pot on my counter that wasn't there before.

I clear my throat, and Miles spins around, a you-caught-me grin on his face. "Good morning," he says jovially, a stark contrast from last night's demeanor.

Pete runs over to me and sits at my feet, pushing his face into my legs so I'll pet him.

"Uh...hi," I say, with a curious quirk of my eyebrow. I ruffle Pete's ear.

"There's coffee." Miles gestures to the new coffee pot. The open box sits on the kitchen table. *He remembered I didn't have a working coffee pot, and he got me one.* My heartbeat flutters.

"Thank you..." I walk over and reach for a mug in the upper cabinet, then go to the sink to rinse the dust out of it. I pour myself a cup of what smells like pumpkin flavored coffee, then whirl around to face him. He's stirring the eggs, whistling. "Miles."

He turns, as if he knows exactly what I'm going to say. His eyes have a mischievous twinkle. *Caught.*

"What are you *doing* here?" I furrow my brow. "I thought you went home last night."

Miles walks over to the fridge and takes out a carton of half-and-half, passing it to me. "Oh, I did," he assures me, shaking his head vigorously.

"Okay..." That doesn't answer my question. "So, why are you here now?"

Miles shrugs. "Pete and I are early risers. I remembered you don't have a coffee pot, so we drove up the parkway and bought you one from Target. You weren't awake when we got back, so..." He holds up his hands as if to say, *here I am.*

I pour some half-and-half in my mug and sit down at the table. Shaking my head in confusion, I look at him. "So...you just let yourself in?"

Miles scrunches up his face and scratches the back of his head. "Okay, yeah, maybe that wasn't my wisest idea. I could have left it on your porch. But I wanted you to have some right away when you woke up." He starts dishing the eggs onto some plates as toast pops out of my parents' ancient toaster.

My heart swells. Miles woke up thinking about me, and we haven't even hooked up. *What on earth is going on here?* "If it were anyone else, I'd be calling the police," I say, with a sigh because I already know I can't be mad at him.

Miles places a plate in front of me and sits down next to me. "I know. But, you should know—it was all Pete's idea." He glances at the dog, sitting like a patient boy, hoping for some scraps.

I laugh. "Well, Pete's heart was in the right place. I guess I can forgive him." I pat Pete's head and take a bite of my breakfast. For the next two minutes, Miles and I eat in silence, smiling at each other like lovestruck teenagers, neither of us knowing what to say next.

Finally, Miles clears his throat and reaches for my free hand. "Jenna," he says, his voice serious.

"Miles?" I grin at him, mocking his tone.

"Would you like to come surfing with me today?" His eyebrows raise and a smile tugs at his mouth.

"It would be my pleasure." I grin. And that's not an exaggeration.

Chapter Eighteen

After dropping Pete off at my condo, I take Jenna back to the same beach where she learned to surf. It's a bit more crowded today, and as soon as we pull into the parking lot, I can tell she's nervous. She's wearing Erin's wet suit again with her wavy hair piled on top of her head. She's chewing on that lip like it's candy. And she is gorgeous. "You good?" I ask with a small smile. I'm excited, this is the first time I will be able to surf beside her. I am looking forward to lying on the board next to her and paddling in for the same wave. Jenna does not appear to be on the same page.

She stares out the windshield, eyes locked on the water. "The waves are really big today."

"They are," I agree.

She swallows hard. "There is a hurricane coming up the coast later this week. That's probably why. I should have checked the surf report." I reach for her hand. "It's okay if you'd rather watch today."

She lets out a sigh of what I assume is great relief. "Oh, thank God." She laughs at herself. "I don't think I'm ready for those waves."

I squeeze her hand and give her a reassuring smile. "I've been surfing my whole life, and I can say, these are big waves. I wouldn't expect you to try these your second time out."

"Okay, good," she breathes. "Maybe I can take some pictures of you."

I laugh, shaking my head. "Whatever you want."

We carry the longboard down the beach and pick a spot. It's another unseasonably warm October day at the Jersey Shore, but I will take it. I spread out a towel for Jenna and get to work waxing the board. Initially, I was going to shortboard it today, but the waves are a little big—even for me. I haven't gotten into the details with her yet, but when I was fifteen, I was rescued in waves much like these. I'm a much stronger swimmer now, but that was a terrifying day. Surviving a near-death experience is part of the reason I never stopped surfing. I have to beat the ocean. I can't let it beat me. If I stop surfing, the ocean wins.

I finish waxing the board and stand, tucking it under my arm. "Are you going to be okay?" I ask Jenna, who appears lost in thought as she watches the surfers in the water.

She smiles warmly. "Of course." She waves me away. "Go, go, have fun."

So, I do. There are about ten other surfers out here, and the waves are a good five to ten feet overhead. A familiar charge of adrenaline surges through me every time I run headfirst into the ocean. My stomach flutters and my heart races—but it's a feeling I've grown to love, to chase. The day my wife left me, I came here, looking for that same rush. The ocean has tried to kill me—yet it has also saved me from myself. It's been a constant in my life, and I can't imagine a day when I won't show up here chasing that rush.

I nod at a few surfers coming out of the water as I head in. "Careful out there," one of them calls.

I snort, giving him a wave. I've got this. I throw myself on the board and paddle out, ducking under each enormous wave until I'm out past the break. Finally, I'm there. I sit up on my board, catching my breath before searching for a wave. Jenna is standing on the shoreline, shading her eyes, no doubt looking for me. I give her a wave and she waves back. I think I see her physically relax once she spots me. This appears to have her a little wound up. It's probably best she's just watching.

I wait for the swell that rolls in rhythmic and powerful,

promising the perfect ride. Then I spot it, a towering well of water swelling in the distance. My heartbeat quickens. Lying flat, I paddle hard, my arms slicing through the water with practiced ease. Even though the sun is bright with not a cloud in the sky, these waves are big and angry. I race against myself, chasing the wave building behind me, like a giant gathering strength.

Then it happens. The wave lifts me, tipping the board forward, and I'm on my feet in one fluid motion. Rushing water fills my ears as the world falls away—it's just me and this angry ocean, moving as one. The ride is pure freedom, a fleeting but eternal moment where I become part of the wave. The ocean guides me back to shore as the wave loses momentum and then I see her. Jenna, on her feet, smiling and clapping for the ride she just witnessed. A smile breaks across my face, and I point at her. Then, I do it again.

Three rides in, my confidence is surging. Jenna has her phone out and is taking photos of me. I'm fire atop a vast wall of water. The next wave I take lifts me and cradles me in its powerful swell. Just like the other rides, I'm to my feet in a single swift motion. I'm on top of the world, flying, riding the wave's energy as it carries me toward shore. Then something shifts. The wave ripples suddenly with unpredictable force, throwing me off balance. The nose of the board dips under the wave, cutting into the water, and for a split second, everything freezes.

Panic rises in my chest and every muscle tenses as I prepare to be pummeled. The wave takes over, launching me headfirst into the churning water. I flail as the wave swallows me whole. The force spins me like an agitator in a washing machine, disorienting me. I fight to regain control of my body and the board, but a sharp sting sears as the board smacks into my cheekbone. Pain blooms across my cheek, a dull throb that is quickly overtaken by saltwater filling my senses and the adrenaline needed to survive. I don't know how long I am under the water but eventually, the wave spits me out. I gasp for breath, clinging to the leash that has me tethered to my thrashing surfboard. I blink, spit out saltwater, and gingerly press my fingers to my stinging cheek. *Blood.* Then

I hear her.

"Miles!" Jenna is shouting my name. "Miles! Are you okay?"

I shake my head and brush water out of my eyes, trying to focus. When I look toward the shore, I see Jenna. She's shielding her eyes and standing on her toes to try and spot me. Several other people stand by her, waiting for a sign that I'm all right. I hold up my hand to them and they cheer. I force myself to swallow the embarrassment of my epic wipeout and trudge out of the water.

"You okay, man?" a surfer asks, meeting me on my way out.

"I'm good," I mutter without looking at him.

"You're bleeding," the guy says.

Before I can answer, Jenna runs to me. "Miles. Oh my God. Your cheek." The worry on her face warms a part of me that up until now was cold and broken. "Come here."

I drop the board to the sand as Jenna pulls me into a hug, running her fingers through the tufts of hair at the nape of my neck. I let myself be consumed by her embrace.

"You're bleeding," she whimpers.

Her fingers graze my cheekbone, and I wince, letting out a hiss. "I'm okay," I reassure her.

"Miles. You scared the *hell* out of me." She swats my shoulder, but I don't miss the trembling of her hand.

"Trust me, it was no picnic for me either," I tell her, sitting down on the board. She sits next to me and rests her head on my shoulder.

"Were you scared?" she whispers, leaning into me.

"Hell yeah, I was scared," I say, my voice frayed. Then softer, "I knew I would be okay though. I always am."

Jenna stays quiet but doesn't lift her head. "Miles, my dad died on this beach when I was nine." Her voice wavers, barely above a whisper.

I straighten, lifting her chin with my fingers. I touch her cheek, and she nuzzles into my hand. "Jenna. I'm so sorry. I didn't know," I say, my voice thick with emotion. I feel terrible. She nods, and I keep my hand on her cheek. I like the feeling of it there. "Do you want to talk about it?"

She shakes her head. "It was a really long time ago. I don't even really know the details," she says quietly. "But I was just so scared when I didn't see you come back up. It terrified me."

Her eyes glisten. She wipes at them and sniffles, not bothering to hold back her emotions.

"I'm okay," I tell her, running my thumb along her jawline.

She sniffles and nods, her gaze drifting from my lips to my eyes. Nothing is holding me back now. Whatever has been building between us was just solidified with her confession. I lean in and so does she, our noses brushing together ever so slightly. I trace my fingers along her cheek, and my thumb lingers on her chin for a moment before tipping it toward my mouth. Her mouth is soft and warm in contrast to my salty, cool lips from the ocean water.

The rhythmic sound of the surf is a steady heartbeat, syncing with my own quickening pulse. I kiss her slowly, giving her every chance to pull away—but she doesn't. *I've waited for this.* The kiss is soft, tentative, Jenna's breath tickles my nose, until it deepens with the unspoken promise of something more—something we've both been wanting. Desire builds in my gut as I wrap my arm around Jenna's hip, pulling her closer. *I want more.* And at the same time, I need *slow.*

Jenna drags her teeth on my lower lip, and she pulls away, a playful smile on her lips. She studies my face, memorizing every detail. "Finally," she murmurs. Then she reaches up and swipes some dripping blood from my cheek. Jenna tips her forehead into mine and whispers, "We really should get this looked at." I'll do whatever she says—except that.

Chapter Nineteen

Miles's cheek is red and angry, with blood drying in small clots. A bruise has already started to blossom from his orbital bone to his cheekbone. I insist on taking him to the hospital or at least an urgent care, but Miles shrugs me off, putting the longboard on his roof rack.

"Miles, come on. You could need stitches," I push, leaning against the driver's side door with my arms crossed.

"No. I've wiped out before. Let's just go back to my place and I promise to ice it," Miles says, trying to pacify me. I think if not for that kiss that still has my lips tingling, Miles would be a lot grumpier.

"Fine," I grumble. "But I'm driving. You could have a concussion."

"From hitting my face? No. But it hurts like hell, so I'll let you win." He rolls his eyes and tosses me the keys.

Driving Miles's car is easy, and I am surprised by how well I'm learning my way around Cape May. I make it there without GPS and without any help since Miles is resting his eyes. We're back at his condo in ten minutes. I pull into his spot and unbuckle, reaching across Miles for my bag at his feet. He grabs my elbow. "Hey," he says with a slow smile, opening his eyes.

"Hi." I bite my lip, smiling back.

"Thanks. I'm sorry I worried you," he croaks.

"You're welcome." We hold each other's gaze for a moment

before Miles leans in, cupping my cheek, and planting a soft kiss on my lips. When he pulls away, I immediately wish he'd come back. I sigh and lean my head on the headrest. Neither of us are in a hurry to leave the car. "We should probably go inside and clean that up," I whisper, gesturing to Miles's face.

"Yeah," he rasps, his voice low. "It hurts."

We climb the stairs to his condo, and I unlock the door. Pete hears us instantly and comes running. Miles fights him off. "Down boy," he says.

I wonder if Miles has to tell himself that too. Seeing him wounded and vulnerable has *my* whole body feeling warm and awake. I ache to be close to him, but I know I need to reel these emotions in.

"Come on, let's have a look." I take Miles's hand and lead him down the small hallway to the bathroom. I close the toilet seat and gently push him down onto it. "Do you have a first aid kit?" I tip his chin to the side, examining the cut.

Miles huffs out a laugh. "Do you know many guys in their forties who keep a first aid kit lying around?"

I shoot him a playful glare. "Band aids? Neosporin?"

Miles shrugs. "Check in those drawers or the medicine cabinet. There might be something."

I step in front of him. Practically straddling him to reach the cabinet above. He holds my hips steady and the skin beneath my wet suit tingles. I grab a washcloth and lower myself back down, but Miles doesn't remove his hands. We stare into each other's eyes, and it takes everything I've got not to climb onto his lap and press myself against him. *I want Miles. Maybe more than I've ever wanted anyone.* I clear my throat, breaking the hold he has on me.

"Let me wet this," I murmur, stepping out of his grasp. When I glance back at him, I can see that he's hard. *I'm glad it's not just me that's turned on.* I turn on the water and soak the cloth. "Warm or cold water?"

"Cold. Please." Miles clears his throat.

I turn off the water and then I'm back in front of him. "Put your head back," I order.

"Yes, ma'am." Miles smirks but does as he's told.

I gently wipe the dried blood from his face. He winces and lets out a sharp hiss. "Sorry," I whisper. Once I have wiped away the blood, I'm able to see that it's just a surface wound. "Let me see what you have in these drawers." I move away and start rummaging, finding some expired Neosporin and a few butterfly strips. I hold my treasures up to Miles. "It's expired, but I think it'll do." I move back in front of him and his hands immediately find my hips again. He digs his fingers into them as if he wants me as close as possible. The feeling is mutual. I go to work, leaning in close and carefully dabbing along the two-inch gash. Miles's breath warms my neck, and all my senses are heightened.

There is no denying this anymore. What *this* is, I'm not sure. Maybe it's a fling, maybe it's more, but suddenly I desperately want to see it through. The feelings Miles evokes in me are like nothing I've felt before. I feel safe and cared for and wildly aroused all at the same time.

Miles interrupts my thoughts. "When I was fifteen, I had a pretty scary surfing accident. It was much like today, except I wasn't as strong as I am now. I was with Leo, and we saw the waves. We knew it was risky, there was no one else even trying to surf. But I was cocky and thought I'd be fine. I got caught in a rip current and I had to be rescued. It was the scariest day of my life. I thought for sure I was going to die," he murmurs. "Today really stirred up those memories." His brow creases and he pushes his lips together.

My heart constricts. *So that's what Leo was talking about last night.* "Oh, Miles." I pull back, resting my hands on his shoulders. "Why did you keep surfing after that?"

"Because if I give up, the ocean wins. I can't let it." Miles's eyes are sharp and assessing, as if he's searching my face for something. Approval? Agreement? I'm not sure.

Now isn't the time to tell him my opinion, so I pull his face into my chest and nuzzle him, running my hands through his saltwater curls. "You really scared me," I purr into his hair.

"I really scared myself," he admits. "But I know I'll be back out there chasing the stars again tomorrow. The ocean knocks me down, but it's also what keeps pulling me back up."

I sigh and pull back, cupping Miles's face in my hands, touching my nose to his. "Miles," I sigh. I'm not sure I can accurately portray my worry for him in words, and I'm not sure it would even matter to him. Miles seems like he'll do what he's always done no matter who likes it.

Instead of saying anything, Miles leans forward and kisses me softly and briefly again, leaving me wanting more. I want to escalate things, but he doesn't seem to want to now. Maybe he's drained. I know I would be.

He pulls away. "I'm going to get changed. Then, maybe we can watch a movie?"

"Well...I thought we'd be going back to my house, but we're here and...I have no clothes. So..." I let my words hang in the air.

"I'll find you something to wear. Come on." He brushes past me out of the bathroom, unzipping his wet suit as he goes. I give myself a quick once-over in the mirror before following behind. By the time I reach his doorway, he is already shirtless. His wet suit is unzipped and rolled down to his waist. I gasp at the sight. His back is all sharp angles and lean muscle. His waistline tapers at the hip. Miles must hear me—he turns and grins, flashing a perfect six-pack. Butterflies swarm my belly, and warmth invades my lower region. This is the first time I've seen him bare-chested, and I am not disappointed.

Miles walks to his dresser and grabs a T-shirt I expect him to put on, but instead, he tosses it to me. It lands on my face, and I get a whiff of laundry detergent and Miles. He chuckles when I pull the shirt off my face and inhale. "Here. Let me get you some pants." He walks to his closet and grabs a pair of jogger sweatpants that will likely fall off me. This time he walks them over to me and places them in my hands.

Miles's hands find my waist and he pulls me close. The folded sweatpants separate me from the warmth of his body, and my insides are screaming for more. I melt into his arms, and we stand like that for several minutes. *What is happening to me?* The raw emotions between us are supercharged and palpable.

"These should work," Miles murmurs in my ear, sending a shiver up my spine.

"These will *not* fit me." I bite back a grin.

Neither of us pull away. It's as if we know that when we do, the moment will have passed us by.

"Roll the waistband." Miles's low voice hums in my ear, he tugs my hips closer to his. He's hard, and when I feel it, I let out a gasp.

"I don't have any underwear," I whisper.

"I like knowing that," he replies, his breath lingering on my neck.

My body reacts immediately, and I pull back to look at him. "Miles," I whimper. "I need you."

"I know," he agrees, pressing his forehead into mine. "But...I don't want to ruin this. I want to take my time with you—make sure it's right. It's not time yet."

I moan in frustration, and Miles cups my face, planting a kiss on my forehead.

"It will be worth the wait," he promises.

It fucking better be.

Chapter Twenty

Miles

Jenna is the only woman I've ever been with who makes me this nervous. My feelings for her are growing with reckless urgency, and I am scared to fully give in to them. I know I can be impulsive. I can give in to lust only to regret it later, when it's quiet and I'm alone. I am having trouble differentiating between lust and falling for Jenna.

We're on my couch, both pretending to pay attention to the Netflix Original rom-com she picked. I could easily turn up the heat. We're laying at opposite ends, trading foot rubs. I'm already better just having her here. And when Jenna leaves to go back home tonight, I know it won't be sex on my mind—it will be her.

What does she do in that house all alone? Does she think about me?

I rub her feet, and she lets out a soft moan that I want to lay claim to forever. No one else should be able to elicit that noise out of her. The credits roll and Jenna yawns.

"Oh, I missed watching a movie on an actual TV." She sits up, pulling her feet back and stretching. She looks perfect wearing my clothes. She is swimming in them, but the outline of her bare breast through the T-shirt has me hard. Knowing she's not wearing any underwear under my sweatpants makes my balls ache.

"We should go get you a working TV," I tell her. I'm not even trying to hide how much I physically ache for her. I am sure she sees it through my sweatpants.

"I don't need a TV right now, Miles." She scoots closer but keeps her feet on the floor. "I should probably go get my car and head home." She almost sounds regretful.

"I don't want you to go," I admit, trapping her body between my legs so she can't leave. "I'll miss you too much. I want you too much." My voice is husky and vulnerable and I don't even care.

Jenna bites that damn lip, smiling up at me through long brown lashes. "I want you too, Miles," she whispers.

That's it for me. I've held back long enough. I grab her wrists and pull her on top of me so she's straddling my hips. "Do you feel how much I want you?" I growl.

She nods and lets out a little gasp. "Yes."

"Are you wet for me under those sweatpants?" I tease, stroking her arm and then letting my fingers linger over her nipples.

"Miles, *please*," she whimpers, and my dick reacts immediately, nudging itself into her warmth.

"We have to go slow," I murmur, sitting up so that she's in my lap and we're face to face. I put my mouth to hers, but I don't kiss her yet. "It's been a long time since I've had these feelings for someone. I want to make sure I can trust them."

"It's the same for me," she says quietly. "I'm out of practice."

"I'll refresh your memory," I say, and then I kiss her the way I have been dying to all this time, since the day I caught her peeking into her house.

Jenna moans softly, and I match it with my own. This kiss unravels everything I've kept wound up tight for the few weeks I've known Jenna. The pull between us is undeniable. I need her in a way I haven't felt before. I pepper kisses down her jaw, to her ear lobe, grazing my stubble against her neck.

"Miles," Jenna says my name breathlessly. "Don't tease me. I need you. I don't want to just make out."

"I need you too, Jenna," I rasp, letting my breath linger. I grip the hem of her T-shirt and yank it over her head, revealing her supple breasts. Her body is better than I imagined, and I'm starving for it. I lean down, taking each of her pebbled nipples between my lips, one at a time, dragging my teeth on their tips as I alternate back and forth. Jenna cries out, grinding her heat over my hardness. I continue to tease her, sucking, biting and nibbling until she is begging. I kiss up her collar bone and jawline. "Can I taste you?" I whisper in her ear.

"Oh my God, yes," Jenna gasps and that's all I need. I ease her back gently onto the couch—right as Pete's pussy radar goes off. He jumps out of his dog bed and sticks his big block head in Jenna's face as I kiss her neck. She giggles. "No, Pete. I'll have time for you later," she laughs, pushing his face away.

"I have a better idea," I growl and scoop her up. Jenna wraps her legs around my waist as I carry her to my room, kicking the door closed behind me. "Sorry, Pete," I call, carrying her to the bed. I tear my T-shirt off in one swift motion and step out of my sweats, leaving my boxers as the only barrier between us.

"You're gorgeous," Jenna purrs, looking up at me.

"You are," I murmur, lowering myself over her. I start back at her nipples, gently sucking each one until she moans my name. Then I kiss down her ribcage, over her belly button to her hip bones. I bite at the rolled waistband of the last thing separating my mouth from her. "Lose these," I say, tugging them down with one hand and supporting myself with the other. As soon as they're off, I trace my fingers through her lips, feeling how aroused she is for me. "You're so wet. Oh my God," I rasp, dropping to my knees and pressing my lips to her thighs. "Don't hold back on me, baby."

"Miles. *Please,*" Jenna moans.

I kiss along her inner thighs, teasing her, my hot breath fanning over her skin. I lick the outside of her bare, swollen lips, dragging my stubbled chin along, eliciting another whimper from her. I slowly drag my index finger through her folds and my breath hitches. I want to slide my dick right in, but I need to taste her first. I gently stroke until I find the button of nerves that has my name falling from her lips. "You like this?" I growl.

"Uh-huh," Jenna cries. "Just like that. Don't stop."

That's the only encouragement I need. I bury my mouth

between her thighs and lick straight up and down, tasting her salty desire. I sink my tongue into her, tasting, licking, and nibbling until she cries out. With my other hand, I slide my fingers inside her, her arousal dripping onto my hand. I pump my fingers into her, stroking and licking simultaneously until Jenna is writhing beneath, unable to hold back.

"Miles, I'm coming. I'm coming. Don't stop." She trembles, her legs tightening around my hand as her body convulses in pleasure. It's exactly what I have wanted to do to her since I first laid eyes on her.

I slide my hand up and hover over her, kissing her cheeks, nuzzling her nose, and finally kissing her mouth. She is beautiful in her post orgasmic glow, and I already can't wait to make her come again.

"Oh my God," she mutters, barely audible. "Miles, you are incredible with that mouth of yours."

I let out an easy laugh and sit up. I brush her hair off her face, gazing at her like the lovesick puppy I am.

She turns to face me, tracing a finger along my lip. "Your turn."

Jenna shoves my right shoulder back onto the bed, guiding me onto my back as she straddles me, starting the same way I started with her. She tenderly kisses around my cut-up face, down along my jaw. When she reaches my mouth, she cups my face and kisses me hungrily. My dick moves in anticipation. She moves down my neck, chest, and ribcage, dragging her fingernails as she kisses. She drags her tongue along the V on my lower abs, and I hiss. She yanks down my boxers, nudging my cock with her nose.

"Now I know how you felt," I groan.

"Uh-huh." She smiles, pressing a gentle kiss just to the left of my dick. She grasps my hardness and continues to kiss everywhere but the head itself, causing me to moan her name. Finally, she takes my length into her warm mouth and hastily pumps. She teases me, licking and dragging her teeth gently up my shaft.

"Jenna, I'm not going to last." I let out a breath. I cover my eyes with my palm. "Oh my God. I've wanted this for too long." I groan when she envelopes the head with the back of her throat, stroking harder. She cups my balls, and I think that will be my undoing—until she pulls back and moves down to take each one into her mouth, pumping my dick and bringing me to the brink of euphoria.

Jenna makes me feel as if I have lost all control. Ordinarily in bed, I take charge, I take the lead. I don't let myself come too fast. All of that is out the window. I am completely enthralled with this beautiful woman, on the edge of a cliff about to willingly dive off. "Jenna. I'm close," I warn, wanting to give her the chance to pull away.

"Good," she murmurs, but she doesn't stop, and that realization intensifies the buildup. Then it's happening and I'm flying, ecstasy ripping through me as my hot liquid fills her mouth—probably more than she bargained for. It's a cosmic transcendence, and I can't believe I waited this long to get this close to Jenna. I close my eyes, riding the wave, and to Jenna's credit, she doesn't move her mouth away, taking all of me. I have stars in my eyes as I open them and gaze at her. She wipes her mouth with my T-shirt, then she grins at me and melts into the crook of my arm.

"You're amazing," I murmur into her hair, kissing the top of her head.

"You are," she breathes. And we stay like that for a long time.

Chapter Twenty-One

Jenna

Pulling myself away from Miles is hard. The feelings I have for him have been building, and today was the culmination of every emotional moment we've shared since the day we met. Miles is, by far, the most attentive lover I have ever had. He made me feel beautiful, safe, and most importantly, seen, all while ensuring the greatest orgasm of my life. I wish I could stay in bed with him from this day forward. The moment we got dressed, I started having anxiety about leaving him. I suspect Miles feels the same way as he drives me back to my car.

We cleaned ourselves up, and then Miles ordered us a pizza. While we waited, I gave Pete the attention he was craving, which gave me a moment to be away from Miles to collect myself a little bit. The separation anxiety I already feel is alarming me. I need to figure out where my head and my heart are, and if they're on the same page. Now that we've been intimate, I worry he'll lose interest in me.

That's not just me being insecure. He told me a week ago that he was worried about that very thing—that he doesn't catch feelings easily. Well, I've caught them. I'm damn near bewitched by Miles and it's scary as hell.

He pulls into the nearly empty parking lot at the brewery and parks next to my car. We sit there for a moment, turning toward each other. I fiddle with the water bottle sitting in the center cup holder. Miles puts his hand on top of mine and intertwines our fingers. I lift my gaze to him, and his lips twitch.

"Have I told you that you're amazing?" he asks me.

My heart flutters. "I believe you have." I bite back a satisfied smile. "Have I told you that *you're* amazing? And that tongue? Oh my." I laugh.

Miles's expression turns serious; he pulls my hand to his mouth and kisses my knuckles. His brows turn together in an agonized expression. "I don't want you to go," he rasps.

I swallow and close my eyes, resting my head on the seat. "I don't want to go either," I utter softly, without opening them. "But you said yourself, *slow*."

Miles groans. "I know, but I want to sleep next to you," he whines, and I almost give in. I'd like to wake up in his condo on the beach again, his legs wrapped around mine, his breath in the crook of my neck. Then we would have coffee on his balcony and look out at the waves.

"It's hard to say good night," I admit, brushing a lock of wavy hair off his forehead. "But this time it's definitely *not* goodbye," I promise, offering a reassuring smile.

"It better not be." Miles smirks. Then quieter and more serious, "I don't think I'll ever be able to say goodbye to you."

I sigh, fighting to control my swirling emotions. "Don't make promises you can't keep, Miles," I whisper.

When he doesn't immediately respond, I take it as my cue to go. I collect my things and reach for the door. "I'll call you tomorrow," Miles murmurs.

"Okay." I shoot him a smile. "Don't go cold on me now," I say it like a joke, but there's a part of me that's terrified I'm going to walk away from Cape May with nothing but memories and a newly broken heart. Miles may be saying all the right things now, but what if he wakes up regretful tomorrow?

"I won't," he says, his voice husky. "I promise."

"Good." This time my smile is easier. "Thanks for the clothes." I push open the door.

"Thanks for the orgasm." Miles grins, his eyes scrunching at the corners.

I bark out a laugh. "Back at ya." I slam the door shut and climb into my cold car. The loneliness hits instantly.

When it becomes apparent that Miles won't pull out of the lot until I do, I shift the car into reverse and head toward my cold, empty house. Today started out perfect, then it got a little scary, and then it was amazing. So why do I feel so empty now?

I get home and take a scorching hot shower that leaves my skin pink. When I get out, I almost put on clean pajamas—then think better of it and reach for Miles's T-shirt instead. If I can't sleep next to him, at least I can fall asleep smelling like him. I climb into bed and fall into a fitful sleep, full of dreams of Miles and a life in Cape May that feels so close but so far away.

☙

I have nothing to wake up for Monday morning, so I sleep in. The mid-morning sun wakes me, shining through the blinds that I forgot to close. I groan and roll over to check my phone on the nightstand. It's nearly ten in the morning. There are several texts from Miles. My heart races as I tap into the text.

Miles

Can I see you for lunch?

I can't stop thinking about you.

I hope you aren't tired of me.

Jenna...

Did I do something wrong?

Without thinking, I dial his number.

"Jenna," he answers on the first ring.

"Hi," I say sleepily. "You didn't do anything wrong." I smile into my phone.

"Sorry. I might have come on a little too strong," Miles says sheepishly, his voice low.

"Just a wee little bit," I tease but I'm smiling. It's been a long time since a guy has fallen for me first. *Is that what this is?* It's almost always me liking someone more than they like me. I need to pump the brakes though. I have no idea if Miles has fallen for me. The last time I even went on a date, my mom was still healthy. Then she got sick, and it was like I pressed pause on my life. It felt selfish to want something just for me. The only consistent relationship I have had the past few years was with my mom's oncology nurse. I have no idea what I'm doing anymore.

"I got worried when you didn't answer. I thought maybe you were having second thoughts about yesterday." Miles's voice sounds tentative, as if he's waiting for me to reassure him.

"I'm not having second thoughts, Miles," I assure him quietly. "In fact. I was dreaming about you until about five minutes ago."

Miles laughs. "Dreaming, huh?" His voice turns sultry. "Was I making you come in the dream?"

I let out a husky laugh. "No. It was much more intimate than that."

"Maybe you can tell me about it over lunch?" His voice is brimming with hope.

"I would love that."

ꝏ

An hour and a half and three outfit changes later, I'm standing outside The Mad Batter waiting for Miles. I have never put so much effort into my appearance for a man—but here I am. Nothing I tried on felt right. Up until yesterday, I never cared—or even thought—about what I looked like around him. I didn't expect things to go the way they did. I finally landed on a pair of slouchy jeans cuffed at the ankle, a gray thermal, and my Birkenstock clogs.

Casual and comfortable. Like I didn't try too hard, even though I absolutely did.

I'm leaning against the railing when he walks up. He's dressed impeccably in a pair of navy slacks and a pinstriped button-down cuffed at the forearm. His wavy hair is tousled and pushed off his forehead. He smiles as he approaches, like his day just got better. I don't know why it's so hard for me to believe that I could have that effect on someone, but it is.

Miles stops in front of me. "Hi," he says quietly. He tips my chin up to his mouth and plants a soft kiss on my lips. "I couldn't get here fast enough," he breathes against my lips. At those words, my whole body tingles. In truth, I couldn't wait to see him either.

It's cooler out today but still unseasonably warm for October this week. Mid-week in the off-season means no wait, even at one of the most popular restaurants in town. Miles grabs my hand and leads me up the wooden steps of the old Victorian house-turned-restaurant. Inside, the restaurant is colorful, bright, and airy.

"Hello!" The cheerful hostess greets us. "Welcome to The Mad Batter. Where would you like to sit today?"

"How about the garden room?" Miles asks, looking at me for approval. I nod, giving him a smile. It's warm enough outside for the terrace today but if I know Miles, he's worried I'll be cold.

The hostess takes two menus and leads us to a small table in a quiet part of the restaurant, where the walls feature art by local artists and rainbow checkered stained glass windows brighten the space. The warmth of the sun shining in feels amazing. Then we're alone again, and my stomach twists itself in knots.

We quietly peruse the menu without speaking. Then Miles reaches across the table for my hand. All of this is perfect—except for the quiet thrum of anxiety beneath the surface. I haven't yet figured out why Miles still makes me nervous, despite everything that happened yesterday and how attentive he is being to me.

Am I terrified of being hurt, or am I terrified of being loved?

I don't think a man has ever truly loved me. At least not the way my father loved my mother. My mother never loved anyone else after we lost him. The strange thing is, when we found out her cancer was terminal, I think she was at peace, knowing she would get to see my dad again. I'd love to find a love like that—someone who would always wait for me—but I don't know if Miles is it. I don't know if it's in the cards for me.

My last relationship ended with him being unfaithful to me—right before my mom got sick. At the time, it was a relief to have something else to focus on. A reason not to take him back. I threw everything I had into caring for my mom. How could I be worried about a breakup when my mom was suffering from terminal cancer? Still, I've always had this nagging voice in the back of my mind that maybe I wasn't enough. That if I had been, he'd have stayed. He'd have shown up for me when it mattered most. He just didn't love me enough. That's what scares me about Miles. He's been nothing but patient and kind. And if I let myself believe that someone could love me like that—like my dad loved my mom—I'd never survive it if I were wrong.

"A penny for your thoughts?" Miles asks, raising his eyebrows and threading his fingers through mine.

I shake my head and smile, my cheeks flushing. I can't tell Miles the thoughts and fears that are swarming my mind so instead, I fib. "I'm trying to decide between pancakes or a burger." I flick my eyes back to my menu to avoid his assessing gaze.

Miles laughs and his carefree smile relaxes me. The server comes over to take our order and I make a last-second decision. Miles doesn't let go of my hand the entire time the server is with us.

"So, I was thinking," he says slowly once she disappears, "Sophie and Liam are having a Halloween party in two weeks. I wasn't going to go. Halloween isn't really my thing, but then, I thought, maybe you might want to." He quirks his brow.

I'm surprised by his question. "Oh. Um, well..." I can't remember the last time I celebrated the holiday.

"It's okay, we don't have to." Miles backpedals. "If you don't want to."

"No, it's just that I haven't dressed up for Halloween in a really long time." I laugh. "Like, decades."

Miles huffs a laugh, his eyes flickering in amusement. "Me neither." He takes a sip of water. "It could be fun," he says with an easy shrug.

A slow smile creeps across my face and I find myself nodding. "Okay. Yeah, it could be fun."

"I'll brainstorm costume ideas for us," he says excitedly, gripping my hand again.

"For us? Like a couple's costume?" I lick my lips, suddenly nervous.

"Why not?" Miles asks, cocking his head at me. "Everyone else will be in them."

Miles wants to be a couple. "Okay. But only because everyone else is." A smile pulls at my lips before I can stop it.

"Sure." He nods, fighting back his own smile. Suddenly, I'm fifteen—on an afterschool date with my crush. The tingles are real.

Our server returns with our food, and we busy ourselves with tasting and sharing bites with each other.

"What are you going to do with the rest of your day?" Miles asks.

"Peel some wallpaper border off the spare bedroom wall. Really riveting stuff." I laugh. "What about you?"

"Well, my meetings are done for the day. I have no showings. I could...peel some wallpaper, too?" His suggestion causes all my loneliness and my desire for him to weld together into a deep, devouring yearning.

I can't hide my happiness. Joy bubbles up, and I laugh out loud. "Yes. You certainly could."

Chapter Twenty-Two

Monday after lunch, I peeled wallpaper with her all afternoon. I left at the end of the day to go surfing, and even though I asked her if she wanted to come, she declined. It killed me to say good night. Still does, every time. But I have to keep forcing myself to slow things down. It won't end well for me if we go full steam ahead only to crash and burn. I want it to work. I don't want her to leave.

The days begin blur after that. A week passes, and I see Jenna as much as possible, but never as much as I want to. She still maintains that she *is* leaving when the house is ready to sell. Sometimes it's just a passing comment, tossed into conversation like it means nothing. But when she says it, everything in me feels paralyzed. My chest hurts, my throat tightens, my stomach winds itself in knots. And when I ask where she thinks she'll go next, she doesn't have an answer for me. I think that's the only thing that gives me hope—maybe I can convince her she belongs here—with me. For now, I focus on the present. The house repairs are underway and Jenna and I are growing closer. I'm planning to tell her how I feel—to let her know I want her to stay. I just have to be careful. I'm learning that Jenna doesn't respond well to pressure, so I'm doing my best not to give her any.

☙

It's the following Tuesday, and we have texted a few times

throughout the day, but I forced myself not to ask her what she's doing tonight. Instead, I decide to forgo my usual evening surf and drive up the parkway to the nearest big-box electronics store. I'm shutting down my computer when I tell Nate this.

"You're doing what?" Nate asks incredulously as I stand grabbing my keys and my jacket off the coat rack by the door.

"I'm going to Best Buy and getting Jenna a TV and a Roku," I repeat, ignoring the insinuation in my brother's voice.

He lets out a low whistle. "First a coffee pot and now a TV. Man, who are you?" He leans back in his desk chair, feigning amusement, but I'd like to think my baby brother is happy for me. It's been a long time since I've wanted to do something nice for a girl.

"Why don't you and Caden come with me? We'll grab dinner," I suggest, knowing Nate could probably use a break from his usual routine.

"Yeah, all right," he agrees.

Two hours later, my four-year-old nephew is running around the electronics store like he took a stimulant while Nate and I mull over our TV options.

"Yo, Caden, settle down," Nate scolds, making an attempt to grab the little tornado's arm. "Well, if you go too big or too expensive, you're going to freak her out," Nate reminds me. Caden buzzes around us again, and this time Nate is successful at gripping him around his torso and tossing him over his shoulder. He dissolves into a fit of giggles.

"I know. I figured a moderate size... If she gets mad, I could tell her it's for selfish reasons. I want to watch TV at her house." I purse my lips, weighing my options.

"You can get a thirty-two-inch TV for less than a hundred bucks now," Nate points out. "That's probably less than taking her to dinner. And probably the least likely to freak her out." Caden squirms in his arms. "You got to decide quick though—this kid isn't going to last much longer. Probably should have skipped the chocolate ice cream." Nate hangs Caden upside down and swings him around, eliciting another loud giggle.

"Okay, let's go thirty-two-inch," I say definitively.

An hour later, I drop Nate and a sleeping Caden off at their house and drive straight to Jenna's. I pull up to the curb and there is only one light on in the upstairs bedroom. My plan is to drop the TV on the porch and then text her, telling her to get the surprise I left for her. It's the perfect plan, but as soon as I'm walking up the front steps, the front door swings open.

"Miles?" Jenna furrows her brow, clearly surprised to see me. "What are you doing here? What's that?"

"I, uh...bought you a new TV." I lift it higher so she can see what is already obvious.

"Huh." Jenna clicks her tongue. "And just why did you do that?" She puts her hands on her hips. "I thought I told you I don't need a TV right now."

I scoff. "Please. This is for me. I need to be able to watch TV when I'm over here," I say matter-of-factly.

"Is that so?" Jenna huffs, an almost hopeful glint in her eyes. "Well, I guess that's fine then." She bites back a smile.

I sigh with relief. If she got mad at me, I'd have to drive all the way back to the store. Then I would have had to figure out how to make her un-mad at me. I move to put the box down on the porch when Jenna says, "Are you going to just leave it here for me to deal with or are you at least going to set it up?" She pulls the door open further and walks inside.

I chuckle. "You drive a hard bargain, lady," I call after her, catching the door with my hip.

The TV from the nineties only needs to be unplugged, but it is insanely dusty and surprisingly heavy. I almost call one of my buddies over to help me move it, but Jenna and I manage to do it together—solidifying her sexiness in my mind—and get it out to the curb. I love a strong woman.

"I can't believe we watched TV on that thing," Jenna mutters, dusting her hands off, as we walk inside.

I laugh, kneeling to unbox the new flat screen. "I know.

Prepare for your mind to be blown."

In ten minutes, I have everything hooked up. Jenna plops on the old tweed sofa with the remote. I'm standing awkwardly, preparing to leave, when she looks up at me, a coy smile on her lips. "Don't you want to stay and watch a movie?"

Do I ever. I grin. "I wish I could...but I have early meetings. I should probably get home." I already regret declining her invitation, but I know I'm in too deep. If I stay with her tonight, I'm never going to leave again. I'm already becoming too attached to her, and if she still plans to leave—and she hasn't said otherwise—I'm the one who will be hurt here. I really need to tell her how I feel.

Jenna juts out her lower lip. "Boo," she whines.

"Don't you have work tomorrow anyway?" I ask.

"I do," she sighs. "Okay, fine. Another night." She stands up to walk me to the door and when we're there, she catches my wrist. "Thank you, Miles," she says, reaching up to peck me on the lips. "For everything."

My smile widens unconsciously. She's not mad at me. I actually made her happy. Maybe she does want a white knight. I know Jenna could go buy herself a TV. But she hasn't yet, so I wanted to do it for her. I want to show her that I'm thinking of her and even if she doesn't need my help, I want to give it. I want to take care of her. "Don't mention it." I tip her chin up and kiss her goodnight again. "I'll be by tomorrow after work with some couple's costume ideas," I say, a slow smile sweeping across my face.

"Oh, *really?*" she teases, "I'll look forward to it."

"Bye," I say, pulling the door closed behind me.

I am out of my depth and it's scarier than the wave that took me out the other day. I know I've been out of the game for a while but...I think I'm falling for Jenna.

Chapter Twenty-Three

"Well, I didn't have Miles Corbin buying a girl a TV on my Bingo card for this year, but what the hell do I know?" Joy quips.

Leo barges out of the supply room. "Hold up. Miles bought you a TV?" He raises his eyebrows and shakes his head in disbelief. "Dude's whipped."

I frown. "Stop it. No, he's not." I fold my arms across my chest. "I'm still leaving anyway," I say, more to convince myself than my well-meaning but disbelieving coworkers. "This thing," I wave my hands around for lack of description, "is nothing more than a little fling."

Joy gives me a pointed look. "Like I have been saying, that's all Miles is known for. So as long as you know that and you're okay with it, then great. Might as well enjoy yourself while you're here."

Leo frowns at his sister, then turns back to me while holding up his hands. "Look—Miles has a reputation. I'm not going to pretend he doesn't. But buying a TV for a girl he's casually seeing? That's...not typical Miles."

"It's just a little fun—I'm still planning on leaving," I say, more to convince myself than them. "I can keep my head in the game." I walk behind the counter and get my travel mug, filled with coffee that I made at *home* in the pot Miles bought for me. I take a long swig of it, willing myself not to swoon over the fact that someone thought enough of me to buy me a coffee pot. *For no other reason than because I didn't have one already.* There I go again. Protecting my heart is going to be harder than I thought.

"Okay. Good. Then do that." Joy holds up her hands, but there is a disapproving tone to her voice that I don't love.

"He did ask me to go to a Halloween party at Liam and Sophie's house," I say, biting back a smile. "He's bringing over some couples costume suggestions this afternoon," I add, just to see their reaction. Their eyes go wide.

"Couples costumes?" Joy's eyes widen in surprise.

"See. Dude's whipped," Leo says, with an I-told-you-so shake of his head.

"Maybe." I look between them. "But that doesn't change anything, I'm still leaving."

"Here we go again," Joy mutters under her breath.

"And what the hell, why am I not invited to this party?" Leo plants his hands on his hips, feigning offense.

"Don't ask me. It's not my party. I'm going to restock," I say, desperate to leave this conversation.

When I am with Miles, nothing else matters. But when I talk about him with Joy, she dampens my, well, joy. It seems like she disapproves of my new relationship, and she's one of my only friends here. I think it's time I call Morgan. She's the only person left who can talk me off this ledge.

☙

Because Morgan's life is far busier than mine, I have to schedule time to talk. I curl up on the tweed couch, pull an old afghan over me, and watch the Roku screensaver when my phone buzzes in my hand.

"There she is," I say, as gleefully as I can muster when I answer the FaceTime call.

"Hi, baby girl." Morgan sounds out of breath but looks happy.

"Why are you breathing so hard?" I ask, scowling.

"Because I am running away from my husband and babies so I can take this call in peace." Morgan cackles. "I'm going to sit in my car with the butt warmer on and soak in every last minute of alone time."

"That sounds nice," I say, wryly. "Says the girl who has far too much alone time,"

"You don't sound good, Jenna Banenna. What's going on? Are those bangs?" Morgan's expression clouds, and concern flickers across her features as she uses my childhood nickname.

Immediately my eyes well with tears. Maybe it's talking to someone who really *knows* me for the first time in a long time, or maybe it's because I've held it all in for nearly a month since probating my mom's will, but the tears fall fast and furious. Morgan's face crumbles as I give in to the wave of sadness overtaking my voice. I let myself cry until my breathing stabilizes and I'm able to swallow the enormous lump in my throat. Morgan waits patiently, without asking questions; the way only best friends know how. I haven't seen Morgan since the funeral, and with how busy she is, I didn't want to bother her in the new parent fog. I haven't even told her what's been going on. When I calm down enough to suck in a breath, I speak.

"It's just been a lot. And yes, I got bangs—huge mistake by the way," I say, my voice catching. "There's so much I didn't know. But the gist of it? My mom never sold our house in Cape May after my dad died. It's been here, closed up since 1997." I sniffle and wipe away another stream of fresh tears. "I only found out when they probated the will. And since I lost my job, I thought, great—now I can sell it and be okay for a while," I mumble feeling hopelessly, desperately sorry for myself

Sympathy flashes behind Morgan's eyes before her jaw falls open in shock. "Wait! You lost your job? Where have I been? When did this happen? Jenna, I'm so sorry. The bangs aren't that bad." She leans closer to the camera, examining me, but her eyes are brimming with unshed tears.

I sigh. "The week after the funeral. They couldn't afford me anymore." I sniffle. "I didn't call because you're in newborn bliss with those sweet babies and you were moving. I didn't want to bother you. But it all feels too heavy now. I need my best friend." I look away from my phone, Morgan's creased brow—caught somewhere between worry and helplessness—is too much for me and I feel the sting of fresh tears all over again.

"Hey," Morgan says firmly, pointing into her phone. "First of all, you are *never* bothering me, Jenna. You hear me? You're my oldest friend. And it's more like a newborn haze, ninety percent of the time." She cracks a smile that relaxes me immediately

I suck in a shaky breath. "I know. But I spent the last few years just...existing for my mom. Doctor's visits, chemo appointments, round-the-clock care. Which was fine, I wanted to. But everything in my life just sort of stopped. I stopped doing anything for me." My voice cracks as the weight of admitting this crashes into me. "Now she's gone, and I have all this free time, and I have *no idea* what to do with it. I forgot how to be me."

Morgan nods, leaning her head on the car window. "Okay, so go back. You lost your job. You drove down to the house. I assume that's where you are now?"

"Yes. But the house wasn't kept up. Everything was covered with drop cloths. There are termites and it needs foundation work. It's not in great shape to sell. So I'm just kind of hanging here, working at a hardware store, until I can list it." I twirl the ends of my hair around my fingers, a nervous habit from childhood.

"Well, that doesn't sound so bad," Morgan soothes. "Living by the beach in the fall. Have you made any friends?"

"I ran into my aunt and cousin, Jake. I hadn't seen my cousin in almost ten years, my aunt in far longer than that. Apparently, we're going to have dinner soon. I have a million questions, but..." I trail off, my chest tightening. "It's probably going to stir up a lot—memories of my dad, losing my mom. It feels like a lot." I flop back on the pillow, suddenly drained.

"I remember Jake from college. Maybe they will have some answers for you," Morgan suggests. "And maybe while you're in a new place, you should start putting yourself out there again. You said yourself, it's been so long since you've done anything for yourself. You took care of your mom for a really long time," Morgan points out, and she's right.

"That's the other thing," I say slowly. "I met a guy." I fight back the smile on my lips, despite my sadness. Even though I am so excited about what's happening with Miles, Joy's reservations steal some of that from me.

"Yay!" Morgan squeals. "Tell me about him."

So, I do. I fill her in on how we met, how he fixed my tire and then paid for another one. I tell her how he taught me to surf, bought me a coffee pot, and a TV, and gave me the best orgasm of my life. Then I tell her he's divorced, and how Joy keeps warning me that he is incapable of being serious with a woman, despite everything that has happened between us. "I'm scared," I admit, feeling the fresh sting of tears again.

"Oh, Jenna. It's normal to be scared. But the things he's done for you? If I've learned anything, it's that guys don't do anything they don't *have* to do, unless they really want to. It sounds like Miles really cares for you." Morgan's words comfort me. "I wish I could reach through the phone and hug you right now."

I laugh, sniffling and wiping the tears that won't stop. "Me too. What if it doesn't work out? What if I end up alone?" I shudder. "I already feel so alone. I'm afraid to give in to the possibility of someone actually wanting me."

"Stop it. You will never be alone. You will always have me, and you can come and stay here any time. As long as you can hold a baby and don't mind spit up," she teases.

I miss her so much it aches. "I will come visit soon." Before I can say more, I'm interrupted by a knock on my door.

"Jenna? Are you home?" A voice calls from the other side.

I hop off the couch, carrying my FaceTime call with me. "I think he's at my front door," I hiss at Morgan.

"Ooh! Let me see him," she squeals, looking giddy behind the screen.

"Absolutely not. Go snuggle your babies and I'll text you later," I whisper.

"Who are you talking to?" Miles's amused voice comes from behind the front door.

"Bye!" Morgan whispers back, and then she's gone.

I swing open the front door, and there's Miles—sexy as ever in jeans and a hoodie, his sleeves pushed up. His hazel eyes glimmer with mischief. He's holding several hangers of clothing and grinning like a schoolboy, but his face falls when he sees mine.

"Jenna, what's wrong?" he asks, concern enveloping his features. "Are you crying?"

I shake my head, sniffling. "No. I was, but I'm okay now." I hold open the door wider so he can come in. "What do you have there?" I ask, hoping he'll drop the subject. Of course, he doesn't.

"Well, why *were* you crying? Let's talk about it." He reaches for me, pulling me into a tight hug, despite everything he's holding. The musty clothes separate us, but I melt into his arms. He smells like saltwater and beach air. He smells like home.

I pull back and gaze up at him. "I don't really want to talk about it anymore. I called my best friend and told her everything that's been happening." I sigh. "It's just been a lot to handle alone."

"You're not alone. You have me," Miles says firmly.

"Miles..." I want to tell him that I can't be sure I *have* him. I can't count on someone I've only known for a few weeks. How could I? But his face is so earnest, I hold back. I shake my head to clear the thought. "Show me these costume ideas."

Miles drapes everything over the couch, taking a few minutes to reorganize the items. He rubs his hands together excitedly. "Okay. First up is this." He holds up a large taco costume and a yellow dress that looks like it might fit me.

I push my lips together, my brow furrowing as I piece it together. "Taco Belle?" I ask, laughing.

"Bingo," Miles says, pointing at me. Next, he holds up a plush red robe, a crown, and a panda bear winter hat.

I stare at him, waiting for him to explain. "What is this?" I ask, unable to hold back my laughter. Just ten minutes ago I was crying, feeling sad and alone, and now Miles is here making me laugh.

"It's Burger King and Panda Express!" he says, holding out his hands proudly. "Fast food, get it?"

"Were you hungry when you were brainstorming?" I ask, giggling. I shake my head. "These are silly."

"Okay, okay, I thought you might say that. My last suggestion is that we both wear all black, and go as Sandy and Danny from Grease. You already have wavy hair!" He lifts his eyebrows and grins, holding up his hands. "What do you think?"

"Done. That sounds like a winner," I say, stopping to take him in. He really put effort into this. I don't know why I'm surprised, but I am. "Do you want to stay and hang out?" I ask, not bothering to hide my hope.

Miles steps closer to me, backing me against the couch. "I wish I could," he murmurs against my lips. "I have to go help my mom put up her twelve-foot skeleton." He kisses me softly, and I melt into it, as if he didn't just say the silliest thing I've heard all day.

When we pull apart, I ask, "What about your dad?" I try not to sound whiny, but I really would love his company tonight. We haven't had any solid alone time since the other day after the beach, and I'm craving more.

"He's a town councilman, and they have a meeting tonight," Miles says, tugging my hips into his. I can feel how much he doesn't want to leave, and I ache for him. He kisses me again, then down my jaw to my ear. "I don't want to go," he groans, letting his warm breath linger. "But I promised my mom I'd help her. My dad hates Halloween."

"Okay, okay." I pat his chest and push him away before I get too hot and bothered. "Go do your thing."

"I will see you soon," Miles promises, giving me one last peck before he gathers up his sample items and heads for the door.

"Miles?" I call after him.

He turns and gives me one of his grins that turns me into putty.

"Thanks," I say. "I feel better."

"I'm glad," he rasps. He blows me a kiss and then he's gone.

Miles and Morgan were enough to quell my tears tonight, but times like this, I really wish I could call my mom.

Chapter Twenty-Four

Miles

I reluctantly leave Jenna's house for my parents', but the whole way there, I can't stop thinking about her. I don't exactly know how I got here, to the place where I can't stop thinking about a girl I just met. I have never been the guy who wants a damn couples costume. I have the overwhelming urge to be near her, to tell my mom I can't come over and drive straight back to Jenna. I wish I could spend the whole night holding her, so she doesn't feel alone. *Why was she crying?* It's gnawing at me that she wouldn't even talk through it with me. I thought we were growing closer these last few days, but I'm worried that it's only me who is invested in this. She's dealing with a lot. Maybe I am just a distraction.

Being with Jenna has made me realize that I take having two healthy parents for granted. I live in the same town as they do, and I can see them any time I want. They were there for me when Erin broke my heart. They invite me over for dinner every night of the week. Literally. It's as if my mom thinks I won't feed myself a proper meal at forty-one. The point is, I have them. I can't imagine what my life would be like without them and my heart breaks for Jenna. She seems so alone, and I don't want her to be. Maybe that's why she was crying.

Halloween is coming up, then it's the holiday season, and I can't help but think, *where will Jenna be?* I want to convince her to stay. I'll be her family. *Whoa, that is an alarming thought.* Yet I can't shake the feeling that there is more to this—that she's somehow a part of me. I'm dying to know if she feels the same way.

I married Erin in my mid-thirties, mostly because if I hadn't, she would have left me. And I loved her, I really did. I fought damn hard for that marriage, until I couldn't anymore because *nothing* was ever enough. With Jenna, I get the impression that *everything* is enough, because no man has ever taken care of her. Maybe it's all in my head, I don't know. But Jenna lets me be who I am. She probably doesn't love that I surf at night just to feel invincible. Or that I'm divorced. I'm sure there are a lot of things *not* to like about me, but if Jenna thinks about them, she never says a word. She accepts me for the man that I am.

When I pull up to my parents' house, my mom is dragging a humongous, heavy box with the skeleton across the front lawn. "Ma!" I shout from the car. "I told you to wait for me."

"I got tired of waiting," she huffs, pushing the box a bit further. "I thought you weren't coming."

I roll my eyes. "I told you, I had to see someone first," I mutter, crouching down to open the box.

"A lady friend?" My mother wiggles her eyebrows. She loves her two sons and her grandson, but I know she wants us to find partners and give her more grandkids before she's too old to enjoy them.

"Maybe. Don't worry about it," I tease, knowing that all she'll do is worry about it until I fill her in.

I get the box open and pull out all the pieces of "Bone Daddy" as my mother affectionately calls him. This is the second year that she's had him, and I swear it's just to drive my Halloween-hating dad crazy. I set the base down. "Is this where you want him?"

"That looks great," my mom says. "Though, I'd really love it if he went right in your father's parking spot." She snickers.

"Well, he can't, you antagonist." I roll my eyes. "He has to be staked into the ground. Pass me his leg poles," I say, and she hands them over. I get to work snapping them in.

"So, you're not going to tell me anything about this girl?" my mother presses further.

I sigh and look at her. "Hip bones." I gesture toward the box. "What do you want to know?"

"Okay, for starters, how did you meet her?" My mom hands me the giant hip bones and crouches back down to pull out the skeleton's ribcage.

"She's a client," I say cautiously, worried she'll tell me to leave it alone.

My mom gives me a knowing look. "Oh, Nate said you were into a client who is just passing through," she says. I get the sense she's holding back.

"That little narc," I scoff.

She laughs. "If she's just passing through, why bother? When are you going to get serious about someone again? I hate seeing you alone." My mother's tone turns patronizing. "Don't you want what Dad and I have?"

I groan, exasperated. "Of course, Mom. But it's not that easy. Divorced at forty-one isn't exactly a selling point."

My mother rolls her eyes. "It could be worse. You could be Ross from *Friends*. 'Three divorces, three divorces.'" She laughs at her own joke, and I crack a smile to humor her.

I grab the ribcage, connecting the wire that makes Bone Daddy's eyes glow. I don't answer her.

My mom's voice softens. "You're a catch. The right girl will see that."

"I am hoping *she* sees it enough to stay here," I mumble, forcing the ribcage into the hip bone until it snaps into place.

"That's what I'm worried about, Miles," my mom says with genuine concern.

I puff out a defeated sigh. "Okay, Mom. I don't really want to talk about this with you anymore. I'm sorry."

"Fine, fine," my mother relents, and we go back to assembling in silence.

We work quietly for a few more minutes, the only sounds the rustling leaves in the fall breeze and an occasional car passing by. At last, I snap the large skull into place and push him up to a standing position. "I have to stake him in, do you have them?"

She hands me the stakes, and once he's secure, we stand back to admire our handiwork. Bone Daddy's blue eyes glow in the dusk.

"Your dad is going to hate this!" My mother shrieks with glee.

"You're insane." I shake my head, laughing. But I have to admit, whatever my parents are doing, it's working. They know the secret to a happy marriage, even if it is lovingly tormenting the other on occasion.

"I know." She grins, and the crinkled lines around her eyes remind me that she's not going to be around forever. "Thank you for helping me. Let's get you some dinner, huh?" My mom links her arm through mine.

I need to cherish these moments, even when she relentlessly probes into my life. I grab Bone Daddy's box and carry it to the porch. "What did you make?" I ask, holding the front door open for her.

"Beef stew, with your favorite biscuits." She winks.

"You're too good to me," I follow her into the kitchen and sit at the same table my parents have had since I was a kid. They are creatures of habit, and if something isn't broken, they're not fixing it just *for the sake* of buying something new. Nate and I constantly tease them about this old, nicked table, but my mom waves us off, saying, *why would I get a new one when this one is perfectly fine?*

My mother busies herself filling a bowl, heating it up, and buttering a biscuit. It's taken me all night to ask the question that's been gnawing at me for days. I clear my throat.

"Ma, do you remember anything about the guy who rescued me?"

I don't know why I suddenly need to know. I never have before, but now, it seems to be life-altering information that I am not privy to. Her back is to me but her shoulders stiffen.

The day I nearly drowned was a bad day in our house. Aside from the obvious, I had gotten an English paper back—and it wasn't good. I was fifteen and only interested in baseball, parties, and girls. My parents and I got into a screaming match over my plummeting grades, and they grounded me. I stormed out, grabbed my shortboard, and hopped on my bike. Leo was on the beach when I got there. He looked as though he was done for the day, but he stayed when he saw me.

"What's up, bro? You look pissed," Leo greeted me.

"I am," I snarled. "My dad sucks. Gonna surf it out."

"It's rough out there," Leo warned, gesturing to the manic ocean.

"You leaving?" I asked. "Ride with me."

"Well, I was, but...okay, yeah. You shouldn't surf alone." Leo's warning did nothing to deter me. The weather channel had been calling for storms all week. They hadn't arrived yet, but the ocean was raging, just like me. There was no one else on the beach at four thirty in the afternoon in late October, except a family with one child. I paddled out, Leo trailing behind. I got a few good runs in, and I felt invincible against the vast, angry waves. My rage was already dissipating, but the waves were big—easily ten feet overhead—and crashed with relentless force. To get past them required every ounce of strength and focus I had in me, but I was up for the challenge.

"You done?" Leo asked after the last good run.

I glanced at the shoreline, where the family was packing up their things. It couldn't be past five thirty. "Couple more," I said, not waiting for Leo to follow.

"If you're cool, I'm going to just watch. I'm beat," he called from the shoreline.

"Whatever," I called back, paddling out.

The ride started like any other. I was strong and had control of the board as my arms sliced through the icy water. I popped up on my board with practiced ease, catching the tip of the wave. I waited for the dopamine hit—that rush of fleeting freedom made even more intangible by my recent grounding. But this time, it didn't come.

My foot slipped and I faltered. My board dug into the wave,

throwing me sideways, the crash of the water swallowed me whole. I flailed as the force of the water sucked me under, the roar of the ocean drowning everything out. Disoriented, I fought to reach the surface, but each relentless wave dragged me deeper and further out. Every time I surfaced, I waved at Leo, hoping he realized I was in trouble. It felt like an eternity before I heard him screaming for help. I will always remember the burn in my throat from swallowing copious amounts of ocean water. The world was a blur of darkness, my strength was waning, and I was about to give up the fight when a strong arm grabbed me and pulled me onto a longboard. I sprawled on the front, and he paddled us back in. Beach patrol and EMTs waited on the shore, and I was immediately put on a stretcher, in pretty rough shape. I never saw the man again.

"Mom," I say when she doesn't reply. "Did you hear me?"

She sighs, turning around and walking over with my bowl of stew. "You know I hate talking about that day, Miles." Her eyes glisten, and I instantly worry that she might cry.

"I know," I croak.

"We nearly lost you. And to think you still ride that damn surfboard." She swats my arm.

"But you didn't lose me, Mom. I'm right here," I urge her. "I just need to know. It feels important. I need to know if you know who he is. What is his name?" I'm almost afraid to hear her answer.

My mom stares at me for a moment too long before she speaks. "Oh, Miles." Her gaze is watery as she takes a deep breath. "He died that day." Then her tears spill over.

I feel like I got the wind knocked out of me. A knot forms in my throat, and I swallow hard. "What?" I whisper. "He died? Rescuing me?" I blink at her—words aren't registering properly.

My mother nods, turning away from me.

Tightness claws at my chest and I press my fist against it. *My savior died rescuing me.*

My fork clatters against my plate as I shove it away. I angrily run my hands through my hair, gripping the back of my neck to hold myself together. I look up, my eyes burning. "Why didn't you tell me this?"

She winces. "I... Miles, we didn't want to upset you. You had been through so much." She wipes her eyes with the back of her hand. "He collapsed on the beach right after pulling you in. Heart attack from exertion they told us."

"Well, who was it?" I demand. My anger is misdirected but I am so mad I can't see straight. "I want a name."

"I don't remember his name, Miles, I wasn't the one who spoke to the authorities. He was gone by the time they brought you to us. I think your father spoke to someone but even then, it wasn't clear." She keeps her voice calm. I don't know why she'd lie but I'm still not sure I believe her.

I inhale a deep breath and nod. My mother pulls out the chair next to me and sits. She covers my balled up fist with her hand, her face softer now.

"After it happened, we contacted the police to ask the man's wife if she would see us. If we could properly thank her. Your father sent flowers on our behalf to a house in town, but I just don't know, Miles. I wish I did. We sent a card with a phone number, in case she wanted to call us. She did." She pauses and sighs. "She asked us to stop reaching out. It was too painful for her and her young daughter." My mother's voice remains steady. "I never did get to meet them."

Daughter. The word echoes in my mind. *The family on the beach.*

I swallow a hard lump in my throat. "How old was the daughter?" The back of my eyes sting.

"I'm not sure. Younger than you for sure." My mom exhales. "Is that all you want to ask?" Her pained expression lets me know that it's time I drop this.

I drag my hands down my face as if I can wipe the raw emotions away. "Yeah. That's all," I grumble, picking my fork back up and taking a bite of stew but it sours my stomach immediately.

I force myself to swallow before pushing the plate away once again.

The front door shuts loudly and I startle. “What the hell is in the front yard?”

Dad’s home.

Chapter Twenty-Five

Jenna

"What if they don't like me?" I wince as I ask myself in the mirror. I've worked hard throughout my life to not worry about what people think of me. As my mother used to say, I'm champagne. I don't need to be everyone's cup of tea. But every once in a while, self-doubt creeps its way back in and I worry I'm not enough—that people won't see the good in me or like me the way I am.

All week after Miles and I decided on our costumes, I stressed over whether people would think it was my cliché idea. Would they think I'm trying too hard? Would they compare me to Miles's ex-wife? Would Miles get to the party and run off with his friends, leaving me to fend for myself? My anxiety is at an all-time high, and suddenly, I don't want to go anymore. Curling up on the scratchy sofa that my mother loved in 1997 and watching my new TV sounds like a much better way to spend a crisp fall night. But I'm sure it's just the nerves talking so I swallow them. Everything will turn out fine, I'm sure of it.

Getting ready was actually kind of fun. I put on my nicest black leggings, a pair of heels, and a black workout top that could pass for Sandy's crop top. I curled my hair and my eyelashes and painted my lips with bright red lipstick. I should feel hot—hell, I can even admit that I look hot—but I'm still feeling a little insecure.

The doorbell rings and a dog barks. Miles. And Pete. Miles suggested bringing Pete over while we went to the party. Then, he could stay over, and we could get an early start on some projects tomorrow. The thought of waking up next to Miles again—now that so much has changed—makes me nervous. I know he'd never force me to do something I don't want to do; that's not the problem. The problem is, I want to do *all the things* with Miles. In the bedroom and out. It's really messing with my plans to leave this place.

I suck in a breath and swing open the door. Miles stands there, looking like he stepped right out of 1956—tight black jeans, black Converse, and a fitted black T-shirt that shows off every inch of his trim physique. His curls are unlike I've ever seen them, slicked back in full Danny Zuko style. He looks hot. Pete barks in excitement and jumps on me, but Miles is paralyzed, looking at me in the same way I'm taking him in.

"Wow," he breathes. "Jenna. You look amazing."

I grin, tension melting away. "So do you."

"Really. You nailed it," he says, snapping out of his trance and walking inside. He tugs me close and kisses my red lips.

"You're going to be wearing my lipstick," I say against his mouth.

"Good. Then everyone will know you're mine," he mutters.

My heart flutters. He could have said *everyone will know you're with me*. Instead, he said *you're mine*. I scold myself for feeling hopeful that I could be his. We get Pete settled with his dog bed and food bowls and then we're ready to go.

"Why don't we Uber?" Miles suggests. The party is closer to downtown than my house is, and it would probably be better not to drive, so I agree. Fifteen minutes later, we're turning onto Perry Street. Miles points out a house with a twelve-foot skeleton in the yard. "That's where I grew up."

I giggle. "Do your parents still live there?"

"Sure do. Bone Daddy was what I was helping my mom with the other night." He gestures to the large, creepy skeleton.

I bark out a laugh. "Bone Daddy?"

Miles holds up his hands. "Hey, I didn't name him. My mom did."

"That makes it even funnier." I giggle.

We pass Ellie's house, and less than a minute later, we reach Liam and Sophie's. The house is decked out in Halloween decor—orange and purple lights, creepy lawn ornaments, and music blaring. Miles thanks the driver and we slide out. "Buddy Holly" by Weezer is blasting, and Liam and Sophie are on the porch greeting their guests. Liam is dressed as Buddy Holly and Sophie is dressed as Mary Tyler Moore. If the song wasn't playing, I may not have gotten it, but I'll admit, I'm impressed.

"Hey guys!" Sophie greets us cheerfully. "Danny & Sandy! How cute!" Her enthusiasm is contagious as she reaches out to hug me.

"Who are you guys supposed to be?" Miles asks, tilting his head, examining them.

"Duh, they're Buddy Holly and Mary Tyler Moore. From the Weezer song that's playing literally right now." I swat Miles's arm with a grin.

"Ohh, I get it," Miles says, walking past them to go inside. "Totally don't get it," he mutters in my ear, and laughter escapes me.

"Drinks are in the fridge," Liam calls after him.

It doesn't take long before the party is in full swing. Sophie, the gem that she is, takes me under her wing, bringing me around and introducing me to the locals as Miles's girl. I'm relieved to see another familiar face, Melanie, as all the ladies gather in a group. I eye Miles across the room. He's standing in the kitchen, leaning against the counter, talking to Danny and some of the other guys. Our eyes lock, and he mouths, "Are you okay?" My heart swells. I actually *am* okay. I can see why Miles loves these people so much.

"So, can we assume that's what you are?" Stephanie, one of the women standing nearby asks. She's dressed as the jelly half of a peanut butter and jelly sandwich.

I get distracted, watching Miles. I shake my head, coming back to the present. "Sorry. What did you ask me?" I grimace in embarrassment.

"Ohh, see? She's so distracted by him," Kristen, Danny's wife, swoons. She's dressed as the loofah to his soap.

"Miles's girlfriend. Is that what you are?" Stephanie repeats herself.

"Oh... Uh..." I'm caught off guard. "I don't really know." I shrug.

"Leave her alone, Steph," Sophie interrupts. "It's new, right, Jenna?"

"*So* new," I agree, nodding my head.

"All I know is, I totally expected Miles to show up alone, dressed as a Ninja Turtle or something. I did not picture him showing up with a total hottie on his arm—one he can't stop staring at." Kristen gestures toward Miles, and we all look just in time to catch him watching us.

His cheeks turn a shade of pink, and he quickly looks away, caught in the act.

"Oh my God! See?" Stephanie squeals, clapping her hands. "He's obsessed with you!"

Melanie rolls her eyes. "What Steph means is, it's been a really long time since we've seen Miles look so happy."

Happy. Miles is happy with me. And his friends notice. Something in my chest shifts.

"Yeah. Sophie, you didn't know his ex-wife, Erin, but she really did a number on the poor guy," Kristen weighs in.

"That's all water under the bridge now," Sophie says, linking her arm through mine. Then I remember—Sophie knows what it's like to be the new girl in town. She's trying to make me feel comfortable.

I take a sip of the punch that's getting warm in my hand and search the room for Miles. A moment later, he's at my side. "How are you doing?" he whispers in my ear, sending a shiver through me. Kristen and Stephanie watch us with great interest. I put my drink on the table next to me and whirl around, putting my arms around his neck and tugging him downward.

"I'm okay," I whisper. "But I missed you."

He pulls me closer and kisses me softly. "You did, huh?"

I nod, resting my head on his chest.

Miles leans down and murmurs in my ear. "How about we Irish goodbye?"

A chill crawls up my neck. Even though it's been less than an hour, Miles is suggesting we leave without saying goodbye to anyone. The party is fun, but I've never liked an idea more. I look up at him, his eyes are fiery, hungry even.

"Let's go," I say quietly, glancing behind me at the ladies who have gone back to their own conversations.

"We made an appearance," Miles says, as if he's reassuring himself—like he can't believe he's part of a couple sneaking out of a party early.

Then we're out on the street, walking in the crisp fall air toward the mall. There is a slight breeze, but otherwise, the night is comfortable. Miles laces his fingers through mine, and I lean into his arm. I haven't let myself relax with a guy like this in what feels like years. It probably has been years. We walk in comfortable silence, but suddenly, I have the overwhelming urge to tell Miles more about myself. For the first time, I want to let my guard down and open up to him. I can't let the feeling pass by.

I clear my throat. "My last boyfriend cheated. I should have known he would—his reputation preceded him—but for some reason, I thought I would be different. I discovered it right after my mom's diagnosis and I ended things. But it's been really hard to date since. Mostly because I was taking care of her, but I guess I also kept my guard up." I glance up, searching Miles's expression, but his face is unreadable.

Miles looks down at me, his expression pained, waiting for me to continue.

"You make me want to let my guard down, Miles." I stop, tugging his hand until he's standing in front of me.

Miles cups my face, his eyes filled with longing. Then his lips twitch into a smile. "Good." He kisses me softly, but it's not urgent. It's as if we're the only two people on the street right now.

I let myself get lost in it. When Miles pulls away, his expression is tender. "Jenna, anyone who would cheat on you would never be deserving of you."

His sensitivity catches me off guard. I wrap my arms around his torso, allowing our bodies to meld together. A breeze blows through, and I shiver.

"Let's get you home," he murmurs into my hair.

Miles pulls up the Uber app as we walk. I take in the scenery of Cape May, the old buildings and mature trees, the quaintness of the town, the smell of the salt air. *Maybe I could stay here.*

I tilt my head back, the night sky stretches endlessly above me, scattered with more stars than I can count. It's like the universe is trying to tell me something. *You belong here.* "Look at all those stars," I whisper.

"Aren't they amazing?" Miles asks, stopping so he can take in the view with me. "That right there is why I surf at night." He points to the sky.

At that moment, a streak of light, sharp and sudden, cuts across the sky—a shooting star. "Did you see that?" I gasp. "I've never seen one before."

"I hope you made a wish." Miles nudges me.

"I don't need to." I meet his warm gaze and bite my lip. This is one of those moments where I feel like I'm exactly where I'm meant to be.

We start walking again and Miles says, "It was supposed to storm tonight...but it sure doesn't look like it's going to."

I glance over at him, longing bursting in my chest. "Nope. It's nothing but a sky full of stars."

☙

The Uber waits on the corner, and Miles opens the door for me. I slide in and he follows. He holds open his arm for me to curl into, and I do. The drive across town feels too slow as Miles slips his arm around my shoulder, tugging me close and letting his fingers skim my thigh, turning my insides to lava. His breath warms my neck as he nuzzles into me, tracing his hands up and down my leg. I want to return the favor and suddenly, we're in the back of an Uber desperately feeling each other up. I slide my hands up his inner thigh and over his zipper where his erection is bulging. We can't get back to my place fast enough.

As soon as we're out of the car, we're kissing on the sidewalk. Miles tangles his hands in my hair, soft moans escaping our throats between feverish kisses. "Jenna," Miles says breathlessly into my mouth.

"I know," I whimper. This isn't like the first time—there's less urgency, more heat. The way our bodies press against each other, his breath warm against my mouth, like he can't get close enough. Need laced with something deeper—something intimate. Something more like trust.

I pull away and make for the front steps, unlocking the door. I grasp his hand and lead him up the stairs to my childhood bedroom, which thankfully has a queen-size bed. We stand in front of the bed, eyes locked, waiting for the other to make the first move. Despite all my past reservations, I let it be me. Miles's breath is ragged and uneven as I tug at the hem of his T-shirt, and he helps me pull it off. He bends down, trailing kisses along my neck, my shoulder, and my clavicle before yanking my crop top down, revealing my breasts. He takes each one in his mouth, sucking until the nipples peak for him. I gasp. "Miles," I murmur.

I undo the button on his jeans, pushing them down to expose his dark gray boxer briefs, his arousal straining against the fabric. He does the same, hurriedly pulling my leggings down, while simultaneously kissing down my torso, my ribcage, my hip bones. He lets out a guttural moan when he sees I'm not wearing any underwear.

"No panties, Jenna?" he growls. "What are you doing to me?"

"I didn't want any lines." I giggle innocently.

Miles hisses, kneeling down and hungrily pulling my folds apart, sinking his tongue into my wetness. I need him so badly. I don't want to wait.

"Miles. I need to feel you," I cry, digging my nails into his shoulders. "Please."

"Let me warm you up, baby," he rasps, sliding a finger inside, eliciting a moan from me that sounds animalistic. "You're not ready yet."

He settles his face back between my thighs and kisses my most delicate parts, gently sucking and dragging his teeth behind, until I can't take it anymore.

"Miles," I say firmly. "I need you inside me."

At once, he's on his feet, scooping me up and laying me on the end of the bed. "Your wish is my command." He hovers over me for a moment, eyes molten and burning into me, before going back to his discarded jeans and grabbing a condom from the pocket.

"Oh, so you planned this?" I tease.

"I like to be prepared around you," he says huskily. He rolls the condom on and at once he's over me again, rubbing his sex against mine. "Jenna, I need you to know, this isn't just tonight for me. This is everything." Miles's voice is raw with emotion, his eyes search mine for confirmation that the feelings of the past month seem to be bubbling over for both of us.

Our breaths mingle, heavy and uneven as we hover on the precipice of something deeper than a physical release. I ache for Miles in a way I've never ached for anyone before.

I swallow the lump in my throat and nod. "I feel the same way."

The moment he sinks into me a wave of emotion crushes me—like nothing I've felt before. Miles thrusts in and out slowly, sending a shiver through me with each new entry. He threads his fingers through mine, pinning them above my head. Our eyes stay locked as we move in sync with each other. Two people connecting on another worldly level. His movements are slow and tentative at first, each stroke sending a shudder through me. "Miles," I whimper. "Harder."

"You feel too good. I'm not going to last," Miles murmurs into my hair.

His breath is warm against my cheek and then his mouth is on mine again, kissing me urgently as his desire amplifies. I open my mouth for him, nibbling at his bottom lip. I wrap my legs around his waist, allowing him to plunge deeper to reach my most sensitive spot. I brush a stray curl off his forehead, and our eyes lock again.

This isn't just desire—it's gravity. It's more than want, it's need, it's an ache, it's everything I've never known I was missing. And I'm done fighting it.

For the past few years, my life has revolved around someone else's needs. It created an emptiness in me that I didn't know was there. Not anymore—now I feel full. Meeting Miles feels like fate. The realization overwhelms me, and my orgasm comes quickly, fueled by the emotion of it all. I cry out his name and my legs tremble as I tighten around him.

Miles drives into me as I come, desperately searching for his own release. It finds him quickly. "Oh my God... Jenna," he cries out my name and collapses on top of me. We lie there, intertwined, sweating and breathing heavily, but content to be in each other's arms.

And then we hear the rain.

Chapter Twenty-Six

It's well after midnight, and I'm lying in Jenna's bed wide-awake. It's comfortable, with a white wooden frame fit for a young girl. The mattress, as I understand it, was hardly slept on all those years ago. Neutral seashore decor hangs on the walls. The room might be any other arbitrary bedroom in a beach house. But it's not. It's Jenna's room and I can't stop marveling at the fact that she's lying on my chest, her legs intertwined through mine, sleeping comfortably.

The soft sounds of her peaceful breathing, the rain outside softly pelting the windowpane, and the incredible orgasm I just had with the woman of my dreams should have put me into a deep, unwavering slumber. Instead, I'm lost in thought. I can't stop thinking about Jenna and how she ended up here with me. Not only that but after my conversation with my mom, I haven't stopped thinking about the day my life was saved at the cost of another.

Something shifted between Jenna and me tonight, what I feel for her is bigger than anything I've ever known. I can't explain it, but I feel connected to her in a way that has nothing to do with how we met. I'm also almost positive that I'm falling head over heels, completely in love with her. The way she dashed into my life and altered everything I thought I knew about love. The way she doesn't want to be saved, yet all I want to do is save her, or at the very least, hold her hand through the hard stuff.

I sigh, and Jenna shifts in her sleep, her eyelids fluttering open. “Why aren’t you sleeping?” she yawns. “I thought I would have tired you out.”

“I can’t sleep,” I say quietly, stroking her jaw. “I’m sorry I disturbed you. Go back to sleep,” I whisper. I stroke her brown hair and Jenna’s eyes close again. My heart constricts. I can’t believe that I’m the one who is lying with her right now. I inch my way down and pull her closer to me. I close my eyes, knowing this is a moment I’ll remember forever. Just as I start to drift off, a large crash startles us both.

Jenna sits up, instantly alert. “What was that?” The fear in her eyes makes me hurl myself out of bed faster than a surfboard sale.

“I’ll go scope it out. Stay here,” I tell her, pulling gym shorts from my bag.

“Miles, what if it’s an intruder?” Jenna pulls the covers up over her bare chest.

I push my lips together, watching fear cloud her beautiful features. “Just stay here with Pete,” I repeat.

I dash down the stairs, poking my head in all the front rooms. I find nothing out of place. I venture down the short hallway to the kitchen—and that’s when I see it. And it’s going to drastically alter Jenna’s plans.

“Uh...Jenna?” I call. “I think you’d better come down here.”

A moment later, I hear her padding down the stairs and then she’s at the entrance to the kitchen, wearing my black T-shirt from earlier, Pete at her heels. I’m momentarily distracted by the sight of her, but her shriek brings me right back.

“Oh. My. God,” Jenna cries. The ceiling in the kitchen is... *gone*. It collapsed, likely from the heavy rain. Wet plaster and drywall cover most of the kitchen floor, and there is a gaping hole in the ceiling. Other parts of the ceiling sag under the weight of the water, telling me that the saturation is extensive. “What the fuck happened?”

“Danny did say you needed a new roof,” I start slowly. “Looks like the damage is worse than we anticipated.” I pull Jenna into a hug. “It’s going to be okay.” I rub her back.

"How, Miles? *How* is this going to be okay?" She pushes away from me and covers her forehead with her hand, pacing around the only part of the floor that isn't covered in wet plaster.

"I'm not sure at the moment," I admit awkwardly. "But we will figure it out. I'm here for you." I inhale sharply and look around the room. "This is some clean up."

"Yeah. You think?" Jenna retorts, batting at her tear-filled eyes. "This house is such a fucking money pit. I just want to sell it as is and run away."

Selfish fear fills my chest and comes up like bile. I swallow hard, willing myself to calm down. "You don't mean that," I say, my voice hoarse.

"I might," Jenna huffs. Then, her face crumbles, and she walks over to me, falling into my arms. Her back shakes with big heaving sobs.

"Shh." I stroke her back. "It's going to be okay. We will figure this out tomorrow, I promise."

"We have to stop the leaking now," Jenna wails. "I'm so tired."

I nod, tucking her head under my chin. "You're right. Do you have any buckets?"

"There are two in the laundry room. And a couple of pots in the cabinet." She gestures to the kitchen cabinet on the other side of the mess. Her expression crumples again and a new round of tears begin to fall.

"Okay, okay." I wrap my arms around her and lead her out of the kitchen and over to the couch. "You rest here. I'll take care of the leaks."

Jenna sniffles, shaking her head. "No, I have to help."

I tip her chin up so she looks my way. "No, you don't. You lie down. I've got this."

"Are you sure?" she asks, but she's already snuggling into the couch, eyes threatening to close.

"I'm positive," I say, passing her the blanket that's draped over the back.

"Thank you, Miles," Jenna says sleepily, settling in the fetal position with the blanket around her.

I pat her leg and then I get to work, putting buckets and pots around the room where there is active dripping. Then, while I'm at it, I take the big pieces of drywall out to the trash, grab some old beach towels from the laundry room, and sop up as much of the water as I can. I'll need a shop vac in the morning though for sure. "Oh man," I say aloud, walking back toward Jenna.

When I reach her, she's curled up under the blanket, sleeping peacefully. She looks so beautiful, I can't resist staring at her for a few moments before scooping her up and carrying her back up to bed. I will fix this for her, and for the first time since we've met, I actually think she wants that.

ଓଃ

I toss and turn before eventually falling into a fitful sleep. It doesn't last long though and I'm awake early. I let Jenna sleep and sneak out of her room to survey the damage from last night in the daylight and maybe call Danny.

It's worse than I thought. The kitchen doesn't have a floor above it, so the hole in the ceiling directly exposes the sky. I'm sure we can get on the roof and tarp it, but with the weather getting colder, it might be a good idea if Jenna stayed somewhere else. *With me.* That may be wishful thinking though.

I pull out my phone and take some photos of the damage, quickly sending them off to Danny. He calls me immediately.

"What the fuck happened?" he says when I answer the phone.

"Uh...the roof caved in," I say, as if it couldn't be more obvious. "You said she needed a new roof."

"Dammit. Well, now she definitely needs one. And fast." Danny groans like he's suddenly awake.

"Are you still in bed?" I scoff, running my fingers through my hair.

"Yeah, man. The party went late," Danny grumbles. "What do you need from me?"

"Let me FaceTime you and then maybe you can tell me the answer to that." I hit the video call button. Danny picks up, lying shirtless in his bed with his wife, Kristen, who's snoozing next to him.

"Miles, what the fuck!" she moans when she hears the call and opens her eyes.

"Sorry, Kris, this is an emergency," I say, flipping the camera around to show Danny.

Danny whistles low. "That's a lot of water damage."

"Yeah. Can I borrow your shop vac?" I ask.

Danny gets out of bed, taking his phone with him "I'll be right there," he says, as if all of a sudden he sees the urgency.

"Thanks, man," I say, hanging up.

☙

By the time Jenna gets up, Danny and I have cleaned most of the mess. We emptied the water-filled buckets, picked up the stray pieces of plaster, and shop-vac'd the floor, which is what I suspect woke her up. We set box fans up to dry out the area as quickly as possible. I'm running a mop over the crusty linoleum when she pads downstairs.

"Miles, you did all of this without me," she says, but it's not a question. She actually sounds touched.

"With Danny's help," I say, turning to her and gesturing at Danny in the backyard, carrying black garbage bags of debris.

Jenna's eyes glisten and she sniffles. "Miles. That's so nice," she whimpers, and I'm afraid she's going to start crying again. Instead, she pulls me into a hug. "Thank you," she murmurs into my chest.

I kiss the top of her head. "It's nothing," I say. "I told you—I'm an early riser."

Danny interrupts us when he comes inside. "Jenna." He nods in greeting. She's still only wearing my black T-shirt, the bottom of it barely skimming her thighs. She tugs at the hem and scootches behind me to hide her exposed legs. A slow smirk tugs at my lips. Danny notices, but he doesn't say anything.

"Hi, Danny. Thank you so much for helping Miles." She peeks around my side, her hands settling at my waist. "I'd hug you but...I wasn't expecting company." She lets out an embarrassed giggle.

"Don't mention it," Danny says with a chuckle. "But I don't think you should stay here. I will call my roofing guys today, but I'm honestly not sure how quickly they will be able to get out here. In the meantime, I am going to nail a waterproof tarp to the roof to hopefully prevent any more damage."

Jenna's brow furrows, but she only nods.

Danny turns to me. "I have some tarps in my shed. I'm going to grab them, then you can help me nail them on."

"Sure. Yeah, of course," I reply, nodding. "Thanks, buddy."

Danny nods and walks toward the door. "I'll be back in fifteen minutes, so if you're gonna get freaky, you better do it now." He chortles at his own joke and then he's gone.

I turn to face her and Jenna and I stare at each other for a moment before I pull her into another hug. "What am I going to do?" she mumbles.

I tip her chin up, guiding her gaze to mine. "Do you want to be rescued?" I whisper, fighting back the twitch of my lips. "I know you can take care of yourself but..."

Jenna bites back a smile and casts her gaze on my mouth. "It might be nice to have some help with this," she murmurs.

"Is that a yes? You want me to white knight you?" I tease.

"Miles." Jenna rolls her eyes, but she's smiling.

"I need you to say it," I say emphatically. "Say, 'Miles, I want you to rescue me.' That way, you can't come back at me later for this."

"I'm not going to come back at—" Jenna drops her arms exasperatedly.

"Ah, ah." I interrupt, wagging my finger at her. "Say it."

Jenna huffs. "Fine. Miles, I want you to rescue me."

I pull her closer to me again. "That doesn't sound very

enthusiastic," I rasp, cupping her cheek. She nuzzles my hand, closing her eyes and melting into my touch.

"Miles," Jenna murmurs.

"Yes?" I ask, grinning.

"Please, rescue me. Please do all the hard things and make all the phone calls I don't want to make." Her voice catches and it causes my chest to tighten.

I take her hand, pulling her into me and wrapping my arms around her. "It would be my pleasure," I whisper in her ear. "On one condition."

Jenna pulls back and looks up at me, her eyes questioning. "What's that?"

"Can we go surfing after this?"

Jenna lets out a peal of laughter. "Absolutely."

Chapter Twenty-Seven

It's nearly four o'clock by the time the guys finish tarping the roof, and Miles and I set off to the beach. The rain passed, and the waves are much tamer, but the air is significantly cooler. That summer reboot we've been experiencing is quickly becoming a distant memory. Soon, there will be no more surfing. For me anyway. I'm sure Miles will still be dragging himself out here mid-winter. *You might not be here to see it,* I remind myself. I really need to make a plan.

Last night with Miles was downright magical. It was the kind of night that doesn't happen to me. The kind of night where the man of your dreams makes you feel safe, protected, cherished... seen. If this is just a fling for him, then Miles is a damn good actor, because I have felt nothing but cared for by him. Now, I need to figure out what all this means for me.

"You ready?" Miles asks, grinning with excitement as he yanks the longboard off his roof rack. He passes it to me before getting his shortboard down.

I suck in a breath. "I'm anticipating the ice-cold water," I admit.

Miles laughs. "Don't worry. Cold water is great for you."

"I'll be the judge of that, thank you," I mutter, following him down the beach.

We crouch down and Miles passes me a block of wax. We get to work, waxing our boards. I'm silently worrying about how quickly daylight is disappearing, but I know Miles won't let anything happen to me. I want to experience this with him.

"Let's do it," Miles says, after surveying the layer of wax on my board. "You're getting good at that."

The waves are baby, beginner waves like the ones I learned on, so paddling out is easy. The icy water stings as my hands slice through it, but I quickly warm up. Once we're out past the break, we turn our boards toward the shore. "Want to just sit for a bit?" Miles asks, looking up at the sky. "The sunset is amazing."

He seems pensive tonight...quiet—it's unnerving. We decided that I'm staying with him until Danny gets the roof fixed, but I'm hoping he doesn't have any regrets about that. I haven't yet let myself think about how I'm going to pay for any of this, but tapping into my 401(k) looks necessary. Today though, I promised myself I would relax. I'll enjoy this time out here with Miles, try to see what he sees.

"The golden hour is my favorite." My eyes catch on the soft golden glow on the water's surface. The only sounds are the soft splashes from our feet dangling off our boards and the waves crashing against the shore.

"It's a close second for me," Miles says, glancing sideways with a wistful smile. Our boards are close enough together that I could reach for him. I let my fingers dangle on the surface instead. He reaches through the water and grips my hand. "I like the stars the best."

"I can see why," I say, looking up at the sky. The first twinkles of starlight are starting to show through the dusk sky.

Miles is quiet for a minute, and I debate whether to ask him what's on his mind. He has been very affectionate, but I can tell that he's lost in thought, too. He seems to be chewing on something, yet at the same time, he can't stop touching me.

I shiver as he lifts my hand to his mouth and kisses it. "Are you cold?" he asks gently.

"A little. I'll be okay," I tell him. "Maybe I need to invest in a warmer wet suit if you're going to be dragging me out here into

November," I joke.

"I like the sound of that. I'll get you one with a hood." Miles smiles but it doesn't reach his eyes. He inhales deeply and says, "Jenna, can you tell me about your dad?"

This catches me off guard and my jaw falls slack. I shudder, bracing for the pain that never really goes away but that still shocks me every time. "What do you want to know?" I ask, swallowing hard.

"You said he died on this beach. Did he drown?" Miles meets my eyes, licking his lips.

I shake my head. "No. I don't know much. We were here all day, and then we packed up to go home. I remember being tired and getting in the car while my parents packed up. My dad must've forgotten something because he ran back down the beach. Literally ran." I shake my head. "I think a storm was rolling in." I pause, glancing at Miles as a wave gently bobs us up and down again. I swallow the lump rising in my throat. "He didn't make it back. He had a heart attack on the shore."

"A heart attack?" Miles repeats, a shadow of disbelief flickering across his features.

I suck in a breath. "Yeah."

"That's not what I expected you to say," he admits, squeezing my hand. "I'm really sorry, Jenna." And he looks it—devastatingly so—as if, all of a sudden, he's seeing straight through the depths of my grief, right to my soul.

I shiver again. "I could never talk to my mom about it without her getting hysterical. Eventually, I just stopped asking." I shrug. "Maybe I'll get the courage to ask Aunt Leona more about it." I pull my hand away and rub my arms to generate heat.

Miles nods. "Come on, you're freezing. Let's ride this next one in and call it a day."

Our boards bob side by side with the swell of the waves, rising and falling in sync, as if the ocean itself is pulling us together. We lie on our stomachs and start paddling, muscle memory guiding me. My arms slice through the water churning in my hands, and then the wave catches me. I pop up, the board steady beneath my feet. For a moment, it's just me and the sounds of the surf. Then, I catch sight of Miles in the corner of my eye, the sunset framing him in a golden haze. He rides parallel to me with expert grace, carving into the ocean with ease, always leaving me enough space to ride the same wave. He mirrors me, laughing and pointing at me as the ocean carries us in. We're both laughing as we step off our boards and walk toward our towels.

I set the board down, and when I stand up, Miles is holding a large towel open for me. I step into it and turn to face him. "You're a natural," Miles murmurs.

"I had a good teacher," I whisper, staring at his mouth.

"Jenna..." Miles lets out a breath. His eyes dart away from me and back—he looks like he wants to say something but he's holding back. *I knew something was preoccupying him.*

"Miles," I say, urging him on. "What's wrong?"

"I..." Miles hesitates and then shakes his head as if changing his mind. "I just want you to know...I really like you."

I grin. "I really like you too, you dummy." I swat his arm. "You scared me getting all serious like that. I thought you were going to dump me."

But Miles grabs my hand again and pulls me closer. He leans down and nuzzles his nose with mine. "No," he says huskily, shaking his head. "I more than like you, Jenna. I'm falling for you."

My heart races. *I'm falling for you* is not something you say to a fling. I know now—this isn't a fling for Miles anymore. If I'm really honest with myself, it's not a fling for me either and it hasn't been for a while. I may have been built up like a fortress, but Miles has slowly but surely been breaking down my barriers and weaseling his way into my heart. And yet, I'm not scared. I'm excited, energized, hopeful...but not scared. Miles hasn't given me any reason to be scared.

"Please say something," he croaks into my ear, my wet hair dripping on his lips.

"I'm falling for you too, Miles," I breathe.

Chapter Twenty-Eight

Well, shit. My suspicions were confirmed out here in this bitter, cold ocean. Jenna's vulnerability when I bring up her dad stirs something in me I wasn't prepared for. It's a question that's been gnawing at me for weeks—what if the man who saved me was somehow Jenna's dad? The way I feel so connected to her. The similarities in the timing of my accident and her dad's death, it's all too coincidental. Now I'm sure of it and I'm freaking the hell out. Her heart cracked wide open at the mere mention of her dad. My chest tightens and the cold seeps in. I try to steady my breathing but I'm spiraling. *I'm the reason her dad's not alive.* The guilt consumes me as I picture that night. Strong arms throwing me on the long board, paddling us in. I never saw his face, but I can almost picture it now. The thought turns my stomach. I have to tell Jenna.

Twenty-five years after nearly losing my life, I find the daughter of the man who saved me. And I'm completely in love with her. That's some serendipity shit. The last thing I want to do is reopen old wounds and hurt her. She deserves to know—but not now. I need time. I need to figure out how I even begin to share this with her.

I surprise us both when I blurt out that I'm falling for her. It's true. But I'm deflecting, shielding myself from this new truth I'm carrying. Because it's heavy. Too heavy to say out loud yet.

We drive to Jenna's house to get her car and her things. She's packing enough clothes for a week. We'll both be in and out of her house checking on the builder's progress. But in the meantime, we're cohabitating—awfully early in the relationship.

"If this is too much," Jenna starts slowly, "you know, me living with you...I can sleep on your couch. We don't have to dive in headfirst." She puffs out her cheeks like she is literally holding her breath, waiting for my response.

I laugh softly and reach for her hand, still cold from the ocean and the late October air. "I just told you I'm falling for you," I murmur, eyeing her carefully while still keeping my eyes on the road. "Why would you think I'd want you anywhere but in my bed with me?"

Jenna shrugs. "I'm just making sure. This is a lot...and you've been single, you know? I don't want to scare you off." Her voice is uneasy, and it makes my chest hurt. *Tell her,* my conscience urges. But I don't.

Instead, I kiss her hand and look over at her. "I'm not scared," I say, hoping it reassures her.

Jenna sighs, resting her head against the seat. "Good. Me neither." The smile she gives me makes me forget I have anything to hide.

I pull up behind her car and throw mine into park. "Do you want me to come in with you while you pack?" I ask.

Jenna shakes her head. "No, it's fine. You go pick up food and I'll meet you back at your place." She glances at the house, smiling wistfully. "It's going to be weird not being here. I was starting to get used to it."

Something shifts inside me, making me uncomfortable. I want her to get used to being at my place—with me. I'm pretty sure she no longer has one foot out the door, but the fear is still nagging at the back of my mind. I give her a tight smile. "Well, you won't be alone now," I say cautiously.

Jenna grins. "I am very excited about that."

I pull my keys out of my pocket and take the house key off the ring before handing it to her. "Pete will be excited too," I tell her. "Fair warning though, he's going to try to sleep in bed with us."

Jenna laughs easily and seems more relaxed. "I like cuddling."

I lean forward and tip her mouth toward mine with my finger. I plant a soft kiss on her lips. "Okay, go get your things. I'll see you at home." *Home.* I didn't mean to say it, but I like the way it sounds.

Jenna is out of the car without a second thought. "Bye!" she calls. "Oh! Don't forget the guac."

I give her a salute and I'm off.

ଓ

I spot Nate's car when I pull into our favorite little Mexican spot. Through the window, I can see him scrolling his phone, probably waiting for a take-out order. I get out of the car quickly so I can catch him.

"Yo," I say, nodding in his direction, as I step inside. I walk up to the counter. "Pickup for Miles," I tell the girl behind the register.

"Okay, it'll just be a few minutes," she says with a smile.

"No problem." I turn and walk toward Nate. "Fancy meeting you here."

"What are you up to?" Nate asks. I notice he's without Caden.

"Picking up food for Jenna and me," I reply, eyeing him curiously. "Where's Caden?"

"With Mom and Dad. I'm grabbing dinner for all of us," Nate says with a smirk.

"What the hell. No one invited me?" I scoff, feigning annoyance.

"I called you. Check your phone." Nate elbows me.

I pull my phone out of my pocket and sure enough, there are a couple of missed calls from Nate and my mom. "My bad. Jenna and I were surfing."

Nate rolls his eyes but he's smiling. "Should have known. Did you convince her to stay yet?"

I shrug. "Maybe. She's actually staying with me for a week or two. Her roof caved in last night." I laugh as I say it because the whole thing is so mind-blowing.

"What? Dude." Nate shakes his head.

"I know. Danny said she needed a roof, but no one expected this." I exhale.

"That's not what I am saying *dude* to. Dude. Miles, you're letting this girl live with you already?" Nate's eyebrows shoot up. "Are you sure that's a good idea? You haven't been serious with someone in a long time. It seems fast."

"So? That doesn't have to mean anything," I say, going on the defensive. "Besides. there are things about her you don't know."

"She likes surfing? Unlike Erin." Nate laughs. This is typical Nate, making jokes to bite back what he really wants to say.

"No." I shake my head, suddenly serious. "I don't think I should tell you." I push my lips together, mulling it over.

The girl at the counter calls Nate's name. He walks up to pay, collecting his bags, giving me a chance to be thoughtful about how I tell him this.

"You have to tell me now," he pushes. "Is she dying or something?"

I gawk at him in confusion. "What? No. She's not dying. At least I don't think so."

"Then what?" He will not give this up, and it's my own fault for bringing it up. Maybe I do need to tell someone. I have to get this off my chest. Nate's my brother. He wants what's best for me. I'm sure he'll have some advice.

I scratch my chin, staring at the floor before meeting Nate's assessing gaze. "You can't tell Mom and Dad. Not yet. I haven't even talked to Jenna about it," I warn, giving him a pointed look.

Nate holds up his free hand defensively. "Okay, okay. *What?*" He's losing his patience with me.

"I think Jenna's dad might be the guy who saved me. Back in '97," I say solemnly.

"What the *fuck*? No way." Nate's jaw drops in disbelief. "That guy died."

"Yeah, I *know*. I just found *that* out a few days ago, actually. Funny that *you* know though and never thought to share that tidbit of information." I frown at my brother.

"What was I supposed to do, randomly bring up something that's painful for you and make it worse? Would you also like it if I sporadically bring up your divorce?" Nate taunts.

"Point taken," I acquiesce.

"Mom told me. She tells me everything." He grins, proud of himself in that obnoxious younger brother way.

"Well. Jenna told me her dad died on the beach. I assumed he drowned. But tonight, she told me he had a heart attack." I sigh. "It might all be a crazy coincidence but..."

"Oh. So, you don't know for sure then," Nate says, frowning.

"I mean...how many people do you think had a heart attack on Cove Beach?" I narrow my eyes.

"It *is* weird," Nate admits.

Just then, the girl calls my name. I step up and pay while Nate waits. We walk out together, both of us mulling over this new information.

"Just...don't say anything until I figure it out, okay?" I say. "I'm asking you as your brother."

"Fine." Nate sighs as he starts walking toward his car. "You just drop a bomb on me before I go see Mom and Dad and expect me to keep it a secret?" he grumbles.

"*Yes*," I say firmly. "Please."

"Okay," Nate says, opening his car door. "I gotta go. This food is probably cold by now."

"Later," I call after him, giving him a wave.

I have to go back for the guacamole.

☙

When I walk through the door, Jenna's curled up on the sofa with Pete beside her, both of them wrapped in a blanket, perfectly content—like this is exactly where they're meant to be. *The only thing missing is me.*

"Hi. You're back." Jenna smiles warmly at me. "I missed you."

I put the bag down and walk over to the back of the couch, leaning down to kiss her. "I ran into Nate. We were just catching up on the weekend," I say. "Sorry."

"It's okay. Pete and I were just making ourselves at home. Well, I guess *Pete* is already at home." She wrinkles her nose, embarrassed maybe.

I lean down and brush my nose against hers, pressing my forehead to hers. "So are you," I whisper, kissing her again.

Tell her. My conscience urges.

Not yet.

Chapter Twenty-Nine

Jenna

Miles and I fall into a steady rhythm that feels unbelievably natural, considering I have only known him a little over a month. Trauma Bangs Jenna would be suspicious, but this new Jenna feels too comfortable to be anything but blissfully naive. The weeks slip by almost without me noticing. Mornings blend into evenings, sun-warmed afternoons giving way to cooler nights.

I don't have work until Wednesday this week, so on Monday, when Miles leaves for work, I take Pete for a long walk along the beach. I throw his ball for him, and he zooms back to me, happy as a lark. He is probably as thrilled to have the company as I am.

On Tuesday morning, we sip coffee in the kitchen before he leaves. "I used to bring Pete to the office with me, but when I left for meetings, he started getting into trouble. So, I had to start leaving him home again. I'm sure he's enjoying all the attention you're giving him," Miles says, pouring coffee into a travel mug.

"Well, it turns out I am enjoying his company too," I say, leaning on the counter and smiling up at Miles. I'm not just talking about Pete.

"Want to come see me for lunch?" Miles asks hopefully. The past two nights we've eaten dinner on his couch in front of *Friends* reruns that he swears he puts on just for me, even though we're both cackling. Then, once we wash the dishes and Miles takes Pete for a walk, we fall into bed and make love before drifting off, our limbs intertwined. We stay that way most of the night, and each morning, I wake up to his breath on my neck. It's unlike anything I've ever experienced, and I am fully aware I could end up with a broken heart.

"Maybe..." I drag out the word, playing coy. "I was going to stop by the house and see if Danny has made any progress."

"I'll meet you there around noon?" Miles suggests. The way he's looking at me is so comfortably familiar that I almost think I'm imagining it. You always hear those stories about people who say they *just knew* the person was the one. I don't know what that feels like—hell, I haven't been in a relationship since the last guy cheated on me. But I am kind of wondering if that's what this is? A comfort, a stillness, that envelops you when you're with the right person. Nothing else in the world matters—not a caved-in roof, a ruined foundation, a lost job—because you have this person by your side to help get you through the hard stuff. I bask in the feeling until rationality takes over, reminding me that I don't *really* know Miles that well yet, as much as it feels that way.

"Jenna?" Miles breaks my thoughts. "You good? I lost you for a minute."

I smile, shaking my head. "Sorry. I was daydreaming, I guess. What did you say?"

"I said, how about I meet you around noon at your house?" He raises an eyebrow.

"Sure. That sounds good," I breathe, standing on my tiptoes to plant a kiss on his lips.

"I'll see you then," Miles murmurs against my lips, and the chill it sends through me makes me want to pull him back to the bedroom and convince him to stay home. He pulls back though and points at Pete. "Be good, boy."

And then he's gone, and I miss him already.

*

After walking Pete, I come back to the condo and bundle up. The Jersey coast finally got the memo that autumn is in full swing. I put on fleece-lined leggings and an oversized chunky sweater. Then I settle next to Pete on the sofa that I've grown quite fond of. It's much softer than the scratchy vintage one in my house. Pete joins me as I power up my laptop and log into my 401(k) account. So far, Danny has been extremely accommodating and hasn't billed me for a thing.

"I'll put it on your tab," he says every time I ask. I am growing tremendously uncomfortable with the idea of a tab, and I feel certain that the number is astronomical by now.

One plus is that I opened a 401(k) at twenty-two, when I got my first job after college, and I haven't touched a dime of it in thirteen years. Surely, I can take a minor tax hit rather than apply for a home equity loan. After three failed password attempts, I finally log in. That shows how often I've looked at it. Though I feel reassured that the number is in the mid-five figures. Perhaps that's enough to pay Danny what I owe him.

I call the account administrator, and after fifteen minutes on hold, I spend the next thirty learning how to make a hardship withdrawal. I might actually be able to pay Danny without a massive tax hit. Relief floods me, making me realize just how much stress I was carrying over this house. I still don't know if I'll stay in Cape May, but it's seeming more and more like a possibility. Miles could get tired of me in another week and break things off, especially since I'm all but moved into his space. But at least I won't be leaving town owing Danny anything. And if Miles doesn't break things off? I'm starting to imagine myself here, with him. Maybe I'll start my own business in the place my parents loved. It's a lovely thought that I'm not letting go of yet.

I close my laptop and exhale. Pete lifts his big block head at the sound and puts it back down in my lap. I ruffle his ears. "Oh, Pete," I sigh. "What does my future hold?" To be honest, I haven't been able to envision it much past these next few weeks. I have been floundering without the responsibility of my mom to care for and a nine-to-five to go to every day. I've been floating around. I think it's time I put some thought into where I'd like to land. I think it's here, but I'm scared.

Pete whines and licks my hand, prompting me to look at my watch. Shit! It's noon. I'm going to be late meeting Miles.

"Sorry, Pete! I have to go meet your da—owner." I scowl at myself. "I guess he's your dog dad," I admit with a smirk.

Pete sits up on his hind legs, looking at me over the couch as I slip into my Ugg ankle boots and jacket. He's practically begging to come with me.

"Okay," I relent. "Come on."

Pete jumps excitedly off the couch and follows me to the front door. I slip his harness over his head, and he pulls me out the door and down the steps to the parking lot.

I laugh. "You riding shotgun?"

When we pull up to my house on Monarch Street, Danny, Miles, and Liam are standing in the front yard. From a distance, they seem to be just shooting the breeze, but as I get closer, I catch Miles's furrowed brow and the way all three men huddle over a notebook in Danny's hands.

I hop out of the car and Pete follows me out the driver's side, pulling me around the car to the front yard.

"I was getting worried about you," Miles says, taking a step toward me and grabbing my hands. He moves closer, ignoring the guys, with a smoldering gaze that looks like he wants to carry me upstairs.

"Sorry," I say, pecking his lips. "I was on the phone with my investment bank," I murmur.

"Why?" Miles pulls back, studying my face.

I sigh and gesture toward Danny. "Because this place is a money pit, and I have to be able to pay for it."

Danny and Liam look up from the notebook. "Hey, Jenna," Danny says.

"Jenna." Liam nods in my direction. Man of few words, that one.

"Hi, guys." I step away from Miles and walk toward Danny. We all stand in a cluster. "Danny, I am ready for you to give me a bill," I say definitively.

"Well, hold that thought," Danny says cautiously. "We've got to go over some things."

Fear envelops me just as quickly as relief did earlier. I should have known it was too good to last. "What's wrong?"

Miles steps closer and puts his hand on my shoulder. "Nothing that we can't work out, right guys?" Miles raises his eyebrows at his friends optimistically.

Danny clears his throat and licks his lips. "The thing is, Jenna, when the ceiling caved in, it caused a ton of damage to the kitchen cabinets. Water got under the linoleum, so now the subfloor needs to be replaced. I have to take a more thorough look at the ceiling in the dining room and just outside the kitchen—it appears to be sagging in spots." He hesitates, and I cut in.

"So, what you're saying is...this is going to cost way more than I was expecting?" I wince.

"Well, you have a few options," Miles interjects. "We could just list the house as is. You might get a decent price if we market the land and sell it to flippers or developers. A developer will come in, knock it down, and build two in its place."

"Knock it down?" I repeat. I am unprepared for the sting of tears at the back of my eyes. I shake my head vigorously. "No. I don't want that. I don't want someone to come in here and tear it down."

Miles groans, rubbing his palm down his face, his jaw ticks in frustration. But then he puts an arm around me, pulling me close and grounding me with the contact—reminding me that we're in this together. "Okay. What else you got, Danny?"

Danny runs a hand through his hair then hands the notebook to Liam. "The other thing is...and I don't usually do this, but Miles really cares about you." He pauses when Miles elbows him and heat floods my cheeks, my eyes brimming with stubborn tears. "You can finance through me. We'll come up with a payment plan and finance what you can't cover."

I take a breath, and then I can't fight the tears anymore. I angrily bat at the one rolling down my face and sniffle. "I don't know what to say," I whisper. "This isn't exactly what I signed up for when I came back here."

"It's okay," Danny says soothingly.

Miles says nothing, and panic rises in my chest again. What seemed doable only an hour ago now seems insurmountable. I pass Pete's leash to Miles. "I need a minute," I say, rushing past the three dumbfounded men.

I think I hear Liam tell Miles to come after me, but he doesn't. I retreat upstairs to my room and pace.

What am I going to do? I never planned on staying here. I didn't ask for this house. I suck in rapid, shallow breaths, panic rising like bile, burning my throat. My chest is constricting, suffocation creeping in. I walk over to the dresser and pick up a photograph in a tarnished gold frame. It's me with my parents at the Washington Street Mall. We're all holding swirled ice cream cones, grinning at the camera. We took this photo right after we bought the house. "What do I do, Daddy?" I whisper to the picture. My dad's memory comes and goes in my mind, after all, I was only nine when I lost him. But what I remember most about him is that he always knew what to do. Much like Miles.

Miles is another problem. I wasn't planning on staying, but in just a matter of weeks, he feels like my partner. And yet I'm up here, freaking the hell out, and he didn't come after me. I let out an involuntary wail and crouch down on the floor against the dresser. Burying my face in my arms, I succumb to big, heaving sobs.

A moment later, the construction noise stops, distracting me from my meltdown. I hear a few voices and then footsteps up the wooden staircase. My door creaks, and when I look up, there he is. Leaning in the doorway, Miles meets my gaze and his expression clouds with compassion and concern. He doesn't wait for me to invite him in. He rushes to me, sits down next to me, and folds me in his arms. He brushes my hair off my damp face and kisses the crown of my head.

"Shh," he whispers. "I'm right here."

Chapter Thirty

Miles

My heart breaks for Jenna, orphaned at thirty-five. She has no one left that she's close enough with to guide her. An overwhelming desire to step up grips me. As I sit here, in her childhood room, holding her until her sobs become soft hiccups, my conscience screams at me. *Tell her what you know!* And yet, I don't, because I don't think Jenna can take anything else today. Every time I want to tell her, I am overcome by my own emotions about falling in love with her and knowing she's choosing to leave. It freaks me out. I don't want her to stay because she feels like she has to, and knowing her, if she learns of any connection to her dad, she will feel obligated to.

Once she's calm, we leave Pete at the house and go for lunch, but Jenna is quiet, undoubtedly mulling over her options.

"What should I do?" she asks, pushing her empty plate away and not bothering to hide the melancholy in her voice.

I push my lips together and meet her eyes, willing myself to put my own selfishness aside. "I think...you should do whatever will be easiest for you," I say as calmly as possible.

"Is that selling it as is, taking what I can get, and running?" Jenna frowns thoughtfully.

"Is that what you want to do?" I ask, my throat tightening. I fight the urge to reach for her hand. It's like we have some unspoken agreement not to let our personal feelings for each other weigh in on this decision she has to make.

"I don't want to run away. It's just, I have never really thought about what I want. I haven't had the chance the past few years, taking care of my mom," Jenna admits quietly. "But I really don't know what I want or where to go. I just feel like I need time to figure it out." Her eyes glisten with fresh tears. I reach across the table, catching one on my index finger.

"I don't want you to run either, Jenna," I murmur. I swallow the urge to confess my suspicions about her father again. "Let's keep this conversation about the house. No other influences, okay? Before you got this news today...what were you thinking about doing?"

Jenna chews on her lip. "I guess I was thinking, let Danny fix everything, DIY the rest of the cosmetic stuff, and then..." She pauses, studying my face.

I open my palm on the table for her to take. Her hand in mind feels warm and reassuring. "Go on," I urge with a little squeeze of her hand.

Jenna inhales sharply. "I still want to fix it up. I don't want to sell it to someone who is going to tear it down," she says emphatically. Then, quieter, "But I was going to wait and see how *we* are before deciding to stay. And if I decide to stay, I have to think about my career. I can't work for Joy forever, as fun as it is." Her expression is so hopeful, I want to grab her face, kiss it all over, and beg her to stay. The fact that she is even considering it is a comfort to me and my vulnerable heart.

Relief floods my veins and something in my chest expands at her admission, as if I finally have reassurance that Jenna is in it with me. She wants to see where this goes too. *Tell her.* My brain won't shut off. "Okay. How about this? Let's take both things...the house and us...day by day? Does that sound okay?"

Jenna nods. "I think so." Then she gives me a wistful smile. "Thank you, Miles."

"Don't mention it," I say, then flag the server for the check, once again swallowing my secret.

I'm not surprised when my mother calls me shortly after I say goodbye to Jenna. She doesn't usually call me during the workday, and that can only mean one thing—Nate opened his big mouth.

"Hey, Ma," I say, tapping the touch screen on my car display.

"Miles, dear. I talked to Nate last night." My mom wastes no time going in for the kill.

I roll my eyes, even though she can't see it. "Let me guess, he snitched," I say wryly.

"I wouldn't think of it as snitching. Nathan is just worried about you." A thing about my mom, she will always tell you that she doesn't take sides, but when she calls Nate Nathan, she is definitely on his side.

"Yeah, well, he doesn't need to be," I growl, leaning back in my seat at a red light, closing my eyes as I grasp for patience. It must be a short light because the cars behind me beep. I glance in the rearview mirror—a middle-aged man is yelling and angrily gesturing with his hands.

"Yeah, yeah," I mumble at him. "Mom, I will talk to Jenna in my own time." I attempt to appease her.

"How do you even know it's really *her* father?" My mother asks tentatively.

I sigh. "Because Mom. How many men have had a heart attack from exertion on Cove Beach in the last twenty-five years?" My patience is wavering.

"It *is* peculiar," my mother admits. She's quiet for a moment. "And you really care about this girl?" she asks cautiously.

"I really do, Mom, yes," I reply emphatically.

"Then you have to tell her what you suspect. You can't keep a secret like this, especially from someone you really care about."

I know my mother is right, but the truth is, I don't know how I am supposed to tell Jenna this. I am falling completely in love with her. Seeing her fall apart on the bedroom floor this afternoon shook something in me. Jenna is my person. I have no doubt about that now. But what if this information freaks her out and sends her running from Cape May for good? Where does that leave me? It sounds selfish, but the moment has to be right.

"I will, Mom. I promise. It's just a delicate thing to bring up. And she is fragile right now. She's been through a lot," I say, turning the car into the office parking lot. I'd love to use this as an excuse to hang up, but Mom is talking to me on the phone, standing on the curb in front of my office, clearly waiting for me. "Why are you here?" I ask, immediately agitated. I hang up the phone and get out of my car.

"This felt like it was too important to wait," my mother says defensively.

"I'm going to kill Nate," I mutter, starting for the door.

She stops me by putting both of her hands on my chest. "Now, no, you are not," she says defiantly. "Nate isn't in there anyway; he had an appointment. I just wanted to talk to you about this myself."

"Well, come on then." I let out an exasperated breath, motioning toward the door.

"I won't keep you," Mom says as she perches on the guest couch in the front of the office. "I just needed to give you my two cents, which is this: *tell her*. If you think her father saved you, you have to tell her. Because if she finds out on her own, it's going to blow up in your face."

"And how do you suggest I tell her, Mom?" I ask through gritted teeth. For someone who couldn't remember the guy's name, she's being awfully persistent that I blow up my entire relationship before I'm ready. I need to channel the appreciative feeling I had for her just the other day. I take off my jacket and hang it on the coat rack by the door, then walk back over to my mother and sit beside her.

"Just be honest. Tell her the exact moment you suspected it." She pats my knee.

"What if she leaves?" I ask quietly. This is another feeling I have been trying to force down every time it threatens to paralyze me. Fear. The fear that I am going to let myself fall for Jenna, only for her to break my heart into a million pieces like Erin did. It's so much easier to be a serial dater than to open myself up to the possibility of getting hurt again.

"Do you love her?" My mother asks.

I sigh and run my hands down my face more aggressively than I intended. "I think...maybe I do," I admit. "God, it's weird saying that out loud. Especially to you."

My mother grins, no longer bothering to hide her relief that I won't be a Casanova forever. "I have to admit, Erin broke your heart so terribly that I never thought you'd fall in love again. I'm kind of excited!"

At this, my guard falls slightly, and I crack a smile. "She is really great." I sigh. "I will tell her. I just have to find the right moment."

"You will." My mom grabs my arm and hugs it to her chest. "You're a good man, Miles." She stands to leave and I think the conversation is over until she says, "Bring her over for dinner on Friday. I'd love to meet her."

"Oh...Mom." I hesitate. "It's soon for that, don't you think?"

"Not if you love the girl," my mother challenges, folding her arms across her chest.

"Well, what if I haven't talked to her about it by then? Are you going to blow up my spot?" I cock my head, raising my eyebrows at her.

My mother scowls. "Don't be ridiculous." She waves her hand. "I just want to meet the woman my baby is so taken with. Please, say you'll come."

I groan and stand up, ushering her to the door. I've had about all that I can take from this conversation. "Fine, Mom. We'll be there," I grumble.

"Six o'clock." My mother turns and grins. She puts her hand on my cheek, and I bend down to plant a peck on hers.

"Bye, Mom."

"Bye, Miles!" She singsongs over her shoulder.

There is no getting out of this one.

Chapter Thirty-One

Jenna

I'm idly dancing around Miles's tiny kitchen to Michael Bublé's "Everything," stirring my mother's homemade pasta sauce when Miles comes in. I don't hear him at first, until he dances up behind me and loops his arms around my waist, kissing my neck.

"Hey, baby," he murmurs, swaying along with me, the closeness of his breath tickling my ear.

Then, like the hidden romantic he is, he grabs my hand and twirls me around to face him, swinging me into a ballroom dance. He swings me around, laughter bubbling out of me, then sings the song softly in my ear, pressing his cheek into mine. I can't say I've ever slow danced in a kitchen before, but now I get the hype. Miles transports me somewhere else, makes me feel as if I am the only thing he sees, and somehow melts all of my troubles away.

When the song ends, he plants a soft kiss on my lips, and I can't escape the sudden feeling that I'm finally home. I belong here with Miles, dancing in his kitchen, making him dinner, and curling up on the couch with him and Pete after a long day. I lean into his chest and wrap my arms around his torso. "You're home," I say, inhaling his salty sea-air scent that seems to be embedded in his skin from living his life in the ocean.

"I'm home," he says hoarsely, and the expression on his face turns my insides molten. He smooths my bangs back from my face, studying me carefully. He looks like he wants to say something, but he just pulls me close again, tucking my head under his chin.

This is new. Miles is extra affectionate tonight, but I don't hate it.

"What are you making?" He interrupts my thoughts. He pulls away and walks over to a cabinet, getting two wine glasses down from the top shelf.

"My mom's pasta and meatballs." I smile proudly. "I was just in the mood to cook something comforting today."

Miles walks out of the kitchen to a banquet-style cabinet in the dining area and retrieves a bottle of red wine. "Do you like Pinot?" he asks, showing me the bottle.

"I like whatever you like," I tell him, dumping a box of rotini in the boiling pot of water.

"Good," Miles says, grinning. "Well, I *like* the sound of that." He pours two glasses of red wine and passes one to me, clinking his to mine. "Cheers to us being here together," he murmurs.

A lump rises in my throat and I force it down with a sip of wine. "Cheers," I whisper, then clear my throat. "Dinner should be ready in a couple of minutes."

Miles comes closer and leans on the counter, watching me. "Speaking of dinner," he says awkwardly.

"Yes?" I ask, smirking and raising my eyebrows.

"My mom and dad want to meet you," he blurts out. "If that's not too weird for you. I mean...I told my mom it's a little early in the relationship...if that's what *this* is..." Miles rambles nervously as he gestures between the two of us. He's awkward and adorable, and my heart swells. He hesitates, running his hands through the mop of waves on his head. "She is just anxious to meet you," he grumbles, and I'm sure it's in embarrassment and not for any other reason that would normally give me self-doubt.

I'm so sure of that, in fact, that I say, "Is that what this is? A relationship?"

Miles's cheeks flush faintly as he meets my gaze. He licks his lips. "It is if you want it to be," he rasps, pushing off the counter and stepping closer to me. I'm frozen in front of the hot stove as Miles stands beside me, hooking a finger through the belt loop of my jeans and pulling me in. "Is that something you might want with me?" he says into my hair, pressing his lips to my temple.

I turn to face him, draping my arms around his neck, and grin. "Are you asking me to be your girlfriend, Miles?" I say playfully.

Miles rolls his head back grinning. "Well, I don't know. Do forty-one-year-olds use the word *girlfriend* anymore?" he teases.

"I don't know, I'm only thirty-five." I grin, grabbing the collar of his T-shirt and yanking him closer.

"Oh, well, in that case. Yes," Miles whispers. "Would you like to be my girlfriend, Jenna Rossi?"

I cannot contain the smile creeping across my face. I bite it back, but it's no use. I give Miles's chest a little shove, forcing him to step back. "Yes, Miles. I will be your girlfriend."

Miles barks out a laugh and lifts me to my feet, spinning me around. "Woohoo! She said yes, Pete!" he calls to the dog who watches us from the couch. Pete barks excitedly. "We have a girlfriend! Woo!" Miles sets me down and cups my cheeks, planting an excited, wet kiss on them.

I laugh, pulling away. "And I'll meet your parents. If it means that much to your mom, I would love to."

"Yes." Miles fist pumps. "It does. It really does."

I roll my eyes, but I can't help smiling. "Okay then. Let's eat."

଼

"He actually asked you to be his girlfriend? Like he is in high school?" Joy gapes at me from behind the counter as I unbox holiday lights in preparation for the upcoming season.

"Yep. And he seemed excited when I said yes." I giggle. Miles absolutely took me by surprise when he asked me to be exclusive with him. I just thought we were taking things day by day. This adds a new layer to my *what do I do?* dilemma. Suddenly, fleeing Cape May with a big, fat sales check doesn't seem so simple. I'm not so sure I want it to be either. Maybe, I can ditch the house and keep Miles.

"Wow." Joy smacks her lips when she says it. "I have to say, I am pleasantly surprised." She walks around the counter and stops right in front of me, taking me in. "You don't look any different," she teases. "Do you feel different?"

I let out a boisterous laugh. "What? Why would I look different?"

Joy reaches out, pushing a stray hair behind my ear. "Just because you're someone's girlfriend now. I sort of thought you'd be glowing or something." She cocks her head at me and furrows her brow.

"Who is someone's girlfriend?" Leo says, barging out of the storeroom, carrying another box of LED lights.

Suddenly Joy looks as if she's bursting to tell this new information. She hops up and down on her toes and shoots me a look that says *are you going to tell him, or am I?* I shrug as if to say, go ahead.

"Jenna is Miles's new girlfriend!" Joy shrieks and then covers her mouth excitedly. "I would have never been able to keep that a secret."

"Wow," Leo muses, frowning. "Are you sure?"

"Am I sure? Of course I'm sure," I say, rolling my eyes. "Why wouldn't I be?"

Leo shrugs. "I don't know, I just never thought I'd see the day that Miles Corbin had a girlfriend." He sets the box down at my feet. "Don't get me wrong, he's my bud, but everyone knows the kind of guy he is. Since his divorce, he dates around." Leo bends down and starts rooting through the box, passing lights to Joy to put on the shelves.

"This isn't like that," I say affirmatively. "Miles and I are different."

"If you say so," Leo says, laughing to himself.

"What? We are," I say, feeling myself get defensive.

"Okay," Joy interjects. "I'm happy for you." She shoots Leo a look that says *shut up.*

"Thank you," I say, exhaling. I crouch down next to Leo and start unloading lights.

"I have to admit, Miles is different than I thought," Joy says quietly. I look up at her and she smiles. "I'm sorry if I seemed unsupportive. I'm really happy for you." She reaches down and squeezes my shoulder.

"Thank you," I sigh. "I'm happy too. It feels right, and I can honestly say, it's the last thing I expected when I came here."

"Well, sometimes life's little surprises turn out to be the things we didn't know we needed," Leo says matter-of-factly. Joy and I simultaneously whip our heads up at him.

"How prophetic of you," Joy deadpans.

I cackle. "Leo, I had no idea you could be so profound."

Leo feigns offense. "Hey. I am deep, okay? I'm not some superficial beach boy with half a brain." He scowls.

"Oh, Leo, I'm sorry." I fight back another giggle.

"Yeah. You both should be." He whirls around and barges back into the storeroom.

Joy chortles, holding her sides as laughter bubbles out of her. I can't help myself, I join in, and before we know it, we're both balled up on the floor of the store laughing through tears and trying to catch our breath.

"Okay, okay," I breathe, pressing my hands to my aching cheeks. "We don't want to

upset Leo."

"You're right," Joy says, wiping a stray tear from her lash line.

"He wants me to meet his parents on Friday. For dinner at their house." I gulp dramatically, but Joy doesn't falter.

"Mr. and Mrs. Corbin are literally the nicest people in the world," Joy says, patting my arm. "It'll be perfect."

"I guess so. And then on Saturday, I'm having dinner with Jake and Aunt Leona. I honestly never thought I'd see that day," I say wryly. "It's going to be an interesting few days."

"You'll be fine—you're you." Joy stands up, reaching for my hand to help me up too. "But more importantly, what are you going to wear to meet his parents?"

Chapter Thirty-Two

The rest of October passes by in a blur. Halloween comes and Jenna buys candy to give out to trick-or-treaters. We only get two at my condo and Jenna ends up giving them the whole bowl. Friday, November first, the entire town switches over to Christmas. The streetlamps have wreaths and angels that light up at night. The Washington Street Mall is ornately decorated with twinkling lights, greenery, and ornaments. The speakers play Christmas music twenty-four-seven for everyone to hear. The excitement in the air is infectious. Even I catch myself whistling along this year.

I would be more excited if I weren't so nervous about dinner at my parents' tonight. I want them to like Jenna as much as I do because I like her *so much*. After only a couple of months, I like her more than anyone I have ever been with. More than I liked Erin at this stage.

Jenna and I have fallen into an easy rhythm, waking up and drinking our coffee together on the balcony overlooking the ocean before going our separate ways for the day. When the end of the day comes, I can hardly wait to get home. I drive as quickly as possible, knowing a hot meal—and Jenna and Pete—are waiting for me. They are both as happy to see me as I am them. To be fair, Pete has always been thrilled when I get home, but I wasn't always in such a hurry. Now, someone is waiting for me—someone I can't believe I've gone my whole life without. Obviously, we shouldn't live together permanently. It would be way too soon. But calling her my girlfriend and coming home to her every day? It feels *so* right.

I don't think I've really been living these past couple years since my divorce. I've woken up, gone to work, gone surfing, and did the mundane adult things that are required of me. But Jenna lights everything up again. I can hardly believe my dumb luck that I found her.

I still haven't gotten the courage to tell her about her dad though. *I know, I know. It's bad.* We're having a great time together, and I am so afraid of what this information will do to us. What if it shakes everything up, and Jenna doesn't want to be with me anymore? The longer I wait, the worse it'll be for me if she finds out before I tell her. That's why I decided after kissing her goodbye this morning, that if everything goes well tonight with my family, I will finally tell her. So, that's the plan.

Nate's already at the office when I get there this morning. He's busy at his computer and doesn't even look up as I walk inside, whistling "It's Beginning to Look a Lot Like Christmas."

"What's with you?" He smirks without looking up.

I scowl at him from across the room. "What do you mean, what's with me? I'm just happy."

Nate grins, "Oh? And that happiness wouldn't have anything to do with a certain client you've been entertaining, would it?" In true Nate form, he can't help himself from antagonizing me.

"I'd say she's far from a client now, wouldn't you?" I frown, pulling out my desk chair and booting up my desktop.

"I don't know, bro. You're the only one who knows the answer to that," Nate says, still not looking my way. He clicks through on a listing he signed yesterday, adding photos and a description of the house.

"Well, considering I made her my girlfriend this week, I'd sure hope so," I say, tipping back in my chair and daring my brother to look my way.

He spins in his chair to face me. "Girlfriend, yeah?" He raises his eyebrows. "So, you told her about your suspected connection to her dad?" The question sounds accusatory, and I know Nate already knows what my answer will be.

I push back in my chair and walk to the coffee pot in the back of the office, selecting a K-cup and pressing brew before I answer him. He clears his throat as if to encourage me.

"Not exactly," I say, hemming and hawing. "I will. But I wanted to see how dinner with Mom and Dad goes tonight."

"Dinner?" Nate's jaw drops. "No one told me about a dinner." He scowls.

I laugh, slurping my coffee and then hissing when it's too hot. "Now you know how I felt the other night."

"Yeah, well, at least we *tried* to invite you. You just didn't answer," Nate retorts sourly.

"Maybe Mom and Dad just want to meet Jenna without your input," I suggest. "Did you ever think of that?"

Nate furrows his brow. "Absolutely not. I'm calling Mom." He crosses his arms indignantly.

"What are you five?" I growl. "I don't care if you come, for what it's worth."

But Nate is already on the phone asking our mom why he wasn't invited to dinner. Mom must give in like she always does with *her Nathan,* because he offers me a smug grin upon hanging up. "Guess I'll see you at dinner." He looks pleased with himself. "Me and Caden."

I smack my lips. "Great."

ᘓ

It turns out that Jenna is putty in Caden's sticky little hands. As soon as he sees her, he is dragging her from room to room, giving her a tour of my parents' house. I follow behind to make sure he doesn't show her anything embarrassing but I'm trying to remain inconspicuous. Jenna didn't get more than two minutes with my parents before Caden latched onto her like Velcro.

Jenna takes it in stride though and seems to be enjoying

my sweet little nephew. I'm standing at the end of the hallway watching Caden show Jenna every bedroom in the house when my Mom comes up beside me. She and I watch them moving down the hallway together for a few moments.

"Now I see why you didn't invite Nate from the start," I joke. "We'll never get her back."

My mother snorts. "You know Caden loves the ladies."

"Like father, like son," I say, glancing sideways at her to see if I can get a rise.

My mother doesn't take my bait and instead says, "She seems lovely, Miles, really."

I grin, draping my arm around my mom's shoulders. "That's because she is."

"And this," Caden bellows from down the hall, "is Uncle Miles's room." He kicks the door open with his foot and turns proudly to Jenna. "Come on!"

Jenna looks at me amused and holds up her hands, following Caden into the room. There is nothing in there anymore but my old full-size bed, my desk with a cork board displaying high school memorabilia, and a few old surfboards leaning against the back wall that I don't use anymore.

Jenna peeks her head back out the door. "How many surfboards do you have?" she asks with a laugh.

I give her a lazy smirk. "A lot."

"Well, you coming? Or can I root through your things?" she teases before disappearing into the room.

I walk down the hallway and into my old room. It's impeccably clean because my mother has nothing else to do. There are some of Caden's superhero toys stashed in the corner.

"This is my room when I sleep over!" he tells Jenna proudly, tugging her arm over to the corner with his things.

I watch them from the doorway, my feelings for her growing with each passing moment. Jenna is crouched down beside Caden, listening intently as he shows her his most prized possessions at Grandma and Grandpa's house. She gives him her full attention but periodically she meets my gaze and smiles. *I am so crazy about this girl.*

We're saved by the bell when, a moment later, Nate peeks his head in. "Mom says dinner is ready."

"Great, I'm starving," I say, gesturing for Jenna to lead the way. "After you."

Jenna grins at me over her shoulder.

☙

"So, Jenna, Miles tells us you came to Cape May after discovering a house that belonged to your parents?" my father, John, asks, taking a bite of pork roast.

Jenna nods as she swallows a bite. "That's right. I didn't know the house was still ours. Miles says your family has been the property managers all these years, so thank you for that." She takes a sip of water.

"Of course. Happy to do it." My dad smiles.

Mom must sense we're in dangerous conversation territory; she interjects before he can ask any more questions. "What is it you do, Jenna?"

Jenna's cheeks blush, and she looks down at her plate. "Oh, well, I'm taking some time off with the passing of my mom but... interior design." She takes a nervous bite of food and chews it carefully.

"Oh, I'm sorry, dear. I didn't realize your mother passed away recently." My mother's face softens with empathy. She clearly didn't realize she was broaching a sensitive subject, as a look of guilt flickers across her face.

"Oh, it's okay." Jenna waves her hand, dismissing my mother's guilt, but I can see the tears glistening behind her eyes. "She was sick for a long time." Her voice wavers, and my heart breaks just a little.

"Still. That doesn't make it easier." My mother pats Jenna's hand from across the table and shoots me a pained expression I can't fully read.

"Let's change the subject, shall we?" my dad interjects.

Jenna swallows audibly. "Great idea." She forces a smile. "Tomorrow night, I'm having dinner with my aunt—I haven't seen her in years. Maybe you know her? Leona Walker."

Dad's gaze shoots to my mom and I watch as a conversation silently passes between them. Jenna doesn't seem to notice. My dad clears his throat. "I do know your aunt, yes," he says, offering Jenna a warm smile. "That will be nice for you to reconnect."

Before Jenna can respond, Caden interrupts with a loud declaration that grown-ups are *so boring* and he wants to talk about the new *Sonic* movie instead. A laugh bubbles out of Jenna, and she looks fondly at Caden who happens to be sitting right next to her.

"Why don't you tell us about it, bud?" I suggest, hoping to lighten the mood.

Things can only go up from here.

Chapter Thirty-Three

"It was so nice meeting you, dear," Miles's mother says, as she walks us to the front door. She puts her arms around both of us. "Please come back again soon." She hugs me into her tiny body, and I marvel for a moment that she actually birthed Miles and Nate, with their tall, athletic frames. Mrs. Corbin can't weigh more than a hundred pounds soaking wet. She's petite but also appears to be in good physical shape.

"Thank you so much for having me, Mrs. Corbin." I give her a genuine smile. It's been a long time since I've had dinner with a real family. It was always just me and my mom. When she got sick, she didn't want to eat much, but I would keep her company on the couch, eating my takeout on a snack tray. A family dinner felt foreign to me initially, but I am so happy Miles brought me along and gave me a glimpse into who he is. Spending time it his family feels like a privilege. "I would love to come back sometime," I add.

"Good. And call me Susan, please." She goes in for another hug, taking me by surprise.

"Okay, Susan. I'll try to do that," I say, smiling into her shoulder.

Susan pulls away and then reaches up to hug Miles, whispering something in his ear that I don't catch. He chuckles. "Good."

"John, come and say goodbye!" Susan yells over her shoulder. "They're leaving."

"Caden pulled him and Nate into a rousing game of Sorry! while you two were cleaning up the dishes," Miles says regretfully. "Too bad we're missing it."

Susan makes a tsking sound with her tongue and shrugs. "Oh well. You'll see him again soon." She smiles.

Miles takes our coats off the hook and helps me slip into mine before putting his on. He leans down to plant a kiss on his mom's cheek. "Good night, Mom. I'll call you this week."

"Bye you two! Be safe driving home," she calls. She stands at the door, waving and looking pleased as we drive away.

As we drive, my gaze drifts to the newly decorated town. Miles reaches for my hand. "Do you want to get out and walk around?" he asks, quirking his eyebrow. "It's nice in Cape May this time of year. The town does a wonderful job decorating."

"They really do," I agree. "Does the town council do it?"

Miles frowns. "I'm honestly not sure who does it," he says with a smirk. We pull into a parking spot and Miles hops out, running around to open my door before I have a chance.

We walk toward the mall and Miles slips his hand into mine. I'm enamored by the lights and the decorations. It's been a few days since I've gone anywhere but to the beach with Pete and work. "Oh!" I squeal. "They're playing Christmas music." Excitement blooms in my chest.

Miles chuckles. "That they are." He sucks in the cold air and looks at me with a tender expression. It's the kind of early November night that promises you winter is coming, without the weight of its chill. Twinkle lights drape the trees in the middle of the mall, dancing across the brick pavers, transforming the town into a sparkling wonderland of golden glow.

Neither of us are talking, we're just taking in the sights. We weren't the only people with this idea, the stores are still busy, restaurants are crowded, and everyone around us seems to be feeling the warmth of the upcoming season.

The sky is inky black and speckled with stars. I don't even realize I've stopped walking until Miles stops next to me. "The stars are so pretty," I whisper.

"They are," Miles murmurs. He laces his fingers through mine, his warmth sending a tingle up my arm.

"You haven't been surfing much after work," I muse, neither of us have taken our eyes off the star-speckled sky.

Miles inhales and tugs me in toward him, so our bodies are flush together and our noses touch. "I've had other things I'd rather be doing," he whispers, tipping my chin toward his.

I giggle. "Oh, I get it. Me."

Miles cracks a half smile. "That's not what I mean, Jenna. Though that part has been nice too." He swallows, and suddenly, words tumble out of him. "Jenna, before I met you, I was barely living. I woke up, I went to work, I took out random girls and moved on quickly." He grimaces. "Then I met you, and everything changed. I feel alive again. I don't care about surfing anymore." He hesitates, lolling his head backward. "Well, okay, I don't care about surfing *everyday* anymore. I still love surfing because it makes me feel alive. But so do you. More alive than I've felt in years," he croaks out that last part and my chest fills with warmth.

"That's really nice, Miles," I whisper, wrapping my arms around his torso and nuzzling into his chest.

He pushes back. "No, Jenna, you don't understand. I don't know what's going to happen tomorrow and maybe I'm reading everything wrong. Maybe you're still going to leave me in a few weeks—but if I don't say this now, I never will." He audibly gulps, licking his lips. "I'm falling in love with you, Jenna. No." He shakes his head. "I'm not falling anymore. I am *in love* with you. So much that I wish I could spend every single second of the day with you. Just to be near you, watch you. I'm enamored with you."

A tear rolls down my cheek. I'm not sure anyone has ever been so blatantly honest with me before, certainly not in a nice way. "Miles..." I sniffle. "No one has ever said anything like that to me before." I blink rapidly to ward off tears, but they fall anyway.

Miles laughs, thumbing away a tear on my cheek. "Okay, good. Because it's true."

I suck in a breath for courage. “I love you, too.”

“You do?” he asks, his voice sounding froggy.

I nod. “I do.”

“I was hoping you’d say that.” The grin that spreads across his face makes my heart burst. He leans down, cups my face, and kisses me hungrily, as if this new declaration has ignited something in him.

I pull away and his thumb lingers on my lower lip. “Miles, take me home,” I whisper and it’s not a question.

“There is nothing else I’d rather do.” He laces his fingers through mine, and we trek the fifty feet back to the car.

Chapter Thirty-Four

Telling Jenna I love her is so freeing. I'm absolutely floored that she loves me back. We can't get home fast enough. My confession has awakened something dormant inside both of us. I'm going to tell her about her dad first thing in the morning. I can't spoil this evening, but I know it's time.

I pull into my parking spot and Jenna is out of the car before I can get around to open her door. She stands on the curb, looking at me like I just hung the moon.

I walk over to her with purpose, cupping the back of her head, tangling my fingers in her hair, pulling her into a kiss full of emotion and need. She opens her mouth for me and deepens the kiss. My desire grows against her, but it's more than wanting to have sex. We've done plenty of that these past few weeks. This means so much more now. I belong with Jenna. I feel it in my bones.

She pulls back from our kiss, her warm breath tickling my lip. Her eyes search mine and she brings her hand up to my jaw, gently running her fingers along my stubble.

"I can't believe you love me," Jenna whispers. "It's been a really long time since anyone besides my mom has said that to me."

"I love you more than I ever thought possible," I murmur, moving her hand from my jaw and kissing it.

"Let's go upstairs." Jenna eyes me seductively and pulls me up the steps to my condo. She frantically unlocks the door and pulls me inside. "Hey, Pete," she calls, but she bypasses him and heads straight for my bedroom.

I follow her, closing the door behind me. "Jenna." I grin. "You're on a mission."

"Shh," she whispers, putting her finger to her lips.

Jenna steps in front of me. Without taking her eyes off mine, she begins unbuttoning my dress shirt. My pulse quickens with anticipation. When it's completely undone, she slides it over my shoulders, letting it fall to the floor. She tugs the hem of my undershirt up and over my head so I'm bare-chested. A chill runs over me as her lips find my chest, and she begins kissing me across my collarbone and shoulders. Jenna takes my arm and kisses all the way down my bicep and forearm until she gets to my hand. Her warm lips press against my palm, and I suck in a breath. She smiles into her kiss before slipping my index finger into her mouth, gently sucking.

I grow hard and impatient, tugging her hips into mine. "Don't I get to take anything off of you?" I growl.

Jenna pretends to think about it, tapping her chin with an index finger. "I guess so." She bites back a grin. "Pick one thing."

I roll my head backwards and before I can choose, she starts undoing my belt and unbuttoning my jeans.

"Hey, now," I rasp, cupping her chin. "It's my turn." I pull her pretty, pink blouse over her head and bend down to kiss her chest, while simultaneously working the clasp on her bra. Finally, her breasts are free, and I waste no time enveloping one with my mouth.

Jenna lets out a hiss. "I said one thing," she teases, gripping my hair, enticing me to suck harder.

"You don't get to be in charge," I mutter with her tit still in my mouth. "I want to explore every inch of the woman I love tonight." At this, I stop kissing her and look her in the eyes. "I love you, Jenna," I murmur, and my voice comes out hoarse.

"I love you, too," she whispers, her eyes glistening.

"Damn right you do." I scoop her up and she squeals. I carry her over to the bed and lay her gently on it. I undo the button on her jeans, and she shimmies them off, revealing a black satin thong. I lean down and kiss from her rib cage, all the way down to her hip bone before sliding off her panties.

"Your turn." Jenna twirls her finger in a gesture that indicates she wants me naked.

"Yes, ma'am." I bite back a smile and step out of my jeans.

"All of it." Jenna sits up and tugs the waistband down on my briefs.

"You run a tight ship." I step out of them and climb onto the bed next to her, wrapping her into a little spoon, letting my dick settle between her thighs. I kiss her neck, running my hands up and down her legs.

She sighs. "Miles," she moans.

"I know," I groan. "But I want to take my time with you tonight."

Jenna rolls over to look at me and I brush her hair away from her forehead. "Tonight feels different between us, doesn't it?" she breathes.

"Because it means more now—at least it does to me. I let myself fall." I pull her into a hungry kiss and lose myself in her until the wee hours of the morning.

ଓ

I wake up Saturday morning with a contentment that I haven't had in years. Jenna is tucked in the crook of my arm, softly breathing on my chest. She sleeps so peacefully, I can't bear to wake her, I am absolutely enthralled by her. I brush hair out of her closed eyes and she stirs, her eyes fluttering open.

"What time is it?" she murmurs.

I lift my head and glance at my phone on the bedside table. "It's nine-thirty," I say. "You can go back to sleep. I know we were up late," I tease, biting my lip.

Jenna sits up and turns over to look at me, a grin on her face. Something happened last night. Aside from just sleeping together, Jenna and I reached a new level of intimacy. We spent the night exploring every part of each other's bodies, multiple times. In between, we talked about our childhoods, our dreams, what we wanted for the future. I've never been so connected to someone in my life. I can hardly believe that it's me she's waking up with. I have no idea how I went my whole life without this woman. "We tired ourselves out." Jenna giggles. "But, I have work today," she reminds me.

It's now or never, I clear my throat. I've got to get this off my chest now that I know for sure that Jenna is who I want to spend my life with. "Jenna, before you go to work...I have to—"

Jenna gives me a sultry grin. "You want more already?" She nuzzles her nose into mine.

I chuckle. "No, I mean, yes. But no. I have to—"

I'm cut off by a knock at my front door. We eye each other, frowning.

"Are you expecting someone?" Jenna's brows knit together.

"Not at all. It's probably a solicitor," I growl, tossing the blanket off my legs.

Jenna sits up so I can get out of bed. She follows suit and finds some clothes in her bag while I rummage around my clean, unfolded laundry basket for something to wear. She beats me to it.

"I'll get the door," she says.

She got dressed awfully fast.

"Maybe I can use my charm to shoo them away." She grins at me as she walks out of the room. "Come on, Pete." I hear her say.

The knocking is becoming more incessant, and I can't help but think this person is very persistent.

"Oh, hello," Jenna chirps from the entryway. "How can I help you?"

The person on the other end must be just as taken aback by Jenna's beauty as I am because it's a moment before they speak.

"Oh, um...sorry. Is Miles here?" The voice is uncertain, and my stomach immediately sinks.

Erin.

I dash out of the bedroom to the foyer, where the woman I love stands face to face with the woman I once loved very much. No one is speaking—they're sizing each other up.

"Erin." My voice comes out hoarse.

Jenna whirls around and meets my gaze, licking her lips. Then, she turns back to Erin.

I clear my throat. "What are you... What are you doing here?" I stutter, raking my fingers through my unkempt hair.

Erin glances awkwardly at Jenna and then turns her eyes back toward me. "Can we... –Can we talk?"

"I'm...going to...just—excuse me." Jenna turns on her toe and marches back toward the bedroom.

"Jenna," I call after her, dragging a hand down my face. "Ugh," I groan. I point at Erin. "Please, wait here."

I don't wait for a response before I dart down the hallway. Jenna sits in the middle of the bed, her legs folded beneath her. She doesn't say anything when I come in, she just watches me warily. I sit down on the edge of the bed.

"Jenna," I manage to rasp out. "I have no idea what she's doing here, I promise."

Jenna licks her lips and nods. "Yeah. Okay." She sucks in a breath and pushes herself off the bed, grabbing her purse. "I should get out of your way so you can talk to her." She starts shoving some things in her bag, deodorant, her toiletries.

I catch her arm. "Jenna, stop it." It comes out like a growl. I swallow the panic rising in my chest—I've upset her, and I haven't even talked to her about her father yet. I pull her into me and cup both sides of her face. "This doesn't change *anything*," I murmur, kissing her feverishly.

Jenna pulls away and meets my gaze with a nod.

"Jenna, I love you," I say firmly. "I don't know what she wants, but it doesn't change anything."

"Okay," Jenna whispers.

"I love you," I say again, this time more emphatically.

"I love you, too," she relents. "I'll see you tonight." She slings her purse over her shoulder and brushes past me.

I follow her out, glancing at Erin, who's already made herself at home at the kitchen island. I ignore her and follow Jenna to the door.

"Call me when you get a break," I say, tugging her close again.

"I'll try." Jenna shrugs, all the warmth from her face gone, replaced with a line of concern over her brow.

"Jenna," I mumble, pressing my forehead into hers. "This is not how I saw this morning going."

"Me neither." She pats my chest, forcing me to take a step back. "You better go see what she wants."

I lean down to kiss her, but she quickly turns and my lips land on her cheek instead. "Jenna," I bemoan, but she's already down the steps.

I take in a sharp breath and close my front door, leaning against it for a moment before facing Erin. With a defeated sigh, I walk back toward the kitchen. Pete watches Erin cautiously from the couch. I round the island and square my shoulders, looking at Erin.

"Bad time?" She lets out an awkward giggle.

"Yeah. You could say that."

Chapter Thirty-Five

Jenna

I close my car door, taking a moment to collect myself before I drive away. It's at this moment I realize how little I actually know about Miles and his previous relationship. But I know I didn't have to leave. And he's told me he loves me no less than fifty times since last night. That seems important. But when I said I was going, he didn't try to stop me. He didn't try to introduce me to her but I also didn't give him the chance.

I let out a frustrated groan and throw my head back against the seat. Life is really unfair sometimes. I lost my dad, then my mom, then my job. I'm underwater in this godforsaken house. Just when I think I might have found happiness with Miles, anxiety creeps back in. He's given me no reason to doubt him but I'm still scared. If Miles was as good to her as he is to me, she probably realizes she lost something good and wants it back. What if when he sees her and wants her back, too? I could just really use a win right now.

I can't bring myself to pull out of the parking lot for a good fifteen minutes. I tell myself it's because I can't calm the anxiety that's camped out in my chest, but deep down, I'm hoping it's a short conversation and I'll see her come back out. I never should have left. I should have asked to stay and hear what she has to say. I know that's irrational though. It's likely a conversation they need to have privately.

I shudder and suck in a breath, throwing my car in reverse. I think about calling Morgan and unloading on her but I know how busy she is. Then I think about calling Joy, but she'll probably say *I told you so, it is Miles after all.* So instead, I drive to my house. I'll get ready for work, put on a brave face, and do the best I can until I can talk to Miles.

I'm surprised when I pull up to find Danny's truck parked in the driveway on a Saturday. He's coming around the side of the house with a large piece of drywall when I get out of the car.

"Jenna!" He calls. "I wasn't expecting—" His face falls and he quickly sets the drywall on the grass before rushing to me. "Jenna, are you okay?"

All I can do is nod—no chance Danny wants to be caught in the middle of this.

Danny steps in front of me. "Is it Miles? Did you two fight?" I can see why Danny has been married for so long; the care and tenderness in his voice immediately puts me at ease.

"Erin came back," I say with a defeated sigh.

Danny's jaw falls open, but he quickly fixes it. His lips form a tight line as if he's thinking about what to say next. "Jenna, listen to me. That means nothing. I'm sure of it."

I shake my head. "I left so they could talk, and he didn't stop me," I mumble.

Danny sighs. "They probably do need to talk but—" he pauses, "Jenna, Miles really cares about you. I saw him married, and I see him now. He's never been this happy before. You have to believe me on that."

I shudder and nod, prepared to step away from Danny and go inside.

"Come on, give me a hug." He pulls me into a big brother hug. "I know he'll call you as soon as she leaves."

"I hope so." I pull back from the hug. "Thanks, Danny. I needed that."

Miles doesn't call me though. He doesn't call me for my entire shift. There is a tiny part of me that expects him to walk through the door at any moment, but as the hours wear on, I lose hope.

Around one o'clock, I text him. It goes unanswered. I text him again at two-thirty, no reply. Panic begins to fill my chest.

"I hate to say it, Jenna," Joy begins tentatively.

I hold up a hand. "Then don't," I snap. "I'm sorry, Joy. I just don't want to hear about what a bad guy he is when less than twelve hours ago, he was telling me how much he loves me." I let out an exhausted sigh.

Joy nods, chewing on her lip. "Okay. I'm sorry," she says softer this time. "Listen, I'm good here for today, why don't you scoot out early? Go see what he's doing."

"Are you sure?" I ask hopefully.

Joy gives me a grim smile. "Yes, of course. Call me if you need me."

ଓ

It's three o'clock by the time I get to my house. Danny's truck is gone, and there are no lights on. I park in the driveway and check my phone. Still nothing from Miles. I can't believe I haven't heard from him. I cave and press the call button on his contact. It rings six times before going to voicemail.

"You've reached Miles Corbin of Cape Reality. I'm either on the phone or away from my desk. Please leave a message and I'll return your call as soon as possible." It beeps.

I immediately hang up. It's only a couple of hours until my dinner with Aunt Leona and Jake. I've got to get myself cleaned up. Maybe by the time I shower and fix myself up, Miles will have called. It's been six hours now. Where is he?

I go inside, and even though the ceiling is patched and there's a tarp on the roof, it's still drafty downstairs. I can't possibly sleep here. I go upstairs and strip my clothes off, stepping into a shower so hot it'll leave my skin raw. I leave my phone on the vanity, and I can't help myself, every few minutes I peek out of the shower to see if I have a missed call. Nothing.

Twenty minutes later, I'm out, dressed in jeans and a sweater, putting on makeup for tonight's dinner. I blow dry my thick waves with a diffuser and for the first time in a long time, I like how I look. *I wish Miles could see me.*

My phone buzzes with a text but it's not Miles; it's Jake.

Jake

Hey, Mom is wondering if you can bring some old photos over when you come tonight?

I haven't even begun to root through them, but Miles mentioned seeing boxes labeled family photos in the attic during the inspection. *How hard could it be?* I clean up my makeup and toiletries, stuffing them back in my tote bag. I'm still hoping to go back to Miles's condo tonight. Coincidentally, Aunt Leona lives on the other side of the same complex. If I haven't heard from Miles by the time dinner is done, I'll go over.

I mosey into the hall and grab the drop-down cord for the attic. I flick on the hallway light and give the cord a yank, revealing a wooden ladder folded up. I tug on the ladder and open it. Once it's sturdy, I climb up into the musty attic. Miles was right. There are boxes and boxes of photos and photo albums. I climb all the way into the attic. The ceilings are too low for me to stand up, but I can sit on the cold plywood floor. I scootch back and pick the first box in front of me.

Inside, there are a variety of photo frames in different sizes wrapped in newspapers. I unwrap the largest one. It's an old collage frame filled with pictures of me as an infant. Some of them are just of me, some are of my parents holding me. I feel a pang deep in my chest and blink rapidly to fend off the tears stinging the back of my eyes. My parents were so in love. My eyes catch on a photo of them holding me in a christening gown. They're gazing down at me as if I'm the most beautiful piece of art they have ever seen.

I sniffle and wipe my nose with the back of my hand. Setting that photo aside, I keep rummaging. More frames fill the box, each wrapped in old, yellowed newspaper. I gingerly unwrap them and find a few photos of Jake and me at the beach, holding our boogie boards. Then one of us with my dad, we must have buried him. He's covered in sand and grinning with a floppy sun hat on. I find one of my dad and Aunt Leona at what looks like my parents' wedding. Near the bottom of the box is another large frame, also wrapped in newspaper, but before I can unwrap it, the headline on the paper catches my eye.

I freeze.

The words blur for a minute before snapping into focus, and when they do, my stomach drops. I unwrap the frame as carefully as possible, so I don't rip the article. I don't even bother to look at the photos.

I run to my phone.

There is still nothing from Miles.

"What the hell, did he *know*?" I ask my empty house. "He must have," I whisper. I grab the article, photos forgotten, and hop in my car.

Chapter Thirty-Six

Miles

I'm so emotionally exhausted from the surprise visit with Erin that I immediately fall into bed. Jenna has work today—I should call her and make sure she's okay. She left here in a hurry when Erin showed up unannounced, marched into the kitchen and made herself at home. As if the last two years never happened. But I'm in no shape to talk to Jenna right now.

My head is pounding and I wince, rubbing my temples as I recall the conversation.

"You can't just show up here like this, Erin." I had said. It came out harsher than I meant it too, but I was already spiraling after the woman I love walked out the door.

Erin looked like she had rehearsed something to say but her face fell at the sound of my voice. "I'm here for Sadie's wedding... she said you aren't going." Her voice was quiet. "I just wanted to see you."

Sadie was one of Erin's first friends when she moved here. I'd been invited too but I declined—I knew better.

Erin cracked a joke about my surfer hair; said I look well. She tried to make me laugh but I kept my distance, preferring to remain on the opposite side of the kitchen island.

"I miss you, Miles," Erin said after fifteen minutes of torturous small talk. She reached across the space for my hand.

I pulled back.

Then she asked if I thought we made a mistake. I shook my

head adamantly.

"No," I said. "We didn't make a mistake. You *broke* my heart." I muttered. "And even still, if this were three months ago, I might've considered...this." I wave at the space between us. "Seeing where it goes." I shook my head. "Not now. It's too late."

"Is it because of her?" Erin asked but she knew the answer.

"Yes," I said.

"Do you love her?" Erin had asked, her expression anguished.

"Very much," I said. I didn't move. I would not apologize for moving on.

That's when she fell apart—loud, aching sobs that used to destroy me. Not anymore. I still felt sorry for her—but not for *us* anymore. When it was clear she wasn't going to win me over, she turned angry. She criticized me for the way I treated her. She said I love-bomb every girl I date until I smother them, and they leave me. But somehow it was still *my* fault we broke up—that I didn't try hard enough to keep us together.

I just sat on the couch and took the abuse. I let her berate me until she tired herself out. I told her I *did* try. But my protests were weak. I gave everything I had to that marriage, and it was never enough. Maybe that's the part I needed to come to terms with: *I was never enough.* When she grew tired of the fight, she left and slammed the door. But instead of feeling relieved, I feel wrecked all over again.

It's not that I want Erin back. Not even close. But seeing her is a stark reminder that I failed our marriage. She reminded me how fast love can disappear. And now Jenna's gone too.

I pull the covers up to my neck and lay on Jenna's pillow, inhaling the scent of her shampoo. It does little to bring me comfort. I close my eyes, letting the weight of the morning pull me under, but I'm haunted by a persistent thought as I drift off. *What if I'm the reason it never works?*

ଓଃ

I wake up hours later in a panic. Jenna's side of the bed is empty. The room feels drafty. I wipe sleep out of my eyes and look around, confused. Some of Jenna's things are gone, the rest are scattered across the room. I reach for my phone and see that it's four o'clock. Jenna has called and texted me multiple times. I haven't spoken to her since she left this morning.

I fucked this up. I can't believe I never called her. "God, you asshole," I groan.

I let Erin get in my head. I let her come in here and make me feel terrible about myself and my new relationship, just because I wouldn't cave to her. She didn't get her way, and she reminded me what a fuck up I am. Now, I'm actually living up to that. I'll never be good enough for Jenna.

A loud banging on my front door startles me. If it's Erin again, I'm really not in the mood. I throw myself out of bed and walk to the door just as Jenna barges through it. Relief floods me—until I see the expression on her face. She's pale, her eyes red and puffy from crying. She's holding a newspaper article. A golf ball size lump forms in my throat.

You have to tell her, because if she finds out on her own, it's going to blow up in your face, my mother's stern voice echoes in my mind.

"Jenna," I breathe, walking toward her, ready to throw my arms around her in relief.

"Miles, what the fuck." Jenna stops in her tracks, and much to my dismay, does not fall into my open arms. She waves the newspaper article at me. "What is this? Did you know about this?"

"Know about what?" The words taste like a lie. I *know* I'm screwed.

"This!" Her voice trembles. She thrusts the article into my hands.

My hands shake as I take it, skimming the page, terrified to look up.

Bucks County man dies after rescuing teen.

By TERRI FLETCHER

The Press of Atlantic City

A Bucks County man is dead of a heart attack on the beach after rescuing an unnamed minor caught in the rip current caused by Tropical Storm Bertha. Nicholas Rossi, 40, of Bucks County, PA was enjoying a beach day with his wife and young daughter when the storm clouds rolled in. "We gathered our stuff quickly and rushed to the car," his wife Anna told The Press. "I wanted to get out of there but Nick said he couldn't leave those boys surfing when he knew how bad the rip currents were. That's when he heard someone screaming for help. He left our daughter and I in the car and ran back to the beach. That was the last time I saw him alive."

Nick Rossi, once an elite college swimmer, had to have known the dangers of going into an angry ocean but he didn't let it stop him. Onlookers say as soon as the boys were safely on shore, Rossi collapsed, unfortunately suffering a massive heart attack. He died a hero.

"We're so grateful to this stranger. He gave his life for our son, and we'll never be able to repay him," Susan Corbin , the minor's mother, told the Press .

"It was my dad." she says, the words barely audible, like it hurts to say them. She swallows hard. "My *dad* saved *you*. Did you know?" Her voice wavers and she wipes at her eyes, waiting for an answer. Jenna's gaze is wide and uncertain, silently begging me for reassurance. Her lips tremble as she searches my face for something—anything—to hold onto. I know she wants me to say I had no idea, and I can't do that.

I can't lie. I look up from the article, sadness enveloping me. I wasn't prepared for this to be over. If she was going to forgive me for the Erin incident this morning, she surely won't now. I press my lips together and stare longingly into her eyes.

"Did you *know?*" she shouts. "Miles. I need the truth."

I swallow and nod, never taking my eyes off her. "I suspected," I rasp. "After the day at the beach." I take a step closer to her.

Jenna lets out a broken sound—half gasp, half sob and then glares at me. "Why wouldn't you tell me?" Her voice cracks. She doesn't wait for an answer. She turns and runs down the hall into my bedroom.

Helpless and ashamed, I follow. She shoves her things into a pile, hands shaking, face streaked with tears.

I lean in the doorway, watching, unsure of where to begin. "Jenna," I begin slowly. *Say something, you idiot.*

"I thought I could trust you!" she hisses. "My world has been falling apart, but it was okay, because I found you. And you love me. But none of that is true, is it? If you *loved* me, you'd never have kept this from me." Jenna crumples to the floor, tucking her knees up to her chest, lost in silent devastation. Her tears fall quietly but the weight of them is crushing. When she manages to speak, she says, "My dad would be alive if it wasn't for you. You have no idea what this feels like. To be hopelessly in love with the man who took my father away."

"Don't you think I know that? Don't you think I feel terrible? Trust me, I'd have rather died if it meant he got to live, and you got to keep your dad." I'm unsure if she wants my comfort or my excuses but this is tearing me apart. Her anger at me confirms my worst fears—I'm a failure at this. I'd never be good enough for her.

When she doesn't respond, I swallow the knot in my throat and continue, prepared to beg. "Jenna, I tried to tell you this morning. Before—before we were interrupted," I mutter.

She looks up from her knees, wiping her eyes and sniffling. "That's another thing. Where were you all day?"

I wince as if I've been slapped. I have no excuses. I left her to worry about me all day, and I have been carrying around this secret for weeks. "I was sleeping." I shrug weakly.

"Sleeping?" Jenna scoffs, standing up. "What? I left here

upset, and you went back to bed?" Jenna scoops as many of her belongings as she can hold in her arms.

"The conversation with Erin exhausted me, I'm sorry," I say defensively, holding up my hands.

"Well, Miles, clearly I was wrong about you," Jenna mutters, sniffling again.

"Jenna, you weren't wrong about me. I love you—don't you want to hear my side of the story?" My chest constricts with rising panic. If she walks out of here, it will be impossible to get her back.

Jenna drops the pile of clothes on the bed and puts her hands on her hips. "Sure, Miles. Let's start with this. How long have you known?"

I audibly gulp and force a steady breath.

"*How* long have you *known,* Miles?" Jenna demands sharply, narrowing her eyes. She must realize it's been a while.

I stare at my feet. "I figured it out that day at the beach. I started suspecting it when you said your dad had a heart attack there," I say hesitantly. "So, I asked my mom. The day I built her skeleton. She didn't remember his name, just that he had a young daughter...and that he died. I didn't know until skeleton day that the man who had saved me had died, I swear." I shift uncomfortably.

"Your family knows?" Jenna's voice rises. "You let me go to dinner with them yesterday, and everyone there knew but me?" Jenna starts collecting her items again.

I exhale. "I don't think anyone knew for sure..." I let my voice drop, unsure how to make this better.

Jenna glares at me. "Miles, you kept a *life-changing* secret from me." Her eyes fill with fresh tears. "How can I trust you now?" She brushes past me. "I need some time," she calls over her shoulder.

I close my eyes, feeling the sting of my own tears. I fucked up. *Of course* I fucked up. It's what I do. I should go after her but what's the use? I'm no good for her. She's better off without me.

Chapter Thirty-Seven

I race down Miles's steps, my vision clouded with tears and the pile of clothes in my hands. I unlock the backseat of my car and throw the clothes on the seat and slide in next to them, taking a moment to collect myself. I need to control my breathing and calm down, but my pulse is racing. I can get through this. I'm used to being on my own. In fact, I might prefer it. Sure, I got swept up by Miles for a bit, but that was just fun. Maybe there was even a part of me that expected this to happen. I was naive to think I could rely on anyone but myself to be my safe space. I can't trust that Miles loves me for me—or if he loves me out of obligation for his life.

Still, I let myself feel it all. I cry harder than I've cried in weeks as reality sets in. I thought maybe I found a place here with Miles, but I was wrong. I am alone. I will probably be alone forever. I know I *can* be alone—but I was hoping not to be. Self-pity settles over me like a thick fog. I have no home to go back to, no job, and I owe way too much money on this house to ever be able to afford to stay here. And how could I? Memories of life with my parents here are reflected in everything.

I love my dad so much.

Why did he have to go back that day?

I lost my dad because he saved the boy who would grow into the man I love.

"I cannot believe this is happening," I cry to no one but myself. My feelings are all over the place. And still, there's a part of me that wishes Miles would come running down the steps. I really believed there was something real between us. Now, I don't know what to believe—I feel so deceived.

As soon as my breathing is under control, I text Morgan.

It's over with Miles.

She FaceTimes me immediately, holding one of her babies in a rocking chair.

"Geez, Jenna," she gasps when she sees my puffy red face. "Are you okay? What the hell happened?"

So, I fill her in. I tell her how he told me he loves me, and dare I say I saw her swoon. Then I tell her how Erin showed up this morning, breaking up our lovefest.

"That bitch," Morgan growls. "I can't even believe that. And he just let you walk out the door?"

"Yes." I wipe at the fresh tears streaming down my face. I fill her in on the photos in the attic, the article, and what happened when I confronted Miles. "Now I'm sitting in my car and dinner at Aunt Leona's is in twenty minutes. I'm a complete disaster."

"Oh, Jenna." Morgan's face crumbles. "I'm so sorry," she whispers.

"What am I going to do, Morg? I can't stay here." I tremble. "I thought I could, but I need to get out of here as soon as possible."

"Well, take some time to sleep on it. You can come here, I told you. We'll help you get back on your feet." Morgan's reassurance immediately sets me at ease. *I'm not alone.*

I'm startled by a knock on the window, but it's not Miles, it's Jake.

"I've got to go, I'll call you tomorrow, Morgan." I sniffle and hang up.

I push open the car door.

"I thought that was you. Mom's condo is on the other side," Jake says cheerfully, but concern clouds his features when he sees me. "Jenna, what the hell? Are you okay? Move over."

I push the clothes I'm lying on to the floor and scoot over, letting Jake slide into the backseat. "What did that asshole do to you?" Jake snarls.

"Do I need to go knock down his door? I know where he lives," Jake growls, gripping the door handle.

I grab his arm. "No, Jake. Don't." I sit up and wipe my eyes. "I have to ask you something." I chew on my lower lip, raw and chapped from tears and the cold air.

"Anything," Jake says, shifting his body to face mine.

"Did you know that my dad died rescuing a kid—and that it was Miles?" I hold my breath waiting for his answer.

Jake sighs, defeated. "I did, yeah. I wasn't sure you knew but that's why I told you I didn't want you to get hurt." Jake looks down at his hands instead of at my face.

"I thought you were worried he was a serial dater," I mumble, wiping my nose again. "It feels like everyone knew but me."

Jake reaches into the pocket of his hoodie and pulls out a tissue.

I smirk, blowing my nose into a tissue. "You just carry these around with you? You really are the son of an Italian lady."

"Hey, I have a cold." He gives me half a smile. "Listen, I only knew because when your mom took you back home all those years ago, my mom was pissed about it. She knows Miles's family and she wanted her to meet them. My mom thought she might feel better if she saw that Uncle Nick saved a kid, helped a family. But your mom refused."

"She was depressed for *so* long. That's all I can remember about that time in my life. My mom never got out of bed. She called out of work all the time. I got myself ready for school, made my own lunches. I would come home from school and crawl into bed with her and all we would do is cry." I let out a breath and close my eyes. The memories are too painful to endure.

"I know. For a while, my mom and dad would call your mom, asking her to move you guys down here. I think my mom really hoped she would at least talk to the Corbins, but one day, your mom flipped out. She told my mom to leave her alone and never call her again...so she didn't." Jake reaches for my hand. "I was so happy to see you at Drexel. To know you were doing okay."

I shrug helplessly. "I mean, I don't know when things started to get better, but they did, eventually. My mom found a therapist. We both went. We healed. But she never wanted to come back here." I sniffle. "So much so, she didn't clean out the house at *all*. I guess that's my job now."

Jake is quiet for a moment before asking, "So, what happened with Miles?"

My eyes fill again, and I use the tissue to catch the falling tears, sniffling. "He knew. I *just* found out that he's suspected for weeks who I am. He never told me."

Jake lets out a puff of air. "Wow. I mean, I knew too. But you aren't dating me, so I get how you might feel betrayed."

"I don't have anywhere to go now. I have no roof on that stupid house. It caved in. I was staying here, but I can't anymore. I'm not sure if I can be with him knowing what I know now." I worry at my chapped bottom lip.

Jake's lips form a tight line, deep in thought. He pulls out his phone. "Let me tell my mom we're a bit late. We'll figure this out." He hammers out a text.

"I think I'm just going to tell Nate to handle the sale and move down south with Morgan. There's nothing here for me." I wipe my eyes and begin to gather myself. "Do you have another tissue?"

Jake pauses mid-text to hand me a mini pack of tissues. Then he looks at me. "Jenna, you have me. My mom. We're here for you." His tone is serious but comforting. "*We're* your family. Don't you remember the fun we used to have?"

I shift in my seat. "I do. But you don't even know me anymore."

Jake laughs, eyeing me sideways. "It doesn't matter. Blood is blood, Jenna. You can't leave. You can stay with me or my mom—God, she would probably love that—at least through the holidays. We will help you figure this out if you let us."

I nod slowly. *Jake and Aunt Leona want to be my family. I'm not alone.* "Okay, maybe."

"Good. I'm starving. Can we get out of here now?" Jake jokes, half-heartedly.

"Yes," I say, shaking my head and wiping at my tear-streaked cheeks. I feel a little better. "Let's get out of here."

ɞ

"Sorry, Mom!" Jake calls, pushing open Aunt Leona's front door.

"It's okay, dear." Aunt Leona walks into the entryway, drying her hands on a dish rag.

I thought I did a pretty good job pulling myself together, but Aunt Leona notices immediately. She rushes forward, wrapping me in a maternal embrace that makes me miss my own mom. "Jenna, sweetheart, what happened?" She pulls back, examining me.

"Why don't we talk about it over dinner?" Jake suggests, making for the kitchen. Aunt Leona has set the table and poured three glasses of red wine. Heavenly-smelling covered dishes sit in the center. It's the portrait of a family meal and something I haven't experienced myself in ages—aside from dinner at the Corbin's last night. The memory makes my throat burn. "Come on, I'm starving."

My lips turn upward, despite my mood. *No wonder Jake is still single.*

Aunt Leona links her arm through mine and leads me into the small dining room. Her condo view isn't as good, and the condo itself isn't as modern as Miles's but it's cozy and warm. Leona's kitchen opens to a dining area, divided by a half wall. The walls are painted a deep beige. She has a brown sectional couch with big, fluffy cushions in front of a gas fireplace that I imagine myself sinking into. Her balcony is smaller than Miles's, but you can still see the ocean.

"You can sit there, dear." Aunt Leona gestures to a seat in the middle of the round table, herself and Jake on either side of me. She makes herself busy, taking lids off the dishes and filling our plates with roasted chicken, vegetables, and mashed potatoes. Jake and I are quiet, watching. When she finally sits down and pulls her chair in, she reaches for my hand. "Please, tell me why you look so upset."

Jake clears his throat. "Maybe she'd like to eat first, Ma?" He raises his eyebrows at his mother.

I shake my head, taking a bite of mashed potatoes. "No, it's okay. There's a lot going on right now."

"She was dating Miles," Jake interjects. "You know, Miles Corbin. She just found out..." His voice trails off.

"Oh, Jenna," Aunt Leona sighs as a look of realization crosses her face. "I'm sorry. That must be very painful for you."

I close my eyes as tears start to well up and then open them again. I swallow the knot in my throat. "It's only painful because he kept it from me. If he had told me right away, I probably would have thought it was some kind of fate." I snort through my tears and blot them away with my dinner napkin.

"Maybe it is." Aunt Leona shrugs. "The Corbins are great people." A wistful look crosses her face. "In fact, the reason they have managed your house all these years is because of our friendship. We used to be much closer but... When everything happened and your mom took you away, Susan was upset. She really wanted to meet her. It became a point of contention between us." Aunt Leona takes a sip of her wine.

"I know they're great people. They're lovely. It's just, I've had a lot of hurt in my life. I really can't take being lied to," I mumble. "It's more than that though. I have nowhere to go. My house is missing a roof. It's a money pit. I lost my job right before I came here. I'm just feeling very lost."

Aunt Leona's face softens, and she scoots her chair closer to mine, putting an arm around me. "I'm sure Jake already told you this, but you aren't alone. You have us."

I nod, forcing myself to take a bite of food so I don't start crying again. My head pounds like a jackhammer, like my brain might explode from overthinking and crying all afternoon.

Aunt Leona scoots her chair back to her side. "You can stay here if you'd like. I have a nice guest room."

"Thank you." I sigh with relief. "Maybe just tonight, until I figure out what to do with myself."

"I think you should stay through the new year," Jake suggests. "What's the sense in uprooting your life now? You can avoid Miles. I'll handle the sale if you want me to. Just don't go running away yet. Let us help you." He offers me a reassuring smile.

"I would love your company," Aunt Leona adds. "I'm practically begging Jake to visit his old mama every week."

Jake scowls. "Not true. I take good care of you," he grumbles.

I glance between the two of them, fighting the swell of emotion that's blossoming in my chest. Miles might have broken my trust, but here is my family, whom I haven't seen in twenty-five years, ready to take me back in. "I am so grateful," I say, putting my fork down. "But, it's been so long. I just... I worry you won't like me."

Jake laughs. "What?"

Aunt Leona ignores him. "Jenna, you're our family. Your mother and I didn't see eye to eye at the end, but your dad was my brother. I loved him very much. I will not just throw you out on the streets to fend for yourself."

I meet her warm gaze and nod. "It does feel really good to be near family."

Aunt Leona squeals. "Good! Then it's settled. You belong with us."

I smile at her, feeling better for the first time today. This morning, I woke up feeling sure that Miles was the one for me. I'm not ending my day with him, and I don't know if I ever will again, but at least I have people to lean on. I may be picking up the pieces of my life, but at least I don't have to do it alone.

Chapter Thirty-Eight

After Jenna left, I took Pete down to the beach and threw the ball for him until my arm hurt. Then I went back inside and fed him before falling into bed, exhausted from the emotions of the day.

Now the sun is casting its morning glow through the gap in my curtains, startling me awake. I slept through the whole night. My hand drifts to the space next to me—empty and cold. Jenna didn't sleep next to me for the first time in weeks. The realization that I may have lost her forever hits me with the brute force of a wave. I fumble for my phone. Jenna's name isn't there—no missed calls, no messages.

I waste no time tapping her name. It doesn't even ring. Immediately to voicemail. *What have I done?* My stomach twists and a wave of nausea passes through me.

I tap back to my home screen—I have other text messages, one is from Erin, the other is from Jake Walker.

I reluctantly open Erin's.

Erin

Miles, I'm sorry for yesterday. I'm leaving town this afternoon. I'd love to see you before I go and clear the air. Call me, please.

I am not in the mood for more of her bullshit but the nice guy in me feels terrible that she was so upset yesterday. There are so many things left unsaid between us—seeing her was like pouring salt on every open wound I still have. I need to stitch them up, once and for all. I text her back:

George's Place - 11:00.

I begrudgingly open Jake's text. *What could he want other than to flip on me about Jenna.* I'm right:

Jake

Stay away from my cousin, asshat.
You really hurt her.

Frustration bubbles in me. I know I hurt Jenna. How could I not? But I had every intention of telling her about her dad before she found out on her own. I'm so angry at myself. I'm afraid it's too late, afraid I'm not good enough, and petrified to let her go. I don't answer Jake; I have to deal with Erin first. I don't have much time before I'm supposed to meet her, so I roll out of bed and head for the shower, hoping to wash away my shame.

When I get out, I don't feel any better. If anything, my chest feels heavier. I call Jenna again. This time when I get her voicemail, I leave a message: "Jenna, please call me. I'm so sorry, baby," I rasp. I pause, caught off guard by the wavering of my own voice. "I love you, Jenna. Please, can we talk? Call me." I hang up and follow it up with a text saying the same thing.

Then, I throw on a pair of gray sweatpants and a hoodie. I feed Pete and take him for a quick walk before going to meet Erin and finally put this to rest, once and for all. I'm jogging down my steps, heading for the sidewalk when I spot Jake, pacing around the parking lot. His head snaps in my direction the second he sees me, like he's been waiting.

"Dude, what are you doing?" I scoff, giving Pete's leash a tug.

"Sit, boy."

"I was hoping to catch you, Miles." Jake walks over. His words come out rough and he faces me with squared shoulders, as if to antagonize me. "I texted you."

"Yeah. I got that." I raise my eyebrows. "What do you want, Jake?"

"You really hurt my cousin." Jake narrows his eyes, staring me down. "I'm not happy about it."

I let out an impatient groan, but I level my eyes with his. "Jake, this is between me and Jenna. We'll work it out." I start to walk away, and Jake grabs my arm.

I turn around sharply. "Are you looking for a fight, Walker?" I shake my arm from his grip.

Jake doesn't falter. In fact, he steps closer. "I always knew who you were, Miles. I warned Jenna, but I should have told her the truth, knowing you wouldn't. If I had, maybe she wouldn't be hurting right now."

I roll my eyes. "You act like I had nefarious intentions, Jake. I love Jenna. If anything, this revelation is even more reason we should be together."

"Yeah, well, she doesn't want you anymore," Jake growls. "You two are done."

I smirk and narrow my eyes at him. "Please, like you have *any* say in what that girl does. Why don't you mind your own business?"

"Jenna is my business. She's my family," Jake says. "And I am asking you nicely to leave her alone."

"Why don't you let Jenna decide for herself if she wants to be left alone, Jake?" I start to walk away again, and this time he doesn't stop me. He knows I'd take him out in a fight. I keep walking though. I wouldn't do anything else to jeopardize my chances with Jenna, no matter how much I want to put my fist in his face.

"Maybe I will," Jake calls after me, but we both know his little intimidation tactic didn't work.

I laugh, shaking my head. "Yeah, you do that."

ঔ

Erin's waiting for me at a small café table when I walk up to George's Place. She's sipping a cup of coffee from the place next door, her posture stiff in the wrought iron chair. It's a breezy mid-November morning and I'm surprised she's sitting outside, but maybe she means for this to be quick. I hope so.

"Erin," I greet her tersely.

Erin stands quickly when she sees me. "Miles, hi."

I gesture to the front door. "Did you want to eat inside?"

Erin shakes her head. "I think it's probably better if we don't share a meal. We don't have to stay long." She sounds uncertain but I'm not going to beg her to stay.

I nod, pulling out my own chair. "Okay, well, let's have it then."

Erin takes a deep breath. "Miles, I'm sorry. I had no right to show up there yesterday."

"No, you didn't. So why did you?"

Erin winces. "Are you sure you want to know?"

I stare at her with wide eyes. "Uh, yeah. You really may have messed things up for me with Jenna. So, I'd love to know your earth-shattering reason for blowing up my life."

"I was afraid of that. I'm embarrassed to tell you this, but some of my girlfriends have seen you around town with her. They said you went to a Halloween party as a *couple*. You never did that with me." She chews on her cuticle before continuing. "I just got jealous. I know I left you but *I'm* the one who's still alone. *I'm* the one who messed up. I thought if you saw me...you might miss me too." She looks down at her cup of coffee.

I rake my fingers through my hair. "I'm sorry, Erin. There's no going back."

"I know. I realize that now. I am really sorry about everything." She looks away, refusing to meet my gaze.

"Thank you," I say quietly.

"Have you talked to her yet?" Erin asks.

I scratch my chin, shaking my head. "No, no. I really don't want to talk about it."

"Okay." She pushes her chair back and stands. "I should get going."

I do the same. *This was easier than I anticipated.* "Okay."

"Can I have a hug?" Her voice trembles when she asks and the sadness on her face tugs at something inside me.

I never meant for things to be this way. "Of course you can," I relent, opening my arms.

Erin steps into them and holds on tight. She pulls back, holding my hand for a moment before turning to go. "Bye, Miles," she mutters softly.

"Bye, Erin." I lift my hand, giving her a half-hearted wave.

Erin walks away, and ease settles over me. Halfway there. If I can just get Jenna to talk to me, maybe she'll see what I see: we're meant to be. But my relief is short-lived when I feel a pair of eyes on me. I look up to see Joy, giving me a death glare. "Hey, Joy," I call, waving.

Joy doesn't reply, she walks into the coffee shop, never taking her narrowed eyes off me. Just great.

I pull my phone out of my pocket as I walk toward my car. There is nothing from Jenna. I hit the call button, and it actually rings before going to voicemail. "So, her phone is on," I say to myself. I call again. This time it goes to voicemail after only two rings. She declined me. I hammer out a text:

Me: Jenna, please talk to me. I love you.

For a moment, the three dots are there, and I get my hopes up, but nothing ever comes. There is nothing else to do but go home. I climb into my car and crank the seat warmer. It's cooler than I thought. As I drive, I find myself going in the direction of Jenna's house. I don't think about it, I just drive. I turn slowly down Monarch Street, anxiety rising in my chest, my heart hammering. My eyes sting from exhaustion, despite ten hours of sleep.

When I pull up to Jenna's house, there's no one there. The house is dark, her car is gone. Where could she be? I assumed she went home last night after her dinner. She must be with Jake. That must be why he came for me. I get out of the car and walk around the house, eyeing the exterior work Danny and his crew have already done. The tarp is still on the roof, but the foundation work looks almost complete. I wander back around front and sit on the stoop. "How did things get so messed up?" I say to no one.

I'm terrified of losing Jenna. At the same time, I'm afraid of her coming back and hurting her. I already failed once. Maybe it's better if I cut her loose now—save both of us from the heartache. I know deep down I won't be able to do that, though. Jenna has changed me forever. She cracked something open in me that I'd thought was sealed shut forever. Before Jenna, I was drifting through life, going through the motions—avoiding anything that required me to feel too much. She brought warmth back into my life, made everything matter again. Her quiet strength, the way she carries on with life despite everything she's been through—even when she's falling apart. She makes me want to be a better man. I just have to hope that I changed her in some way too—that some part of her believes I'm worth staying for.

I groan and walk back to my car. The two surfboards that never leave my roof rack beckon me. I haven't been to the beach for a couple of days. Every time something in my life happens that feels too overwhelming, the waves have been there. I crave the rush of adrenaline, wondering if I can conquer them each time, feeling invincible when I do. I walk around to the trunk, checking for my spare wet suit. It's there. I hop in the driver's side and do the only thing I can when I feel like I'm drowning. I drive to the beach.

Chapter Thirty-Nine

When I open my eyes in Aunt Leona's guest room, I'm confused. I've forgotten everything that happened yesterday, and I'm grappling at the space next to me for Miles's warm body. I don't find it. Then the memory comes crashing into me like a freight train.

Miles lied. He betrayed me.

The panic of never seeing him again rises in my chest, and I have a sudden, desperate urge to talk to him. I grab my phone. He's called twice and texted. I'm just about to hit call when I hear Jake's voice.

"Jenna, are you up?" he calls down the short hallway.

I toss my phone aside and meet him at the bedroom door. "Hey," I say, suddenly conscious of wearing my satin pajamas in front of my cousin.

"I just saw Miles in front of his condo," Jake blurts, pushing his way into the room.

"What were you doing all the way over there?" I frown. "It's the other side of the complex." The color drains from my face as I make the connection. "Were you *waiting* for him?"

Jake shrugs, looking embarrassed. "Maybe. I just wanted to talk to him."

I put my hands on my hips. "Listen, I know you think you're making it better, but you're not." I exhale my frustration and close my eyes for a moment. "Please, stay out of it, okay? Don't talk to Miles."

Jake looks ready to argue but he closes his mouth. "Fine. But you shouldn't either."

I turn away from him and back to my phone. "I'll figure it out," I mutter, picking up my phone.

"I'm just trying to help, Jenna." Jake's voice sounds wounded and defensive all at the same time.

I shoot him an apologetic look. "I know. I get that. I just have a lot going on in my mind and...I have to figure it out." I look down at Miles's text and start to type back, but then something stops me. No matter how much I love him, he kept something huge from me. He might love me, but he wouldn't have done that if he *respected* me. I set the phone on my nightstand and start making the bed. Jake is still standing in the doorway.

"What are you going to do?" he asks me, his voice tight with uncertainty.

"I'm going to have brunch with Joy. And then, I don't know." I shrug. "Maybe go get the rest of my stuff from the house."

"Let me know if you need any help," Jake offers halfheartedly.

"Thanks, but I think this is something I have to do on my own. I'll see you later." I offer Jake a small, weary smile, a polite cue to go.

When he finally does, I get dressed and try to bring myself back to life in the bathroom. My eyes are puffy and bloodshot from all of the crying I did yesterday. Dark circles have settled under my eyes, showing my exhaustion. My face is blotchy, my expression weary, and remnants of yesterday's sorrow linger on my features. I do my best to cover it up and put on a happy face for Joy, my only friend here.

Half an hour later, I'm walking up to the coffee shop to meet Joy, feeling moderately better. That is until I see the melancholy on her face as she leans against the brick building, waiting for me.

"Joy, what's the matter?" I rush to her side. "You look awful."

Joy takes my hand in hers and leads me to a bench. A shiver runs through me—I'm suddenly afraid of what she's about to say. "Let's sit down," she says cautiously. "How are you? Have you talked to Miles?" She chews on her lip.

I frown. "Actually, there's so much more to the Miles story than Erin coming back to town." I exhale deeply. "I was going to fill you in over brunch but..."

Joy looks at me expectantly. "Don't hold back on me now, Jenna," she retorts.

"Well, okay. I don't have a huge appetite anyway," I mumble. I suck in a sharp breath and let it out forcefully. "Last night I learned that my dad died performing a rescue—Miles was the boy. Back in 1997. He collapsed on the beach right after."

Joy's jaw hangs open. "No shit," she murmurs. "Did Miles tell you that?"

The question triggers me, and my eyes well up with tears. I shake my head and Joy puts her arm around me. "When I left the store, he still hadn't called me back. I decided to go to my house and take a shower to get ready for my dinner with my aunt." I sniffle and reach in my pocket for a tissue.

Joy nods. "Okay, go on," she urges.

Everything spills out at once. I tell her how I kept peeking out of the shower to see if my phone was lighting up, and how I worried while I dried my hair, and chose an outfit. Finally, I tell her about finding the photos and the article.

"I hope you confronted his lying ass," Joy cuts in sharply.

I wipe my eyes and nod. "Well, I wanted to give him the benefit of the doubt at first, so I drove over and asked him about it. But he hesitated when he answered, and that's when I knew he had been keeping it from me." A new round of tears starts to fall.

"Oh, sweetie," Joy squeezes me, and I rest my head on her shoulder, grateful for the physical contact.

"Then it occurred to me that he was at his condo all alone, so why hadn't he called me? He said he was *sleeping*," I say incredulously. "Can you even believe that?"

Joy pushes her lips together in a tight line and the expression reminds me that when I walked up, she looked upset. "Actually, I think I can," she mumbles.

When I look at her expectantly, she caves.

"I saw Miles this morning," she says carefully. "He wasn't alone."

My heart hammers in my chest and I suck in a breath, meeting her eyes. "Okay. Was he with Erin?"

Joy nods sadly, pushing her lips together. "I only saw them as they were saying goodbye." She pauses. "But they hugged for a long time and held hands." Joy's face crumbles. "I'm so sorry. I wanted so badly to believe he changed."

I shrug and suck in a cleansing breath. "You know what? It's okay. Knowing that makes me feel a little better." I look down at my tightly clenched fists and slowly open my hands, nodding to myself. I glance up at Joy. "At least, if he gets back together with his ex-wife, it makes his lying to me okay, in some twisted way. Like we weren't meant to be anyway. Does that make sense?"

Joy gives me a grim smile and solemnly nods. "It does, I think." She stands up and offers me her hand. "Come on, let's get some brunch. Carbs make everything better."

"You can say that again," I agree, following her inside.

For the first time in twenty-four hours, I feel like I might be okay.

Chapter Forty

Miles

I spend all of Sunday surfing. I don't know what else to do to take my mind off Jenna and how much I royally fucked everything up. The ocean used to be my place of solace, where I'd go to clear my head. But since I've shared it with Jenna, I can't do that anymore. It's too painful; memories of her bobbing on her board, smiling over at me, her expression open and trusting. She trusted me to teach her how to surf and to keep her safe and she trusted me with her heart, and I let her down. Floating on my board before riding the next big wave is no longer soothing but tainted by the fear that I've lost Jenna forever.

"I'm so stupid," I mutter to myself.

That doesn't stop me from trying though. I surf for hours in the icy waves, chasing that rush of adrenaline—feeling momentarily better when I catch it. Time and time again, my ocean and my beach have been there for me. When I'm pissed off or sad, I come here, and I fight it out with Mother Nature. A knock down, drag out reckoning of my own creation.

The sky turns pink and purple as dusk approaches. I glance at my watch, wanting to catch the first stars tonight, but my body is depleted. The cold November air and the havoc I just wreaked on my body causes convulsions as I hurriedly throw a towel around my shoulders. So much for seeing the stars tonight. I tuck my board under my arm and head toward my car. I'm stepping out of my wet suit and into some sweatpants when my phone buzzes. I tried to forget my phone—and the fact Jenna hadn't responded to any of my messages while I was surfing. Most of this is of my own doing, I know that. Keeping that secret from Jenna—and then her finding out after seeing Erin at my front door—that's all on me. I hate myself for hurting her. I just hope I didn't ruin things with us forever

I climb into the driver's seat and tug a hoodie over my head. I turn on the car and blast the heat to seventy-six degrees before looking at my phone. Jenna's name illuminates my screen.

Bile rises in my throat. I'm sweating, despite the chill in the air. I have a sinking feeling that this text isn't going to be good. I take a breath, willing myself to calm down and tap on the text.

Jenna

Miles, I think it's better if we let things cool off for a bit. Maybe Nate should handle my house stuff from here on out.

"No!" I slam my palm into the steering wheel. "Damnit," I mutter. *I knew it. I lost her.*

My chest caves in and the exhaustion overwhelms me. I don't even have it in me to text her back and fight for her. I can't believe I ruined this. I throw the car in reverse and peel out of the lot. Without Jenna, nothing else matters.

ଔ

I'm late for work the next morning. I arrive just after ten, catching sight of my reflection in the glass windows. I didn't look in the mirror once this morning. I *know* I look like hell—I didn't sleep. My T-shirt is rumpled, my jeans are dirty, and my hair is stiff like straw from the salt water. I brought Pete to work today because I feel bad for ignoring him yesterday, but even he is looking at me with pity.

I swing open the door and our assistant Linda gasps, covering her mouth.

"Dude," Nate deadpans. "Why do you look like your dog died?"

I scoff, raking my fingers through my hair. "He didn't die. He's right here. Aren't you Pete?" I look down at my apathetic dog who plopped at my feet the second we walked through the door.

"Miles, dear, are you okay?" Linda's brow furrows with concern.

"I'm fine." I wave my hand casually, walking over to my desk.

"You look terrible, bro," Nate states the obvious. "You shouldn't be here."

I scowl at him. "This is my business, too. I can show up to work however I want." I pull out my desk chair and flump into it, crossing my arms indignantly.

"I'm going to get us some coffees." Linda announces. She pushes back in her chair and hurriedly makes for the coat rack.

"There's plenty of coffee in the back, Linda." Nate juts his thumb over his shoulder.

"I'll just give you boys a minute." Linda smiles tightly, slipping into her coat, and then she's out the door.

When she's gone, Nate whirls his chair around to face me. "Dude, what *happened?* Why do you look like this?"

I heave out a heavy sigh. "Jenna and I broke up. I think." I slump forward on the desk and bury my face in my hands.

Nate lets out a sympathetic sigh. "Oh man. She found out about her dad before you could tell her, didn't she?"

I lift my head, glancing sideways at him. "Yeah," I mutter. "And..."

"And?" Nate raises his eyebrows expectantly.

"Erin showed up at the condo the day after I told Jenna I love her," I grumble.

Nate lets out a low whistle. "That's bad." He nods, lips pursed.

"I know," I growl, agitated again. I'm going back and forth between exhausted, defeated, and irritated.

Nate pushes his lips together, narrowing his eyes. "So, what did Erin want and how did Jenna find out about her dad?"

I groan and then recount everything that happened on Saturday. When I finish, Nate gapes at me. He lets out his second low whistle in ten minutes.

"Yeah, this isn't great for you." He turns back to his computer. "I'm not really sure I have any helpful advice but dude, I saw the way that girl looks at you. I know you can make things right."

"I'm not so sure," I mutter. "Oh, and she said it's best if you handle the sale of her house." I shake my head, dragging my hand down my face. "Man, I really fucked this up."

Nate turns back to me. "Well, I don't know about that, but I do know you're not going to get her back looking like that." Nate wrinkles his nose. "Go home, bro. Take a shower. The right thing will come to you. It'll be okay."

I frown, then a light bulb goes off. "I know! I'll make her a playlist."

Nate lets out a puff of air. "Bro. That's not exactly what I meant. Go get some rest, will you? Come back tomorrow."

I catch my reflection in the dark computer screen that I haven't bothered to turn on. "Fine. You're right." I push in my chair and put my jacket back on. "Let's go, Pete."

ଓ

Before heading home, I stop by Sunset Blooms. I used to pop in here every Friday to surprise Erin with wildflowers. It got to the point where my bouquet was ready before I even called. Not because I wanted to bring her flowers all the time, but because I was trying to make her stay. Even before she said it, I think she had one foot out the door. I would have tried anything to make her happy. Flowers didn't work for Erin, but maybe they will for Jenna.

I park and check my reflection in the rearview mirror before I go in. I run my fingers through the mop on my head and slap my cheeks to wake up. Then I jog inside. Tina, the owner, is about ten years older than me, and she's a genius with flowers. I could call her with any budget and she'd put together a beautiful arrangement.

"Miles!" Tina greets me with a broad smile that quickly falls when she sees my face. She recovers quickly though. "I haven't seen you in a while. What brings you in?"

I sigh, defeated. "I need a bouquet that says *I'm a giant asshole and I'm so incredibly sorry.* Can you make me something?"

Tina grimaces. "Yikes. What did you do?" She starts puttering around at the various flowers in buckets and tubes behind her, gathering the prettiest ones.

"It's a long story," I mutter, feeling embarrassed, even though I don't need to be.

Tina turns back to me and her expression is reassuring. "Well, whatever it is. I'm sure you'll make it right, Miles."

"Thanks, Tina." I pull out my wallet and lean on the counter. "Do you have a card I can write in?"

Chapter Forty-One

Monday comes quickly, and I wake feeling resigned to what I always knew—Miles and I were temporary, it's over now. I'm okay alone; in fact, I am used to it. I will be okay. But even as I tell myself this, a heaviness settles in my chest. I am a stupid girl for letting myself be hopeful. I thought perhaps Miles might be my person, but I cannot believe how wrong I was.

I never could trust my instincts. Growing up, I often perceived things that weren't really there. In high school, I thought for sure my boyfriend was cheating on me with my best friend. I kept hinting around at my suspicions, but all I did was make them both mad at me. When the relationship ended, they actually did start dating, and I was left with no one. My instincts were wrong then, and they're wrong about Miles, too.

I trudge down the hallway to the bathroom and turn on the shower. While I wait for it to heat, I scroll back through his apologetic text messages. I want so badly to hear him out, but he betrayed me in a way I never expected. I can't help but wonder if there's a reason things worked out this way. Maybe I'm not meant for Miles and instead, I'm meant to stand on my own two feet. All I really know is the only person I can truly rely on is myself. I let myself fall for Miles and in turn, I became dependent on him. And where did that leave me? Heartbroken. It's time I get serious about what I am doing with my life—without thinking about Miles. I don't dare listen to the voicemails he left though; if I hear his voice, I'll cave.

"No," I say to my reflection. "This is how it has to be."

After my shower, I find Aunt Leona sipping her coffee on the couch and watching *Good Morning America*. She smiles and gestures to the TV. A very attractive actor about my age, whose name is escaping me, is being interviewed.

"Isn't he handsome?" Aunt Leona murmurs, nodding toward the screen.

I force a smile before walking over to the coffee pot. "He is," I agree.

I fix my coffee and join her on the sofa, putting my mug on the end table and tucking my feet under me.

"So, how did you sleep?" Aunt Leona asks. "I hope you're finding everything you need."

I nod, sipping my coffee. It tastes burnt. "I am, thank you."

"Are you okay, though? You've been awfully quiet." Aunt Leona's brow softens and she scoots closer to me.

"I'm a little sad," I admit with a helpless shrug. "I thought Miles was different."

Aunt Leona purses her lips. "Maybe he is. Did you give him a chance to explain?"

I shift uncomfortably. "Sort of. I heard enough to know he kept the secret from me for weeks." I exhale. "I just can't believe he kept it from me. And it's my *dad*. I lost my dad and Miles lived and *then* kept it from me. I just don't know how to move past that."

Aunt Leona purses her lips thoughtfully. "I understand. But, did you ever stop to think that maybe he wasn't keeping it from you? That he knows how delicate you are and he was trying to figure out how to tell you?" She doesn't wait for me to argue, instead she gets up and walks back into the kitchen, patting my shoulder as she passes. You have to do what's right for you." She peeks around the corner. "You can stay here as long as you like."

"Thank you." I slurp another sip of burnt coffee. "I'm going to get the rest of my things from the house today, I think."

Aunt Leona comes out of the kitchen and hands me a plate

with a warm blueberry muffin, a melting slab of butter sandwiched in the middle. "That sounds like a good idea,"

I spend an hour with Aunt Leona, drinking coffee and catching up. I will admit, she and Jake are the silver lining in all of this. I came to Cape May feeling lost and alone. Since arriving, I've connected with long-lost family members, and now I know I'm *not* alone. I might be heartbroken, but I'm not alone.

"I better get on with it," I mutter, standing and carrying my dishes into the kitchen.

"I'll be here if you need me!" Aunt Leona calls. *Oh, to be retired.*

My first stop of the day is Cape Realty. On my way out of Aunt Leona's complex, I drive by Miles's side and see his car isn't there. I am running the risk of seeing him at his office, but the sooner I cut ties, the better.

I pull into the parking lot, relieved to see only two cars—neither of which are Miles's.

I look in the rearview mirror, fluff my hair, and swipe on a little lip gloss. It's amazing what a shower and a little makeup can do when you're sad. My trauma bangs are finally growing out. I won't be making that mistake again.

"It's now or never," I tell my reflection. I don't know how long it'll be before Miles is here.

I pull open the glass door and the wind catches it, swinging both me and the door backward—drawing attention to myself.

"Hello, how may I help you?" A sweet voice greets me.

Before I can respond, Nate says, "Jenna." He coughs. "I wasn't expecting you. Miles is...not here."

I clear my throat and suck in a breath. "I actually came to see you."

My words hang in the air before Nate gathers himself enough to respond.

"Oh," Nate says. "Well, then, please come sit." He gestures to the chair in front of his desk.

I offer his secretary a small smile, tucking my hair behind my ear as I walk by. I sit down in front of Nate, and for the first time notice how much he resembles Miles. With the exception of having shorter hair, Nate could be Miles's twin. It's startling, and I have to ignore the twinge in my chest at the sight of him. "So," I say.

Nate offers me a remorseful smile. "So." He meets my eyes. "What can I do for you?" His expression is open and trusting. I trust him.

I chew on my lip for a moment, knowing what I'm about to say will change things in a way I may not be prepared for. "I think it would be a good idea if you managed the sale of my house now..." I pause, wincing, "instead of Miles."

Nate sighs. "Jenna, I know you're upset," he begins.

I hold up my hand. "I'm beyond upset, Nate. I can't work with Miles anymore." My voice catches, and suddenly, I'm afraid I might cry. Something tells me if I did, Nate would handle it with gentle grace.

He nods apologetically. "I get it. And it's probably bringing up all kinds of complicated feelings about losing your dad. I've dealt with loss too, so I understand how you feel." He pushes his lips together, pausing. "Miles knows he messed up. We all warned him keeping that secret would backfire." Nate shakes his head sadly. "This is going to kill him." He meets my eyes, giving me a chance to back out.

I take a deep breath. "I just can't let myself be hurt anymore. Please say you'll help me, Nate."

Nate closes his eyes and then opens them again, scraping his hand down his face. "You're putting me in the middle of you and my brother, Jenna. He's my best friend."

I catch a single tear escaping from my eye with my thumb and Nate notices. He lets out a relenting breath. "Okay. Fine. I'll take over."

I shudder and offer him a shaky smile. "Thank you, Nate. I know it's awkward for you, but this means a lot to me. And I'm sorry for your loss, too." I push back my chair and stand to go. "I'll be in touch when I hear from Danny," I say, walking toward the door.

"Jenna?" Nate calls after me.

I turn back around. His jaw clenches, then loosens. Whatever Nate wants to say, he's struggling with it.

"Yeah?" I ask, waiting.

"For what it's worth, Miles really does love you. You should see the guy. I sent him home. He looked awful." Nate shrugs, helplessly.

My heart constricts at his words, and my eyes well up again. If I talk, the floodgates will break, so all I can do is nod. I put a hand to my mouth as if I can stop the avalanche of tears, and walk out.

ଓ

When I pull into the lot on Aunt Leona's side of the complex, I see him. He's parked diagonally across from me, sitting in his car. If he sees me, he'll try and talk, and I'm not ready for that. I sit for a few moments, watching him, my heart thundering in my chest. Finally, I decide to just make a break for it, hoping he doesn't see me. I manage three paces before I hear my name.

"Jenna." Miles's voice is hoarse.

I close my eyes, stopping in my tracks, and sucking in a breath. Then I keep walking without looking in his direction.

"Jenna, please," Miles begs. "Please talk to me."

I stop, sighing, and turn to face him. He looks like I feel—his hair is disheveled, his clothes are rumpled, and the look of torment on his face matches the storm inside my chest. The sight of him almost has me running into his arms. He's holding the most beautiful bouquet of pink roses, white lilies, and eucalyptus. A small card sticks out of the top of the bouquet

"Please," he says again. "Jenna, I'm so sorry I broke your trust."

It takes me a moment to find my voice and when I do, it comes out wobbly. "I know you're sorry, Miles," I murmur. "But—"

"No." He takes a step closer to me. "No, don't say but." He shakes his head, as if to clear it.

Against my better judgment, I step toward him. He thrusts the bouquet at me, and I take it. I close my eyes, inhaling the beautiful, comforting scent, then slowly meet Miles's gaze.

"These are lovely, thank you," I start slowly.

"Jenna, I love you," Miles pleads.

I shake my head, holding up my hand. "Miles, you don't. You might have thought you did, but maybe we rushed into things. I'm just so sad—about you, about my dad. I need some space." My eyes well with tears, but I rapidly blink them away. I can't let him see me cry.

"No. We didn't rush into this. *This* found us." Miles moves so he's standing in front of me. He catches my elbow, and I force myself to ignore the sizzle bolting up my arm at his touch. Even when I'm mad at him, the chemistry between us is electric. Another few minutes here, watching him plead for forgiveness, and I'll be putty in his hands.

I close my eyes, then open them again, attempting to control my emotions. "I accept your apology," I say calmly.

Relief floods his face, and he runs his hand up and down my bicep, sending a shiver throughout my body.

I take a step back, being this close to him, when emotions are this high, is dangerous to my resolve. I shake my head, and his face falls.

"I just need some time to figure this out. I haven't dated anyone seriously in years and...all of this feels really heavy." I look down, pushing my lips together to fight off the threatening tears.

"Jenna," Miles rasps. "I love you so much. What can I do?"

I slowly bring my eyes up to his and shrug. "I don't know, Miles. Just let me figure this out on my own," I say sadly, averting my eyes to the pavement between us.

"Let me fix it, please." He steps closer, forcing me to back up.

"I can't, Miles. I'm so sorry." I turn and race up the stairs behind me, leaving him staring after me.

Chapter Forty-Two

Miles

A week has passed since Jenna ripped out my heart and stomped on it. After I gave her the flowers, my world came crashing down. I never knew what I was missing until I met Jenna, and now I have to go back to a life without her. The only problem is, I can't. I can't get out of bed. I haven't gone surfing or talked to my friends. I'm a mess, and I don't see the point in picking myself up.

On Monday morning, the week before Thanksgiving, there is a loud knocking on my front door. I'm sprawled on my couch, alternating between sleeping and staring at the ceiling. Pete barks, and the knocking gets progressively louder.

"Miles, let us in." My brother's voice bellows from the other side.

"Go away," I moan. "I'm fine."

"You're not fine!" My mother's shrill voice through the door startles me.

I scowl and roll off the couch. "You brought Mom?" I growl, stalking to the door.

I swing it open. Nate and Mom stand on the other side, worried expressions on their faces. Rightfully so, I guess, considering I haven't been to work all week. I just don't see the point anymore.

"Someone had to get you up and out of the house," Nate mutters, shaking his head. "Miles, buddy, you gotta do something."

"I'm fine," I assure them, turning and walking back inside.

I plop back on the sofa and my mom sits down next to me.

She pats my knee. "Miles, honey, you're not fine."

"I just needed a little time off," I tell them begrudgingly.

Nate sniffs the air. "Does time off mean not showering, taking the trash out, or washing dishes?" His face contorts—nose wrinkling, like he's trying not to gag—as he looks around my disordered condo.

"I'm just tired." I rake my hands through my hair. "You two interrupted my nap."

"This is an intervention." Nate raises his eyebrows. "You are going to get up, get your ass in the shower, and get to work."

"Make me," I scoff, folding my arms across my chest indignantly.

Nate looks to Mom for help.

"Miles, we're just worried about you," she starts slowly. "You're reminding me of how you were when Erin left. That wasn't good then, and it's not good now." My mother's eyes tear up, and something tugs at me deep in my chest. I can't handle seeing her cry.

Nate shakes his head, "No, it's worse. Erin was your *wife*, Miles. Jenna is just a girl you met a few months ago. Pick yourself up and move on." He sits in the armchair adjacent to me, resting his elbows on his knees and eyeing me cautiously.

"She's not just some girl," I rasp, batting at my eyes that unexpectedly sting.

"No, of course she isn't, Miles," Mom soothes, rubbing a hand up my back with a sniffle. "But you can't stay in here like this. You will never get her back hiding in your condo."

"I will never get her back, period," I growl. I didn't lose hope right away. After Jenna left me on the sidewalk, I ran into my condo and made her a playlist. I waited a day or two before I sent it to her, but when I did, she asked me to please give her some space. That's when the last of my hope dissipated. I have never been asked for space before.

"Come on, get up," Nate demands, trekking down the hallway. A moment later, the shower turns on.

I roll my eyes, glancing at my mom as if to say, *Can you believe this guy?*

"You should go take a shower, Miles. You'll feel better. You can't live like this forever." She pats my shoulder. "In the meantime, I'm going to clean up your kitchen." She stands and walks around the half wall into my small kitchen. "Oh my God, Miles, this is disgusting."

I turn around to find her grimacing, repulsed by the state of the sink.

Nate reappears a moment later. "Come on, the water is hot. Don't make me throw you in there." He holds his hand out to pull me up, then follows me down the hallway.

"Dude." I turn around sharply. "Chill."

"I'm just making sure you get in." Nate stifles a laugh.

"I'm going." I hold up my hands in surrender.

I close the door before he can say another word.

I stare at my ashen expression in the mirror. *You can't live like this forever.* My mother's voice penetrates my numb exterior. As much as I hate to admit it, Mom and Nate are right. I don't want to, but I've got to pick myself up. One look at my haggard appearance in the mirror, and I know it's time. Jenna won't take me back looking like this. I strip down and step into the steam, my skin tingling as the warm water cascades over my tense limbs. The hot water is deeply comforting, soothing my tense back muscles, filling me with surprising relief.

I close my eyes, letting the water fall over my face, rinsing away regret and offering a brief solace. It's been seven days of barely moving from the couch, stuck in a haze of guilt, self-pity, and take-out containers, each day blurring into the next. The silence of my phone is deafening, the last message from her reminding me that she doesn't want to see me. *It's probably better if Nate handles things from here on out,* echoing in my head like a song on repeat. But as I lather and wash, my thoughts untangle. *I've been so damn stupid, I've been wallowing in this...in losing her...but she's still in Cape May. And I'm not done yet.*

Renewed hope and motivation twist in my chest, the fog of despair dissipating. I suck in a deep breath, steam filling my lungs. Maybe I can pull myself together enough to get Jenna to talk to me. Who knew I only needed a shower to sharpen my resolve, to fuel my will to get her back.

"This isn't over yet," I say to myself, turning off the shower. I towel off and reach for my phone. We haven't spoken in over a week, I don't even know if she'll respond, but I have to let her know I'm not giving up. I pull up our text thread and take a steady breath.

Jenna, I know I messed up. But I'll do whatever it takes to fight for us.

I hit send and emerge from the bathroom more clearheaded and optimistic than I've been in days.

After I shower, Mom and Nate sit on the couch, waiting for me. They have tidied up and look relieved that I've put on clean clothes. Just gray sweatpants and a black thermal, but I don't smell awful anymore. I sit on the other side of the sectional, my lips slightly upturned to a smirk.

"Do you feel better, baby?" Mom asks, cocking her head at me.

I inhale and offer her a reassuring, albeit grim, smile. "I do, actually. Thank you." I gesture to the kitchen and living area. Nate has taken out the trash and recycling, and now the place smells vaguely of lemon. "And thank you for cleaning up."

"That's what we're here for," Nate says, scratching the back of his head. "But you need to get your ass back in the office next week." He raises his eyebrows at me. "Enough of this self-pity."

"Yeah, okay." I nod my head in agreement. "I'll be there," I promise.

"Speaking of next week..." My mother looks back and forth between us. "It's Thanksgiving!" She grins. She loves Thanksgiving more than Halloween. She spends days prepping and invites her sister, brother, and their families over. It always ends up being over twenty people. Caden loves it—more kids to play with. I usually love it, too, seeing family that we don't see often. This year though, my heart's not in it, and it won't be unless Jenna forgives me.

"We know, Ma," Nate says. "We'll be there."

"Who else is coming?" I ask, forcing myself to sound cheerful.

My mom rattles off a list of names; it's everyone that I expected. "And we're starting early—two o'clock for appetizers and five thirty for dinner."

"That...seems really long," I mutter, glancing at Nate. He shrugs.

"Just promise you'll show up looking like yourself, Miles," Mom begs.

I stifle a self-deprecating laugh. "Okay, Mom. I'll do my best."

"We should go, Mom. Mission accomplished." Nate looks my way. "I'm glad you're up and around, bro."

"Thanks," I say, standing to clap him on the back. "I needed that."

"You did," Nate agrees. "But you'd have done the same for me." He wraps me in a brotherly hug, clapping the back of my shoulder. "Now, go get her."

☙

Around four o'clock, I venture to The Ugly Mug, knowing my buddies will be there for Monday happy hour. I haven't met them here in some time. Aside from last week's wallowing, I spent every waking minute with Jenna. I haven't even opened our group chat or filled them in on what's been happening, but today, I could use their support.

These guys have been my friends since we were ten. They know I'm a good guy. I could stand to be around people who know me well. But also, I could really use their advice.

I park in the back alley and head inside, bracing for their

inevitable jokes. I swing the door open, and a gust of wind pushes me inside. It's quiet because it's November. Even though the town is getting ready for the upcoming holidays, there isn't a lot of street traffic on Monday afternoon. Still, without fail, I find my buddies in our regular corner, talking to Melanie and nursing their beers.

"Holy shit, he lives!" Jack bellows, spotting me first.

I fight back a grin, knowing there is probably more where that came from.

"Look who decided to grace us with his presence," Danny smirks, sipping his beer.

"Yeah, yeah, I know." I hold up my hands in defense, pulling out a bar stool next to Liam.

"I thought you were a figment of my imagination." He elbows me with a laugh.

"She let you out of your cave, eh?" Jack asks, raising his eyebrows.

It's now or never.

"Uh, no." I raise my hand to flag Melanie over. "Jenna and I actually broke up. Last week." I let my news hang in the air as Melanie comes over with my usual.

"Whoa, who died?" she asks, frowning at the four of us.

I clear my throat. "No one died. I just told the guys that Jenna and I broke up." My voice comes out hoarse and I cough away the emotion.

"Oh man, I'm sorry," Jack says sympathetically. "If I'd have known that I wouldn't have made that joke."

I shrug, scooting my stool in and taking a sip of my beer. "It's okay. I fucked up," I say, pushing my lips together and shaking my head.

"What could you have done?" Melanie asks, frowning. "She seemed to really like you."

Danny stays quiet—I'm sure he's seen Jenna and doesn't want to comment. I eye him, wondering what he knows.

I sigh. "I kept a secret from her for a few weeks and she found out about it before I could tell her."

"Oh no, Miles," Melanie whines. "I'm sorry." She pats my hand from across the bar.

"Really?" Danny asks, looking surprised with a lift of his brow.

"What do you mean, really?" I scowl. "Do you know something I don't?"

He scratches his chin and shrugs. "No, it's just, the day I saw Jenna, she was really upset...but not about a secret." He pauses, running his hand up the back of his neck.

"What?" I raise my voice, standing. "You have to tell me."

"Easy, boy," Liam says, chuckling, tugging me back into my seat.

I sit back down and take another sip of beer.

"I was at her house last Saturday working. She came by..." He hesitates. "She was really upset about Erin. I assumed *that's* why you broke up."

"Hold on. Erin? The fuck?" Jack shouts. "Mel, I'm gonna need another beer for this."

I groan and pick up my own, draining it in one gulp. The alcohol takes the edge off, and a fuzzy warmth envelops me. "Settle in, boys," I tell them. "It's a long story."

I fill my friends in on everything—from the realization of Jenna's dad being my savior, to introducing her to my family and falling completely in love with her. They all look so happy for me—until I crush the moment, retelling how Erin knocked on my door and ruined everything. "If Erin had never shown up, I would have come clean to Jenna that morning," I mutter, tangling my fingers in my messy hair.

"So, let me get this straight," Liam, who has been quietly listening up until now, finally speaks. "You told each other you were in love, woke up the next morning to Erin showing up, before you could come clean about her dad?"

I nod. "Yep, you nailed it." I smack my lips together. "I'm fucked, aren't I?"

Liam furrows his brow and pushes his lips together. "But

you're in love. That doesn't just *go away*. I don't think you're fucked per say, but you need a big gesture. Don't you remember? That's how I got Sophie."

"What kind of big gesture? Buy her something?" I glance between my friends.

Jack shakes his head. "No, dude. It's gotta be bigger than that. Even *I* know that."

We're all lost in thought until Danny snaps his fingers, breaking our silence. "What about something for her dad?"

"I don't know," I shake my head. "What would I do for her dad? He died so long ago."

Everyone is quiet again, lost in thought. I'm thinking about the day at the beach and how many times we surfed there together, when a lifetime ago, her dad saved my life. That's when it dawns on me, but I'll need help. I clap my hands. "I've got it." I stand up, throwing some cash on the bar.

"What?" everyone asks at the same time.

"I will explain later, right now, I have to go." I run out of the bar and straight to my parents' house. The only one who can help me with this is Councilman Corbin...my dad.

Chapter Forty-Three

A couple of weeks without Miles in my life feels like I've lost a limb. I can't believe I went from feeling so happy and taken care of to just, not. The funny thing is, most mornings I wake up feeling okay. I get ready for work, have breakfast and burnt coffee with Aunt Leona, and carry on with my day. On days that I don't have work, I research DIY projects to make the house more appealing to buyers. I have also been looking for jobs in South Carolina, near Morgan. My search isn't going so well right now, but that's not stopping me from looking. Occasionally, the loss of Miles hits me with a crashing wave of grief. I think it's really the loss of everything in my life that seemed sturdy. Thankfully, I have Joy, Aunt Leona, and Jake.

It's the week before Thanksgiving and the hardware store has been incredibly busy. Joy gave Leo and me more hours, and I am socking away all the money I can. Helping customers decide what they need keeps my mind off the current indecision in my life. I *am* sad, but I finally feel like I'll be okay, wherever I end up in the new year.

It's almost the end of my shift when the door jingles and in walks Jake and Aunt Leona. Jake is wearing a Santa hat, and I bark out a laugh. "Feeling jolly? You're a smidge early." I giggle.

"We thought we'd see if you wanted to come get a Christmas tree with us," Jake says, sauntering up to the counter while Aunt Leona peruses the LED lights on the carousel in front of me.

"A real tree?" I perk up immediately.

"What else is there?" Jake frowns.

I gesture toward the display of very realistic pre-lit, artificial Christmas trees at the back of the store. "Well, there are a lot of those," I say with a laugh.

"Nah. We need the real deal. What do you say?" He raises his eyebrows expectantly.

"I get off in ten minutes," I say slowly. "Let's do it! I haven't had a real tree since I was a little girl."

"Well, then you're in for a treat." Jake grins.

Aunt Leona comes up to the counter with several packages of multicolored Christmas lights and a star that twinkles. "Jake and I always listen to Christmas music while we decorate the tree, then we order Chinese food and watch a Christmas movie."

I grin, nodding. "That sounds wonderful, thank you for thinking to include me. Christmas may be a little sad for me this year," I murmur. "You know, it's my first one without my mom."

"How could I forget, sweetie?" Aunt Leona asks, patting my hand. "I know we're a little early, but Thanksgiving is so late this year. I like to look at the lights as long as possible."

"Sounds good to me," I say, grinning with excitement. I scan her items.

Joy comes out from the back, whistling to herself. "Oh, hello there!" She greets my family. *I have a family!* "How goes it?"

"We came to see if Jenna wanted to come with us to get a Christmas tree," Jake says, eyeing Joy with a bit of a twinkle in his eye.

"Oh, how fun!" Joy squeals. "I love Christmas!"

Aunt Leona swipes her card, and I hand over the bag of lights.

"You good here?" I turn to Joy.

She nods with a smile. "Definitely. Go have fun." She makes a shooing motion with her hand.

"Thanks." I grin, turning to get my hat and coat from the closet behind me. "I'll see you," I say, with a wave.

"Bye!" Joy shouts. Then a moment later, "Bye, Jake."

I can't help but notice Jake turning over his shoulder, grinning.

ଊ

Two hours later, we pull into Aunt Leona's parking space with the cutest little Douglas fir strapped to the roof. It isn't a huge tree, but it's definitely got some weight to it. Aunt Leona climbs out, and we assess how to get it upstairs.

"Well, I'm going to go order our dinner and get the boxes out of the closet," Aunt Leona says, whirling around and climbing the steps. "You two got this, right?" she calls over her shoulder.

Jake and I look at each other and burst out laughing.

Jake opens the driver's side door and stands on the side of the car so he can reach the rope. "You go on the other side and do the same." He gestures with a nod.

I follow his lead, but I can't reach the tree. "I can't get it," I tell him, groaning.

A throat clears behind me. My blood runs cold. It's been over a week since I've seen him, and I'm not prepared for the backflips my heart does immediately in his presence. I sense him before I see him. He comes up behind me, reaching around my shoulder and tugging the tree toward us. Jake tosses the utility knife without a word, Miles catches it and cuts the rope.

"I would have gotten it," I mutter.

His breath is hot in my ear. "I know you would have," he murmurs.

The back of my neck tingles at his closeness. I want nothing more than to turn my face toward his, kiss, and make up. But I keep my eyes focused on Jake instead.

"Step down, let me help Jake," he commands, but instead of sounding harsh, it's sexy as hell. I do as I'm told, stepping back to give him room.

The two men lift the tree, and with Jake in front and Miles in back, they make for the stairs.

"I really could have done it," I call after them.

Miles turns around, offering me a quick grin that turns my insides molten. *You're mad at him, Jenna. Remember.* I need a pep talk.

When I reach the top of the stairs, they're already inside. I force myself to take a deep breath, willing my pulse to slow down. Miles is just being neighborly. I brace myself and walk in. Jake is on the floor on his side, locking the tree trunk into the stand while Miles holds it up straight.

Aunt Leona is watching, arms crossed, directing them. "Miles, tilt it a little to the right." She points and he does. "There you go, that's it."

"Got it," Jake declares, sitting up. He stands and dusts off his hands before offering one to Miles. "Thanks, man. You made that easier than it would've been otherwise."

I gasp in mock offense and both men turn toward me, silence hanging in the air.

"What? Where's the lie?" Jake smirks.

"Miles, would you like to stay for Chinese?" Aunt Leona asks. Jake and I whirl our heads in her direction simultaneously, and it's not lost on Miles.

Miles chuckles awkwardly. "Thanks, Mrs. Walker, but I really should be going." He moves toward the front door, but as he brushes past me, he stops, reaching for my arm. "Can I talk to you?" he whispers.

My arm is sizzling under his touch. I want nothing more than to go back with him and curl up on that couch with him and Pete. I want to forget his betrayal ever happened. "Okay." My voice is faint.

Miles leads me outside and pulls the front door closed behind us. I lean against the wall for support, but Miles towers over me.

"Jenna, I miss you," he croaks. "Have you gotten any of my messages?"

I close my eyes and nod before meeting his smoldering gaze, burning right through my tough exterior.

He lets out a defeated sigh. “Okay then—” His voice is full of ragged emotion and if I let him continue, I’ll cave.

I hold up my hand. “Stop, Miles, please. I’m not strong enough for this,” I beg. Then quieter, “You broke my heart keeping that from me.”

Miles puts his right hand on the side of the wall, boxing me in. He drops his gaze to his feet, sighing. When he looks back up, his eyes are glistening. “I broke my heart too,” he rasps. “I guess this is it then.”

His body is so near to mine that I can feel goose bumps rising under my sweater. My stomach is in knots, his breath is tickling my neck. *Oh, how I want to stop him and say it’s not over.* The heat between us is scorching. Just because he hurt me doesn’t mean the fire went out. *But I can’t.*

“I got so hurt, Miles,” I murmur, refusing to meet his vulnerable gaze.

Miles pushes off the wall and walks away, raking his fingers through his hair in visible frustration. Then his eyes pierce mine with a determination that makes my insides heat and my thighs ache. “I will make this up to you,” he vows, and then he’s down the stairs, leaving me in dismay.

The delivery driver startles me out of my pity party a moment later with two overstuffed paper bags of Chinese food. It’s enough to feed ten people and far too much for the three of us. I thank him and take it inside.

“Food’s here,” I say, glancing at Jake, flat on his back stringing lights on the bottom of the tree, and Aunt Leona, perched in the chair, delegating.

“Oh yay!” She pops up. “I’ll get some dishes.”

“I’ll be right back,” I call, walking down the hallway to my room. Seeing Miles again stirred something deep inside me. His absence has left a hole in the rhythm of my days. A sharp ache spreads throughout my chest. I wanted so badly to melt into his arms and forget about all of it—nothing matters but the two of us. But that’s not true anymore, and so a quieter, sharper part of me won out, reminding me why everything ended in the first place.

Last week, when Miles brought me flowers, there was a card attached. I shoved it in my nightstand drawer without looking at it, but suddenly, I can't wait any longer. I have to know what it says. I yank the drawer open, pulling out the brown paper envelope, ripping it open in haste. There, in the center of the card is one sentence, written in Miles' scribbly handwriting:

I thought if I told you the truth, you would leave, and I wouldn't be able to take that. —M

A teardrop lands on his jagged handwriting, making the ink run. The truth is, it probably would have freaked me out, but I wouldn't have left. I am constantly looking for glimpses of my mother and father in everyday life. I look for signs that they're with me and that no matter how much I feel it sometimes, I'm not alone. The fact that my dad died saving Miles makes me feel like he's meant for me, if only he hadn't kept it from me.

"Jenna, you coming?" Jake's voice brings me back to the present.

I sniffle and drag my thumb under my eyes, wiping away mascara-tinged tears. "Coming!" I call, glancing at myself in the mirror. I really do look sad. I force a smile at my reflection. "Put on a happy face," I murmur to myself.

So, I do just that.

Chapter Forty-Four

I'm at work on Wednesday when Danny calls. I assumed he wouldn't be updating me on the job now that Jenna and I are over. I figured he'd update Nate, or Jenna herself. I answer anyway.

"Yo," I say, tapping the speakerphone button.

"Hey," Danny says. "Good news—Jenna's roof and foundation are fully repaired. You can list the house."

I glance at Nate who is listening to the call with interest. He raises his eyebrows at me. "That's great, Danny," I say slowly. "Shouldn't you have called Nate though?"

Danny laughs dubiously. "You mean you two still haven't made up? I told Jenna that I'd let you know, and she didn't tell me not to, so..." He makes a noise that sounds like *hmm.*

She agreed? As much as it shouldn't, hope blooms in my chest. *Maybe Jenna wants to see me.*

"Okay, thanks, man. I'll get in touch with her," I tell him, and we hang up.

"You're going to handle this now?" Nate raises his eyebrows judgmentally. "After she specifically asked for *me*?"

I nod, picking up the landline on my desk. "Yeah. I am."

"Okay," Nate says skeptically with a smirk.

I scroll through my phone until I find Jenna's number and then punch it into the desk phone, hitting the speakerphone button.

"Good call," Nate observes, laughing. "She's not picking up if she sees your name."

I ignore him while it rings. "Jenna, hey, it's Miles," I say, eyeing him sideways.

"Hi," Jenna says cautiously. "I was expecting Nate." I ignore the *I told you so* expression my brother is giving me from across the room.

I clear my throat. "Nate's a little busy this week," I pause, looking his way. "So, I thought I'd call you. I know you're anxious to get moving on the house stuff, and Danny says it's ready to be listed."

"Oh, um...okay." Jenna's voice is quiet.

"I could meet you over there, we can look at what he's done and then go from there?" I suggest, not bothering to hide the hopefulness in my voice.

"Oh, Miles." Jenna hesitates. "I don't know if that's a good idea."

I suck in a breath. "Okay, well, if you want to wait until he's back in the office right before Thanksgiving, that's fine too."

"No, you're right. Let's do it." Jenna's voice sounds far away.

"Great," I say, biting back a smile. "I can meet you in an hour?"

"Sounds good. Bye, Miles," Jenna says. She hangs up before I can respond.

"You sure more lying is a good idea?" Nate raises a skeptical eyebrow.

"What else am I supposed to do? She won't agree to see me otherwise." I push back in my seat and stand, putting on my jacket.

"If you say so," Nate mutters. "But if she asks, I knew nothing about this."

Nate, always the good guy. I roll my eyes at him. "Got it, Captain Honest. I'll see you later," I say, walking toward the door.

"Good luck," Nate calls after me.

Once I'm in the car, I dial my dad. I haven't followed up with him since stopping over the other night. Luckily, he picks up right away.

"Miles," he says, happily. "I know why you're calling,"

I let out a nervous breath. "Yeah? Do you have any updates for me?"

"The meeting is tonight," my dad says slowly. "I can't make any promises but send me the copy of what you'd like it to say. I'm going to try to get it passed through as soon as possible."

"That's great, Dad. Thank you," I say, catching the relief in my own voice. "I don't know if it'll make a difference, but all I can do is try, right?"

"That's right, son," my dad agrees. "I'm so sorry about all of this—I want you to know that." There's a catch in his throat that he doesn't bother to hide.

I sigh, gripping the steering wheel tighter. "I know, Dad. But can I ask you something?" My voice wavers as I flick on my blinker and turn the corner.

"Anything," my dad says. I hear him take a breath, slow and heavy, and let it out as if he's bracing himself.

"How come you never told me he died?" My voice hitches on the word and it hangs in the silence that follows.

Dad sighs audibly and I can picture him scratching the back of his neck the way he always does when he's thinking. "At the time, we were just so grateful you were okay. Your mother was a mess for weeks," he says, his voice soft and far away, like he's watching it unfold in his memory. "You know, she and Leona Walker were such great friends. It was a complete coincidence that her brother is who saved you." He pauses and I hear his chair creak. "We tried reaching out to the family through Leona. I had the address, we sent flowers. We asked Leona to help us talk to Mrs. Rossi." Another pause. "But she never wanted to be contacted. Your mom pushed anyway, eventually, Leona snapped. Not long after, they stopped speaking altogether."

I pull up in front of Jenna's house and kill the ignition, but I don't get out. Instead, I fumble with the keys. "So, then how did you come to manage the property?" I frown, a knot forming in my chest. "This isn't adding up."

Dad clears his throat. "After your mom and Leona argued, things got quiet for a while. About six months later, Leona called me at the office. She said Anna Rossi didn't want to sell the house. She paid it off and wanted to have the yard maintained until her daughter was old enough to decide what to do with it." He lets out a slow sigh, the kind that carries years of weight. "I never met Anna Rossi. Or Jenna. Leona set it all up. I respected Anna's wishes. No face-to-face interactions, no contact. And we've never taken a dime for managing the house." He pauses and when he speaks again, his voice cracks slightly. "We owed her your life... at the cost of her husband's. That was more than enough."

My throat tightens. "Wow," I rasp, my voice catching.

"I know you told your mother you figured out who Jenna is before that dinner," he says slowly, carefully. "But I wasn't sure. I didn't think it was possible—but then she said Leona's name. That's when I knew for sure."

A heavy pause settles on the end of the line—thick and final.

Then my dad lets out a chuckle. "Did I ever tell you how I got your mom back after she dumped me?"

I laugh, grateful for the subject change. "No. I had no idea she cut you loose. What did you do?"

A laugh escapes him, fading into a sigh as he remembers. "Our first date was at this godforsaken haunted house that she absolutely loved. I hated every second of it, but she loved it—as you can imagine, considering how much she loves that ridiculous skeleton." He laughs again to himself for a moment before continuing. "I don't even remember what we fought over to tell you the truth. But she told me that she thought it would be better if we saw other people, and I was crushed."

"I can imagine," I say quietly, looking out my windshield at Jenna's little house.

"Well, I got over my pride, and I set her up a haunted house of her own. It was *July*. I got all my buddies and her best friend to help, and we turned her friend's house into a haunted house." My dad is cackling at the memory.

I laugh, raising my brows at my reflection. "That's a gesture all right," I mutter.

"Well, if we can pull *this* off, you'll get her back, Miles. Have faith." My dad is always the optimist. It's one of the things I love most about him.

"I'm trying, but it's hard," I admit, hearing the melancholy in my voice. "I'm about to see her now to go over the listing." I exhale, defeated. "It feels like she's already miles away from me."

"My advice? Don't let on that you're lovesick," Dad says pointedly. "Let her wonder if you're doing okay."

I catch sight of Jenna's car in my rearview, pulling up behind me. "She's here," I tell my dad. A knot builds in my gut—nerves.

"Go get her," my dad cheers me on. "Don't worry, I'll do my best tonight."

I take a deep breath. "Thanks, Dad." I disconnect the call and open my door.

Jenna is already out of her car and standing on the sidewalk when I close my door. I walk up to her but keep my distance. "Hi," I say carefully.

"Hi." She tucks her hair behind her ear but doesn't meet my eyes.

"I'm sorry, I know you wanted Nate." I hold my hands up apologetically.

She nods, pursing her lips. "It's fine," she murmurs.

"Shall we?" I gesture toward the house and start walking. My dad's right. I have groveled already. I have begged her to talk to me. She hasn't wanted to, and there is no point in forcing it. If this last attempt doesn't work, I'll have to move on. For now, I'll keep this as professional as possible.

"Sure." Jenna's voice is quiet behind me.

"Do you have your key?" I turn, meeting her gaze for the first time. "I put mine back in the cabinet..." I trail off. That much is true. I figured I wouldn't need it when she was staying with me—we often came here together. Remembering the day I put it away makes my chest ache. It was the day I accepted that I lost her.

"Oh, yeah." Jenna rummages through the bag she has draped across her chest. I stand about four feet away, waiting. After a moment, she jingles the keys. "Got it." She makes for the front steps, and I follow behind.

I want to make conversation, ask if she's excited about the improvements. I want to be the way we used to be, but at the risk of coming on too strong, I can't. The house is cold inside but clean and stripped of many of the family heirlooms that were here just two weeks ago. Traces of Jenna and her belongings are gone. It looks like any other empty shore house I might sell, but it's not.

We venture down the hall into the kitchen. Memories from the night the ceiling caved in flood my mind, the love we made at the forefront. *Before everything literally and figuratively came crashing down.* I shake the memory away and take in the improvements. The ceiling is repaired and freshly painted. The cabinets have been cleaned and refinished. There is no trace of mess anywhere.

"The cabinets look great." I motion toward them. They are no longer that nineties faded oak, they now resemble the color of driftwood.

"Yeah, Danny knew someone." Jenna hugs herself for warmth. She must have turned the heat off. I want so badly to reach out and touch her, but I restrain myself.

I clear my throat. "Let's go have a look at the sunroom and the roof," I say, gesturing toward the living room. I lead the way, passing the new TV I got her, thinking of the nights we curled up on that damn tweed couch. She trails behind me, and I wonder if she's thinking of those nights too.

The sunroom's drywall is new, painted a neutral gray color that many beach house owners choose. The floor is a new vinyl, designed to look like real wood, and the dated furniture is pushed back into place. "This looks great too," I say, glancing at Jenna. Our eyes meet, and longing tugs at my heart. How easy would it be to take her in my arms and kiss away what's broken between us?

"It does." She looks away, pacing around the room, peering

out the large windows in the backyard. This is a three-season room, now chilly with winter upon us. When she looks at me again, her eyes are glistening. "I love this room," she says wistfully. She sniffles and wipes her nose. "I'll be sad to leave it."

I want to tell her that she doesn't have to; she can stay here, but I stop myself, remembering my dad's words. "Let's go check out the roof," I say, letting myself out the back door before I do something stupid like beg her to stay.

She doesn't immediately follow me. I am on the deck surveying the new roof, shielding my eyes when I hear her come out.

"Miles," she breathes my name. I drop my hand from my face and turn to her.

"Are you ready to talk about numbers?" I ask, trying my best to keep this business as usual.

Jenna shakes her head, wiping her eyes. The sniffle gives her away—she's been crying in the sunroom.

I step closer to her but keep my distance. "Are you okay?" I ask, my voice husky.

Jenna hugs herself and shakes her head. "I just can't believe I'm going to leave this all behind."

My heart constricts. *She's really going.* "You don't have to," I rasp, stepping toward her.

"I don't have a reason to stay," Jenna murmurs, staring at her feet.

I sigh, scratching at the stubble along my jaw. I want to tell her that I'm her reason to stay. I can make her happy. But I've done enough begging. These circles we're going around are ridiculous. Frustration with her bubbles in my chest. "We can do this another time if you want to wait," I offer, bypassing her and taking a seat on the deck steps.

Jenna doesn't hesitate when she sits down next to me. A moment later, she rests her head on my shoulder, soft cries coming from her. I pat her hand, remembering how much she's been through, swallowing my anger. "I'm sorry, Miles," she whispers.

"Me too," I murmur, but I don't let myself say anything else. I don't even put my arm around her. The ache in my chest is hammering. If I can't have this girl, I have to get out of here.

"I miss you." Jenna sits up, her gaze burning a hole through my face. I don't immediately return her gaze.

"I miss you too, Jenna." I sigh. "But you told me you can't be with me." I furrow my brow. Suddenly my frustration is back, and I can't hide it. "It's killing me seeing you like this and knowing I have something to do with it. Knowing that I lost you, and I can't even make it better." I growl, standing abruptly and taking her by surprise. "I'm hurt too, Jenna. I know you don't think that, but I am. I was in love with you."

"Was?" Jenna asks, her expression clouding to something unreadable.

I shrug and drop my hands. "What do you want me to say? I've done enough begging."

Jenna stands up and meets my eyes, frowning. "Say..." She hesitates. "That you'll still be in my life. I can't lose you as a friend."

I open my mouth to tell her I don't want to just be her friend, I want to be her everything, but I close it. "Fine. We're friends, okay?"

Jenna lets out a shuddering breath, nodding. She sniffles and wipes her nose on the back of her sleeve. "Okay."

"Listen, I have another appointment. I have to go." I rake my hands through my hair. I can't imagine what it looks like. "Call me or Nate when you're ready to talk about listing it." I don't wait for a reply. I stalk around the side of the house and get in my car, zooming around the corner before she even makes it around the front. Then, I pull over to catch my breath, surprised at the tears I feel pricking the back of my eyes. *I am so in love with her.* I let myself feel all of the pent-up emotions bubbling to the surface.

Then I man up and head back to my office. It's time to get her back.

Chapter Forty-Five

It was a bad idea to meet Miles at the house. I was doing okay. I actually felt excited when I got Danny's call that the repairs were complete. I wrote him a check and drove it right over to his office. And now, I am free. The house is in a suitable condition to sell. Aunt Leona has persuaded me to stay through the new year, but then, I'm out of here. Nothing is holding me back from starting over, completely fresh. But the second I saw Miles, I knew I would be forever tethered to him and this place. I thought telling him I missed him would open the door for an honest conversation, but I didn't realize until that very moment that he's hurt too. Neither of us meant to, but we hurt *each other.*

After he left, I crawled into my parents' bed upstairs and slept for hours. I don't know what I'm going to do yet, but now I know I am not ready to leave. I'm not ready to walk away from Miles, Cape May, my new friends, or my found-again family.

The days since have passed in a kind of emotional fog. I've kept busy—helping Aunt Leona with dinner plans, taking long walks on the beach, going only to work, and avoiding the places where I might run into Miles. But even in the quiet, he's everywhere. I still hear his voice, his excited laugh as he's catching a wave. I reach for my phone to call him to tell him small things about the house, or how amazing the stars looked the night before.

Now it's nearly Thanksgiving, and I still don't know what to do. But I know I miss Miles. I know my world is empty without him. I think about the night he told me he loves me, under the sky speckled with stars. A love like that doesn't just vanish. Maybe he is missing me too.

I imagine if my dad could have picked a partner for me, Miles is exactly who he'd choose. He's kind and grounded, and even though he carries his own pain, he still shows up for me.

So that brings me to one obvious choice.

If I have to start over, why not here?

Why not in Cape May, where I've found my family again—and finally started to heal? If I stay, maybe we'll find our way back to each other.

Aunt Leona convinced me to shut my brain and my phone off for Thanksgiving, so that's what I'm going to do. The Wednesday before Thanksgiving, a week after seeing Miles, I finish my shift and meet Aunt Leona at the grocery store to finish our shopping. She has invited a few widows from her church group over for the feast, and of course, Jake will be there too.

There will be six of us in all. It seems like we're preparing way too much food, but that is the Italian way. Aunt Leona reminds me so much of my dad that sometimes, I can't even bear to look at her. But the one thing that will always fill me with nostalgia is her love of food and the comfort it brings. *Happy? Eat. Sad? Eat. Worst day of your life? Let me make you your favorite meal. How about a sub tray?* It's exactly what my dad did for me after a bad day at school, or when I didn't make the travel soccer team. I smile at the memory as we walk around the store. Even though I feel pretty low, I'm going to let Aunt Leona mother me, and I'm going to indulge in this Thanksgiving feast—for memory's sake.

Thanksgiving morning, I wake up early, bundle up, and take a walk on the windy beach. Even though it's freezing, I take off my boots and walk along the water's edge. I inhale the scent of the ocean breeze, feel the cold sand between my toes, and breathe. There isn't much that the ocean can't cure, but a pang of sadness hits my chest when I see an early morning surfer catching a big wave. I think of Miles and his desire to feel invincible, to chase away sadness with each smooth ride in. I think about bobbing side-by-side on our surfboards at dusk, gazing at the first stars appearing. Miles made me feel invincible too. If nothing else, I'm thankful for those moments we shared.

It's been a week since we looked at the house repairs, and Miles hasn't called me. I didn't call him either. He left so quickly, I got the impression that I was the last person he wanted to hear from. So there we were, at an impasse, neither of us wanting to be the vulnerable one. Now I can't help but think it should have been me.

I trudge back up the beach, ready to help Aunt Leona cook, knowing it will keep my mind off Miles.

"Jenna." Jake's voice startles me. He steps out of the truck in a wet suit, barefoot and sandy, his surfboard lying in the bed.

"Early morning surf?" I ask, quirking my eyebrow. "It's cold."

"This is a winter suit," Jake says with a smirk.

"Where did you go?" I ask, leaning against his truck.

"The usual...The Cove." Jake hesitates, squinting at me. "Have you seen Miles lately?"

I shake my head. "No. Was he there?"

Jake frowns, like he wants to say something else, but doesn't. "No, I was just wondering." Jake shrugs. "I'm going to ask my mom if she needs anything, go home and shower, and then I'll be back for appetizers at noon."

I nod and offer him a tight smile. "Okay, sounds good."

Aunt Leona planned an early Thanksgiving. She says senior citizens like to eat early and go to sleep. I have to admit, they may have the right idea. Jake and I walk inside together to find Aunt Leona flipping pancakes and listening to Michael Bublé's "It's Beginning to Look a Lot Like Christmas." Jake and I exchange amused glances.

"I haven't seen her this excited for the holidays in a long time," he whispers to me. "It has everything to do with you."

I shoot him a grateful smile and follow him into the kitchen.

"Ma, do you need anything?" Jake asks, kissing Aunt Leona

on the cheek.

"No, but I've made pancakes." Aunt Leona gestures to a foil-covered plate on the table.

"Mom, we're eating a huge meal in like three hours." He rolls his eyes.

"Jenna will eat them, won't you dear?" She gives me a smile that crinkles her eyes.

"I sure will," I say, sitting at the table and putting a few pancakes on my plate. "Then we'll get started on the mashed potatoes."

Aunt Leona glides around the kitchen, Jake excuses himself, and I settle in with my pancakes, soaking it all in. The Christmas tree twinkles, the music creates a soft ambiance, and Aunt Leona places a mimosa in front of me. There's nothing to complain about except... I miss Miles. I miss him with the same familiar ache I feel when I think of my parents. The only difference is, he is still here. *What the hell am I waiting for?* I scold myself.

"Jenna, are you okay?" Aunt Leona interrupts my thoughts. "I'm ready when you are."

"Yes," I say definitively. I carry my plate to the dishwasher. "Just tell me what to do."

☙

Aunt Leona and I cook up a storm for the next two hours. The turkey is making the entire condo smell heavenly, and we have enough side dishes to feed a small army. I absolutely love every second of it. The last few years with my mom, she wasn't strong enough to cook or eat a big meal. I sat with her every Thanksgiving and ate rotisserie chicken and Bob Evans mashed potatoes on a snack tray. This feels special. I must look teary-eyed because Aunt Leona catches me by surprise by wrapping me in a hug.

"I know this isn't easy for you, but I'm *so* glad you're here," she whispers in my ear, stroking my hair.

"Me too." I pull back and examine her face, brimming with

emotion.

"I always wondered about you," Aunt Leona says, cupping my cheek. She's looking at me with the same adoration my mom did.

"So did I," I say softly. "Especially once my mom got sick." I chew on my lip to fight the rising lump in my throat.

Our tender moment is interrupted by Jake and three ladies in their sixties, talking animatedly as they come through the front door. I'm not prepared for guests at all, still wearing my yoga pants and hoodie from my morning walk. We got so busy cooking, I didn't bother to fix myself up, but it doesn't matter. Everyone is excited to meet me, and I have never felt more welcome.

We're sitting around the table, eating a feast fit for the royal family when there's a knock at the door. "I'll get it," I offer. My seat is the closest to the front door. Jake and Aunt Leona exchange a look that I can't read.

I wipe my mouth on the cloth dinner napkin, push my crazy hair behind my ears, and walk to the door. The knocking hasn't stopped; whoever is behind the door really wants to come in. I swing it open and there he is. Miles. His face is drawn, lines of exhaustion carved deep around his eyes, but he is still irresistibly sexy.

He licks his lips. "Jenna," he rasps.

"Miles, hi." I bite back a smile. The truth of the matter is, if he hadn't shown up, I might have gone to his parents' house. I have been pushing thoughts of him aside all day, but I can't escape the longing I feel for him.

"Happy Thanksgiving," he croaks.

"You too." I tug my hoodie down and fluff my hair. Now I wish I took the time to put makeup on. Silence hangs in the air as we hold each other's gaze, neither of us sure what to do next. I finally find my voice and clear my throat. "Do you want to come in?"

Miles drops his gaze, then slowly drags it back up, drawing his eyes up the length of my body. Heat rises up my neck. He looks gorgeous in a nice pair of blue jeans and a button-down with a sport coat over it. He shakes his head. "No. I came here to tell you, I'm thankful for you. And I'd like it if you would come somewhere with me. I have something to show you."

I glance behind me—Jake, Aunt Leona, and our three guests, Barb, Phyllis, and Deb, are all watching with great interest. When I catch them, they all turn away and start yammering at once. "Oh, I don't know... We're in the middle of dinner," I say hesitantly.

"Go on, dear!" Aunt Leona calls. "We'll save you some pie."

Miles bites back a grin. "They'll save you some pie," he murmurs, holding his hand out to me.

"Okay." I sigh. "As long as I don't miss out on pie."

Miles looks at me the way he did the night he told me he loved me, and my stomach is doing backflips. He licks his lips again. "Okay, ready?"

Suddenly, I'm extremely self-conscious about the outfit I'm wearing, the state of my hair, my breath. "Should I change?" I wince.

Miles smiles again, letting out a nervous breath and shaking his head. "No. It's just us and...I think you look beautiful." He swallows audibly.

My face warms and my eyes water, but I blink away the tears before he sees. "Okay, let me get my coat."

I step away from Miles and walk quickly to my bedroom, grabbing my coat from the back of the door. I spritz some perfume, put on some deodorant, and a peachy lip balm. I fluff my hair and slip into my Uggs.

I say my goodbyes to the ladies and Jake, and then Miles and I are in his car, driving slowly, like we're on a Sunday drive. We're quiet at first. Miles seems pensive, nervous even, and I'm looking out the window.

"Where are we going?" I ask, glancing sideways at him.

"We're going to the beach." Miles doesn't take his eyes off the road.

"Okay," I say, because it's the only thing I can think of. *Of course we're going to the beach.*

Five minutes later, we're at the empty parking lot of *our* beach. The waves are calm, the sun is just starting to sink lower into the horizon. Miles doesn't immediately get out of the car.

"What are we doing?" I ask, turning to face him.

Miles inhales sharply. "I have something I want to show you. I thought about blind folding you, but I was so nervous, I forgot the blind fold." He chuckles at himself.

"Okay," I breathe.

"So, I'd appreciate it if you'd close your eyes." Miles unbuckles his seat belt, and I do the same. "I'll come around and get you. Stay put."

I don't get to answer him—he's on my side of the car in a matter of seconds. He opens my door and reaches a hand inside for me to take. I do, and I allow him to help me out of the car. His warm hand sends a tingle of goose bumps up my arm.

"Close your eyes," Miles rasps.

I do as I'm told and let him lead me down the familiar terrain of the beach's path, but we stop at the end without going further.

"Before you open your eyes, I have something to say." Miles's voice quivers, sending a shiver down my spine.

"Okay," I say, surprising myself with the emotion in my own voice.

Miles takes a deep breath. "Jenna, when we met, I had no idea *who* you were. I didn't even know the man who rescued me had passed away. My parents *never* talk about that day. It still makes my mom cry to think about it. So, I never brought it up. When I met you, I wasn't interested in dating anyone—my divorce all but broke me. It made me feel like a failure, and I just preferred not to date anyone seriously. You changed all of that. I fell in love with you, Jenna. I'm so deeply *in* love with you that it makes my chest hurt. The thought of you leaving here without knowing how much you mean to me would have killed me. I need you to know."

No one has ever said anything like this to me before—at least not with such raw emotion. Miles's voice is tender, unsteady, and it unlocks something inside me that I closed off from him. I believe him and suddenly I can't believe I spent so many weeks pushing him away.

He stops talking and takes another shuddering breath. "You can open your eyes." We're standing in front of the pavilion that has been on this beach for as long as I can remember. It's a worn wooden structure with benches under it and sand practically ingrained in the concrete floor.

I blink against the afternoon light and the tears blurring my vision.

Miles gestures toward a large metal plaque at the center of the pavilion's arch. And then I see it. My father's name. It reads, *The Nicholas Rossi Memorial Pavilion*. It hits me like a wave to the chest. My knees nearly give out.

"If you're still going to leave Cape May, I can't let go without knowing what you—and your dad—mean to me."

A gasp catches in my throat. "Miles," My voice is thick with emotion. "How did you do this?"

"My dad's a town councilman, remember? They voted on it last week." Miles drops my hand and steps aside, revealing a fiberglass sign with my father's picture on it and a paragraph of text.

I step forward and read it aloud, my voice trembling:

"In Memory of Nicholas Rossi

September 16, 1957 – October 22, 1997

Nicholas Rossi, a brave and selfless soul, passed away from a heart attack after performing a heroic rescue at Cove Beach. His selflessness and unwavering commitment to others will never be forgotten. His legacy of heroism will continue to inspire all who knew him."

A mix of grief and gratitude crash into me. For so long, I've carried this story alone—my father's heroism, my mother's illness.

Now it is carved here into permanence. I'm not the only one keeping our story alive anymore. I don't know why I didn't see it before but Miles *sees* me. He did this, not just for my dad but for *me*. I don't realize I'm crying until Miles wraps me in a tight hug from behind, pulling me into his chest and kissing the side of my head. I whirl around to face him, and the anguish on his face mirrors my own. He tucks me under his chin.

"I don't know what to say," I whimper, sniffling. "You had the pavilion named after him?"

Miles sniffles too. "I did. He deserves to be remembered."

I pull away and look up at Miles and he leans down, pressing his forehead into mine. "Thank you," I murmur. "This means so much to me."

"*You* mean so much to me." Miles kisses my forehead. "If your dad hadn't rescued me, I might never have met you."

"It feels a little like fate," I admit, sniffling. I've missed Miles so much these past few weeks—of *course* I have. I assumed he'd given up after the day at my house. Being in Cape May, rediscovering my family, sorting through old heirlooms, feeling my parents' presence in every corner of this town—it's given me a sort of closure I didn't even realize I needed. But if Miles hadn't come for me today, I would have gone to him and begged for another chance. Because now I know—it wasn't just timing or coincidence. It was something bigger. It was meant to be.

"Jenna, I love you so much. Please, please give me another chance. I will spend the rest of my life trying to make you as happy as you have made me these past few months." Miles's eyes are shiny, and he blinks back a tear.

"I love you, too," I admit, letting my own tears fall. Miles catches one on his thumb.

"You do?" His voice quivers.

"Yes," I say, smiling through my tears.

"Does this mean you don't want to sell your house?" Miles asks, not bothering to hide the hope from his trembling voice. His palm finds my cheek and he meets my eyes.

"Miles," I whisper. "Take me home."

He kisses me deeply before scooping me into his arms and carrying me back to his car.

Home. That *still* sounds right.

Chapter Forty-Six

Luckily, there is no one on the road this Thanksgiving, because I drive over the speed limit, barely making every light, desperate to get us to Jenna's house. She is leaning across the center console, staring at me, stroking my thigh while I drive. My erection throbs beneath my jeans. I have never wanted anyone so bad in my life. I glance sideways at her, and she gives me a seductive grin.

"You're trouble," I tease, taking the turn onto her street a bit too widely.

"I want you, Miles," she whispers.

I roll the car up to the curb in front of her house. "Your wish is my command." I tip her chin and kiss her softly before hopping out of the car.

I don't even make it to her side before she's on the sidewalk, looking at me with those hazy bedroom eyes. She makes a come-hither motion with her index finger and then takes off for the front porch, laughing.

I chase after her and catch her around the waist, kissing her neck and earlobes from behind. Happiness blooms in my chest and a knot forms in my throat. I can't believe I get to call her mine. She stops fighting me and basks in the desire growing rapidly between us. I let my breath linger in her ear for a second, our pulses racing synchronously. Then she whirls around to face me, the playful mood suddenly gone, replaced with urgent need. Jenna tangles her fingers in my overgrown curls and her mouth finds mine. The kiss starts slow, drawing me in with its quiet urgency. It's as if time itself has paused to make room for the innate connection between the two of us. I'm breathless and longing for more when Jenna pulls away, her lips plump from kissing, curved into a mischievous smirk. She takes my hand and leads me up the front steps. I don't let go while I wait for her to unlock the door.

Neither of us speak once we're inside. The house is drafty, but I'm warm all over. I pull Jenna close to me again, pressing my erection into her and kissing from her neck to her collarbone. Jenna moans softly when I reach the nape of her neck, just above her shoulder.

"Miles, I need you," she whispers. "Take me upstairs."

I don't have to be told twice. I scoop her up the same way I did at the beach, carrying her all the way up to her room, kicking the door open. I stand at the foot of her bed, laying her down gently as she gazes up at me.

"Jenna, you are so beautiful," I croak. "I am the luckiest man alive."

Jenna props herself up on her elbows, biting her lip. "What are you waiting for, then?"

That's all it takes.

The urgency is gone, replaced by something smoother, something to savor. I slip off my sport coat, never taking my eyes off Jenna as I slowly unbutton my dress shirt. Then I hover over her, lifting her hooded sweatshirt up and over her head. Her brown locks cascade around her shoulders. The sight of her in her black bra, wild hair, and seductive gaze is enough to undo me right here and now. Jenna leans forward and starts working my belt buckle, sliding my jeans to my ankles. My dick is begging to be let out, but I push Jenna gently back onto the bed and kiss all the way down her body until I get to the waistband of her leggings. I slide them off and then hover over her, letting the heat of our bodes meld together.

"Let's take our time," Jenna whispers, sliding up to the pillows.

I follow, crawling over her, kissing her neck and jawline. "What about the pie?" I tease through kisses.

"This is so much better than pie." Jenna grins, pulling my face up toward hers. She kisses me hungrily, nibbling on my lower lip. Our breath combines with each tender kiss, a mix of relief to be together and desire to melt into each other.

I move down, unclasp her bra, and take each of her nipples in my mouth, eliciting a moan from her that drives me wild. I swirl my tongue around the erect, pink tip, dragging my teeth gently behind. Jenna cries out, and I groan in response, our noises carrying unspoken pleas to start anew.

"Miles, I need you." Jenna reaches for my boxers and tugs them down, freeing my pulsing erection. She grasps it firmly, pumping up and down, sending shivers through me.

I pull back slightly, tugging down her panties and settling between her thighs. I pin her hands above her head and look into her eyes. "Jenna, I love you so much," I murmur. "Let's never break up again." My mouth finds hers; the kiss is a gentle reassurance that what was broken between us can be put back together.

Jenna reaches down and rubs my dick over her slickness. I groan. "You're so wet for me, baby," I rasp in her ear, sucking on the lobe. "I need to be inside you." I reach down and slide two fingers in and Jenna cries out, grinding against my hand.

"Do you have a condom?" Jenna asks breathlessly.

I push up on my arms. "I was optimistic, but not that presumptuous," I smirk. Then more seriously, "I wasn't sure you'd take me back."

"Oh, Miles," Jenna breathes. "I never want to lose you again."

"Me neither. I'm so in love with you." I murmur. "But..."

"Screw the condom," Jenna groans. "It's me and you...and I need you."

"You don't have to tell me twice." I bite back a smile and then I sink into her, my mouth finding hers. Our movements are slow and sensual, our hands linked together like a lifeline, anchoring us. Skin to skin contact heightens every sensation—I won't last long. "Jenna, you feel too good, I'm not going to last," I whisper in her ear.

"Harder," she hisses. "Come for me."

So, I do, and nothing else matters except the synchronous beating of our hearts, the mixing of our breath, and the weight of unconditional love. Jenna tenses around my cock, her body going rigid, her soft whimper becoming loud moans. I push deeper inside her and we both cry out, finding our release together.

I look down at Jenna, expecting to see a post-orgasmic glow, but her eyes are glistening with tears. A single tear escapes, and I kiss it away.

"What's wrong? Did I hurt you?" I ask, alarmed.

Jenna shakes her head. "I'm just overwhelmed. I love you so much."

I smile and kiss her tears away again as more fall. I kiss her, my smile brushing against her lips. "I love you so much, too," I whisper. "More than you could ever imagine."

Jenna pushes the hair off my forehead, gazing at me. "Really?"

"You have no idea." I grin. "Now, how about that pie?"

ଓ

If I wanted my plan to work, I had to let someone in on it. Earlier in the week, I called Jake and told him what I had done for Jenna. He was shocked and surprisingly impressed, so he agreed to help me. I needed to make sure their Thanksgiving plans weren't at the same time as my family's, and I needed someone to encourage Jenna to come with me when I showed up at her doorstep. Most importantly, I needed Jake and Leona to be on board with bringing our families together again. That's why, when we pull on our clothes, I suggest to Jenna that we go back to her aunt's condo.

She pushes her lips together in thought. "She and Jake have probably cleaned everything up by now. Aunt Leona told me she and her friends like to get dinner over with early." She shrugs with a smirk. "Something about senior citizens going to bed?"

I laugh. *This is going to work out perfectly.* "Okay, would you want to come over to my parents' house?"

Jenna grins. "I would *love* that."

"Great. Pete's there and he really misses you." I offer her a lopsided smile.

We hop in the car and drive across town to Perry Street. The street is crowded with friends and neighbors hosting their own Thanksgivings, but there are a lot of cars in front of my parents' house. I pull into the driveway, put the car in park, and look over at Jenna.

"Ready?" I ask, quirking an eyebrow.

"Sure...but why is Jake's truck here?" Jenna furrows her brow.

"I don't think that's his truck." I play dumb.

Jenna nods emphatically. "No, it is. The surfboard is in the back."

I shrug. "Let's go see."

We hop out of the car and link hands, walking into my parents' house united once again.

Inside is my mother's boisterous family, my parents, Nate, Caden, Jake, and Aunt Leona.

"Jenna!" Caden runs up and throws his little arms around Jenna's legs. She looks around the room, laughing.

"What are you guys doing here?" Jenna's eyes widen when she spots her family.

Aunt Leona stands up and walks over, joined by my mom and dad. "Jenna, there was once a time when our families were close. Your father's death drove a wedge between us for many years." Aunt Leona's eyes fill with tears.

"But not anymore. We're friends that turned into family again," My mom wraps an arm around Aunt Leona, tugging her close.

"Framily!" Caden shouts excitedly.

Everyone laughs.

"Miles asked us to come," Jake says, looking me in the eye. "He set all of this up for you, Jenna."

Jenna turns to me, her eyes tearing again. "You did this? Brought everyone back together?"

I nod, nervously licking my lips.

Jenna says nothing else—she tugs my face to hers and kisses me. Everyone cheers.

When she pulls away, she glances around the room, smiling with her whole face, like she can't believe she's surrounded by family. "Thank you all. This could have been a really hard day, but instead it's perfect. I'm so thankful for each and every one of you." Jenna sniffles, wiping away a stray tear.

A chorus of agreement fills the room as everyone smiles at her.

Jenna shifts, biting her lip uncertainly but then she breaks into another smile that crinkles her eyes. "Okay, enough of this sentimental stuff. Where's the *pie*?"

Epilogue

Jenna

One Year Later

I'm hurrying around my newly renovated kitchen, prepping food for our first ever Christmas Eve dinner in our little house on Monarch Street. Even when my parents lived here, there was never a Christmas celebration under this roof. I could not be more excited. Miles and I picked out the perfect tree from a little farm offshore. We bought all of our decorations from Joy's Hardware, and it feels like a Hallmark movie in here.

It's cliché to say, but I am living my own Hallmark love story every day. After Thanksgiving last year, Miles and I decided we couldn't be apart any longer; we wanted to wake up together every day until the end of time. Instead of listing my house and moving into his condo, we listed his condo. It's beachfront, so it didn't take long to sell. Miles and Pete moved in with me just shy of a year ago, and I have never been happier. Pete has a yard to play in now, but we still take him to the beach. Miles and I have fixed the house up and made it our own—starting with new kitchen counter tops and Miles's furniture from his condo. I haven't vaulted any ceilings yet, but maybe someday.

I put family photos of my parents around the house because I never want to forget that they're always with me. I know this is where they would have wanted me to end up—and who they would have wanted me to end up with.

I've also started my own interior design company. I'm working from home for now, but Miles and Joy have my business cards and hand them out to customers regularly. They have been keeping me busy. I still have to pinch myself—I can't believe that I get to do what I love every day.

Speaking of what I love? This crazy man of mine has embedded a love of surfing in my soul. I can hardly believe it, but he has me out there with him on my dad's beach almost three hundred days a year. I still won't go in when it's ice cold like he does, but now I understand why he chases those stars every night. There's something amazing about seeing the universe from the ocean under the inky night sky. I guess I'm a convert.

"Jenna!" Miles's voice interrupts my daydreaming. He sounds like a kid on Christmas, his voice brimming with excitement.

I put the knife down I'm using to slice cheese for a charcuterie board. "In here!" I call, wiping my hands on a paper towel.

"I have to give you your gift." He marches into the kitchen holding a large, wrapped gift box out to me.

I frown, but a smile tugs at my lips anyway. "Babe, no. It's only Christmas Eve. I haven't even wrapped yours yet."

"Please." He puts the box on the table and folds his hands at me like a begging child. "Pretty please. I can't wait until tomorrow."

I laugh, rolling my eyes. "Fine."

Miles pulls out a kitchen chair for me. It's still my parents' old kitchen table, and I wouldn't have it any other way. "Sit," he orders, pointing to the chair.

"Yes, sir." I tease with a grin.

Miles sits across from me, placing the sloppily wrapped box in my lap. *Hey, at least he tried.* "Open it," he says eagerly, rubbing his palms together.

I tear off the paper and lift the lid, pushing the tissue paper aside...a wet suit. *God love him. He really tried.* "Oh...another wet suit." I bite back a grin. I don't need anything for Christmas, being in our home, surrounded by loved ones with Miles, is all I could ask for. Bless him for getting me another wet suit so we can spend even *more* time together.

"Not just a wet suit. A top-of-the-line *winter* wet suit. You won't feel the cold water at all. There is a hood, gloves, and even booties for your feet!" He grins proudly.

"This is great, baby, thank you." I smile, pulling him toward me for a kiss.

"Can we go right now?" Miles asks excitedly.

"Right now? No. It's Christmas Eve." I laugh incredulously.

"Yeah, but we'll be back. Come on. We haven't been out together in a while. The surf report says the waves are amazing. Please. Plus, it's Christmas Eve and this is the closest I get to religion." Miles does the hands folding thing again and he looks so cute my chest constricts. "It's only three. No one is coming over until six," he urges.

I'm mostly ready for company. We're having a slow-cooked pot roast and vegetables. Aunt Leona is bringing some seafood dishes to keep things Italian, and dessert is off my radar because Miles's mom said she'd bring it. I sigh and then relent, but not without an eyeroll. "Fine. Let's go." I tell him, but his excitement is rubbing off on me too. "But only for an hour!"

☙

Fifteen minutes later, we're pulling up to Cove Beach. It's after three, and the December sky is already turning shades of cotton candy as the sun sinks lower into the horizon. Miles was right though, I'm not cold. This new suit *is* pretty cool.

We trek down to the beach and get to work waxing our boards. I've since adopted Miles's longboard as my own, and he seems to love his shortboard. "You ready?" he asks me with a lopsided grin. He can't contain his excitement.

"Sure," I say, "but Miles, just a few runs. It's Christmas Eve." But I have to force away my smile. This man has stolen my heart in every way possible. If he's happy, I'm happy.

"I know, I know." He pulls me to him and plants a kiss on my lips. "Let's go!"

Then he's off, running full force into the ocean, the one place he feels untouchable. I follow him more slowly; it's been a while since I've been out. But my arms have gotten stronger and no longer feel like limp spaghetti as they slice through the water. I duck under each crashing wave with expertise. The butterflies I once felt coming out here long gone. Now, I feel something like Miles does. Invincible isn't the word, but peaceful might be. I feel at home in the ocean just as much as he does now.

Miles waits on his board, watching as I make my way to him. Once I do, I spin around and sit up. I'm so warm in this wet suit, the cold December air doesn't even give me a chill. *Impressive.* "You made it." Miles grins.

"Are you happy?" I joke, splashing him.

"Hey now," he says, holding his hands up in defense. Then, more seriously, he says, "Coming out here with you has been some of the best times of my life so far."

His emotion catches me off guard. "Mine too, Miles. I love it here," I say sincerely.

"I love you, Jenna. *So much,*" Miles says tenderly. "I never knew it was possible to love another person like this, so selflessly. Your happiness is all that matters to me."

"Is that why you dragged me out here in forty-degree weather on Christmas Eve?" I tease, splashing him again.

Miles ignores my remark and looks up at the sky. "Look, first star." He points to a bright spot in the sky that I am pretty sure is actually Venus and then grins at me. "This is my favorite part."

"Mine too," I murmur, reaching across the water for his hand. He takes it and pulls me and my board closer to him.

"Do you remember last year, when I told you I didn't care about surfing every day anymore because I have you? And you make me feel alive?" Miles's eyes penetrate mine. He doesn't look away until I answer.

"Yeah," I say slowly.

"That's still true. You make me feel alive, every single day," he croaks.

"You make me feel alive too, Miles." I smile, wondering what the heck he is trying to say.

"And you know how I love to surf at night, chasing the stars, because it makes me feel invincible?" Miles asks.

"Miles, I know all of this," I say quietly. "What are you trying to say?"

He grins widely, glancing behind him at the wave building and starts paddling. "Race you!" he calls over his shoulder and then he's gone.

"That jerk!" I say to no one but myself. I laugh and start paddling after him, catching the next wave and riding it in smoothly. When my feet touch the sand I yell, "You stole my wave!"

But Miles isn't ready to paddle back out for another one. He's on one knee, holding a diamond ring, grinning at me. I rush to him.

"Beat ya," he croaks.

"Oh my God," I gasp, covering my mouth with trembling hands. "Miles," I whisper, my heart hammering in my chest.

"Jenna, I used to chase stars, believing on some level that if I could just reach them, I'd find a way to feel invincible. But the moment I met you, I realized I was already there. With you by my side, I don't need to chase anything anymore—because your love makes me feel like I can do anything. You make my whole world as vast and beautiful as gazing at the night sky from the middle of the ocean. Here, with your parents as our witnesses, I'd like to ask you a question." He pauses, licking his lips.

"Jenna Rose Rossi, make me the happiest man in the world, marry me, and be my guiding star? It's the only gift I want this Christmas." Miles's grin is wide, and his eyes are glassy but hopeful.

I'm shaking, both from the cold air and Miles's heartfelt proposal. I rip off my glove and hold out my trembling hand, nodding and crying. "Yes," I whisper. "I would be honored to marry you, Miles."

His eyes light up. "Yes? You'll marry me?" He stands up and wraps me in a hug, swinging me around the beach. "She said yes!" he shouts to the sky. "She said yes!"

I'm laughing and my heart is bursting—I have never been happier in my life. Miles puts me down, grabs a fluffy beach towel, and wraps it around me. I look at the glittering ring on my finger for the first time and my eyes fill with tears. "It's beautiful." I hold back a sob.

"I can't wait to spend the rest of my life with you. I hope we're still out here surfing when we're seventy." He grins, his eyes glistening.

"I hope so too." I stand on my tiptoes and kiss him softly. Our foreheads press together, and I whisper, "Thank you for including my parents."

"I wouldn't have it any other way," Miles murmurs. "Now, let's go see everybody else. We're celebrating."

☙

When we get home, Miles's parents, Nate, Caden, Aunt Leona, and Jake are already gathered in our kitchen. Everyone holds champagne, and Jake passes us each a glass as we come inside. Miles filled them in. They all knew that he was giving me the greatest gift this Christmas—his heart, completely open and unabashed.

It's midnight before everyone leaves, and Miles and I head up to sleep in the master bedroom of our cozy beach bungalow. I slip into bed, pulling the blanket up to my chin, admiring my ring. Miles slides in beside me, pulling me close and taking my hand. He kisses my neck, and we gaze out the window at the starlit sky.

"Merry Christmas," Miles whispers in my ear.

"Merry Christmas," I say with a happy sigh. "Today was the best day of my life."

Miles chuckles. "There's a lot more where that came from."

And I know he's right.

Acknowledgements

I cannot believe the time has come to write acknowledgements again. A year ago, if you told me I'd have two books out within the year, I'd never have believed it, but here we are.

There are a number of people that play an important part in making every book come together. To my agent and friend, Katie Monson. I wouldn't want anyone else by my side on this journey. I can't thank you enough for your expertise, friendship, and for putting up with my daily anxiety.

To Meredith and the team at Page & Vine, Jordyn, Victoria, Jennifer, Amber, and Megan, you are all so amazing. I am so grateful for your knowledge and passion. I cannot wait to continue my literary journey with this team. It is an honor to work with you all.

To my husband, Kevin, I could not do this without your love and support. You are my greatest gift and the rock of our family. Thank you for continually picking up the slack and taking care of *all* of us so that I can work. I couldn't do this without you, and I love you so much.

And to my three amazing kids, Mia, Finn, and Gemma. My "new job" has been an adjustment, but you have rolled with the punches, giving Mommy time to write and not getting too mad when I have "*another* signing." I love you all and I'm so proud of you.

My author journey wouldn't be as successful as it has been without my awesome street team! Thank you, Jessica Walton, Jackie Russell, Kate Kennedy, Alex Lebron, Erica Nassar, Alexa Escapita, Catherine Norselli, Bekah Graser, Kelsey Barton, Jennifer Paoli, Amanda (Mandi) Moore, Kate Fuller, Ashley Spiker, Carson Jones, Courtney Dial, Alicia Kern, Megan Matos, Alyssa Brutlag, Melissa Aleman, Annabelle McGuire, Ashley Martinelli,

Lacey Wallen, Bryanna Thompson, Priscilla Thibodeaux, Charlene Groome, Isabel Cedano, Courtney Chumbley, Krista Harmer, Amanda (Sunshine) Hengen, Emily Leisten, Dawn Cole, Sharon A., Hannah, Erin Ballinger, Kelly Montgomery, Kelsee Hankin, Kristie Reyes, Lauryn Young, Kaitlin Noel, Marissa Hux, Maryanne Parker, Miranda Bourassa, Sherilyn Sinning, Stephanie Torres, Summer Eaton, Julia, Meralys, Jamie Fischer, Cozy Chic Lit Lounge, Whitney ...thebookhermit..., Kerrie, and Kimberly. Thank you for always spreading the love!

To my parents, for telling everyone they know about their daughter, the author. And for coming to countless book events as my support system. I love you both so much. Fair warning, this one is spicier!

To all of my author friends, whatever stage of your journey you are at, I could not have done this without your friendship. To those who went before me, I cherish your guidance in all aspects of the industry. And to those who will without a doubt come after me, I cannot wait to celebrate you all on your paths to success.

To my family and friends who are probably tired of hearing me talk about book stuff, I love you all! Thank you for being alongside me for the biggest thing to ever happen to me. I am blessed to have you.

To my dear readers, thank you for reading and loving my Cape May gang! Thank for you telling your friends about my books and following along on this crazy ride. This whole experience has been beyond my wildest dreams. I am so grateful that I get to take the stories from my head and turn them into books that you will get to read. I will never take a second of this for granted.

About the Author

Linny Mack grew up a voracious reader and writer. She spent her days of adolescence up in her room writing her own stories and cutting her characters out of the Delia's catalog. Now, Linny is a debut author of contemporary romance. When she isn't writing your next book boyfriend, she is spending time with her real-life romantic hero and their three children in New Jersey.

To learn more, visit: www.linnymack.com

LINNY MACK

Choosing You

A CAPE MAY NOVEL

Choosing You

Available March 17, 2026

At forty-one, Melanie Glick has made peace with being perpetually single. She'd rather be alone than be someone's consolation prize. So, she spends her nights tending bar at The Ugly Mug and fills her days writing music, hoping she'll someday find the courage to perform it. Nothing in her life has ever been quite the same since she lost her best friend, Cara, in a tragic accident decades ago, but the music keeps her going. When Cara's brother comes flying into town like a blast from the past, he stirs up old memories, new feelings, and a chance at something she never thought she'd have again.

Country music singer Josh Cote hasn't set foot in Cape May since he was sixteen. After he lost his sister, the charming small town has been a constant reminder of all he's lost. But with the 25th anniversary of Cara's death approaching, Josh decides to pass through on a road trip designed to inspire his first solo album. His first stop? The Ugly Mug, where he comes face-to-face with Melanie, his teenage muse. When he spots the tattoo on her wrist in Cara's handwriting, Josh has the overwhelming desire to get to know Melanie, all over again.

When Melanie offers Josh a place to stay, it feels impulsive—but their connection is instant, rooted in shared grief and a first love that never died. Neither expects the pull between them to grow stronger each day, as their temporary arrangement deepens into something they can't ignore. But with Josh's looming departure and a long-buried secret casting a shadow over their budding romance, Melanie and Josh must confront the ghosts of their past if they have a chance at a future. Can new love truly heal old wounds, or are some scars too deep to mend?

LINNY MACK

Changing Tides

A CAPE MAY NOVEL

Changing Tides

Now Available

After thirteen years of marriage and seven years of infertility with her supposed soulmate, Sophie Bennett's life is turned upside down. Not only does she discover her husband is having a sordid affair, on her birthday, but his mistress is also pregnant with his baby. Seeking solace, Sophie flees to Cape May, New Jersey, a quiet coastal town where she spent many summers as a child. There she encounters Liam Harper, a brooding carpenter who seems intent to keep everyone at a distance. Despite his best efforts, Sophie recognizes the vulnerability under his prickly exterior, sparking a curiosity about him that she can't ignore.

Liam Harper is walking around with the weight of the world on his shoulders. Haunted by a tragedy from his past that changed him forever, Liam doesn't believe he deserves love or happiness. After being unexpectedly awarded permanent custody of his one-year-old niece, Liam's script flips yet again. He doesn't know the first thing about parenthood, and his gruff exterior makes it hard for him to ask for help. When the beautiful and heartbroken Sophie becomes his new neighbor, Liam never expects her to be the one to chip away his defenses.

As the two navigate their attraction and work to heal old wounds, emotions run high. If they want to change the tides of their futures, they must decide whether love is worth the risk. Will they walk away forever, or will fate step in and see them through?

PAGE
&
VINE